SORCERY AND THE
SINGLE GIRL

ALSO BY MINDY KLASKY

The Washington Witches Series (Magical Washington)

Girl's Guide to Witchcraft

Sorcery and the Single Girl

Magic and the Modern Girl

Single Witch's Survival Guide

Joy of Witchcraft

The Washington Vampires Series (Magical Washington)

Fright Court

Law and Murder

High Stakes Trial

The Washington Warders Series (Magical Washington)

The Library, the Witch, and the Warder

The Washington Medical Series (Magical Washington)

The Witch Doctor Is In

Fae's Anatomy

The Lady Doctor is a Vamp

SORCERY AND THE SINGLE GIRL

WASHINGTON WITCHES SERIES - BOOK 2

MINDY KLASKY

PEABRIDGE
PRESS

This novel was first published by Red Dress Ink in October 2007 as a paperback original.

Published by Peabridge Press
P.O. Box 42133
Arlington, VA 22204

ISBN 978-1-95018-414-9

Discover other titles by Mindy Klasky at www.mindyklasky.com

030920mkm

For the Greenhill Girls –
Who fought the battle against the popular snobs

1

O nce upon a time, I thought being a witch would make everything easier.

Yeah, right.

There I was on another Friday evening, leaning against the counter in Cake Walk, the Georgetown bakery owned by my best friend, Melissa White. Over the summer, I'd started helping Melissa close up every Friday night, after I left my job at the Peabridge Library. My assistance gave us a chance to catch up on our weeks, and then we conducted always-needed Mojito Therapy.

I was just waiting until we could turn the sign on the door from "Walk On In" to "Walk On By." I could already taste icy lime juice and rum, mixed with mint and nearly-frozen seltzer water in a chilled tumbler. Summer in Washington was always hot, and this late August day was no exception.

I held a glass of iced tea against the pulse point in my right wrist and tried to forgive the bakery's stuttering air conditioning. After all, it was doing its best to beat back the swampy heat. My red-shot hair frizzed against the back of my neck, and I was pretty sure my kohl liner had smeared around my eyes. So much for drawing out the emerald glints trapped inside my hazel irises. Did that stuff *ever* work outside of fashion magazines?

I probably should have taken a page from Melissa's book and ignored makeup altogether—after all, it was just the two of us girlfriends. The two of us, and a pitcher of icy mojitos.

Since therapy had not yet commenced, however, I took a deep swallow of Mango Mamba iced tea and tried to explain to Melissa. Again. "I know it shouldn't matter. I dated Scott for twelve years—twelve *years!* And I only saw the I.B. for twelve weeks."

I.B. That used to stand for Imaginary Boyfriend. Now, it stood for Idiot Bastard. Or Ignorant Boor. Or Irritating Boil. Get us going, Melissa and me, and we could continue the game for hours.

The I.B. The man I'd set my heart on. My friends and family had all agreed to refrain from using his name. He didn't deserve a name after what he'd done to me.

I sighed. "It's been ten months. Ten months, and nothing. Not a glimmer of a hint of a scintilla of a possibility on the romantic horizon. I'm never going to date again."

"Never is a very long time," Melissa said.

"I don't think I can seriously take romance advice from a woman with fifty-two first dates under her belt in the past year."

"Don't exaggerate," Melissa said with a good-natured shrug. "There were only forty-one."

I shuddered. Forty-one. Forty-one nights of sitting at a table for two. Forty-one nights of coming up with witty and compelling Conversation Topics, five per date. (Okay, I knew Melissa re-used a lot of them, but still!) Forty-one nights of putting on perfect dating clothes, of combing out perfect dating hair, of squelching down perfect dating jitters.

And what did she have to show for it? A Friday evening with me. Me, a DVD of *Casablanca*, and microwave popcorn.

As if she'd read my mind, Melissa brushed her palms

together, a businesswoman ever in charge. "If we don't turn on the upstairs air conditioner now, it'll never cool down."

We might be out of luck anyway. Melissa lived in an apartment above her bakery. Her little home was perfect in every way —except it didn't have central air. In fact, it had a wheezing window unit that was probably Carrier's prototype. You know. Willis Haviland Carrier, the inventor of the air conditioner. I *said* I was a librarian. We accumulate a ridiculous amount of trivia.

Melissa's contraption *could* get the job done, if we gave it enough time. The only problem was braving the oven of an apartment long enough to turn the rattling thing on. She waited for me to volunteer to step into the Sahara that was her living room, but I merely shifted my wrist against my icy glass.

"Come on," she finally said. "Rock, paper, scissors."

Melissa and I settled all our disputes with the childhood game. We might be immature, but we'd never had a serious fight, not in the twenty-five years we'd been best friends. Now, we counted to three, tapping our right fists against our left palms, and displayed our choices—paper for me, rock for Melissa.

"Paper covers rock," I said, trying not to gloat.

"Yeah, yeah," she said good-naturedly. She turned to the steps in the back corner of the bakery. "Keep an eye on things while I'm upstairs. And don't do anything I wouldn't do."

Well that opened up a huge realm of possibilities, didn't it?

I turned to the gigantic stainless steel sink at the back of the bakery, ready to wash a few dishes and get Cake Walk shut down for the night. It was the least I could do, since Melissa was braving the inferno upstairs.

In fact, I'd been practicing a water spell. It should be perfect for a little kitchen cleanup. I'd worked through it with my familiar, Neko, three times in the past week, trying to get my mind around the controlled whirlpool the magic required.

Not that Neko excelled at helping out with water magic.

When I'd first met him, he'd been frozen into the form of a black cat statue. I'd awakened him with my very first spell. He still retained a lot of his feline features, even though he'd remained a flesh-and-blood man for ten straight months. Okay, not *straight* months. Not precisely.

Neko had turned my little home upside down more than once with his parties and his exploits and his boyfriends-of-the-week, but when magical push came to enchanted shove, he'd been there for me, helping me focus my powers and learn new ways to use my gifts.

Even when I wanted to work on water spells, a subset of the the magical world that he detested.

After a week of practice, I'd succeeded in gathering up water from the faucet, and I could consistently get the miniature windstorm spinning in the center of my old farmhouse sink. Each time I tried to factor in dish soap, though, my concentration fell apart, and I was left cleaning up a froth of bubbles. Or a slick river of soap. Or an ocean of foaming water, ankle deep on my kitchen floor.

I bet the Weird Sisters in *Macbeth* never worried about these things. They just hired some sniveling apprentice to scrub their cauldrons clean. Eye of newt, wing of bat…

I decided it was wiser to use conventional cleaning methods in Melissa's bakery. No reason to endanger pastries and pottery alike. Shaking my head and promising myself I *would* master the spell, I reached for a sponge.

Before I could add soap, though, the bell over the door jangled its jaunty greeting. I turned around with a ready smile; I knew how to treat Melissa's clientele when I was at the counter.

And I almost sat in the sink.

The man who stood in the doorway was drop-dead gorgeous. I couldn't compare him to a particular movie star—he was the best of all rolled into one.

He seemed utterly unperturbed by the August heat, not a hint of sweat on his manly brow. His short blond hair lay perfectly, each strand cooperating to set off the strong lines of his cheekbones and his jaw. His eyes glinted in the early evening sunshine, a blue so light they seemed like glass. He wore a crisp white shirt that looked as if it had just left an ironing board, and his jeans fit well enough that Levi's should pay him for the advertising. His shoulders were broad, and his waist was narrow.

He had to come from the Midwest—corn-fed, small-town, a football quarterback if I'd ever seen one. There were country songs written about this man. He'd dated the head cheerleader; they'd been the prom king and queen. He'd wanted to stay on the farm, take over for his daddy, but his mother had presented him with egg money she'd saved through the years, begging him to leave Kansas, to move to Washington for college, for a business degree.

He'd broken his father's heart, even as he'd made the old man wipe away a surreptitious tear of pride. He still called home every Sunday afternoon at four, to catch up with his parents after church, after the mid-afternoon meal they called dinner. He tried to describe the big city to them, to fill them in on his life on Capitol Hill, but they never truly understood.

"I say, are you still open?" he asked.

A British accent.

Okay, so maybe I got a little carried away with my fantasy life for the stranger in front of me. It could happen to anyone. A Brit, though… That was even better than a Future Farmer of America.

I know I was supposed to be a level-headed woman. I had two graduate degrees—in library science and English. I was educated, self-sufficient, competent and capable. I knew better than to swoon over a man's good looks, to melt because he smiled at me, to fall at his feet because he deigned to speak to me.

So shoot me. I'd always had a soft spot for a British accent.

Obviously, plenty of Englishmen were jerks. I knew that too. But, my track record wasn't so great with the standard American issue. And if you asked me to define my perfect man, to write up a quick summary of what I was looking for and place it in an online dating profile, those crisp consonants and plummy vowels would be near the top of my list.

"Um, yes," I said. Smooth, Jane Madison. Brilliant. Witty.

"Have you any Lust, then?"

"Excuse me?"

He winced and smiled ruefully. "A friend sent me. She said you sell Almond Lust, and I couldn't walk by without trying a piece. In fact, I'm to buy up all you have and bring it to a dinner party this evening."

Oh. *Almond* Lust. One of Melissa's specialties.

Well, maybe in some cultures a stinging crimson blush is considered attractive. After all, those British women were all fair-skinned. My dream man was probably used to a gentle companion who flushed the color of a summer sunset. I could hope.

"Of course," I managed to say. I pointed to the pottery plate of shortbread confections, their chocolate layer set off with toasted, sliced almonds. At least my Code Red nail polish was smooth and unchipped. Chalk one up for the colonial team. "We have four left."

"Splendid!"

Again, heat spread to my face. *Pastry*, I reminded myself sternly. He was only commenting on the pastry.

I found a paperboard box beneath the counter and began to transfer the Lust. "Do you work around here?" I asked, intent on drawing him out before he walked through the door, before he disappeared from my life forever.

"I do now. I've just accepted a new position in Arlington."

Arlington. Just over the river. Not in my backyard, but close enough for me to imagine seeing him again. "What do you do?"

"I'm in acquisitions."

Acquisitions. A lawyer, then. My skunk of an ex-fiancé, Scott Randall, had been a lawyer. My shoulders stiffened, but I ordered myself to take a deep breath, to smile, to act like lawyers were my favorite people in the world. After all, if I was going to hate all lawyers, I'd have to move out of Washington. I punched a few keys on the cash register and announced the price. My British friend reached into his pocket and pulled out a money clip with stylized art deco lines that made me think of the statue of Prometheus in Rockefeller Center, the golden god delivering the torch of knowledge to all mankind. I'd never seen an American man use a clip. I bit back a heartfelt sigh.

"Blasted American bills," he muttered with good humor.

Blasted! He said "blasted!" You couldn't get any more British than that!

He shook his head as he slipped off the clip. "You Americans don't have the sense to make your money different colors. Force a poor sod to sort through every last bill to find the right one."

He'd complicated his task by forcing the money clip into double-duty; he had at least a dozen slips of paper tucked next to his cash. He smiled at my quizzical look. "Receipts. I'm terrible about filling out my expense account."

I smiled, anxious to keep even this stilted conversation going. "Receipt!" I exclaimed, like a parrot that had mastered a new word. "Do you need one?"

"That would be lovely, actually." I pressed a button on the register, and it spat out a curl of paper. By then, my Brit had finally found the appropriate bill. I calculated his change, wishing I could think of something else to say.

Downton Abbey. Pride and Prejudice. Monty Python. Bridget Jones. None of those was likely to spark a deep and meaningful conversation. With a sinking feeling, I collected his change from the register. I counted it into his palm, and no one could really blame me if I let my fingers slip against his. The touch lingered only a moment, just long enough for him to curve a smile and say, "With these coins?"

I had no idea what he meant, but I was eager to respond. "Pardon me?"

"It's an old nursery rhyme. Mother Goose, I think. 'With these coins I find you. With these words I bind you. Keep our secret, silent be. Speak to no man, not of me. Diddle dum, diddle dee, fi, fo, fum.'"

When all I managed was a puzzled smile, my mysterious Brit laughed and shrugged at the same time, saying, "I suppose our nurseries had different rhymes." He shot his cuff and glanced at his watch, clearly eager to be heading out to his dinner party. Reluctantly, I made a show of tucking in the lid of his paperboard box. I took a printed sticker from the roll Melissa kept by the register and pressed in onto the box for good measure. At least all the guests at his dinner party would know the source of the delectable treats he carried.

"Good Lust," I said in a cheery voice, and cringed when I heard how stupid I sounded.

"Many thanks." And then he winked at me.

He. Winked. At. Me.

From a lot of guys, a wink would be sleazy. It would be sly. It would be nothing more than a pick-up line.

From my Brit, though, it was a shared joke. A private conversation. An entire future, all wrapped up in one fortuitous twitch of an eye.

And then the bell jangled, and he was out the door, heading back into the steamy DC evening.

"Oh good!" Melissa said, coming back down the stairs. "You killed the Lust."

"What?" I was still staring after the customer, willing him to remember something, to come back, to ask for my name, my number, anything.

"The Lust." Melissa pointed to the empty pottery plate. "It doesn't keep well at all."

I sighed and licked my lips. "Then we would have been forced to eat it all by ourselves."

"What's that?" Melissa reached around me and picked up a white slip from the counter.

I craned my neck and looked at the item in her fingers. It was a card. Like a business card, but with different dimensions —more square than rectangular. It had a dark silver lining, dully reflective, and words embossed in bold, black letters.

GRAEME HENDERSON
ACQUISITIONS

And beneath it, as discreet as a priest in a confessional, a telephone number. 703 prefix. Arlington, Virginia.

I remembered him shuffling through his money, juggling the receipts. He had seemed to take more time than he needed, made the paper more of a production than was strictly necessary. He had wanted me to have this card.

That's what he'd meant by his wink, by the tiny smile on his perfect lips.

Melissa sighed and turned toward the trashcan. Her wrist cocked; she was treating the card as garbage. "*No!*" I exclaimed. She looked at me as if I had two heads. "No," I repeated in a quieter voice. "I think he meant for me to have it."

"He?" Melissa asked.

"The customer who was just here."

"Acquisitions?" Melissa read again. "How pretentious is that?"

"Not pretentious at all!" I rushed to Graeme Henderson's defense. Even as I protested Melissa's dismissal, I realized he couldn't be a lawyer. Not with a card like that. A law firm would have sucked out any spark of creativity, would have bled dry the smooth polish of the silver-lined card. "I mean, it's not pretentious if that's what he does."

"But what does he acquire?"

"Lust," I said immediately.

Melissa gave me a strange look, but she passed the card

across the counter. I slipped it into my pocket, vowing to phone him the very next day.

After all, didn't the dating gods help those who helped themselves?

If I'd known the havoc that one phone call would wreak, I would have thrown away the card right then and there. Lust and everything, I would have just tossed it.

Or at least I would have remembered that witchcraft never made anything simpler. Never, ever, ever.

M elissa and I were well into our second pitcher of mojitos, almost soused enough to join the patrons of Rick's club in singing their rousing rendition of "La Marseillaise," when we were interrupted by a knock at the door. For just a moment, I thought Graeme might have returned to Cake Walk, intent on finding satisfaction beyond Almond Lust, but I realized I was being ridiculous even before Melissa had paused the DVD.

As she opened the door, she sighed in disgust. "Oh," she said, and her tone let me know exactly who stood on the landing. "It's you."

"And it's a pleasure to see you too," Neko said, slinking into the room with the aplomb of his Egyptian feline ancestors. As he glided across the room, he said to me, "I thought I'd find you here. Don't look quite so disappointed to see me."

He leaned over and kissed me on both cheeks—his latest affectation—before settling in the middle of the couch. Sitting cross-legged and stretching back, he looked for all the world like a cat occupying a particularly spectacular sunbeam. After studying his immaculate fingernails, he reached into the bowl of popcorn I'd been sharing with Melissa and extracted a generous handful. He held his cupped palm to his lips and extended his tongue, delicately gathering up a single puffed kernel. He chewed slowly, then cocked his head to one side. "What? You're not even going to offer me a drink?"

I shot Melissa a pleading glance, but she started to shake her head in the negative. She and Neko had scarcely been on speaking terms for the past three months. I mouthed, "Please!" and she recanted, stalking into the kitchen to retrieve a glass. She filled it with our magical concoction of rum, lime, and mint before passing the drink to Neko. "Thank you," he purred, raising the glass to toast her before tossing back a healthy swallow. "Mmmm. Could use a bit more mint, but any port in a storm, as they say."

"*We* thought they were just fine," Melissa said through gritted teeth. "We made them just the way we like them."

I leaned forward to separate them. "Neko, if you'd rather *go home*, I have some chardonnay in the fridge."

He beamed at me. "Not any more. *Jacques* and I finished it last night." He drew out the foreign name as if it were a delectable appetizer. Lowering his eyes and looking up at me through lashes that were longer than any man deserved, he went on, "Or should I say, this morning?"

Melissa huffed in disgust and hustled down the hallway, slamming the bathroom door behind her. I glared at my familiar. "Neko, was that absolutely necessary?"

"What? It was only a bottle of Turning Leaf. Hardly anything to get upset about." A small frown creased the ageless arch between his eyebrows, and his mouth opened into a startled O. "I'm sorry! Did Melissa give the wine to you? Was she upset that I drank a gift?"

"You know why she was upset." I took the bowl of popcorn away from him, before he could devour the rest of our microwaved bounty. "You didn't need to mention Jacques. You know she still isn't over him."

"And once again, I have to say that isn't my fault! I can't help it if Jacques liked me more than he liked her!"

I took a deep breath, ready to explain, again, that Neko wasn't helping matters. I was ready to tell him, again, that Melissa had found Jacques first. I was ready to state, again, that Jacques was the one who had posted on FranticDate.com. I was ready to remind Neko, again, that Jacques had said that his ideal date was a woman—a *woman*—who could bake like his grandmere and who looked like Audrey Tatou. I was ready to scream at Neko, again, that Jacques was the one who had thought that he could cajole himself out of his gayness, that he could "heal" himself, start playing for the other side, if only he found the right woman to lead him onto the straight and narrow path.

But we'd crossed that ground before, back and forth, countless times in the past three months. Neko had come into Cake Walk just as Jacques arrived for his second date with Melissa (a rare second date, I might add—Melissa was pickier than Jacques's sainted grandmere, but she'd been feeling desperate). The attraction between the men had been instant. Jacques had wandered off with my cat-like familiar, barely remembering to say goodbye to Melissa, not even bothering to cancel dinner plans with her that night.

And Neko and Jacques had been inseparable ever since.

I'd tried to remind Melissa that she hadn't even *liked* Jacques that much. She'd been bored by his conversation (all about fashion and designers and life on the haute couture circuit in, um, Gay Paree). She had thought he was self-absorbed and more than a little snobby. She'd found it odd that he had not even tried to kiss her goodnight, despite a first date that lasted until nearly midnight.

But her pride had been injured. Here she was, turning over every stone she could find as she searched for the man of her dreams, and Neko was able to waltz in and pluck the plum from her dating tree, with scarcely a pause to catch his breath.

And I was left in the middle, trying to bridge the gap

between my best friend and my familiar. "Neko, would it kill you not to mention him here? Just until she finds someone else. Until she's focused some new man at the bakery."

He frowned. "It's not like Jacques and I were engaging in hot sweaty man-sex on her sofa." I immediately thought of the cracked leather couch in my basement, Neko's bed every night that he spent in the cottage we shared. I did *not* need that image flickering in front of my eyes, thank you very much.

With a precise moue, Neko leaned forward and touched the remote control to unfreeze the DVD. The rousing French anthem began to pour from the television again, filling both Rick's club and Melissa's living room with the stirring strains of Gallic patriotism. Before I could decipher the buttons on the remote, Melissa stormed out of the bathroom. Her fingers flew over the electronic gadget, and the television crashed into silence. The laboring air conditioner made the only sound in the room. The air conditioner and my pounding heart, as I waited to see if this storm was going to pass.

"Enough!" she said. "We all know how the movie ends."

Okay. So maybe the French national anthem wasn't the best soundtrack at the moment. I guessed we were through watching *Casablanca*. Gulping down a large swallow of mojito, I searched for a new conversational course to guide us into a safe social harbor. Before I could divine one, Neko asked, "And how was *your* afternoon?" And then, in a transparent bid to steer the conversation back to his own love life: "Focused on any new man at the bakery?"

I started to say something, anything to fill the awkward pause. I was even ready to share news about the golden stranger, Graeme Henderson, but Melissa cut me off, snapping, "'Friend-ship is constant in all other things.'"

I stared at her, utterly confused. I knew the rest of the line; it was from *Much Ado About Nothing*: "Save in the office and affairs of love." Melissa and I played the Shakespeare game often enough, quoting snippets of the Bard to each other. We'd used his plays like our own private code since we were absurdly precocious teenagers, gaga over the romance of Romeo and Juliet.

Nodding when she saw that I remembered the rest of the line, Melissa said sweetly, "Jane, could you help me in the kitchen?" She slopped the dregs of mojitos from the pitcher into Neko's glass and practically dragged me out of the room.

"What?" I asked her, as she began dismembering limes with a knife that was large enough to make me take a step back.

"Friendship test."

"What?" This time, I let my voice reflect my utter confusion.

"Friendship test. You know."

Sure, I knew about friendship tests. You could call "friendship test" on your best friend any time you needed to confirm your relationship. You could friendship test the last slice of chocolate cheesecake for example, calling out those two words and freezing the treat on its way to your best friend's plate. You could friendship test packing for a trip, dragooning your best friend into staying up till the wee hours of the morning, deciding whether the strategically ripped jeans or the painfully tight ones were more likely to make your great aunt have conniptions at Thanksgiving dinner. You could friendship test a movie, shoving out the latest blockbuster romance for an action flick that everyone *knew* would be terrible, but it starred Brad Pitt, so you had to go, no matter what the critics said.

But friendship testing an entire topic of conversation? Especially one as innocuous as Graeme Henderson, Acquisitions, and my dreams of British romance?

Melissa rolled mint leaves into a careful pile before employing her knife with the unshakable rhythm of a trained professional. The sharp scent mingled with the rum she glugged into the pitcher, melding with the citrus tang of the limes. She fumbled in her freezer for ice cubes, and when she turned back to me, unshed tears glittered in her eyes.

She wasn't crying for Jacques.

She was upset about all the other First Dates. She was saddened by her endless quest for happiness, her constant search for completeness. And, truth be told, she was probably just a little jealous about *my* relationship with Neko, about my mysterious bond with my familiar. She knew I was a witch, and she understood I had new powers, new abilities, a new life that was separate and apart from the years we'd known each other.

Fine. I didn't have to tell Neko about Graeme Henderson. It wasn't like anything had happened with the guy—he was just a gorge customer who'd dropped in at the end of the day. I'd keep the secret, just with Melissa, if that's what she wanted.

"Friendship test," I said, shrugging. I lifted the pitcher as Melissa rinsed her hands, taking a moment to press her fingertips against her eyelids. "Okay?"

She smiled, and her lips only trembled a little. "Okay."

Neko had switched the television to the Game Show Network, and he was gleefully shouting out answers to an ancient avatar of Alex Trebec. He bombed out at Final Jeopardy, though, and sat back on the couch with a pout. "Stupid game."

"You'll get no argument here," I said.

He started to surf through stations, bypassing anything that hinted of education or drama. When he landed on QVC, they were hawking hideous rhinestone pins. Each was the size of my fist, clustered with fake diamonds, sapphires, and rubies. As we stared at a monstrosity that was meant to represent a peacock, Neko told me, "*That* would make a fantastic addition to your wardrobe."

"It would clash with my brocade petticoat," I said. My job at the Peabridge Library included a colonial wardrobe—rich taffeta and linen, hoops to make my waist look tiny, and delicate embroidery that made my fingers ache every time I looked at the stitches. I wasn't a big fan of the costumes, but I never needed to decide what to wear to the office, and that added up to an extra fifteen minutes of sleep every morning.

The colonial garb had been part of my boss's last scheme to keep the Peabridge budget in the black. She required all of us to dress like Martha Washington, in hopes of bringing in local library traffic. The same desperate measures had led to my living in a cottage on the Peabridge grounds—I had exchanged twenty-five percent of my salary for a fully-furnished cottage. A cottage that just happened to contain a collection of books on witchcraft. Books—and Neko, whose fashion sense (at least in jewelry) seemed twisted from the years he had spent enchanted as a statue in my basement.

From the corner of my eye, I saw Melissa shudder at the hideous rhinestone disaster. "Come on, Neko," I pressed. "Why did you come over here?"

"Oh!" He put down the remote. "Clara phoned."

Clara. My mother. "And?"

"She wanted to remind you that you're both having brunch with your grandmother, a week from Sunday."

So now Clara was my calendar tickler? Brunch was more than a week away. I guess she just didn't want to disappoint Gran.

Monthly brunch meetings had been my grandmother's idea. She thought that if the three of us got together on the first Sunday of every month, then we'd get to know each other better. We'd learn to trust each other more, to share with each other like mothers and daughters are supposed to.

Most of the time, we managed to make it through the meal without outright arguments. It helped when I started ordering Eggs Benedict. I could take out some of my frustration on the English muffin base. I could never make it through a simple breakfast of Special K and skim milk with my mother. Not without shredding half a dozen napkins in frustration.

But I attended our monthly get-togethers religiously. They were a sort of offering to the gods for my grandmother's complete recovery from the pneumonia that had sent her to the hospital the year before. While it had taken months for her to regain her proverbial vim and vigor, she was finally entrenched in her volunteer work again, helping out the DC Concert Opera Guild.

She was also wholly devoted to the cause of strengthening my bonds with my mother. There were now entire weeks when I didn't sulk about Clara abandoning me for twenty-eight years. (I could recite Gran's explanations in my sleep by now. Clara had needed to defeat her own demons. She had needed to grow up herself. She had needed to find the spiritual anchor of her life in the whirlwind world around us. Yeah, yeah, yeah.)

I glared at Neko. "And that reminder couldn't wait until I got home?"

My familiar plucked at an imaginary thread on his black jeans. "There was another message."

I caught Melissa rolling her eyes, and I had to admit I was getting annoyed with my interfering familiar as well. "Yes?" I prompted.

"Teresa Alison Sidney called."

I caught my breath.

"Who's that?" Melissa asked.

Neko cocked his head, clearly asking if I wanted him to elaborate. I fortified myself by filling my lungs and said, "The head of the Washington Coven. The leader of the local witches."

I hadn't met Teresa Alison Sidney yet, but I'd heard her name often enough in the past ten months. She'd been invoked like a saint or a sinner, every single time I strayed from my studies with David Montrose, my warder. Teresa Alison Sidney and her coven had the right to control all witchcraft in their territory. If I didn't measure up, they could stake a claim to all the arcana in my possession—spell books, crystals, runes, and the rest.

Including Neko. My familiar was part of the package. Part of the package I would lose if the Washington Coven deemed me unworthy of membership. I pictured Teresa Alison Sidney as a forbidding woman, wise, waiting—like Whistler's Mother in modern dress. I knew I'd have to meet her eventually, but I'd been perfectly content to put off that reckoning. Put it off until I'd learned more about my powers, until I'd gained some confidence, some courage.

Melissa, not being up on the witchcraft celebrity watch, failed to register the importance of the call.

"What did she say?" I asked Neko, trying to sound nonchalant. After all, the Coven Mother might be calling for any number of reasons. She might... She might have realized she had a sudden need for colonial American recipes. Or she might... She might have been looking for advice on locally grown herbs and aromatics. Or she might...

I couldn't really think of any *good* thing that she might.

"She wants to meet with you. Next Friday. At midnight."

Despite the summer heat, gooseflesh rose on my arms. Midnight. The witching hour. "A—" I needed to clear my throat. "Alone?"

"She'll have the entire coven gathered," Neko said helpfully.

That did nothing to ease the sudden fear that trickled down the back of my neck. I thought of Gran's old-fashioned expression: someone had walked across my grave. "I mean," I managed to say after thinking out each word, "Do *I* have to show up alone?"

"Of course not." Neko's smile was sympathetic, and I could tell he was trying to make his answer light. "I'll be there. And David."

My familiar and my warder. To help me work magic and to protect me. I didn't really feel reassured, though.

"Is this it, then?" I folded my arms around my belly, suddenly wishing I hadn't downed the last couple of minty mojitos. I wanted to rock back and forth, find some comfort in acting like a rebellious toddler. "Are they going to test me?"

"Of *course* they're going to test you," Neko scoffed. His casual dismissal converted my apprehension into annoyance. "You've known that all along. No, this isn't the time for the test itself. They'll choose some important day for that. This meeting is just to lay the groundwork. To tell you the rules."

I nodded. Neko's words made sense. All except for…"Important day? What sort of important day?"

"You know. One of the Witches' Sabbaths. Imbolc. Beltane. Lughnasa. Samhain."

I'd read enough in my collection of witchy books that I recognized the names of the festivals. I was even able to translate Neko's Gaelic pronunciation—"Sow-inn"—to actual spelling—"Samhain." Halloween. But I'd never actually paid attention to the specific witching days, never worried about when they hit the "real world" calendar.

Real world.

This *was* my real world now. I was a witch.

And I was going to be tested by my coven, judged to see if I truly belonged as a new member. I remembered the magical runes and crystals lying in my basement, probably grown dusty, since I'd neglected them for a month or more, while I played with my still-unsuccessful water spell.

Where did the time go? And how was I going to get ready for my first encounter with the Washington Coven, with Teresa Alison Sidney? And what was I going to do once the coven set an actual date for my testing?

Melissa might not have been privy to all of my witchcraft workings. She didn't know the feelings that grew inside me as I practiced my craft. She'd never understand the tremble of power as I worked a spell, the satisfying *snick* of release when my magic hit its target.

But she knew *me*. She recognized my fear. "It'll all be fine," she said, topping off my glass and looking daggers at Neko, sending a sufficiently clear message that even he realized he should keep his mouth shut.

"But——" I said.

"You'll practice," she said.

"I don't——"

"You will," she affirmed.

"I've never——"

"No time like the present," she berated. "Or, more accurately, the future. You'll work with Neko and David. You'll learn everything you need to know. And when you need a bit of support and reassurance, you'll swing by Cake Walk so I can feed you and remind you of everything you *do* know."

She was so certain. So determined. There was no way I could argue with her. She was my best friend, and she knew what was right.

I shrugged and stretched against the back of the couch, shoving my hands into my pockets to help ease the panic-kinks in my spine. My fingers brushed against the card I had hidden away, the silver-edged message from Graeme Henderson. *Acquisitions*.

I felt the message like a gentle electric thrum, like the tension of static charge when you rub a balloon against a wool sweater and make your hair stand on end.

Friendship test. Melissa was my best friend, and she would get me through my meeting with the Washington Coven. Melissa, and Neko, and David. A girl could hardly ask for a better support group.

Melissa plucked the remote from Neko's hand. "Oh well. We can hardly leave Victor Laszlo standing in the lurch, can we?" We watched the end of *Casablanca* without further conversation, waiting until the final screen to toast Rick's famous last words. As one, we lifted our mojito glasses and repeated the line earnestly: "I think this is the beginning of a beautiful friendship."

As I recited the words, my fingers drifted back to the card in my pocket. *Graeme*, I thought. And I let my mind wander over that British accent, that sly wink, and the beautiful…friendship that might await me when I phoned the number on the card. The possibility was almost enough to make me forget about my upcoming meeting with Teresa Alison Sidney and the Washington Coven.

Almost.

But not quite.

3

———

I sat on the edge of my bed and stared at the phone. This was stupid. I'd made phone calls before. Thousands of them. Why should this one be any different? Why should it make my pulse pound? Make my tongue swell up? Make tremors march up and down my arms, like tiny electric soldiers trying to kick me into action?

Or maybe I was just hung over from Mojito Therapy the night before.

I wiped my hands against my jeans and reached one more time for the small white business card. Graeme Henderson. Acquisitions.

This wasn't fair. I shouldn't have to make the phone call. He should have asked me for *my* phone number. *He* should have taken the risk.

But he had. He'd left his card, putting it right on the counter. He'd made the first move.

So, really, it was like he'd already asked me out, and all I had to do was pick up the phone and say yes. Right?

I palmed the card and leaned back against my headboard, hugging my pillow to my chest. Had I ever been the one to make the first move? Well, there was that time in eighth grade, when I'd asked Adam Lehrer to the Sadie Hawkins dance. But that was hardly a date. I mean, there'd been a dozen of us kids, all going to the dance together. We'd stood on separate sides of the gym and told nervous jokes with our friends, waiting until two hours had gone by before anyone was brave enough to take to the dance floor, and that was only because they played the Macarena, and we could pretend like we didn't know each other while we flailed around on the basketball court.

No. I wasn't being fair to myself. I *had* asked Adam Lehrer to the dance. So what was I worried about? This should be old hat, right?

Of course, Adam Lehrer and I had been thirteen years old. And Adam had been a freakish six feet tall, even though he didn't weigh more than one hundred and thirty pounds. He wasn't about to say no to any girl who gave him the time of day. And I never actually *phoned* him for a date. I'd passed him a note in homeroom, asking him to check one box if his answer was yes, and another if his answer was no.

Now, I gritted my teeth. I was being ridiculous. I was a grown woman. A professional librarian. I was experienced, confident, capable, a *witch*, for Hecate's sake.

I wasn't going to let one silly invention—the telephone—get in the way of my finding eternal happiness with the most gorgeous man I'd met since the I.B.

The Itinerant Bellyache. I'd pursued *him*, and look where that had gotten me. I'd even asked him up to Gran's farm, invited him to my family reunion, so my humiliation could be placed on full display for everyone I knew and loved.

Wait. I'd asked the I.B., but only after *he* had invited *me* to lunch. He had asked me out first. He took the lead, and the relationship ended up in the toilet. There. The powers of the universe were clearly sending me a message. They were obviously demanding that I change my ways. Those who cannot remember the past are doomed to repeat it, and all that jazz.

I grabbed the phone and punched in the number before I could talk myself out of acting.

One ring.

I nearly hung up.

Two rings.

I caught my breath.

Three rings.

I started to compose a message for his answering machine, thought better of it, decidedthat I'd just throw away the card, that the universe was clearly reversing its original message. Now it was shrieking: Run! Run! Flee before it's too late!

Four –

"Henderson."

"Madison," I said, before I could stop myself.

I was such an idiot! He didn't even know my name. He was going to think I was mocking him, just for answering his phone with a crisp, business-like precision. "Jane Madison here," I clarified, before he could hang up. "We met yesterday. At Cake Walk."

"Oh yes," he said, and I could hear him smile as he spoke. Yes. *Hear* him smile. Those perfect lips, curving around those flawless teeth... He said, "The Lust girl."

"Er, yes," I said and made a face I meant to be funny. I scowled when I realized he couldn't see me, and then I felt even more stupid. My not-so-becoming flush was rising to my cheeks once again. No wonder I'd sent Adam Lehrer a note in eighth grade—that communication was a thousand times easier than this one, even if I *had* needed to debate the size and shape of the boxes for him to check. Fortunately, Melissa had convinced me that heart-shaped boxes were Not Cool. "I wanted to follow up with you," I said to Graeme, clutching at straws to move this conversation forward. "To find out if the people at your dinner party enjoyed the dessert."

I was *not* going to say the word "lust." Wild horses couldn't make me say it.

"It was everything I'd been told it would be," he said. And then he lowered his voice and whispered, "And more."

Now he was definitely toying with me. He probably left his card on counters all across America. He lured poor unsuspecting shopgirls into thinking he was some harmless football-player frat boy from the Midwest, and then he dropped his sleek Acquisitions card, trolling to see just how many of them—of *us* —were foolish enough to phone him. He probably had this whole call scripted. He already knew what he was going to say, how he was going to lure me into making more of an fool out of myself.

"Well good, then," I heard myself say in a tiny voice that might have traveled all the way from Mars. "Um, goodbye."

"Just a moment," he said, and my heart pounded so hard I needed to open my mouth to take a breath. "Don't be so hasty." Hasty. Did Americans ever say *hasty*? It was a British word. Like naughty. I jerked my thoughts back from *that* precipice.

"I'm truly glad you rang me up," he said. "I wanted to speak with you longer in your shop, but I was late to meet my friends."

"Actually, the bakery isn't mine."

"Oh?"

"It belongs to my best friend. I just cover for her sometimes. I work at the Peabridge Library, just a few blocks away. I'm a librarian." I heard the unwanted note of defensiveness creep into my voice. I'd learned to judge a lot about people from the way they responded to my job title. About fifty percent made "Marian the Librarian" jokes, apparently deluded into believing that they were the first people in the entire history of librarian-ship to make the *Music Man* connection. Another twenty-five percent immediately asked how long it had taken me to learn the Dewey Decimal System. I no longer had a civil answer for either group.

"Ah… 'My library was dukedom enough.'"

"Prospero!" I shouted. "*The Tempest*."

"Quite," he said, and now his amusement seemed warm and friendly, including me in a select club—the cognoscenti, the literati, the something else extravagant that ended with -ti.

I started to make an excuse. "It's just that—"

He was already providing his own explanation, verbally waving off the quotation. "You know. The tedium of a classical education."

"I specialize in that tedium," I said, and then I grimaced. Tedium was not a word I wanted him to associate with me in any way, shape, or form.

"So," he said, when the silence had stretched out a little too long. "Is there a place where we could meet to exchange quips about the Bard? I can find out more about why a librarian offers up biscuits to the public during her spare time, and we could share a cup of coffee?"

I thought rapidly. "How about Bistro Français? It's on M Street, in the center of Georgetown."

"Excellent." I could imagine him writing down the restaurant name in impeccable British penmanship. He didn't seem a smartphone sort of guy. He'd use a fountain pen to write on rich, creamy calendar pages. "There's one small hitch, though. My office is demanding beastly hours just now. Could we make this dessert coffee? Say on Wednesday night?"

Alarms went off inside my head. Office. Beastly hours. I'd heard excuses like that before. Excuses from a married pig of a man.

But, a little voice protested, struggling to be heard over the blaring alarms. Late hours are fine. Late hours are when a married man goes home to his wife and family. Beware the man who *keeps* you from his evenings and weekends and holidays.

"Wednesday night?" I said, and tried to sound as if I was paging through my very busy social calendar.

"Would half past nine be too late?"

9:30. We could chat for an hour or so, and I'd still be able to get home, get to bed, wake up on time for work. "That would be perfect," I said, fighting to balance my enthusiasm against my jaded disillusionment. Damn the I.B.! I refused to let the Incontinent Bogeyman interfere with my current plans.

I'm not quite sure what Graeme and I said to each other then, but I must have made perfectly normal "signing off" noises, because I was suddenly staring at a dead phone and a silver-lined card.

A dead phone, a silver-lined card, and the prospect of my first date since the Ill-bred Bête-Noire had poisoned my love life. I clutched my pillow to my face and squealed, trying to release some of the thrumming, paralyzing energy that rolled over me.

I had done it! I had made the phone call! I pounded my heels against my bed, inordinately pleased with my social bravery.

"Jane? Are you all right in there?"

Neko.

I sat up and placed the phone back on my nightstand, taking care to slip Graeme's card between my mattress and box spring. "I'm fine," I said. "Come in."

My door opened, and Neko poked his head around the corner. His gaze automatically darted toward my closet, to the small metal table that had hosted an aquarium until last October. The glance was so rapid that I would have missed it if I hadn't been waiting. When Neko spoke, he'd carefully trained his face to impassivity. "David is waiting for you in the basement."

My trusty warder.

He must have found out about Teresa Alison Sidney's summons. Neko would have kept him apprised of such a development, even if David's position as warder didn't grant him access to information through other channels. I was a bit surprised he hadn't awakened me at dawn, slavedriver that he was.

"Thanks," I said to Neko, pausing only long enough to twitch my bedspread back into place. I glanced at the edge, envisioning my treasured card tucked safely away. I was pleased to see that nothing looked out of place—a friendship test *was* a friendship test, and Melissa had asked me not to tell Neko about Graeme. Who was I to go back on my word? And the prickly feeling at the back of my neck made me suspect Neko would do *something* to ruin things with Graeme if I gave him half a chance. My familiar and my love life were not a good mix.

Well, I thought, as I descended the stairs to the basement, time enough to think about my mysterious Englishman later. Now, I had to work. At least it was cool downstairs.

David was waiting for me by the bookstand. "Good morning," he said. Somehow, he managed to convey that the morning had mostly fled toward noon, and he assumed I had been lollygagging around—lollygagging!—rather than producing anything worthwhile in the witchcraft sense of the word.

For the most part, David and I had settled into an easy relationship, a surprisingly straightforward give and take. Technically, he was my protector. His job was to keep me from hurting myself when I worked my magic or—more ominously—from being hurt by someone else.

David, though, did far more. He had assumed the role of teacher, guiding me through using my powers, helping me learn more about the strange new world I'd discovered less than a year before.

Whenever I got too stubborn or David got too short-tempered, he threatened to stop teaching me. He told me I needed to go to the coven, to enroll in a magicarium, a school for witches. There, I'd follow the time-honored formula for magic instruction, trudging through the rota, repeating a single spell hundreds of times until I had it down perfectly.

Each time David threatened, though, we managed to make

peace. I didn't like the idea of sharing my magical development with a stranger. I was proud of what I'd accomplished, but also embarrassed by the little things I hadn't quite managed to master. I should have had better control over my spell-working by now, and I was an absolute mess with runes. I hadn't even ventured into the most esoteric aspects of witchcraft.

"Good morning," I said, doing my best to match David's serious tone.

And then we engaged in the Greeting Ballet. We'd done this now, countless times, and it never became more graceful. If he were a friend, I'd throw my arms around him and give him a quick hug. If he were a certain type of casual acquaintance (like Neko's current beau, Jacques), we would peck each other on both cheeks. If he were a work colleague, I'd extend my hand for a quick, hearty shake.

But he was all of those things. And none of them. And so we treated each other with proverbial kid gloves, stumbling into an awkward embrace that left both of us off-balance. I tried to plant a quick kiss on his cheek and ended up grazing the air by his chin. He looked startled and he pulled away, which caused *me* to pull away, backing into Neko.

As my familiar caught my elbow he shot me one of his wry, arched-eyebrow grins, and I bit back the first retort that came to mind. The last thing I needed was for Neko to make smart comebacks about my relationship with David. I brushed my hands through my hair and turned back to my warder. "Good morning," I said again, as if I could erase the entire embarrassing sequence from his memory and my own.

I crossed the room and collapsed onto the black leather couch. Neko's hot sweaty man-sex couch. No. I wasn't going to think about that.

David shoved his hands into the pockets of his khakis and jutted his almost-kissed chin toward the bookshelves. As I'd expected, he said, "I'm here to help you prepare for your Friday meeting with Teresa Alison Sidney."

"Does everyone call her that?" I asked, letting some of my anxiety spill over as annoyance.

"Teresa Alison Sidney? That's her name."

"But do people always use her first, middle, and last name? Why can't she just be 'Teresa?' Or 'Ms. Sidney?' With the triple names, it's like she's a celebrity, and everyone's afraid of sounding either too familiar or too formal when they talk about her."

"Well, she *is* a celebrity," David said. "At least within the Eastern Empire. She's headed up the Washington Coven for twenty-five years, and she's the only witch in history to serve three consecutive terms on Hecate's Court."

"How old *is* she?" I immediately aged Whistler's Mother, pushing her into her nineties, to the outer edges of frail existence.

"Suffice to say, Teresa Alison Sidney got an early start on her career."

"Can you be a bit more specific?" I redrew poor Whistler's Mother again, easing her wrinkles and giving her a red hat and a purple blouse to brighten her day.

"She's thirty-five."

"What?"

"She's thirty-five years old."

"But you just said she's headed the coven for twenty-five years."

"She has. She was a prodigy. She's got strong powers, and she knows how to use them."

I swallowed hard. Thirty-five years old and Teresa Alison Sidney had already led the Washington Coven for a quarter of a century.

You know, I could have handled things if she'd been ancient. I'd been trained since birth to respect the elderly, to offer my seat on the subway, to laugh at a mediocre joke. In the back of my mind, I'd imagined the Washington Coven looking an awful lot like the Concert Opera Guild where Gran served on the board of directors. I *knew* how to handle myself with the opera crowd.

But thirty-five? Teresa Alison Sidney was only five years older than I was! The coven was going to be more like a sorority meeting. A group of my so-called peers, sitting in judgment.

"Why didn't you tell me before?"

"What didn't I tell you?" David sounded exasperated. "I've been trying to tell you about the coven for months. You're the one who always changes the topic of conversation."

"I don't change the topic of conversation. Just the other day at work, Evelyn told me I have the most stick-to-it-iveness of any librarian at the Peabridge. She said she was impressed by my developing a lecture series, and she'd like to grow it into—"

David cocked his head to one side, sparing the half smile that meant he was feeling quietly superior. "Not changing the topic of conversation?" he asked.

"No. I was about to come back to Teresa Alison Sidney. And her age."

David frowned. "Does it really matter?"

I looked at my hands, discovering that I'd clenched them into tight fists. Consciously, I took a deep breath and relaxed my claws. "No!" I said brightly. "Her age doesn't change anything at all!"

"Very well, then. Let's get started."

"What, exactly, are we starting to do?"

David stood straighter. When he spoke, he used his "minister" tone, the deep, rumbling register he saved for the most basic level of my instruction. "Your meeting with Teresa Alison Sidney is really just an introduction. She won't test you this time. But you have to offer up a suitable greeting."

"So, I need to learn the proper witchy handshake? Or is this more of a curtsey sort of thing?"

He swallowed as if bitter wormwood coated his tongue. "Actually, the curtsey isn't a bad analogy." He took a moment to study me, starting at the crown of my head and not stopping until he'd reached my toes. My toes, in their grungy sneakers. My toes that had not seen a pedicure in too many months to count. I tried to curl my feet under the front edge of the sofa. "This will be your introduction to magical society. Your coming out party, if you will."

I laughed. "So, I'm going to wear a white dress and get someone to pile my hair on top of my head? Do I have to scare up an escort?"

"You've already got one of those." He settled his right hand over his heart, as if he were about to recite the Pledge of Allegiance.

"You're kidding."

"I only wish I was." Again, with that head-to-toe survey. "The coven takes these things very seriously. I'm not nearly as concerned about what you'll wear, though, as I am about what you'll bring."

"Bring?"

"It's customary for a new witch to offer a gift to the leader of her coven."

"And I'm guessing a plate of Melissa's Peach Melba Tartlets won't get the job done."

"Hardly." David looked around the room. "You have to present something unique to you. Something that expresses your true nature."

It wasn't difficult to follow his logic. "One of my books."

He nodded. "And you'll have to bind it up in magic."

"Gift wrap won't do? Even if I make a pretty bow and smother it in curling ribbon?"

He pursed his lips as he shook his head, and I knew I was just asking questions to tweak him. To tweak him, and to smother the sudden pang of loss I felt at the notion that someone—anyone—would get to keep one of *my* books. How could I feel so possessive about things I didn't even know existed a year ago?

I further delayed choosing one of my darlings for banishment by asking, "So what do you mean by binding it up in magic?"

"Each witch presents things in different ways, again, unique to her powers and her temperament. If the element of Air spoke to you, for instance, you might surround your book in a miniature storm. You'd temper the winds, so they kept the book safe, and you'd train them to let one specific person—Teresa Alison Sidney—gain access."

It was my turn to purse my lips. I was hardly an expert on Air. In the past year, I'd harnessed it for a handful of spells, but it didn't sing to my powers; it didn't *speak* to me in any meaningful way. Just the same, I couldn't imagine weaving a magical box out of Water—not after my repeated failures with the kitchen-cleaning spell. And I was getting nowhere near Fire. Not with one of my precious books.

Even as I thought of all the magic that I couldn't work, that I *wouldn't* work, an idea took hold in my mind. I spun it about for a moment, testing it mentally, poking and prodding to see if I was an idiot, or merely an idealist. When I still didn't see any flaws, I dared to say, "Earth. Citrine."

David merely nodded as I walked over to the large wooden box that held my crystals. I tried to brush dust off the lid without his noticing, and then I shifted the nested trays inside. I had three good examples of citrine. I liked its clear golden hue, and I was drawn to the steady warmth the stone emanated.

There! The three specimens I remembered. One was small but expertly cut. Another was almost absurdly large, but a whisper of a flaw shimmered in its depths, black and jagged. The third, though, was perfect—large enough to be set in a ring or to serve as an eye-catching center of a necklace. It covered the nail on my little finger.

I lifted it from its velvet-inlaid tray and turned it to catch the light. I could picture it centered above a book, spreading its crystalline power over the bound pages. *Generosity*, citrine said.

Prosperity. Those were its ancient properties, its traditional symbolism. What could be more perfect as an offering to my new magical leader?

I turned to David and said, "Okay. Show me. Show me how to bind a book."

D avid looked at me critically, as if he thought I was mocking this latest chapter in my witchy education. I shrugged and said, "Seriously. Tell me how to start. I *want* to do this."

Still, he didn't respond. I squirmed a little under his attention, barely resisting the urge to raise my fingernails to my teeth, to gnaw away the edge of my nervousness. Fortunately, my Code Red nail polish saved me. It had taken me months to grow out my nails long enough to warrant the expense of Lancôme. I wasn't going to suffer a setback just because David chose to play the part of inscrutable warder.

"All right," he said at last, and I wondered what sort of test I'd passed in *his* mind. "First things first. You need to choose a book. The binding you create, the 'gift-wrap' will depend on the subject you're covering."

I looked around my basement sanctuary. I could still remember shelving every one of the books, creating order from the chaos, applying all my librarian skills for good instead of for evil. I'd been working to heal a broken heart that day—those four days, actually—and I still took pride in what I had achieved.

At the same time that I'd moved the books around physically, I had created a database, listing each one by title and subject matter, so I could find them readily in a pinch. I was tempted to use my laptop now, to fire it up and browse through my records until I found the right gift.

Neko, though, threw the brakes on that train of thought. "Here's a good one! Teresa Alison Sidney should love this!"

I took the volume he offered, a hefty book bound in crimson leather. Ornate gold letters were stamped on the cover: *On the Care and Feeding of Familiars*. The book was relatively new—it was printed rather than handwritten, and the pages were made out of heavy, rag-cotton paper instead of parchment. There was a simple table of contents at the front of the book, outlining chapters on Binding a Familiar to a Home, and Forcing a Familiar to do Your Will in All Things, and Punishing a Willful Familiar.

Neko cocked his head at an appealing angle, looking up through his eyelashes with all the seductive aplomb of George Clooney accepting an Academy Award. He flashed me a brilliant smile, managing to convey that my happiness and satisfaction with his choice were the sole factors that motivated him to continue breathing.

"I don't think so," I said. "There's too much valuable information in that book for me to give it away. Besides," I said when Neko collapsed into a pouting heap, "I'm sure Teresa Alison Sidney's familiar would be too well-mannered for her to ever need a book like that."

Neko grumbled and returned the crimson book to its shelf.

As I watched him scan the rest of my collection, working out some new ulterior motive, I tried to figure out a solution on my own. Teresa Alison Sidney truly wasn't likely to need a guide on controlling familiars. Nor would she need any of my numerous treatises on preliminary spells, or basic crystal-work, elementary rune-reading, or introductory hexes.

I shuddered to think about giving her anything that fluttered around the darker edges of magic. In the best case, she might use my gift to consolidate even more power over the coven—and over me, by extension. In the worst case, she might interpret my gift as a veiled threat. Besides, my collection had precious few resources on the bleaker side of my gifts, and I was loath to give away anything I might conceivably need in the future.

No. I needed to find the witchy equivalent of a coffee table book—a grand volume that sang of riches, of largesse, one that collected fine pictures and minimal text. A book that evoked the spirit of being in another place, of living in another way. A book that Teresa Alison Sidney could display with pride, could invite other witches to peruse, could use to inspire admiration, and maybe just a hint of jealousy from all the members of her coven who weren't lucky enough to own such a treasure themselves.

"I've got it!" I said. I crossed to the far wall and knelt in front of the lowest shelf on the bookcase. I ran my fingers along the spines of three giant volumes, each too large to stand upright anywhere else in the collection. The bottom one was the prize I sought.

I wrestled with it for a moment, fighting to free it from the weight of its cohorts. It was even larger than I remembered, and the cover was more spectacular—green morocco leather stretched over thin wooden boards. It was stamped with an intricate design of pentagrams, circles, and flames of spiritual fire. Decorative brass hinges cupped the spine, echoing the patterns from the book's covers. The hinges were matched by a metal hasp that held the book closed, protecting the treasures within. The brass devices had been charmed magically so they never tarnished; even now, they gleamed like warm gold, whorls and fillips drawing the eye.

I levered the volume against my chest and staggered to my feet, taking care to set it gently on the bookstand in the center of the room. David came to my side, automatically reaching out expectant fingers to touch the fine tooling on the leather cover. Even Neko decided to give up his pouting and show some interest.

"What's the title?" David asked, craning his neck to look around my familiar. There were no words on the spine or the cover.

I worked the be-spelled hasp, admiring the flawless mechanics as the volume sprang open. Perfect rag-cotton sheets were bound inside; the librarian in me knew that some skilled laborer had spent days creating the smooth writing surfaces. I turned to the title page and read aloud: "*An Illustrated History of Witches in the Mid-Atlantic Region, Comprising Maryland, Delaware, the Virginias, and the District of Columbia.*"

I said to David, "It's local history. Especially appropriate for the Washington Coven."

David nodded, raising his eyebrows in appreciation at the lush, hand-colored illustrations that filled the pages. "It looks impressive. It's highly unlikely Teresa Alison Sidney has a copy in her own collection. It has a personal link to you. This is the perfect gift." Involuntarily, I grinned at the praise. "Now, for the wrapping, the binding you'll create. Go ahead and get the citrine."

I dug back in my box of crystals and extracted the stone, resisting the momentary urge to replace the perfect specimen with one of lesser value. If David was right—and I had no reason to think otherwise—if we truly were negotiating my debut in the professional and social world of witchcraft, I didn't dare cut a single corner.

The citrine was warm in my hand as I turned back to the bookstand. Neko came to stand beside me, and I opened my fingers so he could see the crystal on my palm. He exhaled as he bent closer, almost shuddering with the force of his own breath, and when he breathed in again, it sounded like a purr.

The stone glinted, catching every ray of light in the room and mellowing them into a soothing glow before casting them back at the three of us. Without extending my senses or drawing on a shred of my powers, I could feel the waves of emotion streaming off the citrine's cut surfaces—warmth, and calm, and goodwill.

David moved to the far side of the bookstand, pausing to nod when he was centered in front of me and the heavy green-bound volume. "Excellent choice," he said, and the stone's warmth blended with his approval, washing over me like a chamomile-scented bath. He nodded again before he said, "All right. Center yourself for your working."

I was familiar with the process; I'd done it often enough in the past ten months. Neko sidled closer; I could feel the heat of his body radiating against mine. I shifted the citrine to my left hand and folded my fingers around it. Forcing myself to concentrate, to shut out all conscious awareness of the two men in the room, I closed my eyes and took a deep breath.

It felt good to inhale so completely, to stretch my chest and expand my lungs to their full capacity. It felt even better to exhale, to expel all of my stress, my tension, and my worry about Teresa Alison Sidney. I repeated the breathing again and again, each time pulling myself closer to the quiet core of my powers, to a place where I couldn't be worried by mundane details. My final exhalation was long and slow, controlled, emptying my body and my mind of everything that wasn't directly related to the spell I was about to cast.

"Very good," David said, and now he had set aside his minister's voice in favor of a whisper. A distant part of my mind noted his approval, beamed at his compliment, but I remained composed, poised on the magical edge of spellcraft. "Now offer up the purity of your thoughts."

I raised my right hand, letting it drift toward my face as if it were separate from the rest of my body. I touched my brow and felt my physical self settle a little deeper into the cavernous space of magic.

"And the purity of your speech." I touched my throat and sent myself deeper into trance.

"And the purity of your belief." I touched my heart.

I was deeper than I'd been in any of our training sessions, more calm, more poised. A tremendous well of magical power gaped beneath me, buoying me up as if I floated on a super-saturated saltwater sea. I knew Neko stayed by my side, already serving as my familiar before I'd spoken a single magical word. He gathered up my centering and reflected it back at me. He deepened my trance, driving me further and further into my powers.

"Excellent," David whispered, and I knew when I was through with this working, when I came back to myself, I would have to examine this feeling, this complacency, this totally enraptured sense of well-being. "Now. Center the citrine on the book."

I seemed to have developed special vision. Even with my eyes closed, I could see the stone precisely; I could measure the dimensions of the bound volume more accurately than any craftsman with a ruler, with a jeweler's calipers. A tendril of my powers spun out from Neko's magnification. I confirmed that I understood both the book and the stone. Filling my lungs again, I moved the citrine to its precise place and when I set the crystal down, I exhaled until my fingers tingled.

The stone *fit* on the book. The Moroccan leather reached up somehow, embraced the crystal, accepted it and melded with it. Intellectually, I knew they remained separate. They stayed gold and green, stone and leather, but my witchy senses told me they had become more. They had merged. Bonded. Next to me, Neko shivered, and I knew he sensed what we had accomplished as well.

As did David. His voice rich with approval, he prompted, "Now take the power of the citrine, and bind it throughout the book. Meld it with the pages. Spread it through your gift."

I understood his words. I knew that I was deeply enthralled, that I was bound up in my powers, but I also knew I could ask a question without breaking the spell. "Am I trying to create a barrier?"

"You're creating a cover. A protective wrapper. Only you can decide what shape that cover will take. You can craft a shield that only Teresa Alison Sidney can penetrate, so no other witch will know your gift. You can make a layer that's more welcoming, more open. You must decide what you want to say, what message you want to send to Teresa Alison Sidney. To the coven."

What message *did* I want to send?

David had told me a lot about the Washington Coven during our year of training, even though I'd shied away from the topic whenever possible. The coven was the very core of witchcraft in our region. The women members—all witches were women, even if they relied on male warders for their protection—met regularly to educate one another on arcane practice, to learn new spells, new ways to harness the powers of runes and herbs and crystals.

The coven also acted as a social center. Each woman could share the unalloyed joy of magic, the surge of energy that came from using her powers, and each member could commiserate on the frustrations—the spells that didn't work, the magic that couldn't be bridled.

The Washington Coven wove into a network of witches throughout the country, the world. The coven gave its witches a spiritual home, an anchor. It gave them a place to belong, a place where they would be welcomed by sisters, no matter how odd—to a mundane eye—the magic they worked. Behind the coven's walls, a woman could be sheltered, could blossom, could grow, with guidance and protection from others who had walked the same magical pathways.

But I'd never been one to join clubs. In college, I had disliked the chummy exclusiveness of sororities, and I'd actively distrusted any group that required hazing to join. Or maybe that had only been my reaction because my first- and second-choice sororities wouldn't have me. In any case, David had made it clear multiple times: Witches belonged in covens.

Witches were safest in covens. Witches learned more in covens. There were other supernatural creatures that roamed the earth, beings that were policed by the shadowy Eastern Empire. But covens existed solely to foster witches, and I'd be a fool to step away from Teresa Alison Sidney's invitation.

So, how exactly should I present myself to the Washington Coven?

I could be brazen, showing off every last drop of my power and strength, pouring it into the citrine, over the book, building up an edifice that spoke of pride and power and arrogance.

I could be humble, submitting to the coven completely, showing my figurative underbelly and asking for support and guidance, for protection.

I could be rebellious, mining the book with spikes of power, with jagged edges to reflect my refusal to submit to any will not my own.

Each image that rose in my mind was accompanied by a vision of the citrine's field. I could never change the stone's essential aura of generosity, of well-being. But I could groom it. I could shape it. I could craft it into whatever I wanted it to be.

Another deep breath, another gathering of my thoughts. More tendrils stretched toward Neko, reaching for his familiar-power, for his unique skill in magnifying and amplifying my own magic.

And then I shaped the citrine's bonds.

I could place each spark of power precisely, line up my witchery like books on a shelf. I could make every element perfectly straight, place every figurative spine in an exact spot intricately measured from the front of each imagined shelf. I could shape the citrine like the most rigid of academic libraries, creating an autocratic blanket of power to stretch smooth and unbroken over the treasure of my book.

But I wasn't an orderly witch. I wasn't even and heavy, passive and calm.

By nature, I was a wilder person, a more tumultuous worker

of magic. By comparison, I was a children's reading room more than an academic library. I was a series of shelves holding hidden treasures, nooks and crannies, where someone was likely to find an overpadded reading chair and a dozing marmalade cat. I was carefully controlled chaos, not perfect organization.

I laughed out loud as I shaped the citrine. I spread its force over the book like a bibliophile unpacking a treasure trove of boxes. I had *fun* at the edges, stacking new thoughts, new powers, new books into complex designs. I complemented the brass hinges, mirrored the metal lock. I thought of every library I'd ever visited in my life, every sudden discovery of a literary treasure, every serendipitous find in a lifetime of browsing.

The citrine responded well to my light-hearted approach. It captured my sense of goodwill, my hope, my optimism, and it let itself be shaped. I could not say how long I worked with the stone, how many times I checked my design, how often I modified my wrapping.

But I knew when I was done. I knew when the package said exactly what I wanted it to say. I knew when the *Illustrated History of Witches* had been transformed into something that was my unique offering, my special gift.

I opened my eyes at last. Neko stepped away from me, and I watched him shrug his shoulders, regaining his own balance and sense of self. I looked down at my gift, at what seemed to be an ordinary green-bound book, with an ordinary yellow stone sitting on its cover.

And then I looked at David.

He was staring at me. His lips were frozen in a bemused smile; his eyes were locked on mine. He scarcely seemed to acknowledge the book between us.

"What?" I asked, and my voice was too loud for the room.

"Nothing." But he didn't stop looking.

"Why are you staring at me that way?"

"You never fail to surprise me."

"What do you mean?"

"I don't think anyone has ever presented Teresa Alison Sidney with a gift precisely like this one."

"What do you mean?" Suddenly, the goodwill from the citrine dissipated, became a melody I could remember humming but couldn't sing out loud for the life of me. I clutched the edges of the book, recognizing what I had created but suddenly doubting the value of what I'd done. "I should have gone with the academic library, right? I should have made it perfect."

"You did make it perfect," David said. "Perfect for you."

I didn't believe him, though. "This is important. I should do something else. Use my powers another way."

"I wouldn't let you, even if you tried."

"You're my warder! You'd have to!" Self-doubt sharpened my voice.

David only smiled. "Trust me. I know what's best for you here."

"And this is best?" I felt like a child, like a little girl suddenly unsure of herself in patent leather Mary Janes and corded tights.

"This is best," David said. "The best I can imagine you ever doing."

I tried to believe him, but I wished I was meeting with Teresa Alison Sidney then, that very afternoon. I wasn't sure I could stand to wait six long days.

Neko stepped forward, planting his hands on the bookstand. "Well, *I* can't imagine going one more minute without something to eat. Preferably shrimp. With a side of crab salad."

Just like that, I was overwhelmed by a wave of hunger. David had warned me often enough, telling me I needed to ground myself after a major working. Food and drink and calm, quiet introspection—that's what he prescribed. Usually, I tossed off his recommendation, eating a cookie or two, tossing back a glass of water, and delving back into my busy day.

This time, though, I felt drained. Spent. I *needed* sustenance, ached for it in the core of my bones. So I laughed unsteadily and let my familiar lead the way upstairs to the kitchen. Neko knew the contents of my refrigerator better than I did.

But with every step away from the bookstand, I had to resist the urge to look over my shoulder at the citrine-wrapped *Illustrated History of Witches*. I prayed to Hecate it would be enough to get me the welcome I desired.

5

I stared balefully at the pile of clothes on my bed. I had come home from work at six o'clock and immediately discarded my layers of colonial clothing: hoops, jacket, petticoat, neck kerchief, and sleeve ruffles. All were lying on top of my comforter, competing with each other to develop the deepest, most-hard-to-press wrinkles.

On top of my costume lay dozens of other outfits—skirts, blouses, T-shirts, slacks—all in black. After all, black was basic. Black was dramatic. Black was almost all I owned.

I had clingy black and sloppy black, goth black and elegant black, temptress black and too-fat black. I'd spent the evening combining separates that had no business being in the same closet together, much less on the same body. I'd dug out clothes I hadn't worn since I'd last tried to drag Melissa to clubs, years before. I even tried the outfit that used to be my favorite for work, before I was forced into the finest that Martha Washington had to offer.

Nothing was right for my date with Graeme Henderson. Nothing conveyed the energy I wanted, the carefree, devil-may-care insouciance of a girl meeting a guy for late-night coffee.

(Who drank coffee at night, anyway? What sort of strange relationship disaster was I setting myself up for?)

Frustrated, I collapsed on my bed and stared at my nearly empty closet. If I were going to a formal dinner party, I was all set—I still had the emerald sheath dress that Neko had chosen for me last year, the one shot through with golden threads that had made me feel like a princess at the Concert Opera Guild Harvest Gala. Somehow, though, it was a bit much for a Wednesday night get-together.

Green, though. A shot of color. Maybe that's where I'd gone wrong. Maybe I should look at the five percent of my wardrobe that *wasn't* black.

I tugged open my dresser drawers and dug to the bottom of a pile of T-shirts. (Yes, I needed four black ones. What girl didn't?) The aquamarine tee had been a gift from Melissa; I'd teased her at the time because it would look great on her. She hadn't appreciated my sense of humor.

I pulled the seamless garment over my head and checked in the mirror. It was streamlined and sleek. It looked as cool as the water in a swimming pool, promising a refreshing splash on a sweltering summer night.

And there. In my closet. A sapphire blue skirt, also a present from Melissa. Hmm. Maybe she was sending me a message. Maybe she thought I needed to change up my wardrobe a bit.

In this instance, though, I couldn't argue. The tee and the skirt worked perfectly together. They combined to look breezy and fresh, as if I'd simply reached for two garments readily at hand, tossing on any old thing because what girl had time to fuss with getting dressed? No one would be able to tell that I'd decimated my wardrobe to get to this point.

Next up: hair. I could take a quick shower and blow dry my unruly auburn mop. Years of experience, though, told me I'd be fighting fate. The dryer would take nearly half an hour, and my hair would frizz in the late-August heat within seconds of my stepping outside. I decided not to fight reality. A simple barrette would keep my mane off my neck.

I ducked into the bathroom and washed my face. Continuing my theme of summer simplicity I decided to go without a full makeup session. A bit of blush, a hint of indigo eye-liner, a dash of lipstick.

Enough. This was a date. Not a marriage proposal. The paparazzi weren't going to be anywhere in sight.

I grabbed my clutch purse from my dresser and slipped into comfortable, flat sandals. Graeme Henderson might have been the most interesting man I'd met in months, but I wasn't going to waste the pain of high heels on him. Especially not when I was walking to the restaurant, making my way over the scenic cobblestones that still lined many of Georgetown's streets.

I got to the front door before my plan fell apart.

"Sneaking out?" Neko chuckled from one of the hunter green couches. I'd been so intent on leaving that I hadn't noticed him. Him *or* Jacques.

"Not sneaking at all!" I said defensively, looking furtively at the door.

Neko had been resting his head in Jacques's lap, but now he scrambled upright. "Where are you going?"

"Out."

Neko pouted. "I bet you wouldn't answer your grandmother that way."

"You'd lose your bet."

Jacques stepped in before Neko could complain again. "You look quite lovely thees evening, Jane." His accent was strong in the living room's dim light, and I smiled at the Gallic softening of my name, despite myself. What *did* that French hottie find in Neko? Especially given my familiar's rather, um, unorthodox housing arrangement and his invisible means of financial support? Oh well—the things we do for love. Or at least for strong physical attraction...

Jacques asked, "Who ees the lucky man?"

"Who says there's a lucky man?" I answered too quickly.

"Any man who will dine with you ees lucky. And at 9:30. I am turning you eento a proper French girl."

"It's not dinner," I said, although my stomach chose that moment to grumble and remind me I hadn't actually eaten after work. "Just coffee. And dessert."

Neko pounced. "Food. Drink. It *is* a date, then. Where?"

"Bistro Français," I said. After all, they'd get the information out of me eventually.

"Ah, *bon!*" Jacques exclaimed. "They are open until the earliest hours of the morning. Perhaps Neko and me, we will come weeth you?" He nodded, as if this were the most brilliant idea he'd ever conceived. "We will join you there. Make sure that thees man you see ees a good one."

"No!"

I thought of the silver-lined card tucked beneath my mattress, the card that Melissa had made me promise to keep secret from Neko. Even greater than the promise, though, was my terror of the very real romantic damage my familiar could do if he put his mind to it. In fact, even if he didn't—Neko had a knack for saying precisely the wrong thing at the wrong time. Graeme would flee the bistro in short order if Neko had anything to do with orchestrating my love life.

My familiar hid a delicate yawn behind his hand. "Are you ashamed of us, Jane, or ashamed of your mystery man?"

I felt the walls closing in on me. But then, like a ray of sunshine slicing through a fogbank, I saw a way to escape. "If you must know, I'm actually meeting Melissa. She wanted to keep it secret. We're going to try the desserts at the Bistro, to see if there's anything she should duplicate for Cake Walk. We'll be there, sort of in disguise."

Both Neko and Jacques deflated at Melissa's name. But after a moment's blessed silence, Neko twitched his nose. I could almost believe he smelled my lie. "Melissa? Sampling Bistro

Français at 9:30 at night? Doesn't she have to be at her own bakery by four in the morning?"

"All the more reason—they'll never suspect their competition," I said, trying not to sound desperate. "Please, Neko." I looked pointedly at Jacques. "The last thing I need is to have her angry when she's trying to go unnoticed."

Jacques let out a long Gallic sigh, as if all the chateaux in France were weighing on his shoulders. "Poor Meleessa. I never meant..." He sighed again.

Neko stroked the poor Frenchman's hair, flashing a look to me that implied I had overstepped my bounds. "Go on, then," he grumbled. "Enjoy your tarts."

I thought about challenging his tone—or at least his word choice—but I realized I'd won the battle. Waggling my fingers in the guys' general direction, I ducked out the door, pulling it shut behind me.

Time was running short; I had to hurry through the heavy August night. The sun was still setting late; a faint hint of crimson afterglow remained in the sky. Despite the hour, heat shimmered off the sidewalk, and I wondered once again why our founding fathers had insisted on building their capital on a swamp.

When I was a block away from the Bistro, I stopped to catch my breath. I glanced at my watch. 9:25. Perfect timing. I didn't want to get there too early, but I didn't want to be late. Receptive, I wanted to project. Open. But not eager. Not needy.

I resisted the urge to run my fingers through my hair. I even managed not to nibble at my fingernails. I took three quick breaths to calm myself, and then I walked the last block to the restaurant.

"Bonsoir, madame," the maître d' said, his accent challenging Jacques's for continental grace.

"Um, hello." I said. "I'm meeting someone here, at 9:30."

"You are Meess Madison?" I nodded. "Right thees way."

Graeme stood as the maître d' escorted me to one of the booths in the back. The dining room was well-lit, hardly a secret, romantic getaway, but Graeme had contrived to secure a quiet corner. Facing his movie-star good looks once again, I found my breath catching in my throat. His smile lit a tiny fire deep beneath my breastbone, and he said, "I'm so pleased you could make it."

Before I had a chance to worry about how to greet him, he stepped closer and leaned down, kissing me lightly on my cheek. I breathed in the scent of him—fresh air, with just a hint of evergreen—cool and quiet on a summer night. His greeting was more intimate than a handshake, more alluring than Jacques's continental two-cheek kiss. And it was infinitely more satisfying than the awkward dances I shared with David.

Graeme waved me to my seat, waiting until I was settled before he sat across from me. I cleared my throat and said, "I hope you didn't have any trouble finding this place."

"None at all. I'm learning my way around."

"How long have you been in the States?"

"For quite a few years, actually. I'm based here now, although my business takes me back to London regularly."

I resisted the urge to fiddle with my silverware. Instead, I forced myself to look at him, to take in his open expression, the perfect bow of his lips. Maybe, just maybe, I could inoculate myself. If I stared at him long enough, often enough, I might become accustomed to his breath-taking appearance.

Yeah, right. Or maybe I'd just let the conversation lag so completely I'd be embarrassed to ever say anything else, to even try to get it moving once again. "Business!" I said, clutching at a conversational straw. "Your card said Acquisitions. Are you a lawyer?"

I bit my lip, waiting for his answer. *Please-don't-be-a-lawyer. Please-don't-be-a-lawyer. Don't be anything like Scott Randall. Don't be anything like my failed romances of the past.*

"Hardly." His eyebrows arched into an expression that would have been a sneer of disgust on a less refined face.

"I mean, a solicitor. Or a barrister. Whatever they're called."

"They're called both, for somewhat different services. And I assure you, I stay as far away from the law as I possibly can."

I laughed at his rakish grin. "That makes you sound positively dangerous."

"I can be," he purred, and his smile was so intimate I forgot to breathe.

"Madame. Monsieur." I jumped as a waiter made his presence known. The man wore a white apron, and he had a harried expression on his long, droopy face. "Will you be dining with us this evening?"

My belly reminded me it had been sent to dress without any supper, but I firmly squelched a positive reply. Graeme said, "Just dessert, thank you."

The waiter barely stifled a sigh, but his eyes looked deeply pained. If he were an animal, I was certain he'd be a basset hound. A depressed one. "I'll bring the cart."

"Poor man," Graeme said as soon as the waiter was out of earshot. "I didn't realize the Hundred Acre Wood had shipped out poor Eeyore to wait tables at the Bistro Français."

I laughed despite my nerves. "I suppose he was planning on earning a monster tip, hoping we'd order a five-course supper."

"Alas for him. But 'how shalt he hope for mercy, rendering none?'"

My jaw dropped. I mean, it was one thing for the man to know Prospero's line from *The Tempest*; the play was performed all the time. But *Merchant of Venice*? And then, to temper the knowledge of Shakespeare by mentioning my childhood favorite, sagging old Eeyore... My heart swelled inside my chest.

I was spared the need for a witty Elizabethan rejoinder because the basset hound returned with the dessert cart. We were treated to a desultory explanation of the treats—almond cake, baba au rhum, chocolate éclairs, a towering croquembouche, triplets of tiny fruit tarts, crème caramel, napoleons,

Strasbourg cake, St. Tropez cake, profiteroles… I gained five pounds just listening to the list.

When the waiter finished his recitation, Graeme waved an inviting hand toward the cart. "What pleases you?" he asked.

Oh so many things.

Melissa had a long set of rules about foods to eat on dates. I needed to avoid anything that would squirt onto my clothes, that would leave seeds in my teeth, or that would be difficult to cut on a slippery plate with the small fork that would likely be my only utensil. What did that leave? And what could I choose that wouldn't make me feel I'd betrayed Cake Walk?

Charmingly, Graeme misread my indecision. He said to the waiter, "Why don't you bring us a few things. The almond cake, and the chocolate éclair, profiteroles, and…?"

He quirked an eyebrow toward me. How did he maintain his quarterback physique, eating multiple desserts? At least I hadn't had dinner, so I could splurge. Throwing Melissa's cautions to the winds, I said, "The fruit tarts!" They were likely to slip around when I tried to cut them into bites and the berries posed a threat to my otherwise gleaming smile, but I was willing to live life dangerously.

"And the fruit tarts," Graeme told the hound. "And a decaffeinated coffee for me, with a Grand Marnier. Jane?"

"Decaf, also." The waiter nodded and started to wheel his cart away. "And a Bailey's!" I called, abandoning the last of my common sense. He nodded and sighed, as if I had just sentenced his youngest child to a lifetime banishment in the barbarian wilds outside the city walls. I settled back in the booth. "Mmm," I said. "This is so decadent!"

"You see? Hardly the act of a barrister."

"That's right. Now, your card said 'Acquisitions.' What, exactly, do you acquire?"

"Whatever people need." He smiled easily. "Say you read a magazine article, and it mentions a davenport owned by the Countess of Wessex. You decide you can't live without that very furniture in your own parlor. I'm the man to find the piece for you. And I won't even tell the members of your bridge club where I found it. None of them will ever get the same piece."

I laughed, trying to picture myself bidding trump or half-trump or no-trump or whatever it was bridge mavens bid. "I'm not exactly the bridge sort." I wasn't about to say that I had two *sofas*, instead of davenports, and I had a *living room* instead of a parlor.

"What, then? Your book club? Is that what all the librarians go in for these days?"

"I don't know about *all* the librarians, but I've been in a book club or two."

"So you could hire me to find a lamp, say, so you could read great world literature in style. Or a tall-case clock, or whatnot."

"Acquisitions," I said, as if it made all the sense in the world.

"At your service." Graeme's smile blinded me.

The waiter chose that moment to return with our buffet of desserts. He put a large coffee press on the table and shook his head sadly before finding the energy to tamp down our decaffeinated grounds. He poured two cups and set our alcoholic chasers to one side. "Will there be anything else?" he said, and he sighed so deeply that I worried our profiteroles might blow onto the floor.

"Not at present," Graeme said, and then we were alone again. "Cheers!" my acquirer said, raising up his Grand Marnier. I scrambled for my cordial, touched glasses, and then watched him pour his into his coffee. I didn't know if the custom was British or Graeme's own, but my Bailey's quickly met the same fate.

"So," Graeme said, after I had tasted the extremely satisfactory result. "You're a librarian who knows the Bard, and you help out a friend in her bakery. What else should I know about you?"

What else? I could tell him I'd been raised by my grandmother because my own mother didn't want anything to do with

me after my first birthday. Hmmm… Not exactly an upbeat
introduction. I could tell him about the last person I'd spoken to
in London, my ex-fiancé who had broken my heart after twelve
years of dating and the longest engagement known to man.
Yeah, not a great conversation starter, either. I could fill him in
on the I.B., and we could spend the rest of the evening coming
up with more and more horrible meanings for the initials. Yeah.
Right.

I needed something charming, something witty, something
unique that would keep him here chatting with me into the wee
hours of the morning. I sipped my coffee, transferred a rasp-
berry tart to my plate and said, "I'm a witch."

As soon as the words were out of my mouth, I couldn't
believe I'd said them. I mean, it wasn't precisely a secret. David
had never told me not to mention my powers. Nothing I'd read
required me to take an oath of silence. If the Washington Coven
had rules, they'd never told me and, besides, I wasn't a
member yet.

But I could count on two hands the people who knew I had
magical powers. David. Neko. Melissa. My mother and grandmother. My grandmother's friend, Uncle George. The I.B.

There were likely others who suspected. My relatives in
Connecticut had powers of their own to varying degrees, and
they must have noticed the…odd…events surrounding the
unmasking of the Illiterate Booby.

But I had never told anyone before. I had never looked
anyone in the eye and said, "I am a witch."

I waited for Graeme to laugh. I waited for him to look at his
watch, to remember he had somewhere else to be, that he'd
promised to read the collected works of Dostoevsky to his great-
aunt Gertrude that night.

But he didn't.

Instead, he set his fork down, and he said solemnly, "There
are Wyrd Women in my family, going back generations." Wyrd
Women. Witches. "I don't know many of the details, but my da

told me stories when I was a boy. Told me about what his mum could do, when she was angry."

"You believe me?" I was a little shocked.

He swallowed a bite of almond cake. "Why wouldn't I? What possible reason would you have to lie?"

To make myself more interesting. Because I was a delusional madwoman. Because I was an axe murderer, waiting to bewitch him into my bed and then do away with him under the light of the full moon.

"None, really," I said. My voice quirked on the second word, twisting into a semblance of a British accent, and I bit back a wince. I wasn't consciously trying to imitate him, it just happened. I rushed out more words, so he wouldn't think I was mocking. "It's just so strange the way all this has happened. I haven't told anyone. It's not like I'm ashamed or anything, it's just so bizarre I'm afraid that people will think I'm lying. That I'm making it all up."

"When you've seen as many odd things as I have in this world, you start believing what people say."

"Odd things?"

"I'll tell you," he assured me. "But there's plenty of time for that. You go first. I want to hear how you became a witch."

And so I told him. Just like that—I told him about how the Peabridge had been on the edge of bankruptcy and my salary had been slashed, but I'd been permitted to move into my cottage on the library grounds as a sort of substitute for a full paycheck. I told him about finding a secret stash of witchcraft books in the basement—volumes that had been hidden away by a Washington witch named Hannah Osgood, decades before. I told him about finding a statue of a cat and reading a spell and awakening my familiar entirely by accident. And I told him about how I'd used my newfound witchcraft the year before, how I'd poured my magical strength into crystals to help my grandmother recover from a nasty case of pneumonia.

I even told him about my crazy mother and her abilities

with runes, her New Age insanity that had brought her hurtling from the so-called Vortex in Sedona back into my life, even though I'd believed for years that she'd died in a car crash when I was a child. (There hadn't been a car crash, I told him. Just a need to escape responsibility. I managed not to sound bitter when I said it. Or maybe that was the Baileys, coating the sounds of my words in my own ears.) I told him everything I had learned about magic during the past ten months.

He was a wonderful listener. He asked enough questions to keep me going, enough to show that he was truly interested, but he never tried to change the topic of conversation. He never tried to steer me away from the odder bits of my story, the stranger aspects of my powers—crystals, and runes, and the specific spells I had worked.

It felt wonderful to tell someone all of this, fantastic to share. I was grateful when Graeme caught the waiter's attention, when he signaled that we'd both have more coffee. When we'd finished that brew, along with additional supporting liqueurs, I finally glanced at Graeme's watch, just visible beneath the cuff of his shirt.

"One o'clock!" I said. "I had no idea it was so late!"

"The restaurant stays open till four."

"I have to go, though! I have to work tomorrow. I mean, today!"

He smiled at my confusion, letting his grin grow into a laugh when I barely managed to fight off a yawn. "Yes, well. There is that." He got the waiter's attention and asked for the check before pulling out his money clip.

"Wait!" I said, pleasantly surprised again by that clip, by the very Britishness of it. "I never got to hear about the strange things *you've* seen."

"They'll keep. That is, if I may see you again?"

"Yes!" I could hardly believe he thought he had to ask.

"Are you free Friday night?"

"Of course," I said, scarcely wasting a heartbeat to think

only a social reject would admit to being available on a Friday, to having no pressing social plans.

Then I remembered. I *was* busy on Friday. Teresa Alison Sidney. "Oh. No." I hadn't gone so far as to tell him about my upcoming meeting with the coven, and now I was overcome with self-consciousness. "I'm sorry. I do have other plans. Plans I can't break."

He shrugged easily. "I'm afraid I have one of my business trips coming up. I leave on Saturday for England, and I'll be gone for the entire week." I must have looked as crestfallen as I felt, because he grinned and said, "But perhaps the Saturday following?"

"I'd love that."

"I'll ring you up Saturday morning, and we can make plans."

And then he was helping me out of the booth. He was holding the door to the restaurant. He was stepping to the curb and raising a hand, summoning one of DC's ubiquitous cabs. He was handing money to the driver and telling him to take me wherever I requested.

Just before he handed me into the car, he pulled me close. He tangled his fingers in my hair and set his lips on mine. His kiss was soft, gentle, tingling with potential. Before I could say anything, before I could respond, before I could rethink my need to be at work in a few short hours, he pulled back, helped me into the cab, closed the door, and let me drive away.

I lay awake until dawn, watching my clock tick away seconds, minutes, hours—time that could have been spent much more pleasurably, if only I had responded faster to the promise of Graeme's kiss.

6

D avid shrugged as he completed his survey from the top of
my purposely messy chignon to the soles of my practical
sandals. Somehow, it had been much easier to prepare for
meeting the coven than it had been to get ready for dessert with
Graeme.

Women. I knew what to wear for *them*.

I'd pulled on a lightweight knit dress—black of course. Body
skimming, but not skin tight. Appropriate undergarments to
avoid, ahem, the dread visible panty line. I didn't want to
appear too severe, so I'd accessorized with a necklace and
earrings made of fused glass. The jewelry reflected hints of
lavender and crimson, with delicate sprays of emerald.

"Not too much?" I asked.

"I'm sure it's fine."

"You're sure? What does that mean?"

He shrugged. "It means I don't spend a lot of time tracking
women's fashion."

"Neko?" I wailed.

"Perfect," my familiar chimed in promptly. "Trust me."

Trust him. Well, I did. At least in theory. But I still recognized the sparkling feeling in my fingertips as nervousness, and I

reminded myself to take a few deep breaths. I turned back to plead with David. "Promise me you'll stay with me, the whole time we're there."

"I promise you'll never be in danger." That wasn't what I'd asked for. Not at all. But I didn't have a chance to complain before David said, "Okay. Let's go."

I realized I'd overlooked a crucial detail. "The car!" I should have borrowed Gran's Lincoln Town Car after work. I traveled by car so rarely it had completely slipped my mind.

I glanced at my watch and swore to myself. Eleven o'clock. We'd really be pushing it, catching a cab and getting over to Gran's apartment building. I had keys to her car, though, and we could get into the garage easily enough... I just wasn't certain where Teresa Alison Sidney lived or how long it would take to get there. If the car failed to start (not that it ever had in the past), or if the gas tank was empty (even though I'd filled it two weeks before and Gran never drove), or if the garage gates refused to open...

"Relax," David said, producing a keyring from the interior pocket of his summer-weight suit. The silver fob was etched with an intricate torch.

"What's that?"

"My keyring."

"No." My exasperation was only partially rooted in my blossoming panic. "That design."

"Hecate's Torch? Symbol of witches everywhere?"

I *thought* I'd seen it before. It must be printed in some of the books downstairs. I let myself focus on the single silver key that dangled from the device, heavy and reassuring with its black electronics-laden head.

"My car is out front," David said.

"*Your* car?" I was shocked. "How come I've never seen you drive a car before now?"

"'There are more things in heaven and earth', " David said with a grin.

"If that's supposed to make me feel calmer, I'm not sure it's going to work." After all, what did I need with quotations from *Hamlet*? From a play where the main character sees ghosts, goes mad, and litters the stage with bodies before the end of the last act? "Relax," David said again. He spared an inquiring glance for Neko. "Ready?"

For answer, my familiar hefted the *Illustrated History of Witches*. I reached for it, saying, "I'll carry it."

"It's my job," he said. "I serve you, remember?"

"That's the first time I've ever heard *you* say it out loud."

"Mark your calendar, then. I won't repeat it." He scampered to the door, and I realized his banter was intended to help me relax. It didn't help any more than David's quoting Shakespeare. I tried to tell myself it was the thought that counted.

Neither man spoke further as I secured the cottage, even when I double- and triple-checked the lock. I stopped walking when I got to the end of the garden path, turning around to look at my home, at the building that had gotten me into the middle of all this witchcraft business in the first place.

Was it worth it? At the moment, I wasn't sure. I'd choose a dozen awkward first dates over meeting a coven full of witches. Yeah, right. As if I had the choice to make.

When I reached the street, I was amazed by two facts. First, David had found a parking space directly in front of the Peabridge. In Georgetown, that alone required some working of magic.

Second, and even more shocking, was the car that waited for us. A Lexus. Black. With onyx leather that melted under the moonlight, and walnut trim that whispered old money.

David held the passenger door for me as Neko clambered into the back, grumbling about the indignity until David shot him a loaded glance. Neko planted himself squarely in the middle of the wide back seat before he settled the book carefully beside him. He bounced slightly as David pulled away from the curb, and I expected to hear him shout, "Are we there yet?" at any moment.

When Neko failed to fill the silence, I asked, "Do you know where we're going?"

"Of course."

David handled the car expertly. While the streets of DC were never empty, traffic became lighter as we moved out of Georgetown, crossing the Key Bridge into Virginia and the western suburbs. I realized we were heading into one of the toniest neighborhoods around, an area of estates that were set far apart, with long brick fences lining the roads and wrought iron gates that kept the riff-raff from invading.

I wanted to ask David a hundred questions. Where exactly were we going? Who was waiting for us? How many women were in the coven? What would happen once we arrived? How, exactly, was I supposed to prove myself, and what were the penalties if I failed?

I knew, though, that I'd get no further answers. David had already told me precisely what he thought I needed to know.

Just as the dashboard clock flashed 11:45, David took a right turn off the winding road. A wrought-iron gate the height of the Eiffel Tower hung open on massive hinges. We drove up the longest driveway I'd seen this side of *Gone With the Wind*, passing between sentinel ranks of oak trees. The car's high beams made eerie shadows on the trunks, and more than once I caught my breath, expecting some supernatural guardian to swoop down upon us.

I realized my fingers were woven into a nervous clump, and I was rubbing my thumbs against each other like an obsessive maniac. Before David could issue another useless reminder for me to relax, I closed my eyes and took a trio of calming breaths. I leaned back in my seat and tried to imagine Neko standing by my side, reflecting my magical strength back to me, quietly, calmly.

My trick worked well enough that I was surprised when David braked to a stop. "Ready?" he asked.

My eyes sprang open. I was expecting to see Tara—massive columns, solid red brick, and a curving double staircase with servants at the ready. There might even be a barbecue out back, fragrant smoke rising from the grill as belles and beaux flirted with each other. A horse or two wouldn't be out of place, whickering friendly greetings and begging for sugar lumps. And come to think of it, a mint julep wouldn't be half-bad. Or a Bailey's Irish Cream. With or without decaf coffee.

Toto, we weren't at Tara anymore.

The house in front of me might have been designed by Frank Lloyd Wright. The walls were made of stone slivers, set without mortar to form horizontal patterns under the moonlight. I could make out windows high above us, arcane designs cut into their wooden frames. I could see two—no, three—chimneys, rising into the midnight darkness. A walkway led around to our right, hinting at a doorway that remained out of sight.

David led us down that path. I silently congratulated myself for choosing sandals; they were nearly silent on the flagstones, and I didn't need to worry about turning an ankle in the dark. Neko stuck close behind me; I could hear his breath catch as he shifted the heavy book in his arms.

When we rounded the corner, a low voice called: "Halt! Let all who would approach the Washington Coven identify themselves and give good reason for their presence."

I blinked, and then I could make out a man in the shadows. A large man. A large man who wore a dark cloak, despite the oppressive late-summer heat. A large man, who wore a cloak, and held a gleaming, naked sword.

I almost ran back to the car.

What had I been thinking? How had I let David drive me out here, miles from nowhere? Why hadn't I realized I might become the victim of a strange, sword-wielding cult?

My story would be all over the newspapers; it would fill the airwaves for weeks. Gran would put out a weeping appeal for my safe return; even Clara would screw out a tear or two for the cameras. The tabloid press would interview my boss, who would say she hadn't noticed anything unusual prior to my disappearance. They'd shove microphones in front of Melissa, who would push past the paparazzi to get inside Cake Walk, where she would grimly turn the sign to Walk On By in an attempt to free herself from the media circus.

"I am David Montrose, Warder of Hecate." David's voice resonated in the dark nook. He did not seem surprised by the man, did not seem the least bit startled by the sword. He intoned: "I bring with me a Daughter of Hecate, Jane Madison, who travels this path with her familiar."

"You may pass, Warder of Hecate." The man stepped aside, lowering his sword a fraction of an inch. "Welcome, Daughter of Hecate, and be honored in our safehold."

I expected David to step to one side (hopefully, the side between me and the glimmering sword.) I thought he would be a gentleman and let me walk before him. Instead, he squared his shoulders and raised his chin, striding past the armed guardian with only the faintest of acknowledging nods.

As my warder stepped over the threshold and into the house, a silver tracing flared up on the ground. A five-pointed star spread on either side of the door. It was surrounded by a perfect circle, an unbroken line that shimmered with magical force. I knew immediately that the pentagram was a protective field, a barrier even stronger than the man with the sword.

David stepped through the glowing light, shuddering slightly until he reached the far side. He extended his hand, bidding me to come forward, and I knew I had no choice. Compelling silver light glinted off the ring on his left hand. He'd brought me here because I'd been summoned. He'd told me I would be safe.

I stepped over the threshold.

The force hit me like an electric charge. It jolted up my neck and made my teeth rattle in my jaw. It forced me to blink against a sudden brilliant light and then shy away from a crashing, terrifying darkness. My lungs froze; I couldn't draw a complete breath, couldn't break free from the power of the circle.

As I panicked, Neko pressed close behind me. His chest was firm against my back. He shifted his weight so his arm brushed against mine. He edged me forward, out of the circle, to the safety on the other side.

From that vantage point, I could see that Neko wasn't afraid. Not at all. Rather, he was excited—alert and ready, *charged* and in his element. He was a cat, toying with a new mouse. I only hoped *I* could be the predator, and not the prey.

I braced myself and followed David into the house.

A marble-paved foyer opened onto the largest room I'd ever seen in a residence. The space was divided into half a dozen conversation areas, groupings of chairs and loveseats that encouraged quiet, earnest discussion. A variety of tables was scattered about, sporting enough lamps to fill a showroom. All of the light bulbs were subdued, as if the entire room was on a dimmer switch.

There must have been two dozen women present, all talking in voices low enough to match the lighting. I felt as if I'd stumbled into a super-secret midnight meeting of the Junior League. Each woman looked more composed than the one before. There were a few girls, relative youngsters who might be recent college graduates, but most had twenty or more years on me. Three women on the far side of the room looked as if they were in Gran's demographic.

No matter their ages, though, the witches looked fit and healthy. There was an air of determination about them, a razor-edged intensity that marked the multigenerational gathering as *special* in some indefinable way. I'd been so confident in my black dress and my fused glass jewelry. Now, I saw that cashmere and pearls would have been more appropriate.

As if I owned cashmere. As if I owned pearls. I thought about hissing a rebuke to Neko for his approving my outfit, but I knew this was neither the time nor the place.

In one cluster of women, a faint laugh rang out, and I wondered if I would ever get to hear the punchline. I caught a sudden gasp of surprise from another group, the universal sound of shocked gossip that begs for more details even as it warns away the impropriety of telling tales out of school.

A doorway arched to my immediate right, and I could hear a low hum of conversation emanating from behind an oak door. A low hum of *masculine* conversation—I immediately pictured an Edwardian smoking lounge, with well-dressed aristocrats cradling snifters of brandy as they pulled on fat cigars.

"David Montrose."

A woman materialized in front of us. Okay. I shouldn't say "materialized." It wasn't as if a fog swirled into the room, and a woman magically appeared. It wasn't like there was a flash of light before she stepped forward. It wasn't *magical*.

Rather, she approached us with perfect grace. Perfect grace and balance and poise and…majesty. Instantly, I knew this must be Teresa Alison Sidney. Her greeting to my warder toppled the entire room into silence.

"Coven Mother," David said, and he inclined his head in a gesture that would have been a bow in another age, in another land.

Coven Mother. But there wasn't anything the least bit *maternal* about her.

Teresa Alison Sidney was the sum of all my nightmares from high school. I knew instinctively that she was one of the Popular Snobs; she'd *created* the cliques the rest of us could only dream of joining.

She was tall—probably close to six feet—and slender, and she carried herself in a way that advertised the hours she spent at the gym. Her midnight hair fell straight around her face. Its black depths gleamed blue in the dim light, curling in a soft flip just above her shoulders, as if she'd never heard of a breeze, or humidity, or any other summer challenge. I couldn't read the color of her eyes in the darkened room, but I would have given my eyeteeth if they weren't slate grey.

She wore a perfectly tailored cashmere sweater—short sleeves in acknowledgment of the heat outside, but blood red, as if we'd already moved the calendar forward to the heart of autumn. Her charcoal trousers must have had an invisible zipper on the side; they were impossibly slim and cut to exaggerate the length of her legs. She wore a single strand of pearls around her neck, and each earlobe was kissed by an unadorned milky sphere.

"Warder," the Coven Mother said, and the title made David stand a little straighter. "You may join the other men in the front room."

There was no question in her voice, no uncertainty. She was not asking David his preference or giving him any option. He was being ordered from my side, as certainly as if Richard III had sentenced him to the Tower.

Unable to stop myself, I reached toward him, brushing my fingers against his sleeve. He shook his head, once. "By your leave, Coven Mother," he said, nodding deeply before stalking away from Teresa Alison Sidney.

Away from me.

I watched him open the door to my right. There was a momentary pause in the male banter within, and then the noise swelled louder, all greetings and laughter and casual bonhomie. I swallowed hard and reminded myself that Neko had been permitted to stay with me. That, at least, was a mercy.

Teresa Alison Sidney's smile was as perfectly manicured as the hand she extended to me. Her fingers were cool in mine, sleek, as if she spent part of her life as a seal or a mermaid. "And you must be Jane Madison."

"Yes," I said. "Yes, Coven Mother." I answered her perfect nightingale trill with a peacock bray. I knew there was something else I should be saying, something else I should do, but my mind was completely blank. I wondered if I'd lost some basic faculties when I crossed the silver pentagram into the house. Maybe some silent spell had stolen away my most basic social abilities.

I felt a jab in the small of my back and I took a half-step forward. Even as I racked my brain for what I was missing, there was another jab, a poke deeper into my spine. "Jane!"

The whisper broke my trance, and I half-turned toward the sound. Neko was shoving the *Illustrated History* toward me, thrusting it into my arms as if it were an infant needing a diaper change. I scowled, more embarrassed than ever by the awkward presentation of my gift. I should have wrapped it, no matter what David had said.

I turned back to Teresa Alison Sidney. "Coven Mother. I, um... I brought something for you. A small token of my respect."

She turned her head to a perfect angle, her lips twisting into the smallest of smiles. I dared to glance at Neko, steeling myself to take the heavy book from his arms. I forced myself not to picture dropping it, not to imagine the pages splayed and torn on the inlaid parquet floor, in case dreaming had the power to make it so in this strange place of witchy energy.

As soon as my fingers touched the citrine binding, though, a wave of calm washed over me. There was peace in the crystal, confidence. I remembered the power I'd felt when I bound the book. I threw my shoulders back and displayed the volume for all to see.

And I was rewarded with a collective gasp of awe from all the women in the room.

"For you," I said, extending my offering. "Coven Mother."

I'd taken Teresa Alison Sidney by surprise. Whatever she'd thought I'd do, however she'd thought I'd present myself, she hadn't expected this. She hadn't expected the treasure I was offering up.

She looked at me for a long moment, blatantly scanning my face for my intention. I hoped she could see my earnest desire to fit in among my witchy sisters, to find the collective support I'd never known in school, in sorority, in any social aspect of my life. I prayed she could tell I wanted to join this clique, more than I'd ever wanted to join one before.

She glanced down at the volume and completed a tiny nod of recognition. I couldn't say whether she divined the book's name by magic or if she'd studied catalogs of the Osgood collection in the past. But she met my eyes and said, "The *Illustrated History of Witches*."

"I thought you could make good use of it."

"I can indeed." She set her hands upon the green Moroccan leather. "Citrine," she breathed. She closed her eyes and inhaled through her aquiline nose, drinking in the power of my binding.

Now, standing in this magnificent space, surrounded by a showroom of furniture and a gaggle of perfect women, I wasn't sure I'd made the right decision when I wrapped the crystal's power around the book. Maybe I should have been orderly. Maybe I should have been uniform. Maybe I should have followed the letter of the occult law, tamping down every single spark of individuality and creativity in my witchy soul as I bound the citrine to the *History*.

But I hadn't. And it was too late to make any changes now.

Teresa Alison Sidney's expression spoke volumes. I read her surprise at the binding I'd chosen. She'd clearly expected something more traditional—more submissive, more humble. But I also read a flare of greed on her face. She was pleased by the physical gift I'd given, but she was speculating about more, about the collection that nestled secure in my basement, about Neko. Somewhere in the organized chaos of my citrine binding, Teresa Alison Sidney read her first taste of what I could bring to the Washington Coven.

Or what they could take, if I failed to pass the admission test the Coven Mother set for me.

Teresa Alison Sidney said, "Thank you, Daughter of Hecate. Your offering to me, and to the coven, through me, is most valued."

I bowed my head in reply, trying to imitate the precise angle that had symbolized David's proud humility. "You honor me, Coven Mother."

She pulled the book closer to her side, balancing its substantial weight against her hip. But before it could become too heavy or before—Hecate preserve her—it could crease Teresa Alison Sidney's perfect trousers, a shadow glided up to her side. "Connie," she said, not even bothering to look at the newcomer. "Put this in the library."

Connie ignored the dismissive note of command, taking the volume as if it were a valuable crystal vase. She darted a glance at me before licking her lips in quick agitation. Like me, she was dressed all in black, and she seemed to disappear in the room's dim light, even when I looked directly at her. Her gaze skipped around, avoiding direct contact with any of the witches, and her nose twitched like a rabbit.

I felt Neko stifle a move toward her, and suddenly I understood. Connie was a familiar.

Just as Neko betrayed his feline roots every time he moved, Connie expressed her own animal past. She'd been a rabbit, I realized. I shot my own quick look around the room, and I saw that a number of the witches had shadowy companions lurking silently by their sides. The familiars seemed to melt into the room's darkness, almost becoming invisible beside the women they supported.

As Connie carried off my gift, Teresa Alison Sidney treated me to a slow smile. "Again," she said. "My thanks."

And then, a clock began to chime. All eyes in the room swung toward the corner, to the ornate tall-case clock. Witches and familiars, we all listened to the well-known Westminster sequence booming from the magnificent timepiece. After the song was done, there was a pause, long enough for me to measure the sudden, heightened tension, long enough for me to clench my fingers into fists. The tolling of the hours began with deep, sonorous tones. One. Two. Three... Each note resonated through my body, winding me tighter and raising my expectations.

All of the women responded to the clock the same way, even Teresa Alison Sidney. Each of us clenched a little more as the timepiece counted off the hours, and when the twelfth note struck, every one of us was staring at the Coven Mother. Every one of us was waiting.

And Teresa Alison Sidney did not disappoint. "Welcome, sisters," she proclaimed, and her voice was even more resonant than it had been before—deeper and coated with more power. She traced a pentagram in the air. Everywhere her finger passed, a silver streak persisted. "Our midnight coven is met."

The assembled witches repeated: "Our midnight coven is met."

Teresa Alison Sidney raised her voice and intoned, "Let any who would betray us discover the true power of the coven."

The witches took a step closer to their Mother and to me, and chanted together, "So mote it be."

Teresa Alison Sidney lifted both hands into the air. "Let any who would harm us receive the true wrath of Hecate."

The witches took another step, and each said in unison, "So mote it be."

"Let any who would wrong us know no end of earthly grief and loss."

The coven surrounded the two of us. Neko poked between my shoulder blades, and I joined in the chant. "So mote it be."

Teresa Alison Sidney looked pleased that I had found my voice, but she did not interrupt the ritual. "Hecate's Daughters, we gather this evening to celebrate our sisterhood. We join in a circle, in a pentagram of power."

Each of the witches slipped into formation, until they ringed the Coven Mother, Neko, and me. Then, each woman traced her own circle in the air, followed by a personal star. I joined in, only a little behind the others. Neko leaned against my side as I moved my arm, and I felt him mirror back my magic, helping me find a steady flow as all my would-be sisters watched.

I wished someone had given me a rulebook before the stroke of midnight, so I could know what was coming next.

The Coven Mother looked around our group, smiling benignly. "We are all sisters in the coven. Let any who would speak to Hecate's Daughters do so now."

A woman stepped forward immediately. Clearly, her movement was expected; it was probably on the same page of the program as the pentagram tracing we had just completed. This witch was as poised as every other one in the room, as picture-perfect for the private school yearbook photo. Her chestnut hair was cut very short, covering her head like a spiky cap. Her eyebrows were plucked into surprised arches. Her face was tanned, golden, as if she had spent the better part of the summer lying out on a beach. Her lips gleamed in the dim room, and I wondered if she used gloss, or if she had just licked them.

"I would speak to my sisters, Coven Mother."

Teresa Alison Sidney smiled at the woman, a twist of her lips different from any other I'd seen inside this house. *This* smile was real. It was true. It was the sort of smile I might share with Melissa—one I *would* share with Melissa, if I ever got a chance to tell her about this entire bizarre night.

"Yes, Haylee," the Coven Mother said. "Speak to your sisters."

Whatever friendly smile Haylee shared with Teresa Alison Sidney, she cast a harsher look at me. It wasn't *angry*, not exactly. It wasn't rude. But it was *sharp*, like a knife cutting through to some essential core. Haylee cast a look at me, and then she said, "Coven Mother, there is a new witch among us. A sister who asks to join our circle."

"The circle is open to all of Hecate's Daughters."

"All of Hecate's Daughters must prove themselves to the Coven," Haylee said. She relished these words, thrived on them. I thought of my brief, unsuccessful experience rushing a sorority in college. Haylee was the membership chairman, pledge coordinator, and social secretary, all rolled into one.

I pasted a smile on my face, trying desperately to remember that I was long out of college. I didn't need to worry about the silly social games of a bunch of party-hearty girls.

Neko brushed against my arm, though, and I realized I *did* need to worry about these women. Like it or not, I was a witch, just as they were. I was a witch, and I needed my coven. I needed the protection they could offer against arcane challenges. I needed the education they could provide, the wisdom gathered here for generations. But most of all, I needed their acceptance, their imprimatur, which would allow me to continue owning the treasures in my basement—the books and tools and Neko.

Teresa Alison Sidney was acknowledging Haylee's words. "It is true. Each of Hecate's Daughters must prove herself."

"The sisters have met, Coven Mother. We have determined a test for Jane Madison. We have decided what she must do to join our ranks."

Great. Now I was going to hear it. I could only hope my initiation would be as easy as drinking a pitcher of hideous blue cocktails. Or wearing a toga for a week, pretending to be a slave for my so-called sisters. Or calling all the cute boys and asking them out to a party on behalf of the juniors and seniors.

Suddenly I remembered Neko's admonishment the week before, when he first told me Teresa Alison Sidney had phoned. My initiation wasn't going to end in a mere week. It wasn't going to cost me a handful of sleepless nights, a few hungover days. The witches would wait for a major festival. A major celebration.

I wracked my brain, trying to calculate the next major event in the witch-bound year. We'd already celebrated Beltane; Ostara was long past.

Samhain.

Halloween. The traditional marking of the new year for witches, a celebration of change, of transition. A little more than eight weeks away.

Teresa Alison Sidney's smile was slow, and I realized she already knew what Haylee was going to say. She already knew the price for my entrance into the coven. "Speak, Haylee. What have the sisters determined? How should Jane Madison prove her worthiness to join our ranks?"

Haylee's answering smile was almost feral. "She will set the centerstone, Coven Mother. When the sisters gather beneath the moon of Samhain, Jane Madison will set the centerstone for our new safehold."

7

I stood in the dimly-lit kitchen, juggling a plate of finger sandwiches and a glass of punch, contemplating whether I could manage to slip a petit four onto my plate without collapsing my entire carefully-balanced little world. It wasn't just the food I worried about, of course. I was wondering about the witches who surrounded me.

Centerstone? Me? Just how the hell was I supposed to set a centerstone?

I'd pulled Neko aside the first chance I'd had, forced him into a shadowy corner so he could tell me what I'd gotten myself into. A centerstone was the core of a magic circle, a reservoir of protective power. The witch who set one had to be an expert on arcane defenses, on spells and crystals, herbs and runes—any lore that could be harnessed to guard an entire community of witches when they were submerged in their work-ings, when they were, collectively, at their most vulnerable.

For the thousandth time, I glanced over my shoulder at the front room of the house, wondering what the men were doing in there. They must have heard the end of the witches' ritual, the loud crack of thunder as Teresa Alison Sidney traced another pentagram in the air with her whole hand and intoned, "So mote it be."

None of the other witches seemed concerned that their warders were absent. In fact, none of the other witches even acknowledged their familiars slinking around the edges of the table. I had already shot Neko half a dozen glances, silently remonstrating with him not to eat the entire platter of tiny crab-cakes, not to fill his tea-cup with cream, not to suck out the fluffy filling from the exquisite miniature cream puffs, leaving behind desiccated pastry shells.

I was scowling at him again, trying to get him to back away from the artful skewers of grilled shrimp, when Haylee stepped up to my side.

"No hard feelings, right?" she asked, extending her perfectly manicured hand and flashing me a smile. Now that she was no longer encircling me with ritual power, I could see she was as thin as a model. Her collar bones stuck out with a vehemence I'd never seen in person, only on the glossy cover of *Vogue*. I took her fingers as she said, "Haylee James."

"Jane Madison," I said, feeling slightly ridiculous. Every woman gathered around this midnight feast knew my name. I was the reason they had come together that night. Me, and my new mission regarding their centerstone.

"I hope you don't think I was calling you out, trying to give you any sort of special grief."

I had thought just that. I'd thought she enjoyed standing in the center of the circle of witches, taking pleasure in my flash of confusion, in my lack of understanding. I'd thought I was trans-ported back to the worst bits of elementary school, high school, and college all rolled into one, and I hadn't appreciated the sensation that every other witch in the coven knew what was going on while I was attempting to ad lib from a very old, very outdated version of the play we had apparently decided to stage.

"Of course not," I said, and I managed to smile.

Haylee reached past me and took one of the petit fours, popping it into her mouth without worrying about balancing a plate and a glass, without worrying about anything at all. When she'd swallowed the morsel, she leaned closer and whispered conspiratorially, "Teri always does such a nice job with these get-togethers. Half the time, I think that's the only reason we let her be Coven Mother."

Teri.

Teresa Alison Sidney, to me. Terrifyingly powerful, all-knowing leader of the Washington Coven, to me.

Teri, to Haylee.

Once again, I shot a glance toward the front room. Why hadn't David warned me about this? Why hadn't he told me who I'd be dealing with?

Then again, maybe he hadn't known.

Well, that was absurd. He'd been affiliated with the coven his entire life. Warding was the family business, he'd told me. He'd even been temporarily drummed out of the warders corps for breaching the witches' rules. He knew what was going on here. He had to.

If only I did.

Haylee flashed a sympathetic smile. "It's a bit overwhelming, isn't it?"

I tried to match the quirk of her lips, pretending for just a moment that I had her devil-may-care flair. I shrugged and attempted an airy, "Just a bit."

"You'll get used to it."

"Really?" I realized how plaintive I sounded, and I hurried to cover my wistfulness. "I just don't know what's coming next, what people expect of me. I'm not sure what they want me to do."

What was I saying? Why was I talking to this woman? Had she cast some spell to make me confide in her?

As if to confirm that dark thought, Haylee raised a perfectly manicured finger to the base of her throat. I realized she wore an ornament there, a delicate amulet that rested on a silver chain so slight I could barely make it out in the dim light. I could not keep myself from stepping closer, from staring at the device.

A torch. The same emblem I'd seen on David's key-chain. "What is that?" I asked, before I could stop myself.

"This?" Haylee touched the jewelry again, and her voice conveyed a casual shrug. *This old thing?* She said, "It's my Torch. The symbol that I've dedicated myself to Hecate." She looked around the room. "We all wear them. Teri presents them to us, when we're accepted into the coven."

Teri again. "Oh," I said. Well, that made me sound absolutely brilliant. Like I was such a shrewd judge of witchcraft. Or jewelry. Or midnight buffets.

I must be even more tired than I'd thought. As soon as those words crossed my mind, a yawn began to grow at the back of my throat. I thought I could hide it, that I could swallow it away, but I could tell from Haylee's arched eyebrows I wasn't quite successful.

"I know," she said in a voice that wasn't quite sympathetic. "It's all strange when you're new to the coven. Your mother certainly wasn't able to keep up with us."

"Clara?" My voice cracked with incredulity. When had Clara come to the coven? When had she met the witches? And, far more importantly, why hadn't she said anything to me? "What happened with Clara?"

"Let's just say she wasn't given a major assignment, shall we? No centerstones in *her* future. Poor thing'll be lucky if she learns how to read jade runes."

"She's actually quite skilled at jade runes!"

Why was I defending Clara? Well, it was one thing for *me* to challenge her, to say she was a lousy witch and a worse mother. But I wasn't about to let a perfect stranger get in on the game.

"Really." I could tell Haylee didn't believe me. "Well, I suppose we might have been mistaken. Some women are just so nervous when they come before the coven. It didn't help that your mother was so worried about your grandmother. I don't think either one of them had stayed up past midnight in a very long time."

Either one of them. So Gran was in on the silent conspiracy as well. Anger rose in my chest, competing incongruously with another yawn.

Apparently oblivious to my distress, Haylee went on, "I suppose it's *possible* we all drew the wrong conclusion. We might have been thrown by neither of them having a familiar."

Well, of course, neither one had a familiar. Neither one had known she was a witch until I'd spilled the beans last year. And it wasn't as if Gran or Clara could have marched into Macy's to snatch up a magical helpmeet or two at the Memorial Day sale.

Familiars, I knew from my reading in the past year, were only created with the expense of a great deal of magical energy. When a particularly gifted witch died, she could encapsulate her power in an animal, feeding her spectral energy into its body and storing the raw stuff of magic for other witches to draw upon.

As if on cue, Neko chose that moment to abandon his stalking of the food table. He materialized at my side like a ghost, licking his lips. I wondered how many treats he'd stolen while I'd been talking to Haylee. Avoiding my dagger glance, he cocked his head to one side and scratched at his ear. I wouldn't have been surprised if he'd begun to whistle a tuneless little song—anything to make himself seem more innocent.

Apparently unaware of the tension sparking between Haylee and me, he asked, "Do you think Teresa Alison Sidney will bring out any more of the salmon canapés?"

Haylee sniffed, and I immediately realized she did not routinely waste her time speaking to other witches' magical assistants. "Teri is not in the habit of providing extras for familiars." Again, I felt that strange instinct to defend someone close to me, to explain away Neko's hunger. "Especially now that people are heading home," Haylee added before I could speak.

I looked around, surprised to realize there *were* fewer people in the room. The door to the men's club at the front of the house now stood open. While I couldn't see inside from my current angle, I could just make out the shadow of a familiar ducking inside and then, less than a minute later, a tall, sleek man came out.

The warder had clearly been summoned by the black-clad witch's servant. Confident and poised, the man crossed to Teresa Alison Sidney and bowed smoothly, raising her hand to his lips. She smiled tightly, expressing equal measures of satisfaction at the honor and world-weariness at the familiarity. The warder rose from his gesture and offered his arm to his witch, guiding her toward the door without a glance in my direction.

And suddenly, I knew it was time for David to rescue me. It was time for him to make his obeisance before Teresa Alison Sidney, to say whatever needed to be said, to do whatever needed to be done. I was falling asleep on my feet, and the notion of waiting one more minute for my warder to appear almost brought me to tears. "Neko," I said, but he had already sensed my command; he was moving toward the far doorway.

I turned back to Haylee. "Thank you for your...conversation."

"I'm afraid I've upset you. I didn't mean anything negative about your mother or your grandmother. It's just that they didn't have the power we were led to expect. Nothing at all like *yours.*"

"No," I lied, and then I realized she might think that I was agreeing with her assessment of my relatives' witchy abilities. My tongue seemed thick in my mouth as I hurried to clarify, "I'm not upset."

"Good." Haylee smiled and settled the fingers of one hand against the pulse point in my wrist, even as she once again touched the Torch that flickered against her throat. "Because I really do look forward to working with you. Maybe we could get together for coffee some time. I do a lot of business with galleries in Georgetown—I'm an interior designer."

I smiled at the vague invitation. Haylee wasn't actually so bad. She was reaching out to me. She was being sociable. She was welcoming me into the heart of the coven, *assuming* I would join the sisterhood, rather than betting against me. She was being a friend.

And if I had any doubt as to the goodwill behind her words, Haylee smiled winningly and said, "You know you can ask me for help. With *anything.*"

"Thank you," I said, and my response was made almost fervent by David's appearance in the doorway. I was scarcely aware of his steps across the room; I could barely watch him say his farewells. All I knew was he settled his hand on my arm, and I found myself stammering goodbye to Haylee, babbling something to a calm, collected Teresa Alison Sidney. I cut off yet another yawn as I glared at Neko, forcing him to come and stand by my side.

And then, finally, David guided me out the front door of that strange and mysterious house.

The pentagram across the threshold had faded away. As we walked into the wall of humid, late-summer air, I could sense the power that had once been housed in the doorway. Its living, electric thrill was gone, though. The man with the sword had departed as well, and I wasn't sorry to miss his shadowy threat.

I was suddenly so tired I could barely move.

In fact, I was too exhausted to reprimand Neko as he hissed at another familiar, a bird-like man who hovered by his own mistress's car door. I barely understood that Neko was opening the back door of David's car, ushering me onto the long, leather seat, making sure my legs were inside before he closed the door and sat up front.

David was silent as he drove us home, retracing the tree-lined roads until we drove over the Key Bridge, until we worked our way through Georgetown's cobbled streets. Once again, he applied some warder's trick to find another parking space directly in front of the Peabridge.

Neko dashed ahead as David helped me to sit up, helped me to maneuver out the car door, onto the curb, onto the flagstone garden path. My familiar opened our cottage door with his own key. He hovered in the living room, suddenly solicitous, but David shook his head. "I'll help her," he said. "Go to sleep." Neko shrugged before heading down to his basement lair.

"I'm fine," I said, but a yawn betrayed me, and I sounded like a cross child.

"It can be exhausting, entering a safehold for the first time."

"You could have warned me."

"No," he said seriously. "I couldn't. I wasn't allowed to. You needed to meet the coven on your own. Those are the ancient ways."

He led me toward my moon-washed bedroom. I remembered the first time he'd done this, the first night I had ever stretched my powers beyond their natural strength. As if David had a cat's night vision, he removed my fused glass necklace and eased my earrings from my lobes. He loosened my hair from its precarious chignon.

In the past ten months, he'd had occasion to put me to bed a dozen times. He never took advantage of the situation, never brushed against me in a way that conveyed anything more than strictly professional interest.

Not that I wanted him to. He was my warder, not my boyfriend.

But I couldn't keep from leaning against him, couldn't help but turn my face toward his as he helped me out of my dress.

If he kissed me, I wouldn't complain. Hadn't complained, in fact, in the past, the one time he *had* kissed me. The one time he'd made my belly swoop low with a sudden, gasping desire. The one time I'd tasted honest, magical potential on his lips.

What was I thinking?

He was my *warder*. And given my disastrous luck with men, I'd ruin everything if I ever thought of him as anything more than my magical protector. Besides, I was the more recent recipient of another kiss. Graeme Henderson's.

Against my better judgment, I giggled.

"What?" David asked, and I could hear patience in his voice as he waited for me to slip out of my bra. I turned away, suddenly shy in front of him.

"Nothing." But I giggled again, thinking of my secret romance. My Mystery Date, just like the ancient board game Gran had bought me when I was a kid. Graeme was no "Dud Date." That was for sure.

I was going to laugh again. Laugh out loud, for real. I had to think of something serious. Something scary. Something to keep from telling my romantic secret to my warder, who would never approve of the new man in my life. Of any man, distracting me from my studies. "Haylee," I blurted.

"What about her?" he said, easing my faded pajama top over my head.

"She's strong." I took a few deep breaths, clearing my thoughts.

"Yes."

"Stronger than I am."

"Better trained," he said. There was something about his tone, something about the very careful placement of the words that cut through my suppressed laughter.

"But not stronger?" I slurred the last word, as if I'd drunk an entire pitcher of mojitos.

"No," he said. Again, I could tell there was a story there. There was something he wasn't telling me, something lurking beneath his standard warder reserve.

"Teach me," I said suddenly.

"What?" His hands were gentle against my shoulders, but they were irresistible as he eased me back on my mattress. My pillow was like a cloud underneath my head, a cottony bridge to sleep.

"Teach me what Haylee knows. Help me be a good witch, so Teresa Alison Sidney likes me."

"Teresa Alison Sidney already likes you."

"Ha!" I sounded completely drunk now, and I wondered how my hand moved all by itself, how it stabbed the air.

"Well," he amended. "Teresa Alison Sidney *respects* you."

"Teri…" I whispered.

"What?"

"That's what Haylee calls her. Teri."

David pursed his lips in the silver moonlight. "Haylee's known the Coven Mother for a long time."

I clutched at his hand, pulled it close to my heart. I could feel the pulse beating through his wrists, beneath my gripping fingers, slow and steady and unexcitable. "Promise me," I said.

"Promise you what?" He might have been humoring a small child.

"Promise me you'll teach me enough to impress Haylee. Enough to impress Tere– Teri."

He shook his head. "Jane. You can't learn magic just to impress someone. Power isn't a toy. An act. You should know that by now."

"Not just to impress her. Them. All of them." The popular girls. From college age to senior citizenship—all the coven women who had gathered that night. I knew what I was trying to say; I just couldn't get the words out. "For the safehold. For the centerstone."

I could feel the tension in his hand, the wire-taut intensity that corded his wrist and set his shoulders. "Jane—"

"Promise. Promise I'll be stronger than Haylee. I need that. Or I'll never pass."

He sighed, and I felt him give way. "I promise," he said.

I relaxed against my pillow, and my lips curled into a smile. I didn't win very often.

Even as I relished the victory, though, I remembered the man with the sword. I remembered the moonlight glinting on the naked blade, and the silver star that had flared up before the doorway. All that power, all that tradition… I had so much to learn.

Sudden tears rose in the back of my throat. I shuddered, afraid to look out the window. Afraid to see what might lurk in the shadows. Self-doubt, or something worse. "What happens if I fail?" I asked.

"You won't."

"But if I do?" I started to tremble, hard shudders that rippled through my exhausted muscles.

David's reply was as sharp as the stones that made the walls of Teresa Alison Sidney's luxury home. "You know this already. Your collection is forfeit. The books, the crystals, the runes. Everything in the basement. They'll belong to the coven."

My teeth chattered, and I had to force my lips around my next question. "Neko?"

"Gone."

"And you?" He refused to answer, only shaking his head in the moonlight. "David," I whispered. "Stay here tonight."

He passed his free hand over my forehead and smoothed back my hair. I closed my eyes, but I could not still my terrified shivering. "Sleep," he said.

I fought him, though. "Here," I whispered. "Please."

"Sleep," he repeated. And then he took his hand from between mine.

I heard him tug at his shoelaces, heard his wingtips hit the floor. I felt him take off his suit jacket and remove his silken tie. There was a faint jangle as he emptied his pockets, the key to the amazing Lexus jostling with change on my nightstand.

I wanted to open my eyes. I wanted to see if he unbuttoned his shirt all the way or if he pulled it over his head. I wanted to watch him step out of his trousers, hang them neatly on my chair, settling them precisely so they wouldn't wrinkle. I wanted to see if he wore boxers or briefs.

But I was too tired.

I felt him pull my sheet over my shoulders, all the covers I'd need on a sultry night. I felt him lie down beside me, on top of the sheet. I felt him punch my extra pillow, wrestle it into a more comfortable shape. I felt him breathing beside me, slowly, deeply.

His breath evened out my own. It calmed me. Soothed me.

And finally, I slept.

8

I pushed my French toast around on my plate, using my fork to chase it into a puddle of maple syrup. My headache pounded in time to the gospel music that echoed in the Howard Theatre. Clara had been responsible for choosing our brunch location this month.

Ordinarily, I would have been enchanted by my surroundings. The Howard's brunch offerings filled a dozen tables, with choices ranging from cold cereal to omelets made to order, along with a heavy emphasis on Southern home-cooking. One entire table was given over to fresh fruit, and another threatened to collapse under the weight of assorted desserts. A gospel choir enriched the air around us, the women singing loud enough to wake the dead.

Or to wake me, as the case might be.

I'd spent the entire day before—a perfect, work-free Saturday—sleeping off the aftereffects of my meeting with the coven. David had left before I awoke. The only hints that he'd actually stayed the night were the impression of his head on my extra pillow and the faintest whiff of a woodsy scent that might have been soap, or maybe shampoo.

I'd gone back to bed and dozed away the afternoon, the

evening, and all of Saturday night. Even this morning, I'd tumbled out of bed only half an hour before I was supposed to meet my mother and grandmother at the theater. I'd cursed my way through a rapid face-washing and hair-brushing, and I'd pulled on a light khaki skirt with a sleeveless blouse to match— twin concessions to Gran's dislike of my mostly-black wardrobe. I suspected the color washed out my cheeks; my green eyes would definitely have benefitted from a careful application of mascara.

Clara's had.

Clara and I shared the same eyes. Even the manager had commented on that as she showed us to our table upon my belated arrival. "Mother-Daughter Sunday, is it? Have a wonderful meal!"

Both Gran and Clara had descended on the food as if they expected never to eat again, and they'd each gone back for additional helpings while I was still trying to commit to my French toast. My stomach had rebelled at the thought of my customary Eggs Benedict (even now, the notion of runny yolks made me swallow hard), although I *had* managed to gnaw a few strips of bacon. The greasy salt tasted good to me, like hangover remedies should taste.

Not that I was actually hungover. I was just floored by witchcraft.

Gran came back from the dessert table, bearing a slice of cheesecake the size of the Flatiron Building. She graciously accepted a refill on her coffee from a passing waiter before she reached out to pat my arm. "Now tell us, dear. Where were you last night? Some exciting party, I hope?"

My grandmother eternally hoped I would attend exciting parties. That desire must have been the side effect of listening to me moan my way through junior high and high school. I could barely remember those long-ago weekends when an absent invitation to a makeout party drove me into the slough of despond.

Or the pit of despair. Or whatever other deep, dank dungeon of misery I'd inhabited through my teens.

"Yes," Clara chimed in, as if there could be nothing more exciting than my nightlife. I had to hand it to her. She really *was* trying to make these monthly get-togethers a success. I'm sure she only meant the best as she added, "You *do* look a bit bedraggled this morning. You should have taken a moment to purify your aura—a lavender wash would do that for you, you know. Just a spritz of essential oil in the steam from your shower—"

"I didn't have time for a shower," I said, cutting her off at the holistic wellness pass.

Gran's face creased into a frown. I wasn't sure if she was disturbed by my interrupting, or by my failing to bathe. "What did I tell you while you were growing up, dear? One quick shower, and you can conquer the world. Even when you have the flu, there's nothing better than hot water. Hot water, shampoo, and a brisk rub with a face cloth are far better than lying in bed for another few minutes of sleep."

"I met the Washington Coven Friday night."

There. That cut short the Shower Rhapsody.

Gran darted a look at Clara. If I hadn't been watching closely, I might have missed it. I might not have recognized the conspiratorial gesture for what it was, an admission of guilt. Guilt and complicity.

"Coven?" Clara tried.

"Coven," I repeated grimly, as the Rock of Ages crumbled into gospel silence behind us. Diners' applause echoed off the theater walls, and I took advantage of the chaos to exclaim: "How could you have met them without telling me? I thought we were all in this together! Why is that so freaking hard for you two to believe?"

All right. I had to admit I thought the clapping would last a little longer. Or my voice would be a little quieter. Or the silence wouldn't echo quite so loudly after my last angry exclamation.

I felt the families on either side of us lean away, pretending overwhelming interest in their own desserts and coffee. A waiter scurried over and thrust a fresh cloth napkin into my hand, as if starch and cotton would bring me back to my senses. "Can I get you anything, ma'am?" he asked, and I heard his unvoiced plea for me to lower my voice, to behave myself in this public place.

"Just the check," I said, keeping my eyes on Clara.

Her choice of venue. Her turn to pay. She fumbled in her hippie backpack and pulled out a wallet. Slipping her credit card to the nervously dancing waiter, she still avoided meeting my gaze.

Gran, as always, attempted to smooth things over. "Jane, dear, it's not like we *intended* to go behind your back." Well, that protest was enough to release Clara—I turned my hot eyes onto my grandmother. She waved her fingers above her coffee cup, as if she were sprinkling invisible bread crumbs onto the surface. "We didn't choose to go there, dear. They summoned us. They *made* us meet them."

Clara nodded and said earnestly, "It was a month ago. When the moon was full. They brought us out to a house—it was way outside of the city, in Virginia."

Gran backed her up, as if she were suddenly compelled to tell the story, as if she needed to free herself from the memory. "They sent that nice man to drive us. I was so relieved—I never could have found the place on my own. Those narrow roads— I'm not sure the Lincoln could have made some of those turns. Best-looking car on the road, that's for sure, but it's not made for those little rustic by-ways."

Clara was preparing her next line of inane conciliatory babble, but the waiter returned with the credit card slip. He set it down on the table directly in front of Clara and handed her the pen, as if he were afraid she might delay signing. He clearly did not want to chance another outburst from me. I resisted the urge to snarl at him, to curve my fingers into claws and lash out at his tuxedoed chest.

"Have a wonderful day, ladies," he said as Clara finished the formality of paying. "Enjoy the sunshine."

Sunshine. The calendar had slipped to September, but we were still going to melt as soon as we left the theater's air-conditioned cavern. I thought about asking the waiter for a few frosty bottles of water—he probably would have come up with them, if only to get me away from the brunch faster.

Soon enough, we were back in the noon-time swamp. I took advantage of a green traffic light to cross the street and strike out toward the parking lot where Gran had left the monstrous Lincoln. I didn't really intend to get away from my family. If I'd wanted to do that, I could have outpaced them easily enough, leaving Clara to care for my grandmother as I strode off toward the subway.

No, I wanted to finish the conversation I'd begun. I wanted to find out exactly what they knew and when they'd learned it. I wanted to know what the coven had told them. And I wanted to know why they'd kept silent, why they'd left me to face the witches on my own.

Skirting a row of newspaper boxes, I collapsed onto a bus shelter bench, only to sigh with the passion of an aggrieved teenager when I needed to shift over to make room for both of them.

"Don't you understand?" I finally said. "If I'd known you'd already been out there, I could have been prepared. I wouldn't have felt quite so much like an idiot. I would have had a chance at making a good first impression."

"Oh, sweetheart," Gran rushed to assure me. "You always make a good first impression."

I resisted the urge to look back toward the Howard. I hadn't wowed them there.

At least Clara had the good sense to stay quiet. We both remembered what sort of impression I'd made on *her* when we first met. I'd practically fled Cake Walk, I'd been so eager to get away from my own mother.

I took a deep breath.

I was a librarian. My job was to research information and communicate what I learned to patrons. I should be able to speak to my own grandmother, to my mother, and manage to keep a civil tone.

"Here's the thing," I said. "It was so unnerving. I felt like all of them were watching me. Testing me. It was like they spoke a language I didn't know. I was frightened and embarrassed, and if I'd known you two had already been there, it wouldn't have been quite as," I struggled for the right word and then gave up, "as bad as it was."

Clara shook her head. "Jeanette," she started to say, but then she caught herself. My mother was the only person who ever called me Jeanette. That had been my original name before she hied off to Sedona, leaving me with my far more practical, down-to-earth grandmother, and the name I'd used for twenty-nine years. Jane.

Jeanette still rang strangely in my ears—it was the name of an exotic French beauty. Or a pampered American schoolgirl. Not me. Never me.

Clara tried again. "I just don't understand what was so unnerving about the visit. You stay up late all the time, so the midnight hour couldn't be the problem."

Gran chimed in. "And the women themselves, the—" she had trouble bringing herself to say it, "the *witches*—they were absolutely charming. Why, that Teresa Alison Sidney couldn't have been nicer if she'd been serving on the Concert Opera Guild board."

I wasted a moment trying to picture Teresa Alison Sidney among Gran's superannuated opera compatriots. The classiness of the image worked, but something just wasn't right. Teresa Alison Sidney was too...hard. Driven. She had her own agenda and she'd spare nothing—and no one—to achieve it.

Clara, though, was apparently intent on building some new castle of camaraderie, picking up where Gran left off with the Washington Coven Pep Rally. "After we got past the introductions, they were quite welcoming. I was actually embarrassed I didn't have anything to give them after they presented me with my brooch."

"Your brooch?"

Gran clicked her tongue at my incredulous tone, but I ignored her. Clara waved off my question. "Fine, fine, call it a pendant, but I don't think I'll ever wear mine on a chain. It's not really large enough to stand out against my crystals. Maybe I can put it on a lapel, if I'm ever called back to the coven again."

Chain? Lapel?

"What the hell are you talking about?" My question came out even sharper than I intended.

"Jane," Gran protested.

I forced myself to take a deep breath, closing my eyes so I could count to five. The darkness behind my eyelids was crimson-tinged; it dripped reminders of the headache that pulsed beneath my every thought. I tested my words in my own mind, tried them again, and when I was certain they wouldn't sound petulant, I said out loud, "I didn't get any jewelry."

"Well, isn't that odd?" Gran truly sounded perplexed. "We both got identical pieces, your mother and me. They're shaped like a torch. Teresa Alison Sidney said it was a sign of the secret knowledge we possessed."

As soon as Gran said the word "torch" I could picture it. The brooch would have the same stylized flames that had kissed Haylee's throat, that had graced David's keychain. It would call out to me, summon my fingers to try to touch it.

Why had they each received a pin, when I'd received nothing?

"I didn't get one," I mumbled, ashamed to meet their eyes.

There was an uncomfortable pause before Clara said, "I'm sure there was a reason." I knew she was trying to make me feel better. But that didn't help. Not now. Not while I was sitting in the park, dropped once more into all the strangeness of Friday night.

I didn't belong with the coven. They didn't want me. They wanted my mother and my grandmother, but they didn't want me. Not on a permanent basis, anyway. Just to do their scutwork. To set their centerstone.

"Your mother is absolutely correct," Gran said, reaching out and patting my hand, as if she were consoling me about something as unimportant as the bakery being out of chocolate cupcakes. "Someone probably just forgot to have it ready, forgot to call the jeweler, or something like that."

Despite the heat, I shivered as I confessed, "I'm frightened to see them again. To see that guy with the sword."

"Sword?" Clara and Gran asked at precisely the same moment, in exactly the same tone.

"What sword?" Clara elaborated.

I looked from one to the other, wondering if this was part of their being sworn into the sisterhood. Maybe they were supposed to pretend ignorance to us outsiders. Maybe they were supposed to disclaim any concrete knowledge of what went on in the safehold. After all, if I didn't have a torch pin, I could be *anybody*. I could be as dangerous to the coven as…as any of the people who strode by our bench, relaxing on an autumn Sunday.

But no. Gran and Clara weren't pretending. They weren't reciting lines they'd been taught. Looking from my grandmother to my mother, I was willing to swear neither of them had seen a sword the night they'd visited the Washington Coven.

"When I was there, a man stood outside the door," I said slowly. "A large man wearing a cloak, like some sort of medieval nobleman. He held a sword." They stared at me as if I were speaking in tongues. "He had a sword," I insisted, "and he was guarding the safehold. Protecting all the witches."

Clara shook her head. "We certainly would have noticed a knight standing in the doorway."

"Not *in* the doorway," I insisted. "Outside of it. The doorway itself was protected by the pentagram."

"Pentagram?" Gran might never have heard the word for all the shock in her voice.

"You didn't see that either? It was etched in the air. It glowed silver when we entered, David, and Neko, and me."

"David and Neko!" Clara shook her head. "They let you come in with David and Neko?"

"Of course. David's my warder. And Neko's my familiar."

Gran clicked her tongue. "But it was ladies only! That's what they told us." Clara nodded in agreement.

My exasperation began to flow over my determination to stay calm. "You said someone drove you out there! What happened to him? Did he just melt into the ground when you arrived?"

"Now, dear, there's no reason to get nasty," Gran said. "We just didn't see what you did. I understand you're disappointed that you didn't get a Torch. As soon as I get home, I'll give you mine. You can return it when you get your own."

"No, Gran." I shook my head. "I can't take your pin." And somehow, I knew I really *couldn't*. Whatever magic rested in the emblem would object to my handling it. I couldn't explain how I knew that, or what it actually meant, but I was certain there'd be no transferring of torches from one woman of the Smythe-Madison clan to another.

Clara was staring into the middle distance. I could just make out her eyes behind her sunglasses, and I could tell she wasn't blinking. "That man," she said, and it sounded like she was trying to remember an elusive lyric. "He picked us up at your Gran's apartment. He drove us out past Great Falls. He helped us out of the car…" She shook her head. "I can't remember anything else. It's as if he actually did disappear."

"But weren't there warders there? And familiars?"

"Not that I recall." Her tone was perplexed. "You'd think we would have noticed. After all, we've seen enough of your Neko."

So. No warders. No familiars. No sword. No pentagram.

There was a time, back when I was a teenager, when I had

been certain I knew more than Gran. I'd been positive that I was wise in the ways of the world, that I understood how people behaved, how systems functioned. I'd been exasperated with her failure to comprehend the subtle workings of the universe around us.

For example, she hadn't appreciated the importance of passing notes in algebra, even when Mrs. Hock had already issued me two warnings. She hadn't grasped the nuances of who texted whom, and why I was devastated to be pruned from the after-school phone frenzy of one particularly snobby girl whose name I no longer remembered. Gran hadn't understood— hadn't lived and breathed and *known*—why it mattered that Karl Nelson had the locker next to mine but he chose not to use it, preferring to lug around his books in a backpack all day, calling the burden "training" for the football season.

But Gran had learned a lot in the intervening years.

Some time after high school, while I was in college, or maybe even pursuing my useless Shakespeare degree, Gran had become a genius. She read nuances into my conversations; she *understood* my world and the people in it. She knew before I did that Scott Randall was a complete jerk. She would have warned me about the I.B. if I'd given her half a chance.

But now? Today? With respect to the coven?

Gran had nothing. No knowledge. No skills. No witchy sensitivities whatsoever.

And, looking at Clara, I realized she wasn't any better off. Sure, she might have a deft hand with runes. But she thought she could read auras, despite the fact that I hadn't found a single reference to auras in the entire Osgood collection. Clara had glanced through my spellbooks but she quickly dismissed all of them, saying they bored her. She'd shrugged off my attempts to speak about potions or charms.

I looked at my mother and my grandmother, and I realized a terrifying truth.

I knew more about witchcraft than they did. Than they ever

would. I was going to be tested by the coven in ways they could not imagine. Their failure to tell me about their visit to the safehold the month before had not been cruel or mean or even a petty oversight.

They honestly and completely didn't realize how important it might have been for me to know. They had no frame of reference.

And for the first time I could remember, I realized I was going to have to take my next step alone. Sure, Gran and Clara would stand by me, at least as long as the coven permitted them to do so.

But there was no way they could help me. And when push came to shove, come the night of dedicating the centerstone, I was going to be truly alone. Truly abandoned by friends and family. And—worst of all—I didn't have the first idea about how to prepare for the working.

9

I stared into my bathroom mirror, making fish-faces to be certain my lipstick had not coated my teeth. I'd almost reached the end of my tube of Pick-Me-Up Pink. It might be time to graduate—Nars's Fire Down Below had caught my eye the last time I was in Sephora. Sure it was red. Sure it was semi-matte. Sure it would make me look like a hooker if I applied too much.

But I was learning to control myself, learning to master the fine art of lipstick. And if I couldn't handle a grown-up shade of crimson, then how was I ever going to master an entire relationship?

Relationship. I rolled the word around on my tongue as I ran my fingers through my just-trimmed hair. Ever since the Implausible Boob, I'd dreaded the concept of a *relationship*. I wasn't ever going to get involved in a relationship more complicated than the one I had with my dry cleaner. I was never going to put my heart on the line again, never going to let down my guard.

After all, I was a very busy woman. I had a library reference desk to manage. I had a grandmother to assist, a mother to get to know. I had a basement full of books about witchcraft, volume after volume after volume that shouted in no uncertain leather-bound terms that I had better start preparing for setting the centerstone.

But now I'd met Graeme Henderson. I'd been invited out for a dream date, for dessert and drinks at the Bistro Français. I'd shared my witchy secret with a normal man for the very first time since my magical awakening without totally freaking him out.

I'd agreed to meet Graeme Henderson for a Saturday night date.

Not a weeknight. Not an evening when ordinary people might work late at the office, might be called out to a business dinner, to a team-building staff meeting, to some other excuse to avoid a wife.

Saturday.

Married men never made dates for Saturday.

The I.B. had avoided weekend commitments like our Founding Fathers avoided British Redcoats in the woods. Now, with the wisdom of hindsight, I knew he'd been saving those days for his wife. At the time, I'd accepted his busy social life as an indication that the Immoral Brigand was truly desirable, truly admirable, truly everything a girl could ask for in a man— and more.

Okay. So I'd been deluded. A crush will do that to you— especially one delivered with the full force of an anvil dropped from an open window, seven stories up. It was hardly *my* fault I'd been designated to play the Coyote in the Road Runner cartoon of my life. Did anyone think the Coyote really *wanted* to subject himself to the Acme Destruction Tool of the week? The Coyote was a victim, clear and simple.

I sighed. I might be on the road to recovery, but it still wasn't easy to accept a Saturday night date as "normal." My unease was only heightened by the fact that I had no idea what activity Graeme had in mind. He'd told me to dress comfortably, but he hadn't mentioned whether we'd be inside or outside.

Outside on a September night. A night in the swampland beloved of our forefathers, where mosquitoes grew to the size of aircraft carriers, at least until the first killing freeze. I knew from long experience that I reacted poorly to mosquito bites. It wasn't so much that I swelled up when I was bitten. Rather, I developed great puffy welts that looked like globs of uncooked dough. Those bites itched like an entire forest of nettles, too; I couldn't keep from gouging red furrows into my flesh with my still-relatively-new-to-me fingernails.

And I was certain every mosquito in the metro area would be attracted to me. A vitamin B-12 deficiency, my childhood pediatrician had diagnosed. My shampoo. My soap. My scintillating personality. I couldn't say why for sure, but I was an absolute magnet for mosquitoes.

Magic was no assistance. It was too difficult to craft a spell to banish so many tiny lives—each beating mosquito heart (did mosquitoes even have hearts?) would require a separate focus of my witchy attention.

Alas, unsure of my destination for my Saturday night dream date, I did the only sane thing. I slathered my body from head to toe in Deep Woods Off. I protected my vulnerable flesh as if I were preparing for a jungle expedition. I poured lotion onto my arms and legs, rubbing it in with the vigor of the converted. I worked it between my toes, around my ankles. I even ran my fingers through my hair. I was determined not to become The Amazing Swollen Girl of Washington before the night was over.

Slathering completed, I tugged on my newest black T-shirt acquisition. This one was lightweight silk. Its fabric twisted across my chest, accenting my somewhat-lacking cleavage with soft folds. The shirt's hem rode right on top of the waistband of my short black skirt. I twisted to look at my rear end in the mirror. I thought the skirt was slimming, but what if that was only an optical illusion? What if that was only a side effect of my contorting in front of the mirror? What if my skirt was like television, and I secretly gained fifteen pounds just by closing up the side zipper?

I glanced at my watch. There was no time left to change. Besides, I'd already tried on everything else in my closet. Graeme Henderson might be murder on my psyche, but he was great for Goodwill Industries. Each date with him, I found another dozen items of clothing to pass on to the charity.

I grimaced and told myself this dressing-for-dates thing would be a lot easier if there was just a uniform, like the colonial costume I wore for work. I tried to picture Graeme's surprise if I greeted him in an embroidered overdress and hoops. The confining outfits had certainly acted like catnip on the I.B.'s libido.

A sharp knock at the cottage's front door interrupted bad memories of the Immature Baby and his strange attraction to my eighteenth-century attire. I offered up one more fish-face to appease the lipstick gods, and then I took a deep breath, bracing myself to answer the door.

And there was Graeme.

My heart started pounding against my silk T-shirt, and I wondered if he could hear it echo in my living room. He was more gorgeous than I remembered—that quarterback build, the perfect blond hair, those icy blue eyes, with all the intelligence and shrewd good will of a husky.

Without fully intending to, I stepped forward, greeting him with a quick pursing of my lips which he took only seconds to transform into a knee-buckling kiss. I was grateful for his arms around me, for his strong fingers spread across my back. All of a sudden, the air conditioner, which had done such a noble job keeping my cottage cool in the sticky September night, seemed to stop functioning. The heat of Graeme's greeting melted my spine, leaving me winded and desperate for more.

When he pulled back infinitesimally, I gasped, "Good evening."

"Quite," he said, and I felt his gaze on my T-shirt like a physical thing.

I was about to invite him in. I was ready to close the door behind us, lock out the heat, secure us in the air conditioner's chilly grasp. I was already calculating what refreshments I had in the refrigerator—a bottle of tonic water, some salty olives Neko had dragged back from the gourmet grocery store, a jar of Marcona almonds from the same source.

Surely we could survive on cocktail fare for the rest of the night? Cocktail fare and love... Was I even thinking that thought?

He sighed with the regret of a man who must choose his grade-school daughter's princess birthday party over free tickets to the Super Bowl. (Not that he had a grade-school daughter. Not that he even knew the first thing about American football.) He said, "The car is waiting."

"Car?" I tried not to sound disappointed.

"Just a little something I arranged for the evening." His smug smile turned my knees to water.

Curiosity trumped my libido, and I reached for my house keys. Then, I let Graeme steer me down the path that cut through the garden. His fingers hovered above the small of my back; I felt their heat through the sheer silk of my shirt. I imagined them touching my bare skin, envisioned his palm flat against my spine. Once again, my breath caught in my throat, and I forced myself to offer up a little mind-clearing cough.

"Summer cold coming on?" he asked solicitously.

"No!" I sounded too anxious, and I lowered my voice by an octave. "Not at all. Just a tickle at the back of my throat. Maybe some pollen from the garden. The bluestem is out. And the chokeberry. Maybe the Eastern sweetshrub."

I—or he—was spared any more of my demented librarian babble as we rounded the corner of the Peabridge. I looked out at the street and stopped dead.

A limousine. A jet black limousine, stretching half the block, complete with liveried chauffeur. Automatically, I glanced at the license plate, expecting to see the H that indicated a rented car.

No H.

Someone owned this vehicle. "Is this yours?" I finally asked Graeme.

"Let's just say it belongs to a friend of a friend."

I glanced down at my T-shirt and mini-skirt, suddenly feeling underdressed for the evening. "I don't know," I said. "Maybe I should go back inside and put on—"

"Nonsense," Graeme interrupted me, settling a fever-spiking palm on my forearm. "The chauffeur is the one in uniform. We wear what we want. When we want."

I heard the promise purr at the back of his words, and I wondered exactly what proposition was curled inside his English accent. I scarcely had time to blush, though, before the chauffeur was holding the car door for me.

I slid across a leather seat as smooth as polished stone. A bar occupied the space across from my knees, and a bottle of champagne glistened in an ice bucket. Two flutes glinted in the overhead light as Graeme joined me. The chauffeur made a short bow and closed the door. In moments, we were gliding through the Georgetown streets. For the second time in a week, I was being conveyed through Washington, DC in a luxury vehicle.

I took great pride in not owning a car. I was a city girl. I walked where I needed to go, or I took the subway; I even knew the city's bus routes pretty well.

But much more of this fine driving, and I could be converted. I wasted a moment, remembering that my last car ride had taken me to a coven meeting, that I'd come back from that session with an impossible responsibility. I had no business being out and about on a date—I should be learning everything I could about setting the coven's centerstone.

But Samhain was still seven weeks away. And Graeme was beside me right now.

"May I?" Graeme asked, gesturing toward the champagne.

"Please." I couldn't help but smile as he leaned forward. His movements were so confident, so spare. He poured with an expert twist of his wrist, capturing even the troublesome last drop on the bottle's lip. When he passed me my glass, I let my fingers slip against his, and I had to catch my breath against the confusing tremble of heat and cold.

"To the past and to the present," he said. And then, touching his glass to mine, he added, "And to the future."

"Past?" I asked, because I couldn't fold my mind around the word "future."

"I figured we'd take a night tour of the monuments. Your nation's past." Unbidden, I thought of the movie *No Way Out*, of Kevin Costner and Sean Young writhing their way around a midnight Washington while suggestive images of the Washington Monument's obelisk filled the screen. I glanced toward the front of our compartment, but the chauffeur had already raised the opaque window that separated us. Graeme and I were blessedly alone.

I needed to say something, to fill a silence that was rapidly becoming awkward. "I'd like that," I said. I lubricated my enthusiasm with a large gulp of champagne. "Very much."

And so we became tourists. The nameless driver was an expert at his job. He wove his way through crowded streets, stopping at necessary traffic lights but never jarring us, never disturbing the cocoon we wove for ourselves in the back seat. Graeme did his part as well—he kept my champagne flute full, and he produced a series of snackable tidbits, including a tiny crystal bowl of Marcona almonds that nearly set me to laughing because they mimicked the love-nest fare that I'd contemplated in the cottage.

DC's night monuments never failed to impress—the white marble glinted beneath creamy lights, with tourists silhouetted against the stone as if they were placed by some exacting movie director. As we circled around the Greek temple of the Lincoln Memorial, Graeme reached over to tuck a strand of wayward hair behind my ear. "Are you up for a bit of a stroll?"

A stroll? Well, I'd rather stay here in our private air-conditioned retreat, truth be told. But that wasn't very sporting of me, was it? If the man had something else in mind, I should play along. Be more flexible. Even the thought of that word—flexible —made me blush. What was it about this guy? Why did I find him so compelling? I set down my glass with a firm nod. "Of course," I said.

Graeme smiled, and he pushed a button to roll down the compartment window, to speak with the chauffeur. In moments, we were walking around the Reflecting Pool, staring up at the Washington Monument. A pair of red lights blinked at the top, like benevolent eyes keeping watch over us.

Graeme nodded toward the marble. "From here, it looks like the color changes part way up."

"Oh, it does," I said. "They worked on it for about a decade before they ran out of money. It just sat there unfinished for about twenty years, and when they started again, they took stone from a different quarry. They didn't set the aluminum cap until 1888."

"Aluminum?"

"Aluminium, I suppose you'd say. At the time, it cost as much as silver. But of course, it doesn't tarnish."

"Of course."

I winced at his droll tone and realized how much I'd been babbling. "I'm sorry," I said. "I sound like a textbook."

"You sound like a woman with a lot of facts at her fingertips. And *that* is a trait I find quite attractive."

Before I could figure out how to respond to that, Graeme wove his fingers between mine. He started to wander toward one of the side paths, away from the well-lit Reflecting Pool. "Where are we going?" I asked, barely making the words audible above my pounding heart.

"I was certain you could tell me," he said, smiling. "Isn't

there some other monument over here? Something off the beaten path?"

"Constitution Gardens," I said, and then I bit my lip. All right. I *was* a librarian. I knew stuff. But did I have to show off every ounce of knowledge like some completely geeky teen-aged girl? I fought against the urge to tell Graeme about the Monument to the Signers of the Declaration of Independence, or the fact that the Gardens were land reclaimed from the Potomac River Tidal Basin, or any of the other Happy Tourist Facts that sprang to my mind.

Instead, I let Graeme guide me to a wooden bench. "What are those lights over there?" He nodded toward a vague glow that lit the path ahead of us.

"The Vietnam Memorial," I said. *Designed by Maya Lin, completed in 1982*, droned the travelogue in my mind.

"Ah," he said. "What was the name of the woman who designed it?"

"Maya Lin," I said, trying to keep the note of surprise from my voice.

"And how long has it been there now?"

"Since 1982," I said, and my awe definitely flowed into my words.

He didn't care that I knew things. It didn't bother him that I had a stash of trivia tucked away, that I could call up a ridiculous number of facts and figures.

And as I relaxed into the curve of his arm, I marveled at how easy this was. Most guys didn't like to hang out with girls who knew more than they did. I'd spent a lifetime trying to hide the fact that I was smart, trying to disguise my memory, trying to play down the bits and pieces I'd picked up as a librarian.

Even David Montrose wasn't thrilled with my know-it-all approach. Or at least so I sensed. I held back from him. I assumed the role of student and let him play the part of teacher. I gave in to him, regularly, because that was how we related to each other. Those were our *jobs* with respect to each other. He taught. I learned.

I blinked as I became consciously aware of the things Graeme was doing with his fingertips on the back of my neck. The very stimulating things he was doing. The downright *arousing* things, as his lips moved toward my silk-wrapped cleavage.

Toward the cleavage I had liberally doused in chemical-tainted, mosquito-damning poison. "Wait!" I said.

"What?" He pulled back reluctantly.

I let my own fingers travel toward the neck of his white shirt. The cotton glimmered in the dim light, and I licked my lips nervously. At least there was no taste of Off *there*. Who knew what this gorgeous man would think if I let him proceed? If I let him continue on his shimmering little journey of discovery? What a way to kill a romance—literally, with poison.

I undid his top button. "Nothing," I said, aware that his exclamation still hung in the air. "I just thought I should do a bit of the work." I added a taunting smile to my words.

He grinned back at me. "Work?"

"Work," I repeated, and then I shrugged. "Play. Whatever."

I kissed him, to keep the proverbial ball rolling forward. His fingers tangled in my hair, adding an urgency to my lips. I fumbled at another of his buttons, and another. My Englishman had a fine dusting of blond hair on his chest—not one of those movie-star smooth torsos that always reminded me of a boy. No. Graeme Henderson was a *man*. A man who was obviously eager for me to return to my ministrations.

Who was I to disobey? Without thinking, I hitched my skirt a little higher and eased onto Graeme's lap, facing him and the shadows of Constitution Gardens. His indrawn breath told me my attention was more than welcome. I had, indeed, succeeded in making him forget my chemical-soaked skin. I leaned down, determined to continue my successful enterprise. Another button. Another. A tug to free his shirt from the waist-band of his slacks.

I might have ignored the sound of a clearing throat. I could definitely overlook the slap of feet against the black-top path. But there was no way I could avoid the beam of a flashlight.

A flashlight that had all of the intensity of a CSI investigation. A flashlight that immediately picked out and broadcast the fact that my T-shirt had ridden up considerably higher than the waistband of my skirt. A flashlight that showed exactly what a remnant trail of Pick-Me-Up Pink looks like against pale English flesh, especially flesh that was framed by a tousled cotton shirt.

Graeme blinked and sat up straighter on the bench, holding me steady with one confident hand. "Is there a problem, Officer?"

Officer? Crap.

I jumped away from Graeme as if he were a lightning rod channeling an entire thunderstorm of electricity.

The policeman took advantage of the movement to shine his light directly into my eyes. "I was going to ask you the same question, sir." I could hear the smirk behind his words, an infuriating "just a joke between us boys" tone that made my blood boil. "We've had reports of certain…unsavory characters here in the park," the cop went on. "You can never be too careful."

I started to splutter a reply, but Graeme settled a soothing hand on my forearm. "I'm being careful enough, Officer."

I could swear the flashlight beam dipped lower as the policeman made an entirely inappropriate inspection of Graeme's trousers. Or maybe that's where *my* eyes traveled. Oops.

"All the same," the policeman said. "The park isn't safe after dark. You two should move along."

We were being rousted by the DC police. Chivvied along like vagrants. Herded up like streetwalkers. Well, I was the one

being treated like a streetwalker. Graeme was just my unsuspecting John.

I started to protest, to ask if the park was closed yet, if it was
technically after hours. I was going to demand a meeting with
the cop's boss, with the sergeant or whoever-it-was who took
charge of the badge-toting, flashlight-wielding tyrants of the
street.

But then I thought about riding in the back of a police
car. A car that would probably lack the smooth suspension of
Graeme's limousine. A car that would certainly be in short
supply of champagne and almonds, of the miniature chocolate truffles I had glimpsed inside the cabinet of culinary
wonders.

So I let myself be hustled out of Constitution Gardens. I let
myself be marched back to the main path, to the uncomplimen-
tary glare of street lights. I let myself stand beside Graeme as
the policeman waved a jaunty farewell, shaking his head as he
left to search out other miscreants in the night.

I was too embarrassed to hear Graeme's parting words to
Washington's finest. In fact, I was barely aware of Graeme's
fingers on my elbow, guiding me back to the limo. The chauffeur was waiting, standing at attention beside the sleek black
door, as if nothing could possibly be amiss. Before the car's
engine started, Graeme had poured champagne from a fresh
bottle.

But I sat on my half of the car seat, swaddled in my own
private blanket of misery. I felt like a child caught stealing
cookies from the cookie jar. I remembered the time that Gabriel
Kahn had come over to study high school physics, and Gran
had caught us necking on the living room sofa, our textbooks
long forgotten.

Only when the limo pulled up in front of the Peabridge did I
trust myself enough to speak. "Thank you for a lovely evening,"
I managed to say.

"Jane," Graeme said. "Don't be like this."

"Like what?" I started to ask, and I was horrified to hear tears behind my words.

"Hush," he said, and then he pulled me close to his lipstick-traced and now-cotton-covered chest. His arms closed around me, calm and soothing. He wasn't embarrassed. Or at least, he didn't act like he was.

His lips brushed against the top of my head. Against my mosquito-lotioned hair. That was the problem. Deep Woods Off had ruined everything. I pushed back from his chest enough to look into his eyes. "It wasn't like we were doing anything wrong," I said.

"We're both consenting adults," he agreed.

"He didn't have to be so snide."

"He was likely jealous. Miserable sod."

We stared at each other for a long moment, and I realized I could do the responsible thing. The adult thing. I could invite Graeme in, take a quick shower to remove the Off from my tainted skin, and pick up right where we'd been interrupted.

But there was Neko to consider. Neko, and Jacques. And the fact that I'd promised Melissa—*sworn* to my best friend—that I would keep this romance secret from my familiar.

Friendship tests could be a bitch.

"I'm sorry," I said, at the same time Graeme said exactly the same words.

He laughed and cupped his palm against my jaw. "Sometimes, when the moment's lost, you just have to let it go." He sighed as he traced my jaw with one blunt finger. My belly—or something lower—flipped over. "Promise me you'll save next Saturday night for me. Let me make this up to you."

I looked around—at the limo, the champagne, the remnants of a perfect evening. I was acting like a spoiled brat. I shouldn't need Graeme to make anything up to me. If anything, I should be making things up to *him*.

Next Saturday night, he'd said. Just like a regular boyfriend. "I'd love that." I said.

He reached for the door handle. "Let me walk you to your door," he said.

"No!" I pictured Neko and Jacques, staring out the cottage windows. "No," I repeated in a slightly more sane voice. "I want to picture you here. Remember the good things about tonight." I leaned in and gave him one last kiss, a hint of what I wanted to make happen next Saturday.

"Good things," he said with a smile, as he came up for air. And then he reached across me and opened the door.

I was only a little embarrassed to find the chauffeur there, waiting patiently. Of course, he was waiting for me to emerge from the sex lair of the backseat. That was his job. He offered me the slightest bow as he handed me out of the car. "Good evening, madam," he said. He kept his eyes straight ahead, his demeanor as different from the cop's as any two men imaginable.

I forbade myself to look back as I walked down the garden path. Instead, I focused on slowing my breathing, on steadying my pounding pulse. I started to weave together the bits and pieces of my story, the tale I would need to tell as soon as the front door opened.

Earlier, in fact. Neko pounced on me from the front porch. "Where were you?" he asked.

"And who were you weeth?" Jacques added from his own darkened corner of the doorstep.

I wondered how long they'd taken to coordinate their inter-rogation, but I was suddenly inspired to answer with disarming truthfulness. I shivered a little, overcome by my daring. "I had a date," I said, breezily opening the door and letting all three of us into the living room.

"With who?" Neko cocked his head to one side, as if I were a mouse he might bat across the floor.

"Whom," I said, smiling sweetly.

"Whom," he said through gritted teeth, flexing his fingers like a predator's claws.

So much for disarming truthfulness. "Nate Poindexter," I said, tossing off the name as if I'd said it a million times.

"Poindexter?" Neko asked.

Okay, maybe I shouldn't have chosen a surname that made me want to laugh. "Nate," I said firmly. "We went to high school together. I ran into him the other day. He's been living out in San Francisco, but he decided DC's really more his style."

"San Francisco?" Neko asked, making the name of the city sound like an accusation.

"Actually, Silicon Valley. Palo Alto."

Neko nodded, storing away my words. He even stretched, working out every last kink in his seemingly elastic spine. "Where did you go tonight?"

"Morton's. For steak. Apparently no one serves red meat in California any more."

Neko sniffed, and for just a moment, I wondered if he was trying to smell filet mignon on my breath. I wouldn't put it past the little sneak. Before I could come up with another lie to cover my meat-free evening, Neko shook his head. "What *are* you wearing? Eau de Pine-sol?"

"It's not that bad!" I gasped.

"Not if industrial solvents turn you on." Neko made a face. I tried to remind myself he had once been a cat. He was a magical familiar. His senses were more finely tuned than any true human's. They had to be.

"Enough," I said, fighting the blush that heated my cheeks. "I'm going to bed. You boys keep the noise down."

They were quiet enough. But I tossed and turned for hours. Eventually, I got up and took a quick, cool shower—enough to wash away the Deep Woods Off. And the lingering heat Graeme had stirred inside me.

10

Looking up from the lectern, I was once again surprised by the number of people who sat in the Peabridge's conference room. "And so," I concluded, gesturing toward the screen behind me, "you can view our extensive collection of maps, studying them like the founding fathers did in their endless attempts to resolve border disputes, determine effective trade routes, and ultimately break free from British control."

The applause was spontaneous, and I found myself surrounded by eager audience members as I turned off the microphone that was, incongruously, attached to my lace bodice. A middle-aged woman set a hand against her well-groomed silver bob as she said, "Thank you so much! These Monday sessions are the high point of my month."

I put on my best librarian smile. "They wouldn't be anything, without people from the neighborhood joining us."

My words sounded fake in my own ears, but they seemed to please the local matron. As I dug for something a little more sincere to deliver as a follow-up, small hands tugged at my skirt.

"Now, Nicholas, you know we don't do that."

Well, maybe Nicholas's mother knew he wasn't supposed to tug on every last pleat in my colonial garment, but Nicholas himself seemed distinctly unaware of that fine point of etiquette. The toddler's cheeks were smeared with something that looked like strawberry jam, and his tousled hair screamed "Dennis the Menace." Especially the "menace" part.

I had noticed the kid during my presentation because he'd taken advantage of the lowered lights and the quiet crowd to demand his sippy cup, and then had dropped the damn thing on the floor. Repeatedly. Despite his mother's stage whisper that he sit down. Despite the hissed complaints of other patrons. Despite my attempts to incinerate him with glares from the lectern.

His success at prying open the top of the supposedly-inde-structible cup and spilling the contents across the conference room floor was merely an added benefit for those of us who got to maintain the Peabridge's space.

Now, Nicholas buried his face in my embroidered overskirt. What sort of mother uses sticky jam sandwiches as a (blatantly unsuccessful) quietness-bribe? I could only hope the library would consider my dry-cleaning bill a reimbursable business expense. Or maybe I could conjure up some sort of cleaning spell. There had to be something practical in all those books lining my basement walls.

Sometimes, I wondered why I'd launched the Peabridge's program of monthly community open-houses.

"Jane, that was excellent!"

I finally managed to extricate myself from Nicholas's unwel-come embrace as I turned toward my boss's voice. Evelyn stood beside the lectern, resting her hands on the wooden surface as if she longed to take her own place on the podium. She was dressed in one of her boxiest suits, determined as ever to be a grand ambassador for the Peabridge. At least this ensemble featured a cool blue boucle, a soothing complement to her graying hair. She generally favored muddy browns, acid greens, and neon pinks—colors that competed violently against her complexion. I was afraid to rave about the improvement, though, lest she detect my criticism of her past sartorial splendor.

"Thanks," I said, gathering up my notes.

"With ten of these under your belt, I have to say you've really mastered the art of handling this audience."

I stood a little straighter. I *did* do a good job finding topics that would interest our neighborhood scholars. And I managed to keep my training sessions light and informative.

"Stop it, you brat!" The shout came from the doorway, and I looked up just in time to see darling Nicholas standing in the aisle, scrunching up his face in preparation for a deafening bellow. I wondered what poor person he'd attacked. Then, I asked myself if I was a terrible human being for feeling grateful the victim wasn't me.

I settled for making a face and cocking a half-smile toward Evelyn. "Maybe we need to set an age limit on these things."

"And miss out on mothers in the neighborhood, who might not have any other way to get here?"

The worst thing was, she was serious. And no self-respecting Nicholas-terror would ever think to harass *her*. She looked downright evil—like a fairy-tale witch, if I did say so myself. And every little child knew it was a witch who captured Hansel and Gretel, who kept them in a cage and fattened them up for the oven.

Poor Evelyn. She didn't get the benefits of magical powers, but she was stuck with the stereotype.

"I'd better get upstairs," I said. "Some of these people might need coffee to sustain them on their walks home."

"There's the spirit," Evelyn said, and I thought she was going to separate my shoulder as she clapped a pleased hand down on my colonial garment.

I wasn't actually all that eager to staff the coffee bar—I desperately wanted to work on a new research project I'd just begun, involving medical treatments developed in the colonies prior to the revolution. No, lattes were not my friend, but I wasn't about to get stuck cleaning up Nicholas's sippy cup disaster.

The heat was forecast to break tomorrow, but it was still muggy enough outside to curtail the line of brewed espresso drinkers. At the beginning of the summer, Evelyn had tried setting up industrial-strength blenders to make uber-priced coffee milkshakes for our patrons, but even her avarice had been forced to yield to the truth: we *were* a library. People expected some modicum of quiet on our premises, and ice cubes being ground for long, ear-splitting minutes went too far.

And so I ended up just pouring a couple of iced coffees. I wouldn't mind the coffee bar at all, if I didn't need to waste time foaming milk and making complicated cappuccino orders. See? I wanted to say to Evelyn. I was willing to compromise. But she wasn't interested in compromise. She wanted to maximize coffee-based income—a goal that increasingly conflicted with my desire to be an actual reference librarian.

I had just wiped down the counter and straightened the ever-messy container of individually-packaged sweeteners when a familiar voice said, "Is it possible to make a mocha over ice?"

"Mr. Potter!" I hurried around the counter to give the man a quick embrace. He spent a great deal of his time helping Gran with her concert opera work, but the Peabridge's guardian angel never failed to stop by the library for my Monday lectures. I hoped he was pleased with them—it was his generous donation that made the extra sessions possible. The extra sessions, along with the cataloging work that continued downstairs, as we finally started to get our extensive collection under control.

He chortled at my attention, and I couldn't help but notice he stood a little straighter when I stepped back. He even took a moment to smooth his non-existent tie flat against his chest. If my eyes didn't deceive me, he actually sucked in his belly a bit too. Sweet man.

As I stepped back behind the bar to make his coffee drink, I asked, "How is poor Beijing holding up under this heat?"

"Perfectly fine," Mr. Potter laughed. "That little shih-tzu has the entire world wrapped around his paws. I'm trained to turn a fan on for him whenever I leave the house. But we'll both be glad when the weather finally catches up with the calendar."

"I'm sure he repays your attention with flawless loyalty," I said. Knowing Mr. Potter's sweet tooth, I held up the canister of whipped cream. He started to shake his head "no" but gave in to his true desire and held his fingers apart about an inch, to indicate a short dollop. I obliged, giving him the huge serving I knew he really wanted.

"Loyalty." He shook his head. "I suppose that's what some people call it. I say he's just spoiled. This weekend, I'm taking him all the way to Pittsburgh for my brother's birthday party. We're going to a karaoke bar!"

"That should be fun." Not that I thought it would really be fun to drive all the way to Pittsburgh with a yappy shih-tzu in the car to sing karaoke with a bunch of septuagenarians. I'd rather organize my crystal collection.

"Which brings me to the reason I stopped by."

I handed over the iced mocha and smiled inquiringly. Mr. Potter took a moment to sip the beverage and declare it "perfect" before he reached into the pocket of his sports shirt. He handed me a slender envelope, the type that looks like a birthday card containing money from an elderly aunt. "Go ahead," he said. "Open it."

Puzzled, but excited like a little kid, I eased my finger under the flap. Two tickets were nestled inside. I fanned them out against the envelope and read: "Kennedy Center. *Romeo and Juliet.*" The date was for Saturday night.

"I was going to exchange them at the box office," Mr. Potter said. "But then I realized I've seen enough Romeos and enough Juliets for a lifetime. Perhaps you can find someone to go with?"

Someone. Graeme.

All of a sudden, I remembered straddling his lap on the park bench, cringing before the policeman's interrupting flashlight. My cheeks became incandescent.

"Aha," Mr. Potter said. "I see you have someone in mind."

I sighed. I'd have thought my blushing circuits would be burned out long ago. "I do," I said, all of a sudden too shy to mention Graeme by name. I could just picture Mr. Potter saying something to Gran, and then my trying to explain my stunning Englishman to my grandmother and mother both, maybe over another of our infamously strained getting-to-know-each-other torture brunches. Better to keep my secret a while longer. Until I was certain it would survive under the nuclear blast of my family's interest.

As I looked at the tickets, I realized I shouldn't be planning *any* dates around town. I should be thinking about the coven, about setting the centerstone. I needed to start working on my magical test, or Samhain would arrive before I knew it.

But the Kennedy Center? And *Romeo and Juliet?* And Graeme? "Thank you, Mr. Potter! Thank you so much!"

"You'll have to tell me if the play's the thing, then," he said. "I'll be in Pittsburgh all next week, but when I get back, I'll want a full report!"

A full report. Well, he might not get that. Not if an evening of theater became as super-charged as a tourist turn about the monuments. "Absolutely," I lied.

I tried to wave off his money, but he insisted on paying for his iced mocha. "I have an interest in this library, you know. I'd never forgive myself if you went into the red because of caffeine fiends like me."

More like whipped cream fiends, I started to say, but I didn't want to risk hurting his feelings. Instead, I clutched the tickets to my chest and said, "Thank you, Mr. Potter! I really appreciate your thinking of me."

"Enjoy, Jane."

I watched as he walked across the lobby, taking the time to say goodbye to Evelyn. He would never get over the sorrow of being a widower, but the Peabridge had become a sort of second home for him, and I was glad.

When he got to the library's glass double doors, he needed to shuffle left, then right, dancing to avoid a messenger bearing a huge vase of flowers. I shot a glance to Evelyn at the same time she looked at me. Clearly, neither of us was expecting the delivery. Maybe Nancy, helping patrons check out books at the circulation desk? Or the cataloger, working overtime downstairs?

The messenger approached the front desk, set down the elaborate display, and produced an electronic tablet. As Nancy signed for the arrangement, Evelyn and I both zeroed in, drawn like hummingbirds to crimson sugar-water.

Flowers exploded from the vase. There were tall stems of lilies in rich orange and yellow. Daisies brightened the arrangement, and baby's breath ghosted over broad leaves of greenery. A full dozen red roses were tucked into the explosion of color, their broad petals just beginning to open up.

A card peeked out from the midst of the arrangement, and my name was prominently displayed in bold Courier type.

Evelyn sighed. "They're yours." She waited for me to pluck the card from its plastic fork. My belly did a somersault, and I wished she would back away, let me read in peace.

Thank you for an arresting Saturday night.

And it was signed with the initial G.

Arresting. Well, not exactly. I mean, it wasn't as if we'd *actually* been dragged down to the police station. No one had read us our rights or clapped us into handcuffs.

Handcuffs. Maybe that image got me. Or just the memory of the heat that had melted through my short skirt as I straddled Graeme's lap. Or the thought that I'd come dangerously close to being one of *those* women, the type that gets caught having sex in public. (Almost sex. Whatever.)

But suddenly, my cheeks were as dark as the roses.

"What does the card say?" Evelyn asked, holding out a hand as if she expected me to hand over incriminating evidence.

"It's just a little joke," I said, trying to make an offhand shrug. "It wouldn't mean anything to you. I mean, um, to anyone. That is, anyone but me." I gathered up the huge display of flowers and hurried them back to the staff kitchen, where I made a great show of topping off the water in the vase and adding the powdered "life extender."

Don't bother talking to me, I tried to project. I'm much too busy to answer silly questions about flowers. About a card. About a man who would send an entire florist shop to a librarian he'd only met a couple of weeks before.

Fortunately, by the time I came back to my desk, Evelyn was involved in a discussion with Nicholas's mother. It looked like a heated confrontation, and I imagined it involved the uncapped Magic Marker in Evelyn's hand. I didn't see immediate evidence of what Nicholas had ruined, but I didn't waste a lot of time looking.

Instead, I picked up my telephone handset and stared at the keypad.

I could picture Graeme's business card in my mind, even though it was safely tucked beneath my mattress. The bold silver border glinted in my imagination, and I could see the strong font. His name. His phone number.

I punched in the digits before I could chicken out.

One ring.

Two.

"Henderson."

"Hi," I said. "It's me. Jane."

"Good afternoon," he said, his voice suddenly much warmer.

"The flowers are beautiful."

"I figured I owed you something. It's not every evening that ends with such a…bang. Or shall I say, 'whimper.'"

I swallowed hard. What was I supposed to say to that?

He went on before I needed to improvise. "I would have sent

them yesterday, but it was impossible to find a flower shop open on Sunday."

Besides, I thought, it was much more satisfying to receive them at work. Even if the delivery *did* make my boss jealous. Especially if. "Graeme," I said. "I was wondering? Were serious about next Saturday?"

"Quite." I thought I heard a smile behind his reply. Or maybe that was just the British accent.

"A friend just gave me tickets to *Romeo and Juliet.*"

"In fair Verona, where we lay our scene?'" he quoted from the play.

Be still my beating academic heart. "Verona, or the Kennedy Center. Whichever's closest."

"Shall I pick you up at your cottage, then? Before the show?"

I pictured the limousine and the champagne flutes and the professionally blank face of the chauffeur. And Neko's boundless curiosity.

"No!" I twisted my lips and looked down at my desk, certain half the library would be glaring at me. I forced my voice into a more Peabridge-appropriate register. "I mean, I have something I need to do on Saturday afternoon. Can we meet at the theater? Maybe grab a nightcap afterward?"

"I'd love that." The simple way he said those three words tightened my chest so much I couldn't breathe.

"Wonderful," I managed to say. I struggled to add some-thing—anything—but I couldn't string three words together. At last I gasped, "There's someone coming up to the reference desk."

"You'd best go help them, then."

"Yes, I'd best."

But when I hung up the phone, there was no patron in front of me. Instead, there was only the massive bouquet of flowers. As I gazed at them, I convinced myself I could see the rose petals stretching wider, reaching out to the mysteries of the world around them.

Perhaps I should learn a lesson from the natural world. Perhaps it was time to start reaching out. To start taking risks.

I hummed to myself as I straightened my desk and finished up my Monday shift.

11

I tried not to look forlornly at my wallet where it huddled on the countertop beside a half-full fifth of rum. It had cost me almost forty dollars to get Neko and Jacques out of the house, and if I'd had any more cash available, they would have held out for that as well.

But the trade-off was worthwhile. I felt like I hadn't seen Melissa in ages. This was our first Mojito Therapy since the Casablanca get-together. It was only Wednesday night, but we were both free and eager to catch up on work lives, love lives, and other best-friend details.

"What's that?" Melissa asked, pointing toward a smooth, egg-shaped stone on the kitchen table. It was blood-red, mottled with black splotches. The highly-polished rock half-filled the palm of her hand.

I shrugged. "I don't know. I mean, it's an egg, carved out of jasper. At least, I think it's jasper. That's what it looks like."

"What's it doing here?"

"I'm not sure. I found it on the porch when I stepped outside to get the newspaper this morning."

She laughed. "Are you in the habit of finding stone eggs on your porch?"

"You wouldn't believe half the things Neko drags home." I rolled my eyes.

"Um, yes. I would. What are you going to do with it?"

"I don't know." I watched Melissa rub her fingers against it, almost like it was a worry stone. An involuntary shudder rippled down my spine. "Ugh. How can you stand doing that?"

She looked up, surprised. "What do you mean?"

"It's so rough. Doesn't it feel like sandpaper on your fingers?"

"What are you talking about? It's smooth as silk."

I shook my head. It had rasped against my hands when I picked it up. I'd considered throwing it directly into the bushes, but I'd worried about what havoc a contemporary jasper egg might wreak on an eighteenth-century garden. The last thing I needed was Evelyn complaining about my compromising the Peabridge grounds.

I'd originally set the egg aside, thinking I might add it to the collection of crystals down in the basement. But the more I thought about it, the more it seemed like a bad idea. There was something…odd about the jasper egg. Something *off* about it.

I shrugged. It was probably a cheap, mass-produced souvenir, which wouldn't mix well with the witchy treasures in the basement. "It's yours if you want it. Just don't say Neko never gave you anything."

Melissa stuck out her tongue, but she slipped the egg into her pocket. I maneuvered our tray of drinks and glasses into the living room.

"So? Which one was this?" I asked, folding myself onto a couch. As I poured a lime-rich cocktail into Melissa's chilled glass, I couldn't help but look at the giant display of flowers Graeme had sent me. They filled the coffee table, perfuming the room with the heady scents of lilies and roses.

Melissa grimaced in partial reply to my question, but she consoled herself with a sip of minty comfort. "*Washington Today*."

As far as I was concerned, the *Washington Today* want ads

were the weakest link in Melissa's dating scheme. Half the men who advertised in the magazine were married and looking for a little action on the side. About half of *those* bothered to admit the truth up front. Melissa had learned about the others by sad trial and error.

"Married?" I asked, thinking we might as well get the disaster out of the way quickly.

"Oh no," she said. "Not currently."

"Not…currently?" That reply required my taking a healthy swallow of my own drink.

"He got married at the tender age of 23. To his college sweetheart."

I made a face. "Let me guess. She broke his heart, and now he wishes he had his college years back, so he could sow those near-forgotten wild oats."

"Are you going to let me tell this story, or not?"

"Sorry!" I grinned and dodged a waving lily to select one of Neko's Marcona almonds from the pottery bowl on the table. Crunching the salty snack gave me greater satisfaction than usual. If my familiar was going to blackmail me into taking his boyfriend away from our shared premises, the least he could do was keep me from expiring from hunger.

Melissa ran a hand through her honey-colored hair and brought her feet up on the couch, sitting cross-legged like a pre-schooler at reading time. Her overalls settled into place like a favorite flannel nightgown, and I felt like we were staying up late at night at a slumber party. Another swallow of mojito, though, reminded me I was a grown-up and slumber parties were a thing of the distant past.

"Okay," Melissa said. "*Washington Today*. Married at 23 to college sweetheart. For the first time." She held up one finger. "Divorced her at the age of 25. Married—" Another finger. "A woman he met in a bar, one week after he met her, because he thought he'd found true love. Had the marriage annulled six weeks later. Married—" Another finger. "College Girl again.

Divorced her one year later. Married—" Another finger. "His secretary, because she loved him, despite having heard the sordid saga of his love life thus far. And, not surprisingly, divorced her. Spent two years in litigation over the resulting sexual harassment suit."

As Melissa extended her thumb, I said, "Married College Girl again."

"Bingo! Do I need to go on?"

"Where did the count end up?"

"Four weddings to College Girl. Three in-between-girls. I was being auditioned for the role of number four."

"Any possibility there'd be a decent alimony settlement when you two break up?"

"With all those other hands in the pie? He'd probably make me sign a pre-nup a mile long anyway. After all, he *is* a lawyer."

"What type of law?"

"What else? Divorce!" We clinked glasses on that one.

"Sorry to hear it," I said. "Don't you think it's time to give the *Washington Today* ads a rest?"

"And miss out on so many highly-credentialed professionals? What sort of girl do you think I am?" At least she could laugh at herself. Ever a true blue friend, she said, "But come on! Tell me about your date with double-oh seven."

"Double-oh seven?"

"That's what I've been calling him in my own mind. I mean, he's got the accent and the glamor. He's got that slight air of mystery, luring you away from all you know and love." She gestured toward the flowers. "And he certainly knows how to get your attention."

"What do you mean?" A defensive edge sawed into my voice.

"Oh, don't worry. I totally understand," Melissa said, in a tone that said she might not understand anything at all. "He's swept you off your feet. How could you possibly find time for a girlfriend, when you have *Graeme* waiting in the wings."

I started to protest, but then I realized she was right. I hadn't stopped by Cake Walk in over two weeks. Was that possible? Even when I stopped to think about everything going on— Graeme, the coven, family-togetherness brunch with Gran and Clara—I was surprised at how much time had slipped away. Especially since I usually dropped in for at least one sugar fix a day. Graeme might be poison to my friendship, but he was working wonders on my waistline.

"I'm sorry," I said, and I let real remorse color my words. "I won't let it happen again."

"If you do, I'll have to cut you off. You know, never let you have first dibs on eligible bachelors looking for Lust."

I heard the tremor beneath her words, and I leaned forward to clink my glass against hers one more time. "That's a deal. Hey, are we okay about this?"

"Are we okay about your meeting Mr. Perfect while I'm left with the dating dregs?" For just a moment, her face looked pinched.

"Forget about Graeme a minute," I said, wishing I hadn't put my flowers right smack in the middle of the living room. "Are *you and I* all right? I mean, if neither of us ever saw another man for the rest of our lives, are we still going to be friends?"

Her laugh was more bitter than I expected. "We'll always be friends."

I needed to say something. Do something. Break the mood. "Rock, scissors, paper, for getting Neko's olives out of the kitchen."

It took her a moment, but she counted to three and tapped her right fist against her left palm. I chose paper, and she chose scissors. I was glad to let her win.

By the time I'd brought in the olives and refilled our glasses, Melissa had obviously decided to let her dark mood pass. "So," she said. "Tell me about your date. I really do want to know."

She was my best friend. I'd never lied to her before, and I certainly wasn't going to start now. Popping a stolen olive into my mouth, I launched into my sordid tale. By the time I got to the mosquito repellant she was grinning, and when I described the obnoxious policeman, she was laughing out loud.

"You are such a skank!" she said.

"It wasn't my fault!"

"And I'm sure Neko totally agreed, when you dragged your sorry self home."

"I didn't tell Neko."

"What? You didn't tell His Nosy Highness?"

"I promised you I wouldn't. Friendship test, right? Graeme's a secret, between the two of us."

She flashed me a grateful smile. "I wasn't sure you remembered."

"I've got a crush," I said. "Not amnesia. I did have to invent a boyfriend, though—Nate Poindexter. How's that for romantic happy-ever-after name?" She laughed for real, then, and I knew everything *would* be all right between us.

Before we could say another word, there was a knock at the door. Melissa looked at me curiously, but I shrugged. I wasn't expecting anyone.

Anyone but my warder. I opened the door to a rather agitated David Montrose. "I don't know what they think they're doing—" he started, and then he realized Melissa was sitting on the couch.

"Hello there," she said wryly, saluting him with her mojito glass.

I knew my warder well enough to tell he was silently counting to ten. Not because he had a problem with Melissa— they actually got along quite well. Rather, he'd clearly been expecting us to work together, to polish up some witchy routine, something he'd suddenly realized I needed to know, probably about the centerstone. I could tell all that, just from the way his shoulders were set, from the way his jaw tightened when he looked at the fish-chased pitcher of drinks. Or maybe that was merely his taking in the floral display. "Who sent those?" he asked.

A strange shiver stalked my spine. After the quickest of glances at Melissa, I said, "Nate. Nate Poindexter."

"Nate Poindexter?" David asked incredulously.

"He's a guy I went to high school with." I looked at Melissa. "*We* went to school with. He just moved back from Silicon Valley."

Melissa was staring at me, patent admiration on her face. She barely wiped her expression clear before David turned on her. "Do you know this Nate? Does he send flowers to all his high school classmates?"

"I haven't seen him in ages," Melissa said sweetly. "I hear he's changed a lot in the last few years." She gave me a blatant wink.

I don't know if David accepted our ad lib, but he seemed unable to think of another probing question. "Mojito?" I asked.

"Might as well."

Well. *That* was interesting. David never joined my decompression sessions with Melissa. I felt a wave of foreboding as I wondered just what news he bore. Something bad enough to drive a warder to drink? I'd better make mine a double.

I caught Melissa's eye and then glanced toward the kitchen. "I'll get you a glass," Melissa said obediently, unfolding her legs from her half-lotus position.

"I'm sorry," I called after her retreating form. "There aren't any clean ones, so you'll have to rinse one from the counter." I knew Melissa would glance at my well-stocked cupboards, and she couldn't miss the glistening glassware. I also knew she'd give David and me a chance to whisper a hurried conversation.

"What's wrong?" I asked.

He ran both hands through his hair, making the silver at his temples stand out more than usual. "The coven wants to see you tomorrow."

A shard of ice shot through my belly, colder than any mojito in the world. "Why?"

"I don't know," he snapped. Before I could take offense, he sighed and repeated in a drawn out voice, "I don't know."

"But I haven't done anything wrong!"

He must have heard the panic in my voice—I wasn't exactly subtle. I was running over everything I could remember from my other encounter with the witches. The man with the sword, the horrible feeling that I was back in high school, the desire to be friends with the women and the fear they would never accept me...

My apprehension broke David out of his own dark mood. "It'll be fine," he said. If I hadn't spent hours working with him, days, weeks, months learning everything I could about witchcraft, I might have been fooled by the sudden steadiness of his words. He nodded once, as if cementing his certainty. "You have nothing to worry about."

"But—"

Uncharacteristically, he cut me off. "This is actually a *good* thing. The more you get to know the coven before you're tested, the better. We need to start focusing on setting the centerstone anyway. This will give you a chance to build allies. Make some friends."

As if on cue, Melissa returned with a suspiciously dry glass, which she hurriedly filled for David. "The almonds are great," she said, nodding toward the bowl. "And the olives are wonderful." David started to decline, but then she added, "They're Neko's. We've appropriated them for tonight."

David shrugged and helped himself to a handful of nuts. Before I could pretend we had just been discussing something innocuous, the phone rang. I crossed the living room to answer it, taking a healthy swallow of my mojito along the way. "Hello?"

"Are there any policemen in the vicinity?"

"Oh!"

Graeme.

Did David count? After all, he was my astral policeman. At least, he was my astral protector. I half-turned toward the wall, as if David and Melissa might forget I was present. I wondered if there was some way I could drop the name "Nate" into the conversation, without making Graeme think I'd gone nuts. Nothing came to mind. Realizing that approximately three centuries had passed since my startled exclamation, I painted a smile into my voice and said, "None in my current line of sight."

"Perfect." Graeme's voice was as smooth as the rose petals in the bouquet on the coffee table. "I should come over to visit, then. We could continue the conversation we started in the park, before your jack-booted thug interrupted."

"He wasn't mine!" I heard the giggle behind my voice, and I wondered what I must sound like to David and Melissa. I lowered my voice into a more austere register, and offered a silent prayer that the two of them would start talking to each other, would cover my conversation with their own noise. "You must be mistaken, sir," I whispered.

"Sir?" Graeme repeated. "We're going to be formal now, are we? And here, I thought we'd moved beyond that."

I wanted to assure him that his initial impressions were correct. I wanted to tell him we had definitely moved. We'd shifted light-years away from "sir." In fact, I wanted to banish "sir" from our vocabulary forever.

But I couldn't very well say *that*, could I? Not with an audience, suspiciously silent in the living room behind me? Damn Melissa! Why didn't she start some conversation? Why didn't she distract David—after all, *she* was the one who'd extracted the promise of secrecy from me!

I settled for: "There's a lot of territory to move through." I winced. Had I ever sounded this stupid before? If only Neko were here, he'd be babbling about something behind me, keeping the conversation flowing, if only to hear the beauty of his own voice.

God, things *had* gotten bad, if I was actually wishing for Neko's interference.

In the meantime, miraculously, Graeme was chuckling at my miserable attempt at humor. "I realized that after you spurned me—"

"I didn't—" I started, before I realized that there was absolutely no way for me to finish that line—no way that was fit for public eavesdropping consumption. I settled for, "Really. I didn't."

Another chuckle. Great. He thought I was playing games. Annoyed with myself, annoyed with the situation, I said, "What did you realize?"

"You never told me what time the play is on Saturday."

"Eight," I said, thinking my answer was cryptic enough to protect me from prying ears. I gritted my teeth. He could have looked up the time on the theater's website.

"I could have looked up the time on the theater's website," he said. What? Was he reading my mind? Did he have some secret magical powers of his own that let him reach through the phone line and divine my every thought?

"But you didn't because…"

"Because I wanted to hear your voice." I felt a twinge inside me, a swooping shudder as he purred his response. If I'd begged for a more romantic answer, I couldn't have found one. I wanted to slump against the wall, slide down to the floor with the phone still cradled against my shoulder, the perfect picture of the lovesick teenager I'd apparently become.

Speak, I reminded myself. *Say something, before he thinks you've hung up.* "That's very kind of you to say," I finally responded, and I winced before the words were out of my mouth. This was ridiculous. Gran probably had hotter conversations with eighty-year-old Uncle George. Next, I'd be putting on a fake Southern accent and telling Graeme I'd always depended on the kindness of strangers.

"'Kind' wasn't the emotion I was trying for." I could picture his lips as he spoke, his strong chin, those crystalline blue eyes... I sighed. It always came back to the eyes. "Come on, Jane. Am I really not going to see you until Saturday night? Can't we have dinner together tomorrow?"

Was this really happening to me? Was the man of my dreams truly begging me to dine with him? And what else did he have on the menu, besides food?

Of course, I couldn't. David was lurking right behind me. I knew the coven was a command performance.

But Graeme wanted me. He really wanted me. That should count for something, in the Broken Heart Recovery Sweepstakes, shouldn't it?

"I'd love to," I said, and then I added hurriedly, before he could misconstrue my response, "I'd love to, but I can't."

"Can't," he wheedled. "Or won't?"

I was so bad at this. I'd started off all concerned about protecting my conversation with Graeme from David. Now, I needed to figure out a way to beg off dinner with Graeme, without cluing him in to the whole coven thing. I mean, it was one thing for him to know I was a witch. But it was another thing completely for him to learn exactly when the coven met, and why.

It could be dangerous for the other witches. That's why we all had warders, right? To keep us safe from random strangers, from people who hated witches? Not that Graeme hated witches. Not if our dates and my flowers were anything to judge by.

"Can't," I said firmly.

He sighed, and then he was silent for several heartbeats. When he finally spoke again, his voice was so low I had to hold my breath to hear him. "I don't know that I've ever anticipated a play, then, quite as much as I do this *Romeo and Juliet*."

"'Tis twenty years till then," I said, quoting one of Juliet's lines in the balcony scene. I frowned as soon as the words left my mouth. Melissa was sure to get the reference. Would David?

"Sleep dwell upon thine eyes, peace in thy breast." Graeme didn't miss a beat providing Romeo's rejoinder. "Would I were sleep and peace, so sweet to rest."

All right. Even if I was about to face the third degree from the world's most suspicious warder, it was worth it. Graeme seemed to have the entire balcony scene committed to memory—and he knew how to use it to his best advantage.

"I'll see you on Saturday," I said softly. I hung up the phone, but left my fingers on the receiver, as if I could still sense Graeme there. I closed my eyes and let his whispered words linger, like bold wine on the back of my tongue.

"We haven't disappeared, you know."

David. And his tone was the height of warder haughtiness.

"I didn't think I'd be that lucky," I said, before I dared to turn around. "That was…" I cleared my throat. "Nate."

I was startled to see the jasper egg displayed on a handkerchief in the palm of David's hand. He looked so stern I didn't bother spinning out another lie about my long, lost high school love. Instead, I cast a surprised look at Melissa. "So you decided you didn't want it after all?"

She frowned. "David sensed it. I mean, he knew I had it in my pocket."

I turned my attention to David and was startled to see the grimace on his face. "What?" I asked. "What is it?"

"Couldn't you feel it? Couldn't you sense the spell?"

"Spell? It's just a crappy souvenir. They sell them in those import stores on M Street for tourists to bring home to their kids. My parents went to Washington, DC, and all they brought me was this lousy egg."

"It's *jasper*." He almost hissed the word.

"I figured out that much. I was going to add it to my crystals, but it didn't seem…right."

"Jasper guards against witches. It has an affinity for keeping them at bay, for limiting their power. *Your* power." He extended the carved egg toward me, and I had to take a step back. Was that magic, emanating from the rock? Or was it my own apprehension?

"It felt rough to me," I said. "Prickly."

"Then you're stronger than the spell. Apparently much stronger. How did it get here?"

"I assumed Neko left it. He often leaves, um, things on the front porch." No reason to go into the decimation of the local mouse and vole population.

David shook his head grimly. "Neko wouldn't get anywhere near this thing. Not voluntarily."

Melissa chimed in before I could say anything else. "Then who did leave it? Did they mean to hurt Jane?"

"I don't think so." David finally folded the handkerchief around the stone. I could breathe easier the moment it was out of my sight. "I suspect they meant this as a warning."

"A warning?" I repeated.

"Someone has put you on notice. They know you're a witch, and they're watching you."

I rubbed the prickles from my arms. The egg had to be connected to the coven in some way. No one had bothered leaving me jasper threats before Teresa Alison Sidney came into my life.

David interrupted my speculation. "I don't suppose you're going to tell me who that was on the phone?"

"I told you. It was Nate." That came out sharper than I'd intended. The jasper had unnerved me more than I cared to admit. I raised my hands, palms out, silently pleading for peace. "Look, it was nothing. Nothing you need to worry about, I promise." David still looked suspicious. "Please, can't we just forget about the phone call? The phone call, and the coven, and everything else? At least until tomorrow?"

His gaze traveled from my exposed palms to my face. He

looked into my eyes for long enough that I grew uncomfortable. What was Melissa going to think? She was standing right here, watching us have this bizarre conversation, this non-lover's quarrel.

I couldn't tell what David read in my expression but he finally exhaled, like a man resigning himself to a life without sex.

Now, wait. Why had I thought of *that* image? I should have just noted that he sighed, and left the modifiers to a tamer part of my brain, a part that hadn't recently been stirred by champagne and limousine rides and flowers.

"Fine," he said. "But we'll need something more substantial than almonds and olives, if we're going to make another pitcher of mojitos."

David was going to drink the night away with Melissa and me? What *had* gotten into him? Was the jasper that much of a threat?

I couldn't bring myself to ask, though. Instead, I shrugged and included Melissa in my question. "Chinese?"

"Mu shu pork," she said immediately, and I could tell she was trying to pretend that none of the other strange stuff had happened.

"Beef with broccoli," David added.

"Hunan chicken for me," I said. "And we might as well order the salt and pepper shrimp, or we'll never hear the end of it when Neko gets home."

By the time the delivery arrived, we were well on our way through the next pitcher of mojitos, and Graeme, Shakespeare, and prickly jasper souvenirs all seemed very far away.

12

W e were gathered around my kitchen table—David, Neko, and me. I had brought the mortar and pestle up from the basement; the tools crouched in the middle of some yellowish, greenish flowers. The leaves that surrounded the bedraggled blossoms were shaped a little like oak leaves. Their tops were smooth and dark green, but their bottoms were covered with a cottony fuzz.

Mugwort.

I'd walked by the plant for months, completely ignoring it as it grew waist-high in the summer heat. The gardens behind the Peabridge included mugwort because it was used by colonial women to cure for all sorts of problems—bad periods, unwanted pregnancies, stomach and liver parasites, pretty much anything that didn't respond to other medicine.

David had decided to feature the herb in an impromptu training session, filling the time before we headed out to the coven. He was droning on in his best professorial mode: "You'll want to dry all the mugwort you can get hold of. It protects against bookworms—silverfish—that might try to eat through the collection downstairs. You'll use it a lot working with the coven—it's one of the best herbs for cleaning magical implements."

"I make a big vat of mugwort tea and then do the dishes? Like I'm camping?"

I knew he hated for me to be flippant about magic, but I was bored. We'd been at this training session since I'd come home from a full day's work at the library. Neither Neko nor I was at our best—too much MSG in last night's Chinese food accounted for my headache. I could only imagine the escapades my familiar had engaged in the night before. David, of course, was thoroughly unruffled. He'd already drilled me on vervain (a defense against metal weapons), rosemary (protection against the evil eye), and radish (defense against scorpions). Yes. Radish. Scorpions.

I tried to remind myself that a warder's job was to protect his witch. It was only natural that my herbal training would focus on vegetation that would assist him in that duty. Nevertheless, I'd spent the entire evening listening to Simon and Garfunkel inside my head, repeating "Parsley, Sage, Rosemary and Thyme" over and over and over. If I heard about a cambric shirt one more time, I would scream.

Neko took the opportunity of my minor rebellion to shudder delicately. "I am *so* not going camping," he said. I laughed out loud. The notion of my familiar's carefully gelled hair and immaculately groomed fingernails roughing it far from a mirror was so outrageous that even David had to smile.

"You shouldn't cross camping off your list so quickly," David said. "You'd be amazed at what you can find growing in the woods. Besides, mugwort makes a fine mosquito repellant."

Now he told me. "And there are so many mosquitoes inside the house right now," I said grumpily.

"I could open the door," Neko volunteered. "It wouldn't take long for them to track *you* down." With friends like that, who needed enemies—astral or not? I made a mental note to forget tuna on my next three grocery runs.

"Seriously," I said to David. "Why are we spending so much time on herbs? Doesn't it make sense for me to focus on crystals? Or stonework? Something that will help with setting the centerstone?"

"I can't think of anything that will help you more than herbs. You already have an affinity for Earth—for stone. We established that when you helped your grandmother months ago, using the aventurine to heal her pneumonia. You've only added to that knowledge in the last few months. Frankly, the easiest thing about setting the centerstone will be handling the marble itself."

Marble. Of course. A stone known for strength, for protection.

I flexed my fingers. "I don't know. I'm not in great shape. It's not like I spend my time moving large quarry blocks around the house."

"You won't do the actual lifting. We warders will help with that. Part of the ritual will involve introducing you to all of the warders. If you pass the coven's test, then all of us will know you as a witch to be protected, a Daughter of Hecate whom we're sworn to defend."

And if I failed... I knew the answer to that one, so I decided not to bring it up again. Instead, I focused on something I could learn, could control. I forced my voice to be light as I said, "So the marble isn't a problem, and setting it in place is trivial."

"So we might as well have some ice cream and take the rest of the night off," Neko proposed, only to face a glower from David.

I shook my head, shushing Neko as I recognized the method in my warder's madness. "So I might as well learn ways to strengthen the marble. To add to its inherent properties. Each herb we talked about today will help protect the coven, if I use them in conjunction with the marble."

"Precisely," David said, giving me one of his rare smiles.

"Where do the scorpions come in?" Neko interrupted my moment of protégé bliss.

David gave me a quick look, but I could only shrug. Why *was* I concerned about scorpions? The Washington Coven's territory didn't exactly extend to the southwest.

David's expectant gaze grew more wooden, and I forced myself to venture an answer. "Because poisons can hide anywhere? Because a scorpion isn't necessarily a literal arthropod, but anything that lies in wait, ready to jump and poison."

"Exactly!" David's smile was as warm as a cup of mugwort tea, and nowhere near as bitter. I preened and shot my familiar a self-satisfied smile of my own. That pleasure dissipated, though, the instant David glanced at his watch. "We should get moving," he said, "if we're going to get to Teresa Alison Sidney's on time."

I glanced out the window, where darkness had just fallen on the garden. "Isn't the coven gathering at midnight?"

"Not tonight. This isn't a formal working. Just an…organizational meeting. No need for the full ritual. And no need to stay up past midnight on a school night. The meeting starts at nine."

I glanced down at my clothes, wondering what I should wear.

"What are you looking at?" David asked.

"I'm just going to go change—"

"No."

I started to protest, to tell him I would only take a minute, but I recognized implacable when I saw it on his face. "Let me grab some earrings, at least."

He scowled but waved his hand. Neko started to follow me out of the kitchen. "Not you," David said to my familiar.

"I'm going to help!"

"With your help, she'll try on half her closet, just to match the jewelry. 'Help' by cleaning up here."

Neko growled, but he stayed behind.

In my bedroom, I made short work of changing tops,

forfeiting my casual T-shirt for a gauzy blouse. They were both black. I was pretty sure David wouldn't even notice.

Then, I turned to my dresser, where my favorite necklaces were tangled with my most-frequently-worn earrings. I immediately passed over the turquoise—too ethnic for the coven crowd. The jet beads were too fussy. Gold hoops were just plain boring.

And then my eyes fell on my sodalite set. The deep blue stones were veined with white. The earrings were fashioned into miniature wands, elongated rods set in protective silver. The short necklace consisted of polished beads; it was just long enough to go around my throat.

Sodalite was known to enhance self-esteem. It gave its wearer confidence, the ability to think clearly and speak well. I couldn't imagine a better crutch as I went to face the coven. I fastened the necklace around my throat, threaded the earrings through my lobes, and returned to the kitchen.

David was not quite tapping his foot, but his impatience was evident. And he *did* notice the change in clothes. I'd been a fool to think he'd overlook it—even if he was a guy. At least he didn't say anything out loud; he just let me read the disapproval across his face.

Meekly, I herded Neko in front of us as we left the cottage. I shouldn't have been surprised to see the sleek Lexus sitting curbside, directly in front of the Peabridge. As we drove to Teresa Alison Sidney's home, I tried to pay attention. David had explained during our afternoon session that the new safehold would be built on the Coven Mother's property. The home I had visited had not been constructed specifically for witches; it had not been set on foundations poured to line up with the cardinal directions, aligned with the four essential elements.

The new safehold would be built on a plain between the current house and a creek. It would be the height of witchy luxury, harnessing the natural world to strengthen the workings of all the witches within its confines. The centerstone would be the core of those spells, the heart of the safehold's magic. It was important that I understood all the power flowing there, all the ways the land moved around the witches' chosen gathering place.

The suburbs of northern Virginia felt wilder than George-town, as if we'd somehow driven back to antebellum times, or earlier. I tried to center myself for our meeting, becoming consciously aware of the streams we drove over, the folds of fertile land that spread out between country homes. The air was heavy and moist, promising a thunderstorm before morning.

By the time we arrived at Teresa Alison Sidney's, I was nearly in a trance. I didn't know if I was reacting to a day full of library work followed by an evening of instruction or to the calming power of my sodalite jewelry, but I emerged from the Lexus feeling peaceful. Powerful. In control.

At least until I ventured past the man with the giant sword. With a sound that might have been a whimper, Neko moved closer to my side. David contrived to ignore both of us as he escorted us past the guardian, completing the pentagram ritual at the doorway with a rigid formality.

Then, I was back with the coven.

This time, David did not even wait to present himself to Teresa Alison Sidney. Instead, he moved immediately to the front room, opening the door and closing it behind himself before I realized I was abandoned. Neko glanced around nervously, and if he'd still sported his feline tail, I knew it would have been lashing back and forth in anxiety.

I raised my chin, though, and stepped into the sprawling living room.

"Ah," Teresa Alison Sidney said, looking up from a trio of women. "Jane is finally here." She'd added the faintest emphasis on the *finally.*

I started to protest. David had told me to arrive at nine, and it was not yet nine o'clock. I started to explain that it was a long way from my cottage to the safehold, that I didn't even live in Virginia.

Instead, I raised my fingers to my sodalite and took a deep, centering breath. What did any of that matter? I couldn't change things and arrive earlier than I had. I met Teresa Alison Sidney's eyes and said, "Yes, Coven Mother."

It was just as well that I didn't waste time arguing. As Teresa Alison Sidney gave me a frosty nod, the tall-case clock began to chime. As before, its deep, sonorous notes ensnared the witches. Even though no one moved, each woman appeared to stand more still in her place. Each seemed to listen to some distant memory, to gather together a force and energy that was based in the echoing chimes themselves.

When the clock died away, we went through the same ritual we'd done before. The Coven Mother traced a pentagram in the air, and each witch intoned, invoking protection against any who would betray us, any who would harm us, any who would wrong us. I totally nailed the "so mote it be's," blending with the group as if I'd been working this magic for a lifetime. I traced my own pentagram in front of my face when we were through chanting, and energy thrummed around me as the protective circle sealed us off from the greater world.

Teresa Alison Sidney took a deep breath, seeming to feed off the eldritch power we'd raised. Taking a moment to look at each of us, she finally nodded toward the couches. "Sit, sisters. Let us do the coven's work with fairness and with speed. Let us listen to our sisters with compassion and understanding. Let us join our powers together to gain strength from each, to lend strength to all."

"So mote it be," the witches whispered as they followed the Coven Mother's lead. I moved a little more slowly than the others; they apparently had regular, expected seats around the room. For a moment, I felt like a child playing Musical Chairs— I was the odd man out. But then, Neko nudged my elbow and directed me toward a Chippendale armchair that looked as if it had been dragged in from the dining room.

I wasn't sure whether I should edge all the way back on the

slick, upholstered seat, or if I should remain at attention, pretending I was at a job interview. I brushed my fingers against my sodalite beads and settled for ram-rod posture, but I let my spine touch the wooden back of the chair. Neko folded himself at my feet.

Glancing to my left to see if the nearest witch had observed my discomfort, I was surprised to discover Haylee James sitting there. Her Hecate's Torch glittered at the base of her throat, silent reminder of her membership in the coven.

My initial reaction was to bristle—after all, she was the one who had set me my specific task, the one who had demanded I set the centerstone for the new safehold. She was also the person who had criticized Gran and Clara's powers to my face. But she was also the first witch to reach out to me in friendship. I could still picture her right hand cupped around her Torch as she settled her left fingertips against my wrist, friendly and inclusive. Before I could smile at the memory, Teresa Alison Sidney called the meeting to order.

"Sisters, let us begin. Billie, why don't you start with the Treasurer's Report."

Treasurer's Report. Followed rapidly by the Building Fund Report, the Party Fund Report, and the Security Budget Report.

As my sister witches droned on and on about endless accounting details and the need for better management of time and money, I tried to figure out what I'd been expecting. A round-robin tournament of spell-casting, perhaps? A pot-luck of potions? Maybe an exchange of extra crystals, along with examples of how to use the magical stones?

A million hours into the meeting, Teresa Alison Sidney called on Haylee to make the report of the Gardening Committee.

Yes. The Gardening Committee. I felt as if I should be dressed for Ascot, wearing colors like cerise and aqua and a massive picture hat. Haylee stood and cleared her throat.

"The Gardening Committee has been very busy," she said. She ruffled her spiky hair with her perfectly manicured fingers, and I was shocked to realize she seemed nervous. How bizarre. The steady, cut-throat witch that I'd met at the midnight coven couldn't possibly be upset by a report on ranunculi.

She licked her lips and continued. "We've selected the plantings for the new safehold's borders, and we've reserved space in the greenhouse to grow everything over the winter. As soon as we've moved beyond the risk of frost next spring, we'll be ready to give the new safehold complete herbal protection."

"What did you decide on for the borders?" Teresa Alison Sidney asked. There was true warmth behind the question; the Coven Mother even smiled—a courtesy she had not extended to any of the other reporting witches. I was reminded once again that Teresa Alison Sidney—Teri—and Haylee were old friends.

"We'll go with the traditional protective herbs: Parsley, rosemary, an edging of houseleek."

I fought the urge to look toward the front room. I wanted to ask how David had known we witches would discuss herbs tonight, how he had known to train me in the ways of floral defense just that afternoon.

Instead, I nearly yelped as Neko dug his fingernails into my leg, making me focus on the question Teresa Alison Sidney had just asked. "Does anyone have other suggestions for Haylee? Anything else we should work into the border? We're particularly interested in strengthening the power for the spring, when our new safehold will be most vulnerable."

"Radishes."

I heard my voice before I realized I had spoken. In fact, I was only certain I'd said the word out loud when a score of witches turned to stare at me. I fought the urge to curl my fingers around my sodalite for comfort.

"Excuse me?" the Coven Mother asked, and I squirmed like a schoolgirl.

Still, I caught Neko's minute nod of approval. I took as deep a breath as I could manage and I repeated, louder this time, "Radishes."

Teresa Alison Sidney's eyes narrowed, but another woman actually spoke. "That would be wonderful if we're inviting people over for tea and watercress sandwiches."

By the time I tore my gaze away from the Coven Mother's smirking lips, I was unable to determine which of the women had been so sarcastic. I let my hand drift down to Neko; my fingers barely grazed his shoulder.

I don't know if he twitched slightly, or if his focusing ability channeled my own unschooled powers. Suddenly, though, I *knew* which sister had spoken. I turned to face her squarely, meeting her almond-shaped eyes without blinking. Her flawlessly made-up face was perfectly tanned, and I wondered if she exposed herself to ultraviolet rays or just used one of those lotions that would turn me a sickly shade of orange. Her coloring was the perfect complement to her tawny hair, and the velvet-wrapped headband that swept back her bangs made her look like the worst type of Popular Snob head cheerleader from Somewhere Country Day.

Her cheeks flushed as I stared. I kept my voice level and said, "If you're wasting your radishes on sandwiches, then you're ignoring the full herbal power we witches can harness."

I put a slight emphasis on the word "we." I considering saying more—that she might not have enough innate magic to study herb craft, that only an idiot would be unaware of the powers of radishes.

But I remembered how often David had schooled me with a single apt sentence—not to mention the fact that I'd only learned about radishes that very afternoon. Despite Neko quivering beneath my fingertips, despite the pressure of all those eyes staring at me, despite my heart pounding against my ribcage so hard I thought David in the front room might think I was under attack, I managed to say no more.

I could hear the pendulum swinging on the tall-case clock

and Haylee swallowing beside me and Teresa Alison Sidney breathing. At last, the Coven Mother said, "Where did you learn about radishes, Jane?"

"From Hannah Osgood's collection. From the books in my safekeeping." I set the words down carefully, trying not to boast about the materials, but conveying that I was in control of a great deal of witchy wealth. I tried not to think about the fact that all my wealth would be forfeit if I failed to set the center-stone on Samhain.

Teresa Alison Sidney's eyes were even more intimidating than the cheerleader's. But when she nodded, I knew I'd won this round. "Radishes, then. We'll use them for edging, to bolster our protection in the spring.

I exhaled slowly, trying not to let anyone see how stressed I'd been. The rest of the meeting crept by—there were more reports from more committees. Neko curled up against my chair and—for all I could tell—fell asleep.

At last, the Coven Mother asked if there were any other matters to discuss. When no one responded, she stood and led us through the closing ritual, walking in a great circle around the room, gathering up the energy we'd laid out to protect us. She sketched out a spectacular pentagram in the air, tracing silver light with her fingertips, and then she intoned, "So we were met, Daughters of Hecate. Go forth from this circle with peace in your hearts. Go forth with the power of your sisterhood."

"We go forth," the women responded, and I remembered enough from my first visit to join them.

I waited until a thunderclap had echoed through the room and the silver light had faded before I dared to lean back in my chair, closing my eyes for just a moment. I wanted to rub my temples, to curl up and take a nap.

"Would you like some tea?" I heard from closer at hand than I expected. "No watercress sandwiches—with or without radishes—but there's some killer crab dip."

My eyes flew open, and I saw Haylee, extending a cup and saucer like a formal peace offering. I took the caffeine gratefully but was unable to ignore Neko's anxious glance toward the serving table. "Go," I said to him. "But leave some for everyone else." I turned back to Haylee as Neko darted away. "Thank you."

"I'm sorry Kate was so nasty." Kate. She must be the Popular Snob cheerleader. Haylee shrugged. "You've stirred up a lot of the coven. Many witches thought they'd be asked to set the centerstone."

I smiled wanly. "I don't suppose I could forfeit the responsibility?"

"You don't mean that." She flashed me a toothy smile. "You'll do fine. Really." She sipped her own tea. "And radishes *are* an interesting idea. Quaint, actually. A throwback to the herb gardens where so many Wyrd Women got their original powers."

"I know it sounds ridiculous—" I started to defend my knowledge but another quick smile from Haylee implied that no defense was necessary.

"Lots of plants have power." She shrugged. "That's why I like the Gardening Committee. There's so much history in what we do. Have you ever looked at medieval paintings? Or Renaissance, with all those flowers and herbs? Each one was supposed to protect the subject—and the artwork itself—with magical power."

I shook my head. "I don't think I'd recognize half the plants I've read about. I'm pretty good at things in the colonial era, but going that far back…"

"We should go down to the National Gallery of Art some time. We could compare notes from your colonial collection with the paintings there."

Her words were off-hand, but I recognized the thrill that jolted through my belly. It was like being chosen for an elementary school kickball team. Or standing in the high school cafeteria, tray in hand, and seeing a friend wave toward a nearby seat. Or staying up until dawn, clutching pillows and eating nacho cheese Doritos and gossiping about all the cute boys.

"I'd like that," I said.

"Oh, God!" she said. "I shouldn't have said anything! My schedule is *insane* for the next week, week and a half."

"That's right. You're an interior designer, aren't you?"

"Yes, and I'm finishing up a kitchen renovation for a major client. Can you wait till a week from Sunday? We could get to the Gallery at two and avoid the morning tourists?"

I nodded. "That would be wonderful."

Haylee matched my shy grin with another stunning smile. Her fingers flickered to the Hecate's Torch at her throat, as if she were grateful for my agreement. "Fantastic!"

Eager to continue the conversation, I nodded toward her Torch. "I can't wait until I have one of my own. Just hearing about Gran's the other day made me realize how much I want one. *Need* one. It was so hard not to accept Gran's as a gift! As *if* that would work for me!"

"As if," Haylee repeated, and she reached out to pat the back of my hand, making my fingers tingle as if she were sprinkling them with magical pixie dust. For just a moment, I thought I must look ridiculous to her. I must seem petty, jealous of my weak, witchy grandmother. What had even made me bring up Gran? There was no reason to dwell on the coven's dismissive attitude about my distaff relations.

"It's normal for a witch to want a Torch," Haylee said. "Almost as normal as getting hungry at one of these meetings. How about another cup of tea?"

I laughed and offered to fetch drinks for both of us. Maybe this coven thing was going to work out after all.

13

"Have another muffin, dear." Gran pushed the plate of lemon-poppyseed treats closer. I shifted a little on her kitchen chair, grateful that I hadn't yet donned the whalebone corset that would keep me sitting straight for the rest of the day.

Corsets. Whalebone. We *had* come a long way, baby.

Consciously deciding to celebrate my liberated sisters' battles, I helped myself to a second muffin. It was still warm from Gran's oven.

I'd been skipping enough desserts (I'd still been too busy to wander over to Cake Walk) to justify the additional breakfast. I even thought I might have dropped a couple of pounds. Before I knew it, I might start to look like the svelte Teresa Alison Sidney. Well, at least I might have a touch more confidence the next time I met with the coven for committee reports. What more could a girl ask?

I reached for the butter. It would be rude not to celebrate fresh-baked muffins, right? It wasn't every day I got invited to someone's house for a home-cooked meal.

Gran cleared her throat and said, "Your mother and I have been trying to figure out the best way to talk to you about something. I convinced Clara we should just broach the topic instead of beating around the bush."

So much for the loving care of a home-cooked breakfast.

I should have realized this was something big. When I'd returned from work the night before, the light on my answering machine had been flashing. Instead of the usual "Jane Madison's grandmother", Gran had actually steeled herself to say she was expecting me for breakfast the following morning, and she wouldn't take no for an answer.

I pushed my plate back, ignoring an inviting trickle of melted butter over the crisp muffin crust. I tried to convince myself I'd never been a big fan of lemon poppyseed—the seeds always got stuck in my teeth. My stomach growled, though, as restless as my mind had suddenly become.

"Yes," I prompted, when no further confession seemed forthcoming.

"We've been worried about you. About us. It's been difficult enough for the three of us to get to know each other, and now..."

Irritation pricked at the back of my throat. I'd been a fool to think Gran and I could chat like light-hearted friends. I should have realized I would end up sulking here like a sullen teenager. What *was* it about coming back to Gran's house that pushed me into this long-abandoned role?

"What have I done to upset Clara now?" I heard the obnoxious tone beneath my words, but I felt no need to modify it.

"Now, don't blame your mother. I've been concerned too."

"So, what? The two of you get together to talk about me? Did you bake for Clara also? Set out the fine china, so both of you could figure out exactly what I'm doing wrong, and how you want me to change?"

Okay. So the vehemence of my tirade even surprised me. I mean, I'd come to realize during the past year that Clara *was* my grandmother's daughter. Gran was going to do everything she could to help Clara on her quest to return to the normal world.

Clara herself was trying—she *had* moved back to DC, leaving behind her meditation group and the vortex near Sedona, and all the strange New Age concepts she'd adopted to disguise her true witchy nature.

But I really didn't want to feel any sympathy for Clara. Not now. Not this morning, when Gran was practically admitting the two of them had plotted against me.

Gran tsked and lifted the tea cosy to top off her cup of Earl Grey. She settled the quilted cover back over the china teapot before she met my eyes. "Make me a promise, Jane."

Gran and her promises. Over the years, I'd promised any number of outrageous things to ease her ever-more-bizarre fears. She'd made me swear not to eat fugu the first time I'd gone to a sushi restaurant, as if poisonous Japanese blowfish were the only thing on the menu. I'd vowed not to ice-skate on the Potomac during one of the rare winters when the river had frozen over—as if I'd ever considered taking my weak ankles out on the ice. I'd promised not to sneak into the National Zoo at night, and I'd even offered up a special, auxiliary oath not to try feeding the pandas—because they only *looked* like people in panda suits, and they were actually dangerous wild animals with claws and a temper to match Tyrannosaurus Rex. And just last year, I'd promised not to lick any toads—an oath that proved surprisingly challenging, in light of my more obscure witchcraft paraphernalia.

Gran had perfected her promise extraction, making each vow seem simple and straight-forward and logical, even as I rolled my eyes at the absurdity of her disaster scenarios. She was going to prevail in the end. So, I should just go ahead and agree. Forget to fight. Move on with my life.

I dug in my heels.

"What are you asking, Gran?"

She stopped fiddling and looked me straight in the eye. Uh-oh. This was going to be a doozy. "Stop seeing the coven."

"What?"

"Don't see those women anymore. Clara and I don't think they have your best interests at heart."

"Of course they don't have my best interests at heart!" I sighed in exasperation. "They're *witches*, Gran. They're a coven. They're a sisterhood, banded together to protect the magical group, not the best interests of any individual. And *definitely* not the interests of an outsider, like me."

Gran blinked. I don't think she'd ever considered I might agree with her in principle. "Then why are you so intent on working with them?"

"I don't have a choice."

"You always have a choice."

I shook my head. "Not this time." I tried to think of how I could phrase this, how I could make Gran understand. "This isn't a group I've chosen to belong to. It's not like the Concert Opera Guild, or the Friends of the National Zoo. This is *more*. It's deeper. I was born a witch. Magic is in every fiber of my being."

"But you don't have to associate with those women!"

"I do, though." I clenched and unclenched my hands. "I've been trusted with great power. Now, I've got great responsibility." Wonderful. I was reduced to quoting Spiderman to justify myself. "Gran, I don't have to agree with everything they do. I don't have to be involved with every project they undertake. But I *do* have to work with them. David says the only alternative is registering with the Eastern Empire, formally declaring myself a loner, an outsider for life. I don't even know what that means, really. But I'm pretty sure Teresa Alison Sidney wouldn't take it lying down."

"That Teresa Alison Sidney—" Gran said, and she shook her head in disapproval.

"What, Gran? I thought you liked her." Wasn't Gran the one who had been so enamored of the Coven Mother? Hadn't Gran contemplated inviting her to join the Concert Opera Guild? What had changed?

Gran pursed her lips. "She was rude to me. And to your mother, too. You might not think we care about this witchcraft nonsense, but we do, on some level. We care because you do. And we don't like to be made fools of in front of everyone."

Her voice trembled. Tears had actually gathered in her eyes. My heart clenched, and I felt truly miserable, like I was leaving my family to seek my fortune, like I was turning my back on the woman who had raised me. "What happened, Gran?"

My question flustered her. She removed the cosy and lifted the china teapot, gently sloshing it from side to side to test how much water remained. "Do you want some more tea?"

"No, Gran." I waited for her to tell me.

"Now, you've let that muffin get cold. Let me pop it into the microwave, freshen it right up."

"No, thank you, Gran." I tried to keep an edge from my voice.

"Maybe you'd like some fruit? I've got some lovely pears—first ones of the season. Let me slice one for you."

I settled my hand on her wrist, keeping her from flying off to the refrigerator. "Gran, what did the coven do?"

She fretted at the edge of her napkin. "Clara got a phone call yesterday afternoon."

Yesterday. The day after the coven's business meeting. "Who was it?"

"One of the witches. She didn't give her name, but her voice was older than Teresa Alison Sidney's."

"How did Clara know it was someone from the coven?"

"Who else begins a conversation, 'I speak as the messenger of Hecate?'"

Well, Gran had a point there. I said, "What else did she say?"

"She told Clara the coven had reconsidered. Teresa Alison Sidney decided to take back the jewelry they gave us."

"The Torches?" I immediately thought of my conversation with Haylee. Had I said something to make the coven act? But there'd been no indication that my longing for Gran's Torch was a problem. Besides, the witch who'd phoned couldn't be Haylee, not if her voice had been old. And Clara had received the call. Not Gran. Not the grandmother I'd inadvertently framed when I said I longed for a Torch.

No. Hayley's fingers had tingled against mine. She was my friend. She would never turn the coven against me. Against Gran and Clara.

Gran shook her head and sighed. "I mean, neither Clara nor I thought they were so important in the first place. You know I was willing to give you mine."

"But the coven shouldn't be able to just demand you return them, for no good reason. Did the witch give Clara any explanation at all?"

"She only said the coven had reconsidered. That the two of us aren't worthy of membership. Our powers aren't strong enough."

I went back over last night's meeting. Maybe this had nothing to do with me at all. Had there been a report from a Membership Committee? Something about tossing out underperforming members? I might have missed the details, if they'd been buried in some minutiae when my attention was wandering.

But no. I would have paid attention to a discussion about coven membership. Gran and Clara's status had not been part of the meeting. It must be something separate. Personal.

But I still couldn't yield to Gran's request. This was one promise I just couldn't make. I took her right hand between both of mine, squelching a moment of surprise when I realized how thin her bones were, how papery her flesh had become. "Gran, I'm so sorry. But I can't promise. Not now. Let me try to make this right, from inside the coven. Let me explain to them that they're wrong."

Gran sighed. "Jane—"

"Gran, you have to let me go ahead with this. Once I'm in the coven, I can learn things. And change things too. They were wrong to treat you that way, even if your—" I caught myself just in time, stumbling before I turned "your powers are weak" into "you're new to your powers."There was no reason to rub in Gran's and Clara's limited abilities.

Gran sat back in her chair. She took her eyeglasses from the bridge of her nose, spending a long time polishing them against her apron. "It's just that I love you, Jane. *We* both do, Clara and I. And we want what's right for you."

"I know that, Gran. I really do." I leaned forward and kissed her cheek. "And now, what's right for me is getting to work. Evelyn will kill me if I'm late."

Gran took a deep breath, and then she pushed herself up from the table. "Take her some muffins, dear. She'll forgive anything with a fresh-baked muffin on her desk."

Yeah. A fresh baked muffin and a half-caf, half-decaf latte with an extra-large cap of whipped cream. But the conversation bothered me as I walked all the way home. I could have taken a cab and saved some time, but I wanted a chance to think about what Gran had said. Besides, it had rained the night before, and the city streets shimmered with the first hint of true autumn chill. (And Gran was absolutely right about one thing—Evelyn *would* forgive my late arrival if I sweetened that news with a treat.)

Did I really want to be a member of a club that intimidated my closest family members? That invited people to join and then took away their membership on a whim? Did I want to be one of the Popular Snobs?

The problem was, every time I asked myself the question, the answer kept coming up yes. I could still feel the thrill of realizing Haylee was inviting *me* to go to the National Gallery. (*Me!* Silly, new-witch, me!) My fingers tingled as if she were still touching me with her cool, steady hand.

And aside from the new friendship, I could remember the power I'd felt at the midnight coven, the silver-traced energy that had bound the women together. There was strength in their rituals, traditions that gave them roots. My entire body could still remember the *pull* of the tall-case clock, the expectancy that grew out of its deep chimes.

A part of my witch's soul longed for that sense of togetherness, that bonding with others. There was a reason witches came together in covens. We *were* Wyrd Women. We did experience the world in strange ways. We needed to share those experiences with each other, order them, make sense out of them. We needed the sisterhood to sustain us.

By the time I got back to the Peabridge, it was already 9:00. I ducked into my cottage and donned my colonial attire in record time. I was still pinning my mob-cap to my hair as I burst through the library's front doors.

Fortunately, Evelyn was away from her desk so I could slip the muffins onto her blotter without her ever being aware of my late arrival. I powered up the coffee bar, grinding a batch of beans so I was ready to greet the first customer of the day.

"Excellent!" my boss said, as she returned to the main reading room from the cataloging office downstairs. "It's a pleasure to see you so prompt and responsible."

At first, I thought she was mocking me, but a quick glance at her close-set eyes convinced me she really meant to deliver a compliment. I shrugged. "You know, anything for the Peabridge."

"That's the spirit!" Evelyn said. "Now, when you get a moment, come into my office, so we can discuss your next Monday Session."

For once, I was actually grateful to see a trio of customers approach, and I took my time brewing their complicated requests. I hadn't settled on a lecture topic yet; I'd been a little preoccupied the past two weeks.

Covens in colonial life, I thought, trying to generate a suitable topic.

Social hierarchies amid closed-membership eighteenth-century cabals.

Secret societies and the Founding Fathers.

Secret societies and the Founding Mothers. And daughters. And granddaughters.

I laced a mocha with whipped cream, nodding to myself. That was actually a possibility. Oh, not the secret society part. But mothers and daughters and the tug of filial duty through the ages. Evelyn would be sure to love the idea.

By the time I got back to my desk, even *I* was brimming with enthusiasm for my session topic. I could bring colonial mothers and daughters to life. I could present an interesting lecture about the pressures of multiple generations living and working in the same house, competing for respect in the same territory.

I sat at my desk and smiled at the icon in the lower right corner that said new mail had arrived. My fingers moved automatically, clicking on the flashing yellow envelope.

To: Jane.Madison@peabridge.org

From: Warning@example.com

Subject: We Are Watching You

How much does the coven mean to you? How much are you willing to invest in their safehold? How much is the centerstone really worth?

Beneath the words was a picture: a red jasper vase, black veins ugly against crimson stone. Four sprigs of herbs were stuck in the vase, herbs as familiar to me as Gran's battered copy of *Joy of Cooking.* Feathery dill. Fennel, turned upside down, so I couldn't miss its branched white bulb. Oregano, with its simple, flat leaves. Thyme, all woody stem and tiny, spiky leaves.

This time, I didn't need David to tell me I was being warned. I didn't need my warder to recite medieval texts. Dill, fennel, oregano, thyme. All were popular in contemporary cooking. All had survived to the twenty-first century because people

believed they held extraordinary properties. Life-saving properties. The ability to stop a witch in her tracks.

My hand shook as I forwarded the message to David.
Someone didn't want me to place the coven's centerstone. How
far was he—or she—willing to go to stop me?

14

I stared at the Potomac River, trying to will my tears not to trickle down my cheeks. I could sense Graeme standing beside me, but I wasn't ready to look at him yet, wasn't ready to talk. Instead, the Kennedy Center fountains chimed away behind us, filling the silence with water sounds. Half the lights on the marble terrace had already been turned off; the huge entertainment complex was going to sleep now that its last evening performance was over.

How many productions of *Romeo and Juliet* had I seen in my lifetime? How many versions of the star-crossed lovers had I watched flit across a stage? How many times had I screamed inside my head, warning Juliet not to drink her potion, begging Romeo not to fall on his sword?

But tonight's show had been special. Well-acted. Well-designed. But something more than that—it had *moved* me. For the couple of hours I'd spent watching the play, I'd forgotten I was surrounded by red velvet and gilt lighting fixtures, that I had a library job to worry about, a coven to occupy my spare time.

The characters had lived and breathed and *been*, and now they weren't, and I could barely keep from sobbing as I stared out at the night-time lights of Georgetown.

Graeme passed me an immaculate linen handkerchief and said, "They were wonderful, weren't they?"

"Yes," I managed, and then the tears did break loose, and I was looking away, trying not to let him see me act like a fool.

Maybe I was just overwhelmed by everything that was happening in my life—the coven and its centerstone (which I still hadn't learned enough about), Gran and Clara and their demands that I back away from the witches, the Peabridge and the increasing hours that I spent brewing coffee when I should be researching colonial history, Graeme...

Graeme...

He rested his hand against my back. I could feel the warmth of each finger as his palm settled between my shoulder blades. I was wearing a light cardigan sweater, emerald green over my black sheath dress.

I resisted the urge to lean back, to feel the taut muscles of Graeme's chest, to fold myself inside his arms. If I let him touch me, I truly would start sobbing like a child. He'd see mascara blobbing around my eyes like a raccoon mask, and he'd realize I was a sentimental idiot, and he'd know for sure that he didn't want anything more to do with an hysterical, gibbering woman.

Better to stare out at the water. Better to focus on the flickering lights and stopping the tears that leaked from my eyes. Better to wait until I could talk without sobbing, until I could force myself to be coherent.

"Do you know what gets me every time?" he asked, mercifully filling the conversational gap.

"Hmm?" I managed to make a questioning sound without actually shaping any words.

"The nurse." He shifted his weight, and the motion exposed my side to the steady breeze that blew off the river. I couldn't believe I was actually chilled out here on the marble patio. Every year, I thought we'd be doomed forever to eternal sweltering heat and every year I was surprised by the sudden autumn change in September's weather.

I rubbed my arms to tame the goosebumps that had sprung up under my sweater before I asked, "The nurse?"

"She's the only person in the Capulet household who truly loved Juliet, who truly understood what that girl was willing to do for love. She's the only one who isn't surprised the morning after. But she's the only one who isn't allowed into the crypt at the end."

I sighed. Graeme really *did* understand. The young lovers had been so hopeful, so certain of themselves. Life—and love—could be so unfair.

And that thought led me into very dark places. Places I didn't want to go—not with a gorgeous man standing by my side. A gorgeous man who was waiting patiently for me to recover from my morose sadness. Waiting patiently while I dabbed my eyes with his handkerchief and hid the mascara-streaked evidence inside my clenched fist.

Another gust of wind picked up off the Potomac and—despite my best intentions—my teeth started to chatter. "Come along now," Graeme said, his British accent rising to the surface more clearly than I'd heard all evening. "Let's get you out of this weather."

"No!" I said, and then I realized that I sounded like a five-year-old spoiled brat. "I mean, it feels wonderful, after all the heat we've had. Do you mind very much staying a bit longer?"

Mind very much? I was starting to sound British again. I gritted my teeth. I hated the way I picked up other people's accents. I could watch a few episodes of *Downton Abbey* and sound like an English lass for hours. And watching an evening of Shakespeare certainly didn't curb the tendency one bit.

Graeme didn't seem to notice. Instead, he smiled and slipped off his jacket, draping it over my shoulders with a protectiveness that made my heart skip a beat. Half a dozen beats. Nearly stop beating altogether.

Had any other man ever watched out for my comfort this way? Certainly not Scott, my former fiancé and philanderer extraordinaire. And the I.B.? It would never have crossed his Infantile Brat mind to protect me.

"Mmmm," I said, and then I *did* lean back against Graeme's chest. I let his arms fold around me, felt the warmth of his fingers spread like fans across my hip bones.

"I've been thinking," Graeme whispered, his lips close to my ear.

"Yes?" I managed to say, barely remembering that I needed to hold up some small part of the conversation.

"You're going to say I'm daft."

What? Graeme had fears about what *I* would think? Me? The woman who bathed in Deep Woods Off and then attracted the entirely unwelcome attention of the Park Police? The woman still recovering from *Romeo and Juliet*, like some lovesick teenager? "I doubt that," I said.

"It's just that you've told me about your…powers."

My belly went cold as I heard his hesitation—colder than the breeze off the river, colder than my memories of Scott and the I.B. How long had Graeme been considering me "other," "different," "strange?"

"Yes." I pushed the word past the lump that suddenly threatened to close my throat. I didn't want him to believe I was some bizarre creature, something he couldn't relate to, couldn't speak to. Didn't want to spend time with.

"You've told me about them, but I've never seen you use them."

Yeah, like that had gone so well, with men in the past. I thought of the Impressive Bother, and the times he'd seen me use my witchy attributes. The first occasion, in my cottage's kitchen, he'd been so unable to cope that he'd ascribed my magic to his own confused senses. And the last time, up at Gran's farm… Well, there'd been no confusion then. The Impetuous Blackguard had understood exactly what he was seeing. And he'd been terrified.

With good cause, I might add.

Showing off my skills as a witch was not exactly at the top of my "One Hundred Ways to Win the Man of Your Dreams" list.

Of course, providing a small demonstration wasn't exactly forbidden either.

"What are you saying, Graeme?"

His fingers clenched slightly, effortlessly turning me around to face him. "I'm saying I want to see you. I want to see what you can do. I told you about the women in my family, the powers they've had. I want to see that power in you."

His blue eyes seemed silver in the shadows on the terrace. The lights were behind him, so his face was carved in planes. I felt his urgency in his fingertips, sensed his earnestness in the heat that radiated from his chest.

"It's really not much to look at," I said, trying to make a joke so I didn't have to respond to the raw desire he stirred inside me.

"I want to look at it. I want to look at you."

Oh. My. God.

The heat in his words would have made me do just about anything. A striptease, here on the back porch of the Kennedy Center? No problem! Bring him home to my bed, ignoring the inquiring looks of my familiar and his lover? Hop on in! Present him to my grandmother, my mother and my best friend, and tell them he was the man I was going to spend the rest of my life with, come hell or high water? Absolutely!

Oh. Wait. That last option wasn't really on the table. Yet.

"You want me to work a spell?"

"Just something small."

"Now?"

"Please." He made the request sound like an offer.

I licked my lips and looked out over the river. I'd spent so much time working with David, focusing on crystals and herbs, that I'd ignored the original aspect of my magic, the spells I'd learned to work from the library in my basement.

I thought back to the endless rows of books I'd cataloged,

the pages and pages of magical words I'd examined, at least in passing. As the breeze picked up over the Potomac once again, I realized I had the perfect little working, ready at hand.

"I shouldn't do this sort of thing," I said, suddenly embarrassed.

"I won't tell if you don't." Graeme's white-toothed smile made me blush, as if he were promising to keep more secrets than my magic.

"It's just that I should have my familiar here. Or my warder."

He looked surprised. "I didn't mean to suggest anything inappropriate. If you're not allowed to use your powers without their permission…"

He trailed off, probably driven into silence by the angry set of my lips. Of course I was allowed to use my powers! David Montrose was not the boss of me. And Neko? He might think he could run my life, but I was *his* master. Mistress. Whatever.

Neither David nor Neko could stop me from using my powers. At least with regard to something as minor as the spell I meant to work now. I mean, if I were to try something *major*, like setting the centerstone—well, of course, I'd expect my magical cohorts to be present for that.

But a few words, chanted on the night-time breeze?

I wouldn't ask permission to have a slice of cake for dessert. And I wasn't going to turn to David and Neko for something equally as mundane. I forced my frown into a smile. "No," I said sweetly. "I certainly don't need their permission. Watch this."

I felt his eyes as I turned back toward the river. I heard him catch his breath as I reached out for the essence of Water, the strength and power of the basic element that flowed past our marble perch. I imagined him stepping back in surprise as I raised my arms dramatically.

And there he was, behind me, catching his jacket before it slipped from my shoulders to the ground. "Damn!" I said. Why hadn't I realized what would happen, the instant I moved my arms? What sort of idiot witch was I? "I'm sorry," I said, my concentration shattered.

"No harm done." I heard the laughter beneath his words, good-natured humor meant to carry me along. He wasn't poking fun at me. He honestly meant for me to feel more comfortable. He held out the jacket as if it were a coronation robe. "Perhaps if you wear it properly?"

I smiled and accepted the offer. And then, before I could lose my nerve, I turned back to the river and closed my eyes, the better to concentrate. I touched my forehead, offering up the power of my thoughts. I touched my throat to give the power of my words. I touched my heart to present the power of my belief. And I said:

> "Flowing water, flowing stream
> Capture moonlight in a beam
> Pass close to the quiet shore
> Open up a magic door
> Offer up your strength as heat
> Beat back chill, cold breeze defeat
> Let fast current turn to frost
> Heat us, now that summer's lost."

I knew the spell was working even before I heard Graeme's indrawn breath. A suddenly warm breeze skirled off the Potomac, brushing my face like a promise of things to come. When I looked out at the water, I could see a silver path condensing all the way from the marble porch to Roosevelt Island in the middle of the river.

Anyone who happened to look down on the Potomac at that precise moment would have thought the water was reflecting moonlight. Reflecting with an odd precision perhaps, providing a cleaner line than expected, but reflecting, all the same.

I knew the silver was not reflected light, though. The silver was ice. Rime settled on the water as I drew forth the river's warmth, as I created a silky summer breeze with magic.

I turned to Graeme, a smile broad across my lips. "And *that* is a little spell."

He was struck dumb by my working. I could see the surprise, flat across his face. What had he expected? Thunder? Lightning? Flashes of eternal hell-fire spawned by my witchy demonstration?

"But… You…" He swallowed and tried again. "You stopped the flow of the entire river."

I frowned. I didn't think he would notice that. "Only for a moment. I took too much water into the spell right at the start. As soon as I found the proper balance, I let the rest of it flow back."

"You let…" He stared at the silvery path in front of us. "That's ice, isn't it?"

"Ice. Frost. Whatever you want to call it. It's not that thick. It doesn't go down to the bottom of the river-bed."

"But you can keep it there, now. While we're talking?"

I'd left a tendril of my powers attached to the frozen streak across the water. In fact, my warm breeze did continue to blow, harvesting the river's power, draining the water's heat for our personal convenience. I shrugged. "It doesn't take much power to maintain. Casting the spell is the hard part."

"I see. I'd always thought…" He shook his head slowly. "But what do I know about magic, eh?"

"I should probably let it go. I wouldn't want to confuse any fish or anything."

"Oh! Yes! By all means!"

I closed my eyes and imagined the heat diffusing, sinking back into the river. I let the ice break up as quickly as it had developed. When I stared out at the river again, ordinary moonlight flickered over ordinary current.

"That was incredible," Graeme breathed.

"It was nothing," I said, embarrassed by his attention.

"No," he contradicted. "Thank you. Truly. Thank you for sharing that with me."

I don't know what it was about those words, but he made them sound...intimate. As if I'd shown him something substantially more personal than a mild weather-working spell. Before I could respond, Graeme was kissing me. His embrace held all the urgency of our encounter on the park bench, all the heat of that fast-banked desire. His fingers tangled in the hair at the base of my neck, and I opened my lips, eager to get the full taste of him, the full feel of him.

And something jangled against my thigh.

Startled, I leaped back. "It's nothing," he said. "Only my mobile." His cell phone. Apparently set on "wake the dead" for its vibration mode. "There," he said. "They've rung off."

I laughed nervously, but neither of us wasted time returning to where we'd left off. His knee forced its way between mine, and his arms closed around me, keeping me balanced, or at least on my feet, even as his lips began doing extremely unsteadying things to the base of my throat.

And his phone jangled again.

"Dammit!" he swore, slamming his hand into his pocket to pull out the offending appliance. He glanced at the number on the screen and muttered something I didn't quite catch. "I'm sorry," he said curtly. "I have to take this."

He stabbed at the screen to answer as he strode across the marble portico. The chilly natural breeze had returned from the river, blowing his words away from me so I couldn't have eavesdropped if I'd wanted to.

If I'd wanted? Of course I'd wanted to.

I pulled his jacket closer and waited for him to finish his rather animated conversation. He ran his fingers through his hair twice. He shifted his weight from foot to foot, like a tiger preparing to pounce on some unsuspecting prey.

At last, he slammed the phone into his pocket and turned to face me.

"I'm sorry," he said. His eyes flashed anger more than sorrow. "I have to go."

"Go?" I was so surprised I repeated the word like a mynah bird.

He shrugged angrily. "I have some work to do."

"Tonight?" I asked incredulously. "It's Saturday. And it's almost midnight."

"11:30," he said, as if I'd really been asking the time.

"Whatever. Can't it wait till morning?"

He shook his head grimly. "No." And then he repeated, "I'm sorry." He put out his hand, cupping my cheek as if he truly wanted to continue the, um, conversation we'd begun before we were so electronically interrupted. "Let me get you a taxi home."

I was so surprised that I let him lead me off the marble terrace. We passed through the now-darkened hallways of the Kennedy Center, moving among the last of the maintenance crews preparing the vast hall for its night-time sleep. We walked out to the street, and Graeme managed to hail a cab instantly, applying the ancient masculine art of transportation management.

Just before he handed me into the back seat, he pulled me close for a kiss, so fiery that I moaned like a silly heroine in a book. Then, he whispered against my ear, "I'll make this up to you. I promise."

And before I could say anything, he handed money to the driver and closed the door behind me. We pulled away from the curb, taking the corner at breakneck speed. By the time I righted myself on the seat, Graeme was gone. I gave my address to the driver and sank back against the door.

Acquisitions. That's what Graeme's business card had said. What sort of acquisitions emergency happened at 11:30 on a Saturday night?

I tortured myself with scenarios until the driver pulled up outside my cottage. As I fit my key into the lock, my phone started ringing. I pushed my way into the living room, barely shoving the door closed behind me. Two rings. Three. I sprinted into the kitchen and grabbed the handset before the answering machine picked up.

"You've resolved the emergency faster than you thought, and you're ready to make it up to me now?" I remembered to smile as I spoke, so Graeme would know I was only kidding, that I wasn't a screaming harpy, furious with a single change in plans.

"That was a very bad idea."

David.

Not Graeme. David. A shiver rippled down my spine.

I kicked off my heels and sank onto one of the kitchen chairs. "Oh. It's you."

"Yes, it's me." I heard his frustration, loud and clear. "What the hell were you doing at the Kennedy Center?"

"You don't have the right to spy on me like that!"

"I wasn't spying. You were broadcasting your location to anyone with the faintest hint of magical ability. What were you doing, working a spell in public? Trying to impress your Mr. Poindexter?"

I flushed at my dating subterfuge, but I wasn't about to tell David Graeme's real name. Just the thought of sharing that confidence made me queasy. I swallowed my discomfort and let it sharpen my words. "It wasn't anything major. I've been able to work that spell for months. It was no big deal."

"Have you received any more emails, Jane? Any more 'gifts?'"

I never should have told him about the herb-o-gram. He'd become completely paranoid. Now, thinking back to that email, I was ready to laugh it away. Someone was playing a joke on me, trying to make me nervous. It was probably just a coven thing, a hazing, like a sorority sister being "kidnapped" from her dorm room on rush night.

"No," I answered David. "But if I had, you would be the first to know."

"I wish I believed you, Jane. Look, this is not a joke. If you expect to be ready to deal with the coven on Samhain, we have to work every chance we get. You can't waste your energy on games."

I rubbed my face with a hand that still smelled of Graeme's cologne. Wistfulness actually stiffened my resolve. "David, I already told you, I'm not giving up my entire social life for the coven. You and I are meeting, what? Tomorrow morning?"

"At seven."

I could have sworn I'd agreed to nine. I never would have let him bully me into seven o'clock on a Sunday morning. "That's a little early, don't you think?"

"You know if I had my way, we'd have been working tonight. And now you'll be drained of power, in addition to short on sleep."

"It wasn't anything major!"

"Is that what Nate Poindexter said?" He drew out the name, as if it were a grammar school taunt. Next thing I knew, I'd be sitting in a tree, K-I-S-S-I-N-G.

"David, my personal life is my personal life."

"That worked out so well for you last year, didn't it?"

"That's a terrible thing to say!" I was truly surprised. David was often pushy. Over-protective. But he never said things specifically designed to hurt my feelings. To make me remember just how foolish I'd been, how irresponsibly I'd acted.

Now, he sighed. "Just be careful, Jane."

A long silence stretched between us, as I tried to think of something to say, something that would tell him just how much I'd learned from the I.B. Graeme, er, Nate, was different. I was certain.

David warned, "Just make sure you take care of yourself."

"I'm doing that, David," I said, suddenly certain I had to

end this phone call immediately. End it, or be sobbing into the phone. "You can be absolutely certain I am doing that."

I hung up without saying anything else. As I stepped out of the kitchen, I caught a flash of movement as the door to the basement slipped closed. Great. Neko had overheard every word.

I stomped off to my bedroom, making every effort to send the echo of my footsteps thundering into the basement. I slammed my door closed, finding a little relief in the way the entire wall shook.

As I threw myself onto my bed, I realized I was still wearing Graeme's jacket. I took it off and buried my face in the satin lining. I fell asleep breathing in his smell, telling myself that anyone could have a midnight occupational emergency. If it had been an omen, or a ruse, or a trick to break things off, then he would have demanded his coat back before sending me home. Right?

All night long, I dreamed of walking toward him, jacket extended, as my feet slipped and slid on a silvery strip of ice that never ended.

15

_____

A week later, I would have given anything to work a spell as simple as the one that had frozen the Potomac River. David and I had trained together every day for the past week. Ever since our midnight conversation about Graeme, er, Nate, my warder had insisted that we make up for lost time, preparing for Samhain and the centerstone working. He'd even gone so far as to commandeer three of my lunch hours at the Peabridge.

Sometimes I wasn't sure if he really believed I needed that much work on witchcraft, or if he was just trying to make it impossible for me to see Nate, er, Graeme. Every single day, I vowed to confront David about his interference with my love life. But every single day, I succumbed to shivers of apprehension when I imagined the actual conversation. I knew David's position on extracurricular activities. I knew we had magical priorities. I _agreed_ on those arcane goals.

But I still indulged in late-night phone conversations with Graeme, long after Neko had retreated to the basement and David had gone…wherever David went when he wasn't being my warder. Lying back in bed, feeling my phone grow warm against my ear, I tried to stifle unwanted yawns as I told Graeme about my day. Not _everything_ about my day, but as much as I could share. And when I finally fell asleep, I dreamed about November, after the centerstone was set, when I could be an ordinary librarian, going out on ordinary dates with my so-much-more-than-ordinary boyfriend.

Boyfriend. Graeme. I loved putting those words together in one sentence.

So what, if I used a beginner's spell to banish my fatigue in the morning—three times in the past week? If I was only pretending to be bright and perky and inquisitive on a Sunday morning when I would have much preferred to crawl back under my comforter to sleep uninterrupted, dreaming of the incredible man who had kissed me an entire week before?

I had a warder to impress. So I brewed my pear oolong tea. I pulled my hair back into a serviceable ponytail. I tugged on a T-shirt and jeans, in a testimony to my willingness to work. And I threw open the door to the basement, slamming on the over-head light and calling out in a dulcet alto, "Neeeeko! David's will be here in a moment! Up and at 'em!"

I pretended not to hear Jacques grunting Gallic obscenities, and I ignored Neko's scowl as he climbed the stairs, pawing sleep from his eyes. I couldn't believe Jacques tolerated the strangeness of Neko's life—the odd basement room, the lack of a traditional job. And yet the Frenchman seemed more devoted than ever. Perhaps Graeme would turn out to be as tolerant when I could tell him everything.

I succumbed to a delicious shiver of anticipation as David knocked at the front door.

By noon, I wondered if the coven was worth all this. I was exhausted—physically, mentally, and emotionally. Even as I considered working yet another surreptitious banishing fatigue spell in the kitchen, I could hear David's implacable voice in my mind, bolstering me for yet another lesson. The coven was the center. The coven was the core. It helped its members, protecting them against mundane authority. It was the very reason witchcraft had persisted through the ages, through the centuries of suspicion and persecution. No other institution in the Eastern Empire was dedicated to preserving witchcraft per se. In the supernatural tangle that ran beneath the fabric of the mundane world, the coven was warp and weft for women like me.

I shook my head, dragging my thoughts back to the morning's lessons. I'd spent the last four hours working magic on a gigantic chunk of marble. David had kept his promise; as a warder, he'd carried the stone into the cottage. He'd hefted it onto the coffee table, grimacing once he was free of its weight.

But *I* had been tasked with purifying the damn thing, with securing it against malevolent forces. I'd siphoned off my energy, dram by dram, pouring it into the microscopic crystals of the stone as I whispered a variation on a spell I'd known all my life:

"Protect and keep all safe from harm
Watch o'er my coven like a charm."

I'd sealed that magic into the marble, balancing the Earth energies of the stone with Water's purifying aspects. I'd needed to account for the effect of Air as I washed its surface with radish tea. And as the purified water soaked into the edges, I felt the protective marble *change*. Not in any scientific way, not in a manner that could be measured with thermometers or calipers or any other mundane tool. But I could *sense* the transformation. A bearer of poison (a scorpion, a liar, whatever) could not move past the invisible barrier I'd created.

Neko had helped. He'd mirrored my strength back to me, fracturing it with a thousand different lenses, allowing it to coalesce into a greater reservoir, a deeper pool. When that almost proved insufficient, he'd adopted the role of World's Most Sadistic Personal Trainer. At one point, he'd crouched in front of me and chanted, "*Channel* your energy. *Commit* yourself! You're not as weak as you think you are!"

I'd seriously considered turning him back into a statue.

But in the end, the marble was sealed. It was marked with my unique astral signature. It was secured against evil. And I sank onto the hunter green couch, light-headed and heavy-limbed, exhaling completely for the first time since David's arrival.

My warder nodded slowly as the last filaments of my cleansing spell dissipated from the air around us. "How did that feel?"

How did it feel? Like I was hefting the Capitol dome onto my shoulders. Like I was balancing the Washington Monument on my forehead and staggering to keep my footing. Like I was trying to drain the entire Reflecting Pool with a single bat of an eyelash.

"Fine," I said, managing a smile that I hoped didn't look too fake. I let my fingers touch Neko's shoulder, and if he realized I was stabilizing myself there, he didn't let on. "I think I'm getting the hang of this."

"Excellent," David said. "I have to admit you've made major strides this week."

Prickling pride burned off my pleasure at his compliment. "Not what you expected, I know."

He raised his hands, palms out, offering up a peaceful apology. "Why don't you just take my words at face value?" he asked reasonably, settling back on the couch. "So. Take it easy this afternoon. You'll be surprised by how much power you spent this morning. Why don't you read a book, maybe take a nap? Eat a light supper and get a good night's sleep."

Neko nodded helpfully. "At least the museum café should have a light supper. They serve a lot of salmon. Will you bring me some salmon?"

"Crap!" I'd completely forgotten that I was supposed to meet Haylee James at the National Gallery of Art. Where had the week gone? Oh, that's right. I'd spent it with my warder and my familiar.

I glanced at my watch. It was 12:30 now. If I ate a quick lunch, I could still jump in the shower, dry my hair, throw on something elegantly casual, and meet Haylee by two.

David shook his head.

"What?" I asked.

"What do you and Nate have on the social calendar?"

"If you *must* know, I'm meeting Haylee James at the National Gallery of Art for a tour of their Renaissance collection."

"Haylee!" He couldn't have been more surprised if I'd said I was meeting the President for tea in the Rose Garden. He recovered quickly, though. "What could you possibly have in common with Haylee?"

"Aside from the fact she's a witch?" I let the words drip with more sarcasm than a sixteen-year-old challenging her parents' most unfair curfew. "And part of Teresa Alison Sidney's coven? And the only friend I have in that entire group?"

David didn't rise to my bait. His voice was deadly calm as he said, "Haylee James is not your friend."

"How can you say that? You've never even seen us together!"

"I know Haylee. And I know you. Friendship is the last thing on Haylee's mind if she's making plans with you."

"That's a terrible thing to say!" And the more I thought about it, the worse it was. Was David saying I wasn't good enough to be friends with a witch as accomplished as Haylee? Or that she was too popular, too close to our Coven Mother to waste her time being friends with me? The options were opposing sides of the same coin, and I didn't like heads *or* tails.

David grimaced. "Haylee has said a lot worse things about me in the past. Said and done."

"Aww," I said, irrationally stung. First, David was trying to keep me from seeing Graeme. Now, he was interfering with my hard-earned friendship. I lapsed into the most annoying baby tone I could contrive. "Did Haywee huwt your widdle feewings?"

I heard Neko's jaw drop. I had never challenged David so directly.

He reacted to my ridicule instantly—his face snapped closed, and his jaw tightened like an iron brand. "Do *not* come to me when you have problems with Haylee James," he said, and his voice was so low I had to lean forward to make out his words. "Don't expect me to clean up the mess you're making."

"Fine," I said. He didn't know she was the only witch who talked to me at coven gatherings. She was the only one of my so-called sisters who bothered to give me the time of day. He didn't know, because he abandoned me every time we entered Teresa Alison Sidney's home.

"Fine," he repeated. He waited a long moment, as if he thought I would take back my word, but then he shrugged. "And so we're done for the day."

I showed him to the door without making any attempt to smooth things over.

Okay. So, there wasn't enough time to dry my hair. But if I hurried, I could still take a shower. And I could eat an entire box of Triscuits as I hailed a cab to the museum. The soda? I was better off without it anyway.

But I got my soda late that afternoon, in the upscale café at the National Gallery.

Haylee and I had wandered through the Renaissance paintings at the museum. I was astonished by the collection—I hadn't been there in ages. In fact, the last time I'd visited, I'd been on a school trip. The boys had stared at statues of all the naked babes, and the girls had made unkind comments about Rubens' models. I remembered standing in the rotunda, looking up at the statue of winged Mercury and wondering why no one ever sent *me* any secret message.

Well, I was long on secrets now.

"So?" Haylee asked, as we sipped Coca-Cola over tiny ice cubes. We had poured our beverages from little glass bottles—the nostalgia component almost justified the outrageous cost. A steady stream of museum visitors filed by the gelato bar, and I reminded myself that I did not need a cup of stracciatella to make it through the day. "What did you think?"

"I have a lot to learn," I said. "I never realized how much information is...embedded in the world around me."

There were hints to our witchy powers buried everywhere in the museum. The marble columns that sheltered the artwork were only the first harbingers of magic, creating a protective arch around the space, around the temple of humankind's learning and accomplishments. I could sense further power in the flow of the Mercury fountain—in the round pool that centered the power of the museum's protective dome.

And the artwork! Sure, I'd put in my time learning to parse symbolism in paintings. I'd suffered through Art 101 in college, mastering basic vocabulary and belaboring the meaning of the open window behind Mona Lisa's shoulder. I'd served my sentence with Monet's waterlilies and Dali's melting clocks.

But the paintings that Haylee had just shown me... I'd had no idea how much information was conveyed in each and every brush stroke. "Just that peacock alone," I said. "I could spend days working out what the artist meant."

I was thinking of a round painting, one that was attributed to Fra Filippo Lippi. It showed the presentation of the gifts of the Magi, the three wise kings adoring the Christ child. In the center of the panel, at the heart of the swirling imagery, a peacock stood on the roof of the manger.

I smiled at Haylee over my Coca-Cola. "I just can't get over how wrong I was. I don't know where I came up with the idea that the peacock was a vain bird, that it was silly because it showed off its tail." There was more, something that I couldn't quite remember about the peacock. Something that lurked in the back of my mind, in my cluttered closet of academic knowledge.

"Oh, those stories *are* told. But that's because people are afraid of beauty." She said the words simply, as if she weren't aware of the effect her gamine hair and her high cheekbones had on half the men who walked by while we drank our soda. No, those men weren't *afraid* of beauty. They were attracted to it. Attracted to Haylee. She toyed with her Hecate's Torch, fingering the charm on its silver chain.

"People are afraid of the things they don't understand," I said. "The things they can't control."

Haylee's lips set in a grim line, and I had to lean closer to catch her next words. "That's why we witches get such bad press. Oh, we're amusing and fun at Halloween, when people can show us with warts on our noses and cobwebs in our hair. But ask about us any other time of year, and you're likely to hear about the evil eye. Spells. Charms. And witches burned at the stake for all the evil things we do."

Well. I hadn't expected the conversation to take quite so grim a turn. I cleared my throat and said, "The evil things we're *alleged* to do." I smiled, so she'd know I wasn't chiding her. So she'd know I was her friend. Or trying to be one.

She fiddled with the wrapper from her straw. "Alleged."

An uneasy silence pooled around us, spreading like a puddle of viscous tar. I reminded myself to breathe. To relax. To say something to break the dark flow of our thoughts.

"Lovely weather we're having lately," I said, forcing a laugh so she'd realize I was making a joke.

Haylee's eyes were dark, serious, as she asked, "Do you know how to change the weather?"

Immediately, I thought of standing on the Kennedy Center terrace with Graeme. I remembered the heat of his arms around me, the warm breeze that I had crafted, wafting off of the chilling river. I thought of the passion that had risen between us, the promise mounting until his cell phone jangled us back to the real world.

"Um, I can work a few minor spells," I said.

Haylee must have seen my cheeks flush. She pounced like a peacock discovering the tastiest of wormy morsels in the gravel at its feet. "What?"

"What what?" I tried again for humor, chiding myself for acting like I was thirteen years old.

"Why are you blushing?"

I shook the ice cubes in my glass, wishing I knew a spell for making more Coke appear. For making minor earthquakes happen. For distracting a witch when she was hot on the scent of gossip. "It's nothing," I said.

"Your lips say 'nothing', but your eyes say more, more." She laughed at her corny words, and I couldn't help but join her.

I stared at her Torch, unable to meet her gaze. "It's just this guy I met, a few weeks ago." She arched a perfect eyebrow but remained silent, forcing me to take a deep breath and continue. "We've only gone out a few times…"

Haylee's smile was soft. "But you like him."

I let myself nod, but I looked away shyly. "A lot."

"Tell me all about him!"

Tell her about the cute boy I liked. That's what friends did, right? I would tell her, then she'd tell me about some guy *she* had met. We'd commiserate over past mistakes. We'd remind each other of the good things about guys, warn each other off about the bad things. Share and share alike. That's how girls made friends.

I thought of poor Melissa, with her parade of Mr. Wrongs. As miserable as those men had made her, they were one of the key reasons she and I had bonded over the years, one of the reasons we continued to get together for Mojito Therapy and commiseration. Except it had been ages since we'd found time for cocktails and gossip. Almost two weeks had passed since that weird night when David had joined us, and it had been months since we'd spent time alone, just the two of us, catching up. I'd just been too swamped.

"Go on!" Haylee pressed, leaning closer.

And so I did. I told her how Graeme had come into Cake Walk a month ago. How we had laughed about Almond Lust. How he had left me his card. How we'd been on three dates, and each had left me a little more intrigued. Okay. A *lot* more intrigued. How we'd teased each other over the phone for the past week.

"He sounds like something," she said, when I trailed off.

"He is," I said, and I sighed. "If we could only keep from getting interrupted. Maybe I should wear beryl the next time we get together."

"Beryl?"

I heard David's voice in the back of my head, droning on in professorial authority, and I thought about the ancient guide to crystals that even now was opened on the bookstand in my basement. "Beryllium aluminum cyclosilicate." I might as well have been speaking Greek, given Haylee's opaque expression. "It's a crystal that increases motivation. It gives confidence to the wearer, but can reach beyond that person. Maybe that's all Graeme needs. A bit of clarity of vision, to keep us both on track."

"Clarity." Haylee said the word decisively. "Beryl. Where *do* you learn this stuff?"

I was shocked. Didn't every witch know about crystals?

But of course they didn't. Most witches didn't have the hoard of books I had in my basement. Most witches didn't have my librarian's compulsion to organize information, to pull together facts and details, to memorize, memorize, memorize. Haylee's strengths must lie elsewhere.

"I'm not sure where I picked that up," I said. "Just something I collected along the way, I guess."

"I'll have to remember it. And I'd love to learn more about crystals from you."

"Any time!" I said, and I meant it. Here was a witch—an honest to goodness witch, and my first friend within the coven. I would do almost anything to keep building our relationship.

Haylee glanced around us, and for the first time, I noticed that the café was emptying. She said, "Well, it looks like they're about to throw us out of here."

I frowned. "I wanted to go back through the painting galleries one more time."

"Not today." Haylee pushed back her chair. "You're not still thinking about that stupid bird, are you?"

"It's right on the tip of my tongue…"

"Peacocks," she said, and the started ticking points off as she slung her purse over her shoulder. "They're symbols in every major world culture. They represent the glorification of the soul. They stand for saints, because medieval people thought their flesh didn't rot."

"Their voice!" I finally remembered, as we walked out of the museum into the early autumn evening. "Hearing the peacock's cry is bad luck."

Haylee paused on the marble steps. "Isn't that the owl? I heard the owl call my name?"

"Peacocks, too," I insisted. "That's what I've been trying to remember all afternoon."

"Well, at least we don't have to worry about accidentally overhearing one here in the city."

"How did you know the rest of that stuff?" I asked.

"I'm an interior designer, remember? You wouldn't believe the number of people who want to know the spiritual meaning of the things they put up on their walls."

I thought of Clara, and her obsession with harm~ ˙
Age interpretations of every last thing around i
said. "I would."

We took another couple of minutes to chat ab

ings we'd seen, and then we promised we'd get together again. Soon.

By the time I got home, I was exhausted. I might have impressed David by being ready for that morning's session, but I had definitely awakened too early. And invested too much energy into the centerstone training. I glanced around the living room, grateful to see that Neko was out, somewhere, presumably with Jacques.

Dinner was going to be a giant bowl of microwave popcorn.

I had already changed into my pajamas and burrowed my feet into my bunny slippers when I realized the message waiting light was flashing on my answering machine. I pressed the playback button and almost squealed when I recognized Graeme's voice.

"Hello there, Lady of the River. I hope you enjoyed the Gallery with your friend. If memory serves, I still owe you from last week. I hope you'll let me make it up to you. Maybe you can even show me a little more of what you can do. Soonest, Jane."

Show him what I could do.

The notion excited me. I thought again of how I'd hidden my powers from the I.B., kept him from knowing the extent of my abilities until I needed to use my magic against him. The idea of being honest with Graeme filled me with a glow of happiness.

He knew about me. He understood. He was even more attracted to me because of who I was.

I should play things cool. I should curl up on my couch and read a book. I should go to bed early, prepare for my busy workweek.

But I couldn't keep from dialing his phone number. The digits were now firmly memorized, burned deep enough that I no longer needed the silver-lined Acquisitions card. I caught my breath, ready to say something witty and entertaining, but the 'ine went immediately to an answering machine.

He must be on the phone.

I tried back a few minutes later, and a few minutes after that. By then, my popcorn had gotten cold, and I realized I was too tired, even for that snack of a dinner. I tried to reach Graeme one last time, but nearly broke my jaw biting back a yawn as his machine picked up yet again.

I should listen to the signs of the universe, I told myself. I could always reach Graeme in the morning. I should go to sleep.

And so I did.

16

Some mornings, even the coffee machine had it out to get me.

The first time I attempted to grind Colombia's finest, the grinder detached itself from the main machine, sending coffee dust into my eyes, ears, and nose. When I finally stopped coughing, I wiped the tears from my cheeks, leaving brown smudges across my face. Keeping Health Board regulations in mind, I cursed at the mess, ran downstairs to the restroom, cursed at the dim light, washed my hands, cursed at the skin-drying soap, rinsed my fingers, cursed at the raspy towels, and then climbed the stairs to begin the process all over again.

The second batch of coffee stayed in the grinder—along with one of the blades, a screw, and a strange metal flange I'd never seen before. It took me the better part of half an hour to reassemble the machine. And, of course, I needed to curse, wash, curse, dry, curse, and start all over again.

By that time, I'd already turned away three mothers and their precious children, a total of five brats—ahem, Junior Colonial Explorers—who had arrived early for my weekly American Family reading hour.

American Family had seemed like a brilliant idea when I'd

first thought it up. I'd imagined sitting on the floor, surrounded by a circle of adoring fourth- and fifth-grade children who all longed to learn about the history of our country. I had pictured myself choosing favorites from my childhood, books that would stretch elementary school reading levels—*The Witch of Blackbird Pond, Johnny Tremaine*. I could still remember laughing at Johnny's short temper, crying over our colonial battlefield losses, learning without ever realizing just how much history was being slipped into my daily entertainment quota.

Reality was a little different from my dreams.

First of all, I wasn't reading to ten-year-olds. They were all in school, of course.

No, I played hostess to a circle of toddlers, along with the occasional four- or five-year-old who was home sick from regular school. The neighborhood mothers all looked upon me as a free baby-sitter. I had actually heard one shriek into her cell phone with unrestrained glee when she discovered the Peabridge's amazing community service.

Each week, the mothers collected their coffees (usually demanding an inordinate number of special requests—one pump of chocolate syrup rather than two, nutmeg sprinkled on top instead of cinnamon, anything to break the routine that just barely managed to keep me sane as I staffed the coffee bar.) One woman, the bane of my barista existence, ordered skim milk in her drink and full-fat foam on top. She acted like I was attempting murder when I got the order reversed. Twice.

Okay, I took pleasure wherever I could find it at the ever-more-hated coffee bar. So, sue me.

Each week, the mothers lingered in the reference area until they had all been served their caffeinated treasures. Then, they retreated to the basement exhibit space, feigning an unholy interest in whatever diaries we were highlighting downstairs.

Downstairs. Where it was peaceful. Quiet. Child-free.

"Sit down, Jonathan!" I said for the seventh time in ten minutes. "No one else can see the book if you're standing up."

Jonathan finally obliged, crossing his chubby legs. I smiled, pleased that I had finally gotten through to him. He smiled back with his milky baby teeth, and then he plunged his index finger into his nose. He cleared the second knuckle easily, but I fought the urge to say anything. After all, by the time I found a Kleenex and got him cleaned up, there was no telling what the other kids would do.

As if on cue, three-year-old Kayla stood and grabbed at the crotch of her adorable corduroy pants. "Potty," she said, groaning for emphasis.

The word inspired two of her classmates, who also began clutching themselves and whining. Jonathan's younger brother—what was his name? Aaron?—started to crawl away from the group. His mother had promised me he wasn't ready to crawl yet. He'd only just mastered rolling over two weeks before. (Yes, I had been thrilled to be the sole adult witness to *that* milestone, let me assure you.)

"Potty, potty, potty," Kayla chanted, turning the two syllables into an eloquent dissertation on struggle and deprivation, broken dreams and strangled futures.

I glanced toward the stairs, willing the mothers to return. Surely they were attuned to their own precious offsprings' needs. They must realize how much time had gone by. They had to require another freaking cappuccino, just to make it through the day!

Evelyn came out of her office, clearly distracted by the noise. She gave me a disapproving glance and then loomed over Kayla. "Young lady, we do not sing in the library."

Kayla burst into tears. As if on cue, the infant Aaron collapsed onto his belly, looking like a startled turtle for the split second before he added his own shriek to the fray. Jonathan continued excavating his right nostril as if he hadn't a care in the world, and the two other children resumed and amplified Kayla's chant.

Evelyn shot me an accusing glance. I smiled as sweetly as I

could under the circumstances and said, "Their mothers are right downstairs. Do you want to get them, or should I?"

Evelyn spun on her heel, as if she couldn't leave the room fast enough. "Come on," I said to Kayla. "There's nothing to cry about."

"I'm afraid of w—w—witches!" she said.

I looked down at my pinafore, noticing a streak of coffee grounds I'd somehow missed in my earlier disaster cleanup. "Me?"

"The witch!" Kayla said again with even greater urgency, and she pointed after Evelyn's departing back. In fact, she inspired Jonathan to add his own slimy digit to the mix, and they repeated to each other, "The witch! The witch!"

"So, they've found out the truth."

Neko. I'd know his smug voice anywhere.

I turned to face him with a speed that might have been misconstrued as desperation. Momentary distraction was all Aaron had been waiting for. "Stop that baby!" I cried as the infant started to race past my familiar. Neko looked down in horror, but it was Jacques who cornered the squirming child, trapping him between two wooden chairs.

"Kayla!" I shouted, loud enough that I shocked the girl into silence. "There isn't any witch."

"There isn't?" Neko asked, apparently unaware of the chaos that surrounded him. I shot him a look that threatened to jolt him back to his statue form.

"There isn't any witch," I said again. "The nice lady who went downstairs is a librarian. She works here just like I do."

Neko's mouth stretched into a precise O, and I saw him recognize the error in his ways. He turned to me and mouthed, "E—ve—lyn?"

I nodded grimly. Neko reached toward Kayla and patted her head with delicate fingertips, as if he feared contracting chicken pox—or some more horrific childhood scourge—from the contact. "You poor little girl. No wonder you were frightened."

I glared at my familiar and took advantage of a momentary lull in the cacophony to ask, "What do the two of you want?"

"We just woke up," Neko said, adding a delicate yawn to illustrate his words, "and you were out of coffee at home. We thought we'd come over here and have you make us some."

"The coffee bar is closed during American Family hour."

Jacques looked at his wristwatch. "American Familee. Is over at eleven, no?"

"Yes." I glanced at the clock on the wall, thrilled to see that this week's purgatory had finally ended. "Yes, it is," I repeated with relish.

As if on cue, Kayla resumed her chant: "Potty, potty, potty." Neko jumped back as if she were threatening to steal one of his lives. Jacques took a moment to process what she was saying, and then he, too, took a large step away.

"You," I said, pointing to Neko. "Take those two by their hands. And you," this time it was Jacques I pinned with my evil librarian eye, "pick up that baby. And Kayla, that is *enough*! Jonathan, come with me. We're going downstairs now."

Like the Pied Piper, I led the procession down the library stairs, trying to ignore the glares from the patrons who were actually trying to get academic work done at the reference room reading tables.

Evelyn had created this problem, I tried to tell myself. Evelyn had turned the reading room into a café, complete with child-care. Evelyn. Not me.

I scowled.

Neko seemed terrified to disobey me. He recognized the tone I'd used; he probably realized I was only a shade away from snapping out a magical Word of power. I could do that, too. I'd read enough to know how to freeze everyone into place, with a single well-formed syllable.

At the foot of the stairs, I found Evelyn chatting breezily with the mothers, laughing as one finished up a droll little tale about a family trip to Colonial Williamsburg. "Well," my boss said, fanning herself and exclaiming as if the patron were the most brilliant storyteller ever to grace the Peabridge halls. "How were *you* supposed to know the cider was alcoholic?"

Kayla launched herself at her mother's knees, keening about her toileting needs. I accepted Evelyn's glare, considering it worthwhile to get rid of the child, even at the cost of some professional standing. I jutted my chin from Jacques to the well-coiffed mother of Jonathan and Aaron. I let my voice freeze as I said to her, "You'll be thrilled to know Aaron has mastered crawling now."

She smiled like a grateful saint. "These mornings at the Peabridge do him so much good. You really should host American Family sessions every day."

"Every day?" Evelyn asked, as if the idea had never occurred to her.

"What?" I said quickly, hoping to dig out the idea before it could take root. "And lose out on them being so special?"

"Jane!" My name echoed in the stairwell, and I recognized the voice of Nancy, the circulation clerk. "Jane, we need you up here! There are some patrons who want coffee!"

What the hell? Who said I was the only person who could make a fool out of myself at the coffee bar? When Evelyn had stumbled on the coffee brainstorm, she'd intended all of us to learn how to grind the beans, how to foam the milk, how to make the endless variations on a steaming cup of joe. Somewhere along the way, though, I had been designated chief coffee-maker. And child wrangler. And bottle washer. It was a minor miracle I even remembered how to use our online catalog.

"Excuse me," I said, barely keeping an edge of professionalism in my voice. "Jacques, you can hand Aaron over to Mrs. Duchamp now."

"Duchamp?" he repeated, perfecting the nasal pronunciation I had not dared attempt. "Madame Duchamp?" He squealed at the prospect of meeting a fellow countryman.

Rolling my eyes, I left him and Neko to the joy of the Peabridge American Family community.

As I climbed the stairs, I watched my feet. The last thing I needed was to slip on the steps—my dignity had been injured enough by spending the morning babysitting. I smoothed my mob-cap and made sure the muslin was still centered on my head. Wouldn't that be perfect, if it slipped into someone's latte?

"Good morning."

My heart stopped. One moment, I was a harried librarian, wondering how I could move a coffee bar out of my library and into the nearest Starbucks, where it belonged. The next, I was a lovestruck woman, staring into all-too-familiar light blue eyes.

"Graeme," I said.

He smiled, obviously amused by the startled expression on my face.

"What are you doing here?" I whispered.

This wasn't right! He was part of my real life. My important life. The private life I lived away from the Peabridge. I didn't want him here in the library, didn't want him to see me surrounded by screaming kids and temperamental coffee grinders. He was supposed to think of me as smooth and witty, urbane and experienced.

Yeah, right.

I yielded to the inevitable. "Can I make you a coffee?"

"I'm sorry," he said. "I shouldn't have come by. But I wanted to see you here. Where you work. It makes it easier for me to imagine you." He lowered his voice to a whisper so soft I couldn't hear his British accent. "To think about you when we're apart."

Could a girl make a coffee drink when her knees had melted? "It's fine," I managed to say. "I'm glad you came by. Even though there really isn't much to see."

He looked at my embroidered silk dress, and I imagined his fingers on my whalebone stays. "Oh, I think there's more at the Peabridge than meets the eye."

Desperate to defeat the blush that was spreading up my neck, I said, "Please! What do you want to drink? I have to look like I'm working!"

He grinned wolfishly. "I'll have a mocha, then."

"A fine drink," another voice said. "My favorite, in fact."

"Mr. Potter," I said, recognizing the speaker before I could even turn around. "How was Pittsburgh?"

"Exhausting. But a mocha would be just the thing to pick me up. Little did I expect to find someone else ordering my drink." He laughed at his little joke.

"Oh!" I said. Graeme was standing patiently, as if he were accustomed to waiting for flighty women to remember to introduce their elders. "Mr. Potter! This is Graeme Henderson. Graeme, Mr. Potter gave me the tickets for *Romeo and Juliet*."

Mr. Potter's smile was wide. "And I take it, you are the young man who escorted Jane to the performance?"

"Yes, sir," Graeme said, managing to connote a tiny half-bow behind the two words. Something about the answer made him seem like a nobleman, a knight, a regal protector in shining armor.

I took a deep breath and moved behind the coffee counter. I contemplated harnessing some sort of spell to make the machinery function properly, but I couldn't figure out a way to mutter the words without being too obvious. And the way my day was going, I didn't have any confidence my magic would work. I settled for crossing my fingers with all the passion of a third-grader hoping for a passing grade on a math test.

"And how was the production?" Mr. Potter asked.

I missed Graeme's reply as I poured milk into a stainless steel pitcher. Whatever he said, it clearly pleased Mr. Potter. Both men laughed, and Graeme started to describe the costumes for the ball scene in the first act.

The men's conversation was easy and smooth, and I relaxed enough to create two perfect mochas. I topped Mr. Potter's with extra whipped cream, just the way he liked it, and then I turned to Graeme. "Whipped cream? Er, chantilly?"

His smile was just sly enough to make my heart pound as he accepted a dollop.

I handed over both cups and was about to join the conversation about the Friar Lawrence scene, when I realized that disaster loomed.

Neko and Jacques must be close to finishing with the American Family mothers. They'd come over to the coffee bar when they were done. They'd get the drinks that had lured them here in the first place. They'd stand at the counter and ogle Graeme.

And Neko would ask me questions. Questions I had promised Melissa I wouldn't answer. Questions I had no intention of sharing with David Montrose or anyone else involved in my witchy life. Worse yet, Neko would jump to the conclusion that Graeme was "Nate", and I'd be left making excuses to everyone, excuses that sounded feeble even as I tested them in my own mind. I shivered, suddenly chilled to the bone.

"Here!" I said, my voice a shade too shrill. "Mr. Potter, you must be exhausted after your trip back from Pittsburgh! Why don't you sit down at the reference table!"

Graeme looked at me curiously, but he obligingly helped our elderly library benefactor over to a seat. I managed to arrange things so Graeme's back was to the coffee bar, so Neko would not see anything suspicious when he came upstairs.

Now, if I could just have Neko's and Jacques's drinks waiting, I could get them out the door that much faster. Neko was easy—steamed milk, with just the smallest drop of coffee. Ecru, he preferred, he'd told me often enough. Not beige. Not ivory.

And Jacques? He was getting a latte whether he wanted one or not.

I made the drinks in record time, digging into my own hidden colonial pocket to extract money for the cash register. It was worth it, just to hurry them on their way.

Sure enough, Neko and Jacques accompanied the American

Family mothers up the stairs. "Yes," Neko was saying. "A daily reading session does make sense to me. I'm certain the children would get much more out of it." He smiled winningly and waggled his fingers at Kayla's mother as the entire troop of miscreants left the Peabridge.

Then, he pounced on the coffee bar.

"Here," I said, thrusting one cup into his hand and another into Jacques's. "Go ahead. Take them with you."

"It was cold downstairs," Neko complained. "We'll just sit down at that table in the sun, to warm up for a moment."

That table. Next to Graeme and Mr. Potter.

"No!" I shouted, and then I remembered that I worked in a library. "No," I repeated in a stage whisper. "Why don't you take your coffee outside and warm up there."

"Eet's too cold," Jacques said, stirring four packets of sugar into his latte. "The weather, eet has turned to autumn."

"Fine," I said, knowing better than to push the matter. "Stay inside." Before I could figure out some other way to speed up my familiar's departure, I saw Graeme push his chair back. As he started to stand, I said to Neko, "Wait here! I have to help a patron!"

I sailed across the room, grabbing the first book that came to hand. "Here!" I said, setting it down on the reading table between Graeme and Mr. Potter. Graeme had turned toward me as I approached, but I maneuvered myself into an awkward position toward the foot of the table, forcing him to turn away from the coffee bar. Away from Neko's curiosity. Safe from prying eyes. I took a seat, and Graeme sank back into his own chair.

"I thought you might be interested in this!" I said, glancing down to see which book I'd grabbed.

Ports and Harbors of Colonial America.

Mr. Potter looked up with a perplexed smile. "Why am I interested in ports, Jane?"

Why, indeed? I opened the book at random, hoping to find

an intriguing map. "You were in the Merchant Marines, weren't you?"

"Me? With these eyes?" Mr. Potter laughed and waved a hand toward eyeglasses that would make Coke bottles seem fragile.

"I could swear Uncle George said you'd served with them." Okay. So I was desperate. I could not let Graeme turn around, could not let him draw Neko's attention in any way.

Involuntarily, I glanced toward my familiar, only to find him staring at me intently. If he were still in his cat form, his tail would have twitched back and forth. He took a single step toward me, and I forced a bright smile. "Whoops! Another patron. I'll be back in a moment." Graeme started to stand again as I left, and I resisted the urge to press my fingers onto his shoulder. Neko would certainly notice that level of attention. "No, no," I said. "Don't get up!"

And then I was back with my familiar. "What?" I asked.

"I was just wondering?" He scuffed his shoe along the floor, looking for all the world like a schoolboy caught red-handed with the answer form for a multiple-choice test.

"Yes?" I wanted to glance toward Graeme, wanted to make sure there wasn't anything suspicious about him and Mr. Potter, anything that would make Neko question my personal dedication to that particular pair of patrons. No. I must not look. I must not turn.

"Could I lick the pitcher?"

I glanced at the stainless steel container that I used for foaming milk. It had already been wiped spotless. "Neko!" I said in exasperation. "You shouldn't have done that! This isn't our own kitchen."

And then, like a nervous twitch, I couldn't help but look over my shoulder. Couldn't help but see Mr. Potter yawn and stretch and climb to his feet. I lunged forward, throwing myself into the space so Neko could not look across the room.

"Jane, are you all right?" Jacques asked with Gallic solici-tousness.

"You're acting strange," Neko said, much more frankly.

"I'm acting busy," I insisted. "I have library work to do."

Another quick glance—Mr. Potter was coming our way. For some reason, though, Graeme, was paging through the ports book, keeping his head lowered over the pages. Yes. There was some luck left in the world.

"No," Neko said. "I've seen busy. You're not busy at all."

I made myself look toward Evelyn's office. "I know whether I'm busy or not. Come on, you two. Get going."

"Jane," Mr. Potter said, and I was forced to turn around. "I must be going. Time to walk Beijing and read the newspaper. It was a pleasure meeting your young–"

"Yes," I interrupted loudly. "Yes, you *should* be getting home. Beijing needs you."

"Your young what?" Neko started to ask, but I was already rushing Mr. Potter across the room.

"Have a wonderful day, Mr. Potter. And thanks again for the theater tickets. I'm glad you had a wonderful time in Pitts-burgh!" And I finally hustled him out the door.

By the time I got back to the coffee bar, Neko was eyeing another stainless steel pitcher. I slapped the back of his wrist. "Out!" It would take me ages to sterilize the one he'd already defiled.

"What was that man saying? A pleasure meeting your young what?"

"A pleasure meeting my boss. Evelyn. The woman who will fire me, if she sees me spending more time talking to you."

Neko looked dubious, but Jacques chose that moment to reach out for my familiar's arm. "Let us go," he said. "Eet ees time to get to work."

Work? What did Jacques do? He always seemed available to lounge around the cottage with Neko. But I wasn't about to look a gift Frenchman in the mouth.

"Goodbye," I said firmly. "And good riddance," I muttered under my breath as they finally left the Peabridge.

"Jane!" Evelyn stepped out of her office before I could cross the room and collapse on a chair next to Graeme. "Come in here for a moment. I think the idea of expanding American Families is brilliant. Positively the best notion you've had all year."

I looked wildly toward Graeme. He had finally stood up and turned to face me. He must have understood my pantomimed frustration. He made a great show of shooting his cuff, of glancing at his watch. He smiled slowly—sexily—and then he shrugged. "Later," he mouthed.

And then he headed out the Peabridge doors.

Defeated, I slumped into Evelyn's office, determined to find a way to torpedo daily American Family sessions.

17

"I don't know how you do it," I said to Melissa, watching her swirl the foam on top of a customer's latte. With a few deft twists of her wrist, she created one of Cake Walk's trademarks —a perfect heart of white foam layered against the darker coffee base.

She reminded me of clowns who create balloon animals at children's birthday parties. They could take one four-foot balloon and twist it into a tyrannosaurus rex. If I, on the other hand, attempted to do something as simple as a sword, I'd end up creating some phallic sculpture that would make a mother scream and demand that her child drop the so-called toy immediately.

Melissa handed off the latte and accepted a few dollars in exchange. As she rang up the sale, I took a delicate sip of my own tea—hot Mango Mamba, in an effort to battle the dank day outside. Staring out at the gloomy weather, I was grateful I'd taken a mental health day from the office. Some Fridays were meant to be spent away from work.

September had slipped into October and today's rain had fallen without a break, tugging leaves from the trees and melting them into a slippery mash on the sidewalks. The weather matched my mood. I sighed and said, "Melissa, we need to talk."

Almost two weeks had passed since I'd juggled patrons at the Peabridge. I'd invested a dozen more training sessions with David and Neko. I felt like I'd memorized every book in my basement and worked the spells in at least half of them.

I'd only managed to see Graeme on one night, and then I'd practically fallen asleep over a late dinner and a single glass of burgundy at "our" restaurant, Bistro Français. I probably would have embarrassed myself a few more times, but Graeme had fled on another business trip to London. He'd been gone seven days, and I was going quietly crazy. Our nightly phone conversations left me eager for his return, slated for next Wednesday night.

The spellwork was exhausting me. But I was equally worn down by the double life I was leading, the secrets I was keeping —from Neko and David about Graeme. From Graeme about the coven. It was long past time to relieve some of that pressure. Long past time to be released from my friendship test. Hence, my mental health day and my presence in Cake Walk on a Friday afternoon.

"Sounds serious," Melissa said. She frowned with a best friend's sympathy and leaned against the counter. Before I could dig up the words I needed, the front door opened.

Three women jostled into the store. Their cheeks were flushed, and their dripping hair was pulled back into limp pony-tails. Water pooled on the floor from their running shoes. Melissa smiled automatically, as if to say she could imagine nothing more than fun than a Friday afternoon spent mopping up after her customers. With a rueful glance to put my intended conversation on hold, Melissa called out to the customers, "Nothing like an afternoon run to justify something from Cake Walk! What can I get you, ladies?"

Their orders bubbled up, and I watched Melissa handle

both food and drink with an easy efficiency. She was *good* at what she did. Her coffee grinder never broke at crucial moments. It wouldn't dare, given the smooth control of her hands on the levers. The runners took their snacks and conquered a table, falling into over-oxygenated chatter about their workout.

"You were saying?" Melissa finally settled down, once again leaning against the counter.

I was saying… I sighed. I didn't want to confront my best friend, didn't want to seem as if I valued the man in my life more than her. I grimaced and looked over her shoulder at the calendar on the wall. There were lines of X's crossing off the days, the weeks, since I'd last hung out at the shop. A twinge of guilt crinkled the skin around my eyes, especially when I saw two red X's in the mix.

Two more first dates. First dates that a best friend should have known about. I nodded toward the wall. "What did I miss in the first date department?"

Melissa shrugged. "Are you sure you want to know?"

"That doesn't sound good." It didn't sound good on a couple of levels, I thought. Melissa would already have gushed about complete romantic fulfillment, about pledging the rest of her life to some man of her dreams. More importantly, though, Melissa shouldn't worry about censoring herself, about telling me *anything* related to her dating life. After all, we were best friends.

So-called best friends. I'd been falling down in that department for a while.

"Come on," I said, suddenly afraid at the distance spreading between us. "What happened?"

I saw the precise instant she decided to share with me, decided to overlook the evenings I'd spent with Graeme, the nights I'd spent under David's tutelage. Her smile was as warm as the ovens at the back of the shop. "Sequin?" she asked, nodding toward a large pottery plate of Ginger Sequin cookies.

She knew how much I loved them—they were as thin and

crisp as sugar cookies, but the crystallized ginger on top gave them an added bite. Melissa didn't make them often because the dough was tender, and the finished cookies had an unfortunate tendency to break across the middle. Unfortunate, that was, for Cake Walk's bottom line. It was a downright boon to those of us who helped Hoover up the so-called culinary disasters.

I nodded, and Melissa produced a plate of "rejects" from beneath the counter. I smiled as crunchy ginger goodness melted over my tongue. "Thanks," I said. "Now come on. Spill. Who was the first guy?"

She sighed. "A Dedicated."

That would be Dedicated Metropolitan Singles. A group of unattached men and women who got together to do good deeds on a regular basis. The organizers of each project accepted volunteers, then distributed a list of names and numbers afterwards, so workers could get in touch if they'd hit it off during the event.

Usually, Melissa's Dedicateds were earnest young men. Too earnest. Melissa had been lectured by a vegan for conducting the abattoir of her bakery, sacrificing all those eggs and pounds of butter that kept innocent chickens and cows in servitude. She'd been bullied into writing large checks to several Dedicateds' favorite charities. She'd been shamed into spending weekends patrolling local waterways, cleaning up other people's messes.

I wasn't a big fan of the Dedicateds, but I mustered a best-friend smile and asked, "So? Where did you go?"

"Dinner at Luna Grill and a movie."

I smiled cautiously. "So far, so good."

"Oh, the dinner was fine. He ordered the pasta—with three toppings, so I knew he wasn't a tightwad. I had the veggie panini."

"Melissa," I said, using a mock-warning tone. She knew I wasn't interested in the menu.

"And then we went to a movie."

"Which one?"

"That new documentary? About the crazy old man who built the Taj Mahal in the Nevada desert?"

"The one who saved tin foil since he was a boy?"

"Yep." She nodded grimly, as if a mock Indian monument were the greatest threat to mankind's safety and peace of mind.

"I take it the movie was lousy?"

"I wouldn't know. I couldn't see it. I spent the entire evening wrestling with the octopus sitting next to me. I mean, it's not like we're in junior high any more. Sometimes a movie is just a movie, you know?"

I knew what she meant. And I also knew the date hadn't been a complete disaster. It wasn't like the Dedicated had broken her heart. He'd merely wasted her night. She clearly hadn't liked the guy from the get-go; I could tell from her half-hearted description of the date. When Melissa really liked a guy, her disaster stories were much more elaborate.

Once again, a pang of conscience tweaked the skin around my eyes. What sort of friend was I? I should be indignant on my best friend's behalf, even if her bad night out hadn't been the disaster of a dating lifetime.

Melissa spread her hands flat on the counter. "I think I'm ready," she said.

"Ready for what?"

"To become a nun."

"Weren't you raised Jewish?"

She snorted. "Jewish. Catholic. I've got enough guilt for either. For both."

"What do you mean?"

She wouldn't meet my eyes. "I feel guilty about Cake Walk."

I was shocked. Melissa had never expressed the slightest hint of doubt about her bakery before. "What do you mean?"

She picked up a clean rag from the stainless steel sink and ran it over the already spotless countertop. "I'm worried about it. About me. I'm afraid I'm just indulging a hobby, when I should be working toward a career."

"What are you talking about? Cake Walk is *amazing!*"

"I need to grow my business." She managed a tremulous smile, and I saw just how much that admission had cost her. "I mean, I love what I'm doing here. I love running the shop and testing new recipes and stocking whatever I want to stock."

"But?"

"But it won't be enough in the long run. I need to expand."

"Open up another bakery?"

She shrugged. "Like I'm going to find the time to do that? The only reason I can make ends meet on the rent here is I staff the place myself."

"So what's changed?"

This time, she *did* meet my eyes. "What if I don't find some-one, Jane? What if I never meet the man of my so-called dreams?"

"What if you don't? What difference does a man make? You're running your own business, living your own life."

She sniffed. "That's easy for you to say. You've got Graeme. And even if things don't work out with him, you'll always have David and Neko."

There it was. The perfect window for me to address the friendship test. But I could hardly ignore the source of my best friend's distress. "Melissa! You're being ridiculous. You'll always have *me!*"

"You know that's not the same. And you're definitely not going to support me in my old age." She shook her head and tossed the rag back into the sink. She scored a perfect two points, but I don't think she cared. "I need to save more, if I'm ever going to retire."

"Retire? Melissa you aren't even thirty yet!"

"If I'd gone to law school, I'd be a partner by now."

"Maybe. But you'd also be exhausted and miserable and

hating every second of your life." I did some quick mental math. "And you'd be putting in twelve hours a day."

She looked around, taking in every corner of the funky little bakery. "Like I'm not doing that now?"

"Melissa, you're scaring me. I've never heard you talk like this before."

"I guess I've never been quite as tired of the dating scene before. Quite as ready to admit I'll probably be on my own forever." She took a deep breath, and I watched her exhale slowly, like a yoga master. "Enough," she said. "We aren't going to settle all my problems this afternoon. Why did you stop by? What did you want to talk about?"

Ach. This was not a good time to bring up my successful dating life. I took a Sequin and crunched it methodically. Only after I had swallowed ginger-scented crumbs did I say, "Look, it's nothing. We can talk some other time."

"Ja—ane." She drew my name into two syllables, the familiar wheedling of a best friend.

I took a deep breath and braved her gaze. "I-need-your-permission-to-tell-Neko-about-Graeme."

"What?"

I forced myself to speak more slowly, to enunciate the words so something slower than a hummingbird could actually understand me. The effort made me shiver, a bone-deep trembling, as if I'd been caught outside in a storm. "I need to tell Neko about Graeme. I've been going nuts, trying to keep them from finding out about each other, and it's just going to be worse when Graeme gets back from London on Wednesday."

"It was a friendship test!"

"It was. And I've kept it so far. But I think this is something real, Melissa. Graeme's going to be around for a while. I've spoken to him every night while he's been away, but I can't keep hiding what's going on. Neko lives in my *basement*, you know."

Whoops. Wrong thing to say. Melissa winced when I mentioned my familiar, and I knew she was thinking about how

Neko had stolen Jacques. Not that Jacques had ever really been up for grabs, but... Before I could figure out a way to make my argument stronger, the door opened and Siamese twins walked in.

Oh. Wait. They weren't actually joined at the hip; they only looked like it. While Melissa waited to take their order, the pair of young Goths took a long minute to kiss, intent on raking each other's tattooed shoulders with their black-painted fingernails. The taller girl finally came up for air, and Melissa took advantage of the break in the action to say, "Can I get you anything?"

"Um, yeah," the shorter one said. "Two plain coffees."

"Sumatran Samba or Colombian Caramel Cream?"

The customers had a whispered conference, requiring much nuzzling and a quick dart of his tongue studs against teeth. "One of each," came the final answer.

"With lots of room for cream," the other girl added helpfully.

Melissa nodded and poured two cups. The tough Goths proceeded to take them to the fixings bar at the end of the counter, adding enough milk and sugar to simulate coffee ice cream. Steaming coffee ice cream.

The rain chose that minute to pick up. Rather than risk their eye makeup running down their faces, the Goths huddled at a corner table, slurping their coffee like five-year-olds with glasses of chocolate milk.

Before I could resume my argument in favor of telling Neko about Graeme, the door opened again. I bit back an exasperated sigh. This was the bakery Melissa worried wasn't busy enough? The newcomer was a regular; Melissa grabbed a carryout cup before the guy even reached the counter.

Money changed hands, and I cleared my throat, anxious to make my point before yet another customer could interrupt us. "It's just that I feel like I'm lying," I said, keeping my voice low enough that the Goths couldn't hear me. Not that they'd be listening all that carefully. They seemed intent on breaking whatever law of physics said two bodies couldn't occupy the same point in space and time. I turned so I couldn't be distracted by their acrobatics. "Lying to Neko *and* lying to Graeme."

"'Lying' is a pretty strong word," Melissa said. She was going to fight me on this. The whole long-term life plan thing must really be bothering her. And the fact that Neko's current boyfriend was another stop on her long road of dating failure only heightened her resistance. I gritted my teeth. I was sorry about Jacques—I really was. And I was sorry about the octopus Dedicated, and sorry about every other bad date Melissa had ever suffered. But it wasn't fair for her to put the kibosh on my own happiness.

I opened my mouth to say so, but the damned bell above the bakery door jangled again. Melissa served up four Cinnamon Blondes to go. As the harried young mother added the paste-board box to her shopping bags, I almost offered to open her umbrella for her, to get her out of the shop and back into the rain. My fingers twitched, eager to turn the sign around on the door, to change it from "Walk on In" to "Walk on By".

Instead, I delved back into my argument, no, my *discussion* with Melissa. "It *feels* like lying," I insisted. She continued to look unmoved. "How would you feel if I hadn't told you about Graeme?"

"But you *did* tell me. You had to. I'm your best friend."

My sigh of exasperation threatened to burst into an angry shout, as yet another crowd of customers came in. There were four this time, and each wanted a complicated coffee drink, along with one of Melissa's trademark sweets. As the inevitable clanging and banging began, I forced myself to stop thinking about the friendship test, to set aside my frustration with Melissa. Today just wasn't the day.

Besides, I had plenty of other things to worry about. I glanced at her calendar again. October 6. I had three and a half weeks left. Twenty-five days until Samhain, until I was tested by the coven. Of course, if I lost my books and Neko in the testing, then I'd hardly have to worry about divulging the secret identity of my boyfriend.

"There!" Melissa exclaimed, and I realized we were once again alone at the counter.

"What?" I looked behind me to see what had caught her attention.

"You were doing it again."

"Doing what?"

"Zoning out. Going somewhere. Dropping out."

I hunched my shoulders defensively. "I don't know what you're talking about."

"You get this look in your eyes. Like you're staring inside instead of outside."

I forced myself to smile. "No great inside outside thing going on here. I'm just trying to enjoy a great cup of tea."

"You don't even like Mango Mamba that much. Listen, you've got to stop dwelling on things."

She was one to talk. "I'm not dwelling!" I realized how loud my voice had gotten, and I glanced at the Goths. I was only marginally comforted by the fact that they were busy testing each other's tattoos for secret Braille messages.

"You *are* dwelling. You're stewing. Look. Keeping Graeme a secret from Neko is not that big of a deal. It's not like you and that cat-freak are lovers or anything. He's a tool, right. A familiar. You don't owe him anything."

"That's a terrible thing to say!"

This time, the Goths did look over their shoulders, staring at me like I was a madwoman in some bizarre zoo. The taller one whispered something to her companion and they gathered up their leather jackets to brave the great outdoors, leaving behind cups, stirrers, and a litter of extra sugar packets.

Melissa clicked her tongue. "Come on," she said. "I didn't mean to hurt your feelings. It's just that you've become so distant. Sometimes I feel like if we didn't have the friendship test, we wouldn't have any friendship at all."

"I'm not distant. I'm busy!"

Melissa cocked one eyebrow at me—a gesture that always made me jealous, because I couldn't do it.

"I have been!" I said. "Nothing's changed between us. You're exaggerating to justify your stupid test."

"All right," she said, spreading out a hand-towel on the glass-fronted refrigerated case. "Tell me what I've got inside here."

"What?" Her question made no sense.

"Yeah. It's a Friday afternoon, and you've been standing here for over an hour. If you've paid any attention to me, to what's important to me, you'll have an idea of what I've got in the case."

I didn't have the least idea what was underneath the towel. "That's ridiculous," I said.

"Come on. Don't stall. You usually notice right off the bat."

"I've usually heard you talking about it, all week long."

"That's my point, exactly."

Oh.

I closed my eyes, trying to remember what I'd seen when I'd walked into the bakery. Nothing. I didn't have any image in my mind, no thoughts at all.

I thought about nudging behind the towel with my witch-craft. I should be able to do *something*. Maybe a mirror spell, working off of the chrome finish on the sides of the refrigerated case...

I glanced at Melissa's set jaw and realized that using my powers would only make things worse. Well, I knew her repertoire. I could make a guess—an educated one. Like best friends make.

"Hazelnut Claires de la Lune, Latin Lemon Merengues, and Savory Basil Cremes."

"Wrong, wrong, and wrong!" Melissa shook her finger at me with each incorrect guess. She was really angry. Really, truly hurt. And when she pulled back the towel, I began to understand why.

Devil's Nips—rum-drenched chocolate truffles.

Lime Stars—miniature key lime tarts, built on star-shaped pastry.

Mint Pillows—mint-infused meringue floating on a bed of home-made chocolate pudding.

Rum, lime, and mint. The ingredients of mojitos, our bonding cocktail of choice.

Melissa's voice shook. "The rum would have kept, but the limes were drying out. The oil in their rinds only last so long. And the mint was absolutely on its last legs."

"Oh, Melissa," I said, suddenly realizing how much I'd missed our evenings together. How long had it been? Over three weeks.

And then, before I could justify everything I'd been doing, before I could explain about Haylee and Renaissance art and the Kennedy Center and the centerstone—if I even *could* explain about the centerstone—the door to the bakery opened yet again.

This time, it was a mother with two adorable children, both under the age of five. Both barely able to see the baked riches spread out on the counter and in the glass case. Both afflicted with a terrible case of indecision, as they weighed the relative merits of Lemon Bears versus Chocolate Dreams, with the Mint Pillows thrown in for good, guilty measure.

I waited for the mother to badger them along, but she seemed in no hurry. I waited for Melissa to make some excuse, so she could at least turn back to me, at least acknowledge my awkward discomfort. I waited for the children to make up their minds—this wasn't the last time those kids were ever going to eat!

And when another minute ticked by, and another, and another, I realized I couldn't wait any more. I couldn't stand there, as if nothing was wrong. I couldn't hang out, and try to come up with an apology that would mean something.

I felt trapped. And that made me angry.

I shoved my tea mug back on the counter, and I gathered up my soggy umbrella. Melissa flashed me a "wait" look, but I only shrugged. What good would it do for me to wait? What could I really say, to justify myself? Why should I *have* to justify myself, when I had so many other things going on? And how the hell was Melissa worried about her long-term savings when she had so many customers that a friend couldn't get a word in edgewise?

When I got to the door, I turned back, but Melissa was smiling down at the indecisive little girl. The Devil's Nips glared at me from the refrigerated case, like baleful eyes witnessing my departure.

I stomped onto the cobblestones, my feet slipping in the sodden remains of a pile of leaves. I cursed and forced myself to walk a little more carefully. I'd been right to leave, I told myself. I needed a friend who had time to listen to *me*. Time to help. Not someone who sublimated her passive-aggressiveness into freaking baked goods.

I ducked into the lobby of the giant bank on the corner. While my umbrella dripped onto my shoes, I dug deep in my purse, fumbling until I found my phone. I punched in Graeme's number, taking a perverse pleasure that I remembered the digits, that I didn't need to rely on the phone's memory. I didn't have any idea what time it was in London, but this was an emergency. I needed to hear his voice.

One ring. Two. Three. Four.

Voicemail. I swore under my breath and hung up. No reason to leave him a message. No reason to tell him I'd just had a fight with my best friend. A fight she wasn't even fighting.

Before I jammed the phone back into my purse, I got another idea. I scrolled back through my recent calls. Of course the number was still there, from when I'd called to confirm our earlier meeting.

"Haylee?" I said when she answered on the second ring. "It's Jane. I know it's short notice, but I are you free for dinner tonight?"

18

W ell, at least the rain had stopped falling during my training session the following day.

Not that I could be certain, locked away inside my basement, kept company by no one but my warder and my familiar. David had insisted we extinguish the overhead lights for our all-day Saturday session—we needed to distance ourselves from the modern world and focus on ancient power. Blah, blah, blah.

We'd already burned through our first set of six tapers, tall dripless candles that had been brand new when we started. I'd just replaced them in the matched silver candlesticks that were part of my collection of witchy books, magic wands, and other artifacts. Part of the collection that would be forfeit to the coven if I failed to set the centerstone.

Let's face it—I enjoyed a romantic candlelit dinner as much as the next girl, but this was a little ridiculous. There was nothing romantic about trying to read by candlelight. In fact, in the past several hours, I had gained a healthy respect for Abraham Lincoln. I wouldn't have lasted one week, doing school homework by firelight. Our former president supposedly made it through *years*, studying in his log cabin.

That was then. This was now. My fingers itched to turn on the 60-watt bulbs above our head.

"You need to concentrate," David said.

"You've been saying that for hours," I groused. Neko winced and shifted a little farther away from me, as if he didn't want to be caught in the backlash of my warder's anger.

"You've needed to do it for hours." David sighed and pushed back from the table. "This isn't just some theoretical study, you know. That jasper egg was real. That email was a threat. Setting the centerstone will make you vulnerable in ways you've never been before. You must be able to defend yourself magically."

"I know," I said automatically. I hadn't told him about the three other email messages I'd received, all with similar pictures and messages. I knew self-defense was important. I needed to learn how to protect myself from ghoulies and ghosties and long-legged beasties. And things that go bump in the night.

But really. How many consecutive hours could one girl spend studying?

My stomach rumbled, and I cringed with embarrassment. My lunchtime peanut butter and jelly sandwich seemed a long time ago. Even *if* I had eaten a huge dinner with Haylee the night before.

She had agreed to meet me for supper, and after a bit of back and forth, we'd decided to get together in the city. Between the rain and my non-confrontation with Melissa, I was feeling deeply in need of comfort food, so we descended on Chez Billy Sud, a French bistro just off Georgetown's main street. I started with French Onion Soup and moved on to spicy lamb sausages, all served with fresh, crusty baguettes. There was no need to observe First Date Rules of dining decorum—it wasn't like I needed to worry about looking foolish as I struggled with strands of melted cheese from the soup. Or at least, I didn't worry a lot.

Haylee and I weren't through talking when we finished our main courses, so we ordered dessert (chocolate mousse for her, a homemade apple dumpling for me, complete with caramel sauce and fresh whipped cream.) I actually found myself quite pleased with my ability to smother my sorrows in a blanket of fat.

I'd told Haylee about my spat with Melissa, and she'd confirmed that my bakery-obsessed friend was out of her mind. There was no need to expand a business that was so busy the owner couldn't find five minutes to converse with a friend.

Haylee had asked me about how things were going with Graeme. I told her he was out of town and I was going a bit insane, waiting for him to get back. She'd laughed knowingly. Sympathetically. No, *empathetically*, like she knew how hard it was to wait for a loved one to return.

And there was something else.

Haylee taught me a new spell.

It had started as a joke. We'd wanted to linger at our table, long after ordinary customers would have paid their tabs and left. When the waiter came by to refill our mugs of tea for the fourth time, Haylee had touched his wrist with one of her long, perfectly-manicured fingers, cupping her Torch with her other hand and muttering a few words under her breath. "We'll call you if we need you," she said.

I'd watched as he blinked, confused and unbalanced for just a moment. He stumbled when he stepped back from our table, as if he'd been sleeping on his feet. Haylee repeated her touch and the hastily spoken spell when the hostess stopped by to see if we needed anything, and again when the manager drifted over to see why we were lingering. Each person who approached left with a dazed look and an inability to remember that we were sitting at the table.

Which wasn't a problem until I'd tried to pay our bill. I attempted to catch the waiter's eye, with no luck whatsoever. I waved to the hostess. I actually reached out to touch the manager's sleeve. At that last gesture, Haylee had laughed. "Don't worry," she'd said. "You can't reach them."

And we'd left—like high school kids skipping out on a meal of burgers and fries. I'd felt totally guilty, but also strangely thrilled by the power. In fact, my fingers tingled when Haylee accidentally brushed against them, our hands meeting in mid-air after I tried to flag down the manager. "How long will they be like that?" I'd asked before we parted ways by Haylee's Mini Cooper.

"Until I release the spell. I'll do it before I go to sleep tonight." I frowned, uncomfortable with the notion of shoplifting an evening's food and drink. Haylee's laugh was clear as the rain-freshened air. "Don't worry! They'll be good as new in the morning."

I'd waved as she drove off, but then I sneaked back into the restaurant to leave some cash on our table. There'd been no need to sneak, though. No one had noticed me at all, and our dishes still sat on the abandoned tabletop. I'd sighed and told myself someone would be able to notice the money in the morning.

"There," David said, jerking me back to the present. "You were doing it again."

Wasn't that exactly what Melissa had said the day before? "I was not." I sounded like a stubborn toddler, and I waited for David to dig in with a suitably immature, "Was too." Neko seemed to anticipate something equally sophisticated; his entire face tightened as if he'd received too many Botox injections.

Our brilliant banter was interrupted by a deep vibration, a thrum that shook the entire basement room. I glanced up nervously. "It must be raining again. Thunder."

Neko shook his head sharply, and I was reminded of a real cat's predatory concentration. He climbed to his feet and paced behind my chair, taking a couple of tight, controlled steps in each direction.

And then, I realized the "thunder" had not stopped. The low growl continued, barely at the edge of my hearing. It sounded as if the entire house was humming, as if the stone foundation beneath the cottage was vibrating. The note was deep enough that I wasn't certain I could hear it with my ears, but my body had no doubt. I felt it in my bones.

And it was getting closer.

Or larger. Or louder. Something.

I glanced at David, hoping he was ready to laugh off the vibrating threat. My warder, though, offered no hint of comfort.

Instead, he stood on the other side of the table. His feet were planted solidly on the ornate silk carpet; he looked as if he had manifested from its swirling design like a genie. His hands hung loose at his sides, his fingers extended downward. I tried to tell myself that if we were in real danger, if something truly threatened us from the astral plane, he would clench his fingers into fists.

But then I realized I'd never seen David make a fist. He channeled energy when he worked as a warder. He guided flows of power. He needed his hands relaxed, available to direct anything that came his way. Even when he had encountered the sword-wielding guard at the safehold, he had kept his body loose. Alert, but loose. Like he was now.

The noise—if it really was a noise—grew stronger. I could feel it with my entire body, sense it the same way that my eyes saw, that my ears heard. It was oppressive and large, like a wave of power rolling over the house.

But it wasn't a wave. It didn't rise and fall back. It didn't ebb and flow.

It only grew stronger. Steadier. Pushing like a crowbar against a padlock hasp.

This was magic. Magic I had never seen before. Magic I couldn't measure, couldn't predict. I tried not to picture it as a wall of carved jasper, blood-red stone cut through with jagged black lines.

"Neko," I said, gesturing sharply. He quivered, but he obeyed, coming to stand by my left side. I settled my fingertips on his shoulder, immediately feeling the familiar augmentation as he bolstered my powers, as the lens of his inherent abilities mirrored my strength back on itself, focusing my magic desires, my goals.

I tried to distract the vibrating force, to change its direction, break its concentration. There wasn't anything to touch, but I raised my hands in front of me, splaying my fingers wide.

I could feel the pressure of the malevolent force, sense it with every strand of my body and my mind. I imagined my fingers pushing against it, forcing into a doughy solid. Not stone. Not jasper. Anything but jasper.

There was a familiarity about the energy, a vaguely discernible *recognition* that let me move into even closer contact. I melded with the wall of power more closely than I would have thought possible. It felt like a physical thing, an object I could push against, something I could move.

I glanced at Neko, making sure he was still close enough for me to draw on. His almond eyes were huge in his face, and his cheeks were pale. He stared at me steadily, without blinking, and I thought he'd stopped breathing.

David, too, was completely still. Watchful. Ready. Waiting to see what I could do with my powers. Waiting for me to save us from whatever this strange attack might be.

I took three breaths to calm myself. I touched my forehead, to offer up the strength of my thoughts. I touched my throat, to offer up the power of my astral voice. I touched my heart, to offer up the devotion of my spirit. I took a deep breath, and I declaimed the words Haylee had whispered in the restaurant the night before:

> "Looking, thinking, sensing—be
> Elsewhere, somewhere, someplace. Free
> Your mind from what you see here,
> Let your thoughts be empty, all clear.
> Turn away.
> Turn away.

Turn away."

There was a flash of darkness.

It was the same flare of power I'd experienced countless times in the past, but it seemed all the more dramatic for our surroundings. For just an instant, everything in the basement—even the basement itself—disappeared. The six new-lit candles were sucked into darkness, even the orange afterglows of their wicks extinguished into nothingness.

My entire body ceased to be. I could not hear the sharp panting of my breath, couldn't feel the drumbeat of my heart. I could not smell the nervous perspiration that pricked beneath my arms, couldn't feel Neko's shoulder, couldn't see David's rigid warder body, interposed against the vibrating threat.

And then sensation flooded back, rushing in with a purity and a power that made me stagger. The candles guttered as if a tornado had passed overhead. My ears filled with the sound of my own galloping heart, as if I'd just stumbled across the finish line of the Marine Corps Marathon. I tasted salt at the back of my throat, and I realized I'd bitten my tongue.

The vibration was gone.

The oppressive force had dissipated, shattered into a million shards. I could sense their remnants, glimpse them from the edges of my witchy senses, like fog drifting away after sunrise. I struggled to gather up a handful, to study the ghostly remains, to figure out who had attacked us and why.

Before I could succeed, though, David stumbled and fell to his knees. He gripped his head with both hands and rocked back and forth. Even before I ran to his side, I could see that he was trembling, shaking like a man caught in a fever.

"Oh my God," I said. "Neko! Turn on the lights!"

I blinked as the overhead bulbs burst on. David flinched and buried his face in his hands, moaning like the wind around an abandoned castle's towers. I gripped his wrists, held them tightly, willing strength and power and calm into my warder.

Neko crouched beside us, glancing rapidly from my face to David's.

"David!" I said, desperately hoping he retained enough reason to answer me. "What should I do? How can I help you?"

"Wait. A. Minute." With a superhuman effort, he stiffened his fingers and raised them from his face. He let me move his hands into my lap, cradling them gently. His lips were grey; all of the color had drained from his flesh, leaving terrifying, bruised-looking pools beneath his eyes. If I hadn't known better, I would have bet good money he'd been ill for weeks, that he'd been recovering from the worst of the flu, bronchitis, and pneumonia combined.

"Let's get you upstairs," I said matter-of-factly, needing to do something, anything, to set things to rights. "Neko, put his right arm around your shoulder."

I wouldn't have sounded so calm, if I'd realized what a task I proposed. One witch with no upper body strength and a familiar who spent more time lounging on a couch than at the gym were nearly outmatched by a fit, well-muscled warder. The diet books always said muscle weighed more than fat, and David seemed determined to prove the rule.

I don't think we induced more than half a dozen bruises by knocking him against the stair railing on our way up. And his head was certainly already aching when Neko let it bang, hard, against the doorframe. And he honestly wasn't any paler than he had been by the time we dropped him on the sofa, wrestled his shoes off, and manhandled his feet up onto the couch.

"Run downstairs and blow out the candles," I said to Neko. "I'll get a damp towel from the kitchen."

By the time I returned with the towel in one hand and a glass of water in the other, David had pulled himself up into something resembling a sitting position. He winced as he leaned against the sofa's arm, but I had to admit he looked better than he had in the awkward position Neko and I had managed. He took the glass of water and swallowed with painful-looking bobs of his throat, but he batted my hand away when I tried to wipe the towel across his face.

I could have persisted. I could have done anything to his weakened body without even bringing my powers into play. But his lips had begun to return to a remotely normal shade, and the green-blue shadow of veins had faded from his forehead. I decided he was recovering, and I crouched back onto the edge of the coffee table.

"Thank you," I said, and my voice trembled as I thought of what might have happened downstairs. "Thank you for fighting that thing."

"What in the name of Hecate's own private hell did you do down there?"

Neko arrived at the top of the stairs, just in time to hear the end of David's furious question. I wasn't surprised to see my familiar turn tail, pulling the basement door closed behind him.

Coward.

I tried to understand the venom in David's voice. I assumed he'd been frightened. I knew he was exhausted. I could only guess how much his body ached.

But anger? Outright, untamed rage?

"I was trying to save us?" I cursed inwardly when my answer came out sounding like a question.

"By using Dark Magic?"

"Dark—"

"What gives you the right to work a Will Breaking spell?"

"Will—"

"And how did you think I wouldn't notice, when it was directed against me?"

"Stop!" I said, as he pulled himself up straighter against the armrest. He was shifting to expand his lungs, to get more volume so he could continue his excoriation. "Just stop for one damned minute!" I said. Whether he heeded my demand, or was merely too weak to go on, I took full advantage of his silence. "Directed against *you*? I was fighting against that...that thing! That pressure! The jasper wall that threatened all of us!"

And then I realized what was going on. I remembered David's stance as the thrumming power approached. I remembered his legs spread wide, his back strong and straight. His hands hanging loosely at his sides, fingers extended. And I recalled the odd familiarity of the magic I'd opposed, the way I had known it, somehow, some way.

David had been working a spell.

Some sort of warder's magic. I'd seen him use his powers before—finding a parking space when the streets were crowded, banishing fatigue, lighting candles and extinguishing them with a brush of his hand. I'd been the recipient of his headache-banishing spell several times, when I'd pushed my own powers beyond their natural scope.

But the thing that had threatened in the basement? That was an entirely new range of activities. That was completely beyond anything I'd seen from David before.

Without thinking, I threw the damp towel at him, hitting him square in the middle of his chest. He reacted slowly, grasping for the cotton cloth as it slid onto the cushion of the couch. "You bastard!" I said. "*You* were the power! You were pretending to threaten me!"

"I had to do something." His words were nearly as heated as my own. "You weren't bothering to practice."

"I've had enough practice!"

"*I* decide when you've had enough practice. I'm the teacher."

"And I'm the witch!" I sprang to my feet and paced between the coffee table and the front door. Dammit! He had really frightened me. He'd made me believe something malevolent was after us, that something truly evil was converging on my cottage.

"Now that we've established our roles," he said, ignoring the furious glare I shot his way, "Maybe you'll deign to tell me where you learned a spell that Hecate's Court has banned for public use?"

Haylee.

Haylee had taught me the illegal spell by working it on the unsuspecting staff at Chez Billy Sud. She hadn't *intended* to teach me; I had just observed. Apparently, I'd paid close enough attention to master the magic on my own.

Or *had* I mastered it?

Haylee's spell had certainly not had the same effect as mine. Everyone at the bistro had gone about their evening's business physically unharmed, waiting on other tables, collecting other patrons' money. No one had been hurtled to the floor; no one had been left bruised and breathless.

"Who?" David said again, and I could measure his recovery by the amount of raw rage behind the word.

It wasn't Haylee's fault my working was too powerful. It wasn't her fault that I threw my powers around. I couldn't throw her under the bus. "It doesn't matter who," I said. And then I had some insane impulse to distract him. "You shouldn't be angry. You should be proud of me."

"*Proud* of you?" I flinched at the volume of David's roar, even as a tiny corner of my mind was relieved by his rapid recovery. Surely Neko could hear downstairs. My familiar would *have* to interrupt if a life-and-death battle erupted up here. Wouldn't he?

"Proud of me," I repeated, with a bit less confidence. *In for a penny, in for a pound.* "We were working on self-defense, right? Well, I protected myself. I used my magic to keep myself safe. That's what you want, right?"

"I *want* you to be able to take your place as a witch, to keep the Osgood collection. Do you have any idea what would have happened if I hadn't contained your brilliant little working? Do you have a clue how quickly Hecate's Court would have swarmed here?"

The last smidgen of certainty drained from my mind. "H—
Hecate's Court?"

David sighed. "Jane, there was enough power behind your
spell to make it felt from New York to Georgia."

I couldn't think of a single response. How had I summoned
that much force? With one little spell, that I'd never even tried to
cast before?

David struggled up to a full sitting position, and I winced
with him as he rubbed the back of his neck. "You should know
this by now," he said. "The Court monitors Dark Magic.
There's a whole group of witches who watch specifically for
breaks in expected power. Your little show would have been off
the scale."

"So you stopped it?"

"I absorbed it. As best I could. I broke it up, anyway. If
anyone was already looking here, already focused on you, they
could see that something happened. But I kept the energy from
flowing out in one massive flood. The ripples will last for days. I
can't do anything about that."

"I'm sorry," I said, even though two words were completely
inadequate. But I was. I truly was. If my spell had been as
strong as David said—and I had no reason not to believe him—
then he had been my lifesaver, keeping me safe from the Court's
justice. I collapsed onto the other couch. "I thought I was
protecting us. Stopping that thing, whatever it was."

"You certainly did stop it." He managed a ghost of a smile.
For the first time since coming upstairs, I took a deep breath.
Everything was going to be all right. We *were* safe.

But that just made me return to my original question. "What
was it? What did you summon?"

His skin returned to its normal tone, and I realized he must
be blushing. David Montrose. My warder. *Blushing.*

"What?" I pushed.

"It was nothing."

"I felt it. Don't tell *me* it was nothing."

"It was just...you."

"Me?"

"You." He started to shake his head, but winced before he really got the motion going. "It was your stubbornness. Your refusal to work. Your rebellion. I gathered the energy and pushed it back at you."

My stomach dropped. "All of that came from me?"

Instead of answering, he closed his eyes and eased his head to the back of the couch. "I shouldn't have done it. I just wanted you to feel a touch of danger. A hint of what could be arrayed against you. Placing the centerstone isn't a game, Jane. It's the most serious working of magic. You're going to build a safe haven for witches, a protected place for generations of practitioners to come. You'll be vulnerable at that working. You have to be prepared for the worst."

I spluttered for something to say, fighting against the chilly finger of fear that traced my spine. "So, you think I'm the worst."

He smiled, even though he didn't lift his head. "I think you are your own worst enemy. For now." Before I could muster a response, he did sit up, and he looked straight at me. "Jane. This is important. Who taught you the Will Breaking Spell?"

"No."

My fingers jangled, like limbs awakening from a sound sleep. I couldn't tell him. There must be some mistake. Something I had done wrong. I must have twisted Haylee's working when I attempted to reproduce it on my own. After all, Teresa Alison Sidney certainly wouldn't let Haylee run around working Dark Magic. The strongest Coven Mother in recent history wasn't going to let her best friend violate the laws of Hecate's Court.

David's voice was persuasive. "Jane, if I'm going to keep you safe, I need to know."

For just a moment, I was thrown back in time. I was sixteen years old and sitting on Gran's couch. I was explaining that she needed to give me the car keys, needed to trust me with her

Lincoln so Melissa and I could drive to a friend's party. I'd pulled out the big guns: "Gran, you taught me everything I know. Now you have to trust me."

It had worked well enough then. Melissa and I had gone to the party, and I'd drunk nothing stronger than water, afraid that even caffeine would rattle my nerves for the drive home.

Now, I looked David straight in the eye. "David," I said. "You taught me everything I know. Now you have to trust me."

It was a great line.

"Fine," he said at last. "I trust you. But don't do anything stupid, Jane."

"Stupid!" I managed to sound scandalized at the notion.

"Stupid," he repeated, and then he waved toward the table. "Could you get me another glass of water? And open up the basement door. Tell Neko it's safe to come out."

I did just that. And as I filled David's glass at the kitchen sink, I wondered what I was going to say to Haylee when I saw her again. And how long it would be before David left, so I could call Graeme. Just to talk. Just to share the craziness of my witchy day. Like any friends did. Any good friends. I pasted a smile on my face and counted the days till Wednesday.

19

"Well, well, well," Gran said. "It's hard to believe another month has gone by."

Clara joined in with, "And it's so nice that the city has finally cooled off."

Great. We were reduced to chatting about the weather. The weather and the calendar. Were those proper conversational topics for grandmother, mother, and daughter? For three generations of witches?

But that was the problem. We couldn't talk about witchcraft. Couldn't talk about the single most important thing in *my* life. Ever since Gran had asked me to abandon the coven and I had refused, I had felt unable to mention anything to do with magic. Yet, as autumn gained its true grip on our shortening days, I felt I had fewer and fewer topics to share. Setting the centerstone always lurked at the back of my mind.

I certainly wasn't about to mention the telephone conversation I'd had with Graeme the night before, after David had finally left, after Neko had gone off with Jacques, intent on making the Gallant Gaul stop sulking about an entire day lost to witchy business.

I took a quick sip of my water, trying to cool the heat that rose to my cheeks. After all, it wasn't every evening I threw myself across my couch, whispering into my phone. It wasn't every evening I could have written a letter to a porno website. "Dear Hotmamas.com: I never thought I'd be the sort of girl to seduce a man over the telephone..." It wasn't every evening that I pleaded—begged—a man to catch a transoceanic flight and come up and see me some time.

Graeme had laughed and told me he couldn't break away. He was in the middle of a business deal. I could hear him typing away on a computer keyboard, hear the chime of incoming email. When I'd complained that it was the middle of the night in London, that no sane man would be working, he'd told me that just proved he was insane.

So, he wouldn't hop an earlier flight. But that hadn't stopped us from talking. And after a while, I didn't *want* him to appear on my doorstep. I would have been too embarrassed about some of the things I'd said.

No, I wasn't going to repeat any of *that* conversation to Gran and Clara. That certainly wasn't what our monthly bonding brunch was all about.

Before I could think of suitably neutral tinder to toss on our dying conversational embers, the waitress brought our meals. Luna Grill was known for its build-your-own omelet brunch—I'd been reminded of the restaurant when Melissa recounted her disastrous date with the Dedicated. Looking at our current plates, I couldn't imagine a more clear depiction of our personalities.

Gran had ordered the heart attack special: a three-egg omelet with ham, bacon, and sausage folded in, along with cheddar cheese. She'd shrugged when she ordered, accepting my gaping disbelief with a gentle smile. "If cholesterol hasn't done me in yet, it's not going to get me now."

Clara was going through a vegetarian phase. It had to do with discovering the true balance of her Pisces nature, with recognizing complete respect for all living things. In fact, she had initially declared herself a vegan, but since she had no idea how to cook tofu, tempeh, or beans (without the addition of a good piece of salty ham), she'd retreated to a broader definition of spiritually healthful eating. Egg white omelet for her, then, with spinach, mushrooms, and sautéed bell peppers. I'd wanted to ask if she could hear the vegetables, weeping for their lost siblings, but I thought that might only increase the friction between us.

I had been looking forward to a good egg dish when I got to the restaurant, but my relatives had put me off my game. I decided to abandon omelets altogether and stick with my ongoing theme of comfort food. Therefore, I was feasting on French toast, with a gallon of maple syrup dumped on top and enough whipped cream to make butter superfluous. I'd added a side of fresh fruit. After all, breakfast was the most important meal of the day.

Okay. So we'd finished with the calendar. With the weather. I couldn't talk about the coven, and I wouldn't mention Graeme. What did that leave?

"Things have been busy at work," I said, promptly filling my mouth with a giant bite of maple-soaked bread to avoid any immediate need to reply to their inevitable questions.

"I wanted to go to your Monday lecture, but I got busy with opera things," Gran said. "Did I see you were discussing mothers and daughters in colonial times?"

"Where did you see that?" I asked, surprised, and a little impressed that Gran stayed in the Peabridge intellectual loop.

"On the library's website, of course" Gran said, taking another dainty bite of her Lumberjack Special.

I almost choked on a strawberry. Gran? On the Internet?

"Don't look so surprised," she said. "You did set up my computer for me."

"I thought you just used it for email."

"For email. But when I get bored, I skate the Internet."

"Surf," I said.

"Surf. That's right." Gran nodded happily. "Have you ever heard of Wikipedia?"

"Um, yes," I said, carefully keeping my tone neutral.

"Your Uncle George showed me Wikipedia. I'm working on correcting some of the opera entries. Can you believe someone actually wrote that Tosca has *four* acts?"

Clara answered before I could. "Scandalous," she said. Her eyes met mine over her coffee cup, and I could tell we were both trying to keep from laughing. Sarah Smythe, Wikipedia editor. My grandmother never ceased to amaze me.

Gran said to me, "I've been trying to get your mother involved. There are hundreds of entries about astrology. Someone should make sure they're accurate."

"And I'm just the person for the job," Clara said, clearly quoting Gran's recruitment speech as she pushed food around on her plate.

I asked, "Is there something wrong with your omelet?" If the kitchen had messed up, I wanted them to correct things—I felt responsible for the meal because it was my turn to pay.

"Oh, no." Clara sighed and speared a wilted leaf of spinach. "I just don't like vegetables in my eggs. Eggs cry out for cheese. And maybe a bit of ham."

She looked forlornly at Gran's omelet, and Gran obliged by pushing her plate across the table. "Help yourself, dear. I can't eat another bite."

Clara speared meat from Gran's plate and augmented her own breakfast, while Gran and I refrained from commenting on the shocking collapse of Piscean vegetarianism. In fact, I helped myself to a bite of the meaty omelet as well, mentally justifying that I had to balance my sweet breakfast plate with Gran's savory one.

Gran, undeterred from her earlier topic of conversation, said, "Clara, you *are* the person for the job. I can't imagine anyone with more knowledge than you about the signs of the Zodiac."

I sank back on my wooden bench and glanced up at the mural of a sun painted on the opposite wall of the restaurant. He was smiling as if he approved of our conversation. All was right in this little world. Gran was meddling quietly in our lives, expressing her absolute certainty that Clara and I could both conquer whatever we had in front of us. And, if history was any guide, it was just about time for the spotlight to turn on me.

"And you, Jane," Gran said without missing a beat. "You should take a look at their article about coffee. I'm certain you could add something, given your experience at the library."

Great. I wasn't an expert on colonial history. Or even on clothing in eighteenth-century America. Nope. Gran wanted to crown me latte queen of Georgetown.

And I wasn't even that. Melissa could pour rings around me any day.

I wasn't going there. I wasn't going to mention Melissa, to let Gran and Clara sort through our little friendship wrinkle.

As if she were reading my mind, though, Clara chimed in. "You could ask Melissa, if you had any questions."

So much for that plan. I made my voice firm. "I have no intention of editing the coffee article. I drink tea." To prove my point, I tried to to catch our waitress's eye, to solicit a new pot of hot water.

Clara dug in. "I'm just saying that between the two of you, you have a lot of information. You and Melissa could work very well together."

"If we were speaking to each other."

Oh. I guess I really *did* want to talk about Melissa. Why did my conversations with Gran and Clara always steer toward whatever one thing I was absolutely, positively certain I didn't want to talk about?

Gran pounced. "You had a fight with Melissa?"

"Not so much a fight. Just a...gap."

"A gap?" Clara looked as if I were speaking a foreign language.

"We've both been busy," I said, after stabbing another bite of Gran's omelet to buy time for a reply. "She thinks I'm too tied into...other things." No reason to drag Graeme into the fray. Clara would want to work up his star chart, and Gran would have us married off in a matter of hours.

"And you think?" Gran prompted.

"I think if she has a problem, she should talk to me directly." I excavated another sliver of ham. "She avoids me, and then she tries to make me feel guilty. We just need some time apart from each other."

"It sounds to me," Clara said, fishing for the last piece of sausage on Gran's plate, "as if you need to spend more time *together*."

"Ha," I said, without a trace of humor. "I don't think that's going to happen any time soon." I was determined to get the conversation away from my Melissa. "Anyway, no matter how you slice it, I'm not an expert on coffee. If I have one more fight with the stupid coffee grinder at work, I might walk out of the library altogether."

Gran clicked her tongue. "That doesn't sound like you, Jane. You love the Peabridge."

"But I hate what it's become. Or what I've become, working there. We're a victim of our own success. Evelyn's little coffee bar is so popular that I spend more time making fancy coffee drinks than I do researching colonial history."

"Maybe you need to get rid of the coffee drinks."

"Like Evelyn would ever go for that." Everything was so simple in Gran's world. She could just dust her hands and be free of any little problem, like coffee grounds, or steamed milk, or chocolate syrup, or whipped cream.

Clara chimed in, and I could tell she was trying to be reasonable, trying to act as peacemaker—a novel role for her. "Why did Evelyn add the coffee bar in the first place?"

I decided to play along. "To add money to the operations budget. It's amazing how much we make with overpriced caffeine. Starbucks has already done our job for us—they have everyone conditioned to spend four dollars on a cup of coffee. If we charge five and offer the convenience of drinking it in the library, they're only too eager to pony up."

Gran nodded. "But what if you simplified things? Cut back to regular drip coffee? That would make things easier for you, wouldn't it"

"Our profits would plummet. Even if we charged three dollars a cup, there wouldn't be enough takers to meet Evelyn's bottom line."

"But drip coffee and a sweet? A cookie or a brownie or something like that?"

That wasn't a bad idea. We'd had patrons asking about scones or muffins to go with their ill-gotten coffee gains. And if I only needed to slam a brownie on a plate after I poured regular old coffee... "Where am I going to find the time to bake?" I argued.

Gran smiled. "It takes fifteen minutes to make an entire tray of brownies. You know that. We made enough for school activities while you were growing up."

I glanced at Clara to see if the reference to my mother-deprived childhood had rattled her. She was intent, though, on sneaking a strip of bacon from the ruins of Gran's omelet. Oblivious, Gran went on: "If you don't have time, I'm sure Melissa can help you out."

"Melissa is the one that doesn't have the time," I said flatly.

"Well, I'm sure you could manage without too much difficulty," Gran said.

A line of Shakespeare came to me, from the scrambled depth of my literary mind: *Thou art a mocker of my labour.* It was from *As You Like It*, said by Orlando. I didn't bother saying the words out loud—neither Gran nor Clara would have recognized it.

Melissa would have. I shoved that thought aside.

Besides, Gran wasn't mocking me. Maybe I *should* consider a little baking at home. The more I toyed with the idea, the more it made sense. If we could get people to fork over five dollars for a cup of fancy coffee, what would people pay for a brownie? A couple of chocolate chip cookies? I didn't have to produce anything as complicated as Cake Walk did.

Sure, we might lose a buck or two by dropping the expensive lattes and cappuccinos, but we'd still make a relative fortune on drip coffee. And we'd make up the difference—and more—on baked goods, even after we paid for the ingredients.

More importantly, if I were freed from the tyranny of foaming milk, I could return to my true love—working as a reference librarian. It was worth fifteen minutes spent baking each night, if that meant I could work as a librarian during the day. I sat back on the bench, enamored with the notion of trading in my coffee bar apron.

Sure, there would be complications. Mr. Potter would have to give up his mocha—although I bet I could convince him to accept a shot of chocolate in a regular cup of coffee. And he really *should* cut back a bit on whipped cream. And we'd have to limit the children's access to sugar. One cookie apiece, and only after the American Family sessions were over, with the little darlings back in their mothers' tender loving care.

"Okay," I said. "I'll think about it. Brownies and cookies aren't a bad idea. Maybe we could start in November."

"November first," Gran said, as if we'd reached a firm agreement. "Nothing like the start of a new month for a new venture."

The waitress came by to take our plates. I had left two slices of French toast. Clara had abandoned the vegetarian dregs of her omelet. But Gran's plate was completely clean, thanks to all of our help. The waitress gave my grandmother a new look of respect. "Can I get you ladies anything else? Dessert, maybe?"

Before anyone could decline, I said, "We'll see a menu, please." After all, brunch without dessert was…breakfast.

We ended up ordering one slice of apple pie and another of

cherry. At the last minute, Gran broke down and ordered the special of the day, turtle cheesecake. The waitress shook her head in obvious amazement as she wandered back toward the kitchen.

Only after we were safely ensconced with enough calories to support an entire football team did I see a meaningful glance pass between Clara and my grandmother. Gran inclined her head once, silently issuing an invitation for Clara to speak.

When only silence followed, I said, "What?"

"What what?" Clara countered.

"What are you supposed to ask me? What are you afraid I'll get upset about?"

"I don't know—" she began, raising her hand to her to the kunzite crystal that she had started wearing around her neck months ago. Kunzite. Unconditional love. Family harmony.

At least she was trying.

Gran cut in. "We wanted to ask about the coven. Are you still seeing those women?"

Those women. Gran made it sound like they were prostitutes. Or child-murderers. Or worse. (What was worse? I'm sure suburban witches headed up some sort of nefarious list.)

I took a deep breath and held it for a count of five before daring to answer. "I have to. I'm one of them. And I'm setting the centerstone on Samhain."

"Samhain?" Gran asked.

"Halloween," Clara answered before I could. All her years with the New Age folks had served her well. She shook her head at me. "It's just that the coven causes so many adverse ripples in the ether."

That was a new one, even for Clara. "Ether?" I finally managed. "I'm not sure I can sense the ether."

Nope. I didn't quite get the tone right. Clara's shoulders stiffened and her lips pulled into a tight little frown. Gran leaped into the breach. "The ether doesn't matter, dear. We're much more concerned about whether they're being nice to you."

Ah... They wanted to know if my play-dates were working out well. If anyone had pulled my hair or told me I was fat or twisted my name into a taunting playground chant. "Actually," I said, "I had a great dinner with one of them just the other night."

And we left without paying the bill. And she inadvertently taught me a dark magic spell that nearly knocked out my warder and made my familiar quiver in the basement with terror.

I rushed past those details. "I think we're actually becoming friends. We went to the National Gallery of Art a few weeks ago to look at the Renaissance paintings. I don't think I've done that since I was in high school."

"That sounds lovely, dear," Gran said. I saw the look she flashed Clara, the silent command to accept what I was saying, to support me.

Clara swallowed hard and asked, "What's her name? Your friend?"

"Haylee. Haylee James."

"Isn't she the one with the short hair?" Clara jumped on the recollection immediately. "The snooty one who's best friends with Teresa Alison Sidney?"

I stared at the jovial sun mural on the opposite wall and took another five-count. A slow one. "That's the one. She's actually been quite nice to me. The nicest of the bunch."

That wasn't saying much.

Okay, neither Gran nor Clara said those words out loud, but I could read their faces—printed in size forty-eight bold Times New Roman.

"Hey," I said, anxious to change the topic of conversation. This brunch had gone too well to be sacrificed to the coven and its politics. "Did you know that in the Renaissance, the peacock was a symbol of saintly purity, because people thought the birds' flesh didn't rot?"

Clara took the conversational bait. "In Eastern art, peacocks counteract venom. The birds ate snakes, so they were thought to protect people from poison."

I actually beamed at her. She'd given us a clear path out of the coven discussion. "I've been learning a lot about antidotes lately," I said. "It's amazing the powers that people ascribe to different herbs. We might plant the Peabridge gardens differently next spring, to reflect some of the colonial beliefs I've uncovered."

And that was it. We made it through the last of brunch without another uncomfortable silence. Neither Gran nor Clara asked anything else about Haylee, or Teresa Alison Sidney, or David, or Neko, or anything else witch-related. When the waitress brought our bill, I slapped down my credit card. It was good to be able to treat when it was my turn, good to continue this new-found family tradition.

After the meal, I walked my grandmother and Clara to Gran's massive Lincoln. Clara opened the driver's door while I walked Gran around to the passenger seat. I put my fingers on the handle, but she stopped me by settling her palm against my cheek.

"Call Melissa, darling."

I glanced away. "I will."

"Good friends are hard to come by. We can't afford to let any slip away."

Unexpectedly, tears rose in the back of my throat. What was up with that? After a great morning, a fine breakfast, and some good conversation, I was surprised to find myself on such an emotional edge. "I won't," I whispered.

Gran stretched up and kissed me on the cheek. "Promise me, Jane. Promise you'll call her."

Another Gran promise. Well, she hadn't specified *when* I needed to call Melissa.

"I promise," I said.

I just wasn't ready yet. Besides, I wasn't even sure Melissa would have time to talk to me. Not with Cake Walk as busy as it was.

The queasiness in the pit of my stomach had to be a reaction to French toast and omelets and dessert and cups and cups of tea. What else could make me feel so miserable as I walked away from the best looking car on the road?

20

I glanced around the cottage one last time before answering the knock at the front door. It wouldn't do to keep Haylee waiting. Not when I had barely summoned the courage to invite her into my home in the first place. Not when I was hoping she'd distract me from staring at the telephone, waiting for it to ring, waiting for Graeme to announce he was home from his business trip. Not when I'd spent an hour and a half straightening, neatening, getting everything in order.

If Melissa had been coming over, I wouldn't have cared. She'd seen me at my worst—dust bunnies under the bed, mascara streaks under my eyes, broken hearts under fake smiles. But I hadn't spoken to Melissa since she'd brushed me off in the bakery. Of course my promise to Gran niggled at the back of my mind. I *would* keep it—eventually. When I had time.

"Haylee!" I said, throwing open the front door.

"Oh my," she said, stepping into my living room. "Isn't this *quaint.*"

Quaint. Not a great word. She probably thought the place was tiny. Bizarre. Inconvenient. But as I looked around, I thought it looked like home. I said, "I'm so glad you could come by!"

"I'm glad you phoned," she said, with a confident smile that helped me forget she probably had a dozen names on her dance card. After all, she was an accomplished witch and the best friend of Teresa Alison Sidney. Why *wouldn't* she have a million plans for a crisp autumn evening?

I made myself grin and say, "I was just going to mix some drinks. Come into the kitchen?"

"Can I help?"

"No!" This was ridiculous. I was as jumpy as if this was a date. I forced myself to take a calming breath. "I've got everything I need. Please. Just make yourself comfortable. Tell me what you did today."

Haylee obliged, sitting on one of my ladder-back chairs. She'd gone shopping that morning, she said, trying to find a little black dress for an evening wedding next month. She was looking for something velvet, something wintry, but it had to be comfortable in an over-heated ballroom.

I made polite listening noises as I went about my hostessing business. I found the fish-decorated pitcher on my first try and almost yelped with success. What a great sign! Neko sometimes hid it, and I was reluctant to summon him upstairs, to beg for his help in any aspect of entertaining.

I reached under the sink and prowled through my stash of alcohol. There, toward the back, was my fifth of rum. There was a two-liter bottle of soda water as well. Perfect. I looked calm, cool, and collected. Organized. Prepared. Mojitos R Us, twinge of Melissa-guilt be damned.

And then, I opened the refrigerator.

I reached for the bowl of limes that I'd left on the top shelf, but it was empty. No problem. I must have put them in one of the crisper drawers. I tugged open the fruit drawer and was greeted by one sickly lemon and some desiccated husks that might have been grapes in a former life.

Before I could question my sanity, I saw a single Corona

beer, nesting in a cardboard six-pack container. Corona. Mexican beer. Most frequently served with a sturdy slice of lime. I grated my teeth and told myself that Neko would pay for his unsanctioned little Cinquo de Octubre celebration. Especially since it was already October 11.

Fine. Hayley and I would have mojitos made with lemon instead of lime. A new drink. For my new friend. I reached to the back of the refrigerator, for the tall glass of water that was holding my mint and keeping it fresh.

No glass. No mint.

I had the presence of mind to wait until Haylee reached a breaking point in her story—she'd found the dress she wanted, but she couldn't find the proper heels. Everything was four inches high and slutty; she was looking for two inches and seductive. I smiled and laughed and agreed that fashion designers hated women.

Then, I politely excused myself and marched to the basement stairs. I flipped the light switch on and off twice, an agreed signal that told Neko to get his paws off Jacques and prepare for me to descend the steps.

And when I reached the foot of the stairs, it was immediately clear what had happened to my mint. "What are you two doing?" I cried.

Their faces were covered with a bright green paste. They looked like creatures from the Scope lagoon—their hair was slicked back and their eyes peered out from identical pale white circles.

Jacques barely moved his lips as he answered me. "Mees Jane! We should have saved some of the mask for you!"

Neko nodded in cautious agreement, tilting his head back to preserve his cosmetic application. "Jacques said that these mint facials would do wonders for our pores. I can feel everything tightening up!"

I wanted to tighten *him* up. Instead, I looked over at the

bookstand, at a precariously balanced cutting board strewn with denuded stems of mint, balanced by a bowl rimmed with a hardening paste. At least they'd shifted my crystals handbook to one side, closing the cover to protect the valuable parchment pages from mint facials.

No time to argue. No time to rant. Haylee was waiting upstairs. "Did you save me anything at all?"

"I think there's still a beer in the fridge," Neko said helpfully. "Beer is good at relaxing people. You look like you could use a good relaxation regimen."

I stalked upstairs before I could waste my time telling him what I thought of his "relaxation regimen."

I forced a smile at Haylee when I came back into the kitchen. "Sorry. I thought I had more mint downstairs."

"Oh! There's a basement in this place?"

"It's fully finished. That's where Hannah Osgood's books are. Neko stays down there, too."

She looked doubtful. "And Neko keeps a supply of mint?"

"No," I said ruefully. "Not tonight." I turned back to the counter. All right. I'd already decided to make a new drink for us—it was just going to be a little newer than I'd planned. Lemon. Rum. Soda. How bad could it be?

That bad.

Haylee smiled politely after she took her first sip. But then she set her glass down on the table. Firmly.

I tried mine, to figure out what was wrong.

Nothing—if you liked watery, fizzy rum. My single desiccated lemon had added no measurable flavor. I'd tried to compensate by pouring the rum with a heavy hand, and I'd dumped in a generous amount of sugar, but the result was a cloying mess.

"Well," I said. "At least we have something to eat." I extricated a plate of vegetables from the fridge, pleased that I'd outsmarted my familiar by choosing something healthy. "We might as well go into the living room. Make ourselves comfortable."

And so we did. But I couldn't really *get* comfortable. I was nervous, afraid I wouldn't seem witty enough, engaging enough, plain and simple *fun* enough for Haylee to bother wasting an evening in my company.

All of a sudden, I remembered Melissa's dating strategy, the Five Conversational Topics she cultivated before each blind encounter. I should have come up with a similar list for Haylee, fallback for conversational lulls like the one we were weathering.

Maybe those Lemon Monstrosities weren't so bad, I was beginning to think. At least they'd provide a little social lubrication. And then, the basement door opened.

"Bueno sera, muchachas!"

"What the—" I couldn't keep from exclaiming. The creatures that sashayed into the living room had some vague resemblance to Mexican peasants—they had huge sombreros and brightly colored blankets thrown over their shoulders. But they would only be cast as Mexican peasants in a gay porn film. One that put a premium on black silk shirts open to display waxed chests. And tight leather pants. And perfectly hydrated skin, with expertly relaxed pores. "Um, hello?" I managed to squeak.

"Mi burro es muy perezoso," Neko enunciated carefully in a schoolboy Spanish accent.

"Mi burro es su burro," Jacques confirmed.

"And where the hell are you going?" I asked, not at all certain I wanted to know the answer.

"Julio is throwing a party," Neko said. "We're late. We missed the first three days."

"Days?" I asked, trying to rein in my shock.

"He's celebrating Juan Peron's birthday." When I just gaped, he continued, "Juan Peron? The little Mexican man who sells coffee? Think, Jane! Why else would we be drinking Mexican beer? And wearing sombreros? And serapes?" He trilled the "r" in the last word.

I somehow managed to form an answer. "Juan *Valdez* sells coffee. And he's from Colombia. Juan Peron was from Argentina."

"Argentina?" Neko sounded scandalized.

I glanced at Haylee, to see how she was handling this. She looked shocked, but I couldn't tell if she was overwhelmed by Neko's geographic ignorance, or if she was overcome by his sartorial splendor. I grimaced and said, "Juan was married to Eva." Blank stare from Neko, and a baffled shake of the head from Jacques. "Little Eva?" I prompted. "Evita?" And I braced myself for the inevitable connection.

"Don't cry for me Argentina!" Neko belted out, with such enthusiasm that his sombrero tumbled to the floor.

"Argentina." I nodded.

"Do zey drink Corona een Argenteena?" Jacques asked.

"I suspect they will tonight." I shrugged. Nothing I said was going to change their costume. And at the tail-end of a three-day birthday blast for a dead South American demagogue, who would care what country they represented? "Be careful, you two. Don't stay out too late."

"We weell go back to my apartment after zee party," Jacques said. "Julio leeves right upstairs."

Who was I to argue? I certainly didn't relish the thought of my noisy, inebriated familiar stumbling around the house at three in the morning. "Fine," I said, but then I tossed a last warning glance toward Neko. "Don't forget, though. David wants to work tomorrow afternoon. I'm leaving work a couple of hours early."

Neko tilted his sombrero to a more flattering angle. "Afternoon," he said. "*Noche*."

"No. *Tarde*. Afternoon. Don't keep us waiting."

Neko frowned for a moment, but then he seemed to remember his battle against unsightly facial lines. He swooped over to me and air-kissed both cheeks before he and Jacques tumbled out the front door.

As silence drifted back over the living room, I winced and turned to Haylee. She was staring at the door with a look that could only be horror. "That was your familiar, wasn't it?"

"Yes." I couldn't quite meet her eyes.

"And he goes out on his own?"

"I awakened him on a night of the full moon. I, um, didn't know any better at the time."

Her eyes narrowed for just a split second. "And that man with him?"

"Oh, that's Jacques. He's just a friend."

"A...friend." She shook her head. I somehow suspected Haylee's familiar lived a different life from Neko's. A very different life.

"More carrots?" I asked brightly, desperate to change the topic.

Haylee shook her head again. "No. No more carrots." She finally pulled her gaze away from the front door. I hoped she could forget the image of our twin Argentine-Colombian-Mexican peasants, debauching their way through the streets of Georgetown. I was doing my best to do so.

"Hey," she said at last. And her voice was the one that I remembered from Chez Billy Sud. Inviting. Gossipy. Friendly. "Tell me more about that guy you mentioned. What's his name? Graeme?"

I felt the familiar giddy crush-rush, the breathless swell of excitement that came from talking about the cute boy in study hall, the handsome captain of the football team, the dream date for prom. "What about him?"

"Why do you like him so much? What makes him different from every other bad-date single guy in town?"

"I can't describe it." I shrugged and tried anyway. "When I'm with him, I have this feeling that he's paying attention to me. Like I'm as important to him as he is to me. Like he thinks about me even when we're not together."

Haylee scrunched her pretty face into a comic nightmare. "Sounds like stalker-time to me."

I thought of my magic flowing across the Potomac, washing over Graeme and me after we had watched *Romeo and Juliet*. I remembered the safety I felt when I was with him, the enveloping calmness as he placed his arms around me. I felt the spark he raised deep inside me, with the brush of a kiss on my lips, with the fire of his palm against the small of my back.

"This is different," I protested. "*More*. Not creepy. Besides, I haven't even seen him in a couple of weeks. He's been out of the country on business."

"When does he get back?"

Busted. "This afternoon, actually. At least he was supposed to."

"Then he hasn't called yet?"

"No. But I'm sure he's exhausted, with travel and everything."

Haylee nodded, and I thought she was going to let the topic drop. Then she asked, "Have you even seen his house?"

I was immediately defensive. "No."

"His office? Anything about his private life?"

She had no way of knowing she was touching one of my hot buttons. The I.B. had kept his private life secret from me. Every aspect of it. Including his wife. I raised my chin defiantly and said, "He's told me *a lot* about his private life. Haylee, he says that women in his family were witches. He's not afraid of me. Not afraid of my powers. He *honors* me for my witchcraft."

"Honors you?" Her smile was sly, and the knowing look on her face made me blush. Before I could retort, she said, "Let's go."

"Where?"

"To Graeme's house."

"I don't even know where he lives!" I shrieked, forgetting the power of that confession.

"Are you saying the Peabridge reference librarian can't locate a simple home address?"

"I'm saying—" But I stopped myself mid-sentence. I *did* want to find out where Graeme lived. I wanted to visit his house. I wanted to know more about him, to prove to Haylee—to myself—that he was the man for me. I pushed myself up from the couch's deep, comfortable cushions. "I'm saying," I repeated, "that going to Graeme's house is an excellent idea. Besides, I still have his jacket. From that night at the Kennedy Center."

"It's only polite to return things that don't belong to you," Haylee justified for me.

"Only polite," I agreed.

I don't know why tracking Graeme suddenly seemed like such a good idea. Maybe I was trying to impress Haylee. Maybe I was trying to convince myself—reassure myself that Graeme and I *did* have something special going on, something real. Maybe I was trying to exorcise the Insufficient Bad Boy once and for all.

Or maybe I was just desperate to get out of my "quaint" little cottage, with my boring plate of healthy vegetables, and my undrinkable pitcher of sugary rum and soda.

Before I knew it, I'd fired up my computer and completed a quick Google search or three. Then, Haylee and I were in her Mini Cooper, driving to the Virginia suburbs, following directions from her GPS. We pulled up in front of a brick colonial and stared at its lush green lawn, its welcoming porch light, its stone walkway and late-blooming marigolds.

Marigolds, I thought automatically, with an attention to detail that would no doubt have thrilled David Montrose. Useful for healing wounds and resolving stomach ailments. And for brewing into an aphrodisiac tea. And those day lilies over there, I thought frantically, mentally steering away from aphrodisiacs. Good for treating wounds and burns and snake bites. And nervousness.

Not that there was anything to be nervous about. Nothing at all.

"Wait!" I cried, reaching out to touch Haylee's arm as she pulled up to the curb in front of the house.

She braked to a stop, then looked at me questioningly.

"Drive around the block!"

She smirked, but she obliged me. And then she complied with my request to park four houses away, so we could casually walk past Graeme's front door, trying to catch a glimpse through his gauze-curtained windows. (No luck—the sheers were just heavy enough to keep us from seeing anything useful.) And she kept me company as we strolled down the block, trying to snag more of a view from the side of the house. (Still no luck—not enough space between buildings.) His back yard. (Yet more no luck—a locked gate barred our way.)

I thought about cajoling Haylee into walking around the block, trying to count off the lots, to figure out which house backed on to Graeme's, which backyard would be even with his. Before I could even try, though, Haylee shook her head and walked up the stone path to the front door.

Just like that. Brazen. Confident. Like she owned the place.

She ignored my chittering excuses, waiting only long enough for me to fold Graeme's jacket over my arm and come stand beside her on the marble flagstone. Then, she raised the brass knocker (shaped like a perching gargoyle), and let it strike— once, twice, three times.

My throat went as dry as Neko's so-called wit. My heart pounded so loudly in my ears that my entire body throbbed. I tried to remember why I had let Haylee drive me here, what I had thought to gain by hunting down Graeme in his home. His private home. His personal space. On his first night back in the country for nearly two weeks.

"This was a really bad idea," I whispered to Haylee.

She smiled at me, calm as the cloudless sky above us. "I think you'll be surprised."

Before I could swear off surprises, before I could vow to live a boring life forever, a life of humdrum, stultifying ordinariness, the deadbolt whispered back. The doorknob turned. For the first time since our little field trip began, I thought to push my hair out of my face, and I wondered what had possessed me to leave home without even the quickest foray into my stash of makeup.

"What—" Graeme's eyes fell on Haylee, and he looked surprised, shocked at this stranger standing on his front porch. She inclined her head toward me, and his gaze automatically followed. "Jane!" He glanced back and forth between us, rapidly processing what had to be an astonishing sight. His killer smile quickly banished any look of consternation. "And to what do I owe this pleasure?"

His accent seemed thicker in the evening air, and my knees went trembly all over again. "Welcome home!" I said, realizing both of them were waiting for me to say something. To *do* something. "Haylee and I were out, um, having dinner. We thought we would just stop by and say hello. And I wanted to return your jacket. And welcome you back to town." Well, that sounded idiotic, even to me. To compensate, I thrust his coat toward him. "Here!" He took the garment reflexively.

"I didn't realize you had my address," he said. But he smiled when he said it. I had to hold on to the fact that he smiled.

"I'm a librarian," I said.

"How could I forget?" He extended a hand to Haylee. "Graeme Henderson," he said.

"Haylee James." She shook with the efficient disinterest of a business executive. "Pleased to meet you."

"The pleasure is all mine." He looked back at me before I could even think about being jealous, before I could contemplate what my hair would look like if it were cut as short and spiky as Haylee's. Or how my eyebrows would appear, if I plucked them so carefully. Or how my cheekbones might be coaxed out with just the right combination of blush and toner.

"Where are my manners?" Graeme asked rhetorically. "Won't you come in?"

"We don't want to be any trouble," I said. But Haylee was already smiling her cool smile and striding into the foyer. It would have been rude not to follow her. Downright uncivilized.

"No," Graeme said. "No trouble. No trouble at all." He closed the door after us and gestured toward the living room. "I just finished unpacking upstairs. I was going to catch up on some work." He nodded in the general direction of an oversized roll-top desk. Spreadsheets drifted across the horizontal surface and an adding machine anchored the paper storm. "Day, night, hour, tide, time, work," Graeme quoted, crossing the room to pull down the roll top and hide away his labor.

"Play!" I said, finishing off the quotation. I couldn't help but flash a triumphant smile toward Haylee. "It's a line from *Romeo and Juliet*," I explained.

"I see," she said. Her cool voice dampened a little of my enthusiasm. I caught her sideways glance toward Graeme, and I knew she was measuring his blond good looks. I stood a little straighter.

Graeme, apparently oblivious to the inspection, waved us toward the couch. "Please. Have a seat. I'll just be a moment."

And he was good as his word. Haylee perched on one of the oversized armchairs, while I (exercising girlfriend's prerogative) actually sat on the couch. She and I managed to chat about the coffee table book—*Washington DC, Then and Now*—and she was just urging me to look up the Peabridge, to see if there were any photographs of my home, when Graeme returned with a serving tray.

"I trust you both drink red wine?" We nodded, and he made a little show of pulling the cork and pouring the pinot noir. He passed around a small plate of chocolates, and I selected the perfect truffle, pleased beyond all reason that my boyfriend— yes, I was feeling confident enough now to think the word—my *boyfriend* had such sophisticated treats ready and waiting for random visitors.

Graeme settled back onto the couch beside me, looking utterly comfortable and relaxed, as if madwomen showed up here unannounced more evenings than not. "Sometimes," he said, "It's best to go with the simple pleasures in life."

I thought of my disastrous attempt at cocktails and nodded agreement.

"So, Haylee," he said, turning his attention to my friend. "I'm afraid I don't recall Jane telling me what you do."

He was right, of course. I hadn't mentioned her to Graeme, because I hadn't realized she was going to be important in my life. Going to be my strongest link to the coven. Going to be my new best friend (at least until I kept my promise to Gran and ironed things out with Melissa.)

Haylee sipped from her wine before she answered. "I'm an interior designer," she said.

Graeme glanced around, as if he were seeing his own living room for the first time. "I'm embarrassed to think of what you'd say about this place."

She laughed. "It's actually quite well done. Strong. Masculine. Except for that lamp, there." She pointed toward a rather delicate stained-glass lamp sitting on a table in the corner. "It doesn't quite fit in with the rest of the place."

What an eye, I thought. I wondered what impression I'd made with the eclectic collection in my cottage.

Graeme scowled at the lamp. "That thing. I'm keeping it for a friend."

"Ah. The hazards of friendship." Haylee raised her glass, as if she were toasting someone, or something. Before I could decide whether I should join in the toast (possibly implying that Graeme had bad taste in friends) or stay silent (letting Haylee take an odd, controlling hand in our conversation), my witchy new best friend changed the topic herself. "Your accent," she said to Graeme. "I can't quite place it. North of London, isn't it?"

Graeme nodded. "Cambridge. You've got a good ear." I wondered if I would ever be able to pick apart British accents so accurately.

And that led us into a discussion of travel. They were both much more worldly than I. I managed, though, to parlay my one trip to London into an entertaining tale about being lost in airports and almost missing not one, not two, but three different planes.

Hearing Graeme speak wistfully of home, I began to plot another trip to England. Maybe I'd go with him on his next business trip. We could go to Stratford, see William Shakespeare's birthplace for ourselves... Wander through towns that still had thatched roofs and Tudor half-timbering... Sit in a pub and eat steak and kidney pie...

Well, steak pie, anyway. I would pick out the kidneys.

All of a sudden, a clock chimed twelve from somewhere deep inside the house. I hadn't heard it earlier, but the deep, steady toll of the hour immediately made me think of Teresa Alison Sidney and the safehold, somewhere farther out in the Virginia suburbs. I darted a glance at Haylee, but she didn't seem to make the same connection.

In fact, she seemed not to make any connection at all. She was stifling a yawn against the back of her teeth—a move made obvious by her thin, elegant bone structure. "I'm sorry," she said, when she realized both Graeme and I were staring at her. "I must be more tired than I thought."

I started to jump up. "*I'm* sorry! I'm so inconsiderate! And Graeme, you must be exhausted, after your trip!"

I wasn't quite sure how the night had gotten away from me, except that I was enjoying being with Graeme—with Graeme *and* Haylee—so much. I'd been mesmerized by the conversation —by Haylee's cool wit and by Graeme's charming... Charming everything.

Haylee shrugged. "I should drive you home and then get back out here."

"Out here?" I asked.

"I live in Arlington, too."

I was mortified. Here it was a work night, and Haylee would be stuck ferrying me around for another hour after I'd already kept us all up too late. "Here," I said, reaching for my phone. "Let me call a cab."

"We can do better than *that*." Again, that perfect Graeme smile. It made me shiver at the same time it melted something deep inside me. "Why don't I give you a quick ride home?"

"I—" I couldn't even think of a lie. I wanted him to drive me home. I wanted him to do a lot more than that.

Haylee must have sensed the meaning behind my hesitation. "Well," she said, giving in almost too quickly. "If you truly don't mind…"

Graeme glanced at me and closed his hand over mine. "I truly don't mind." He excused himself to get his car keys and Haylee took advantage of his absence to flash me a wicked grin. "You look *smitten*," she said.

"I am," I confessed.

Graeme returned and made short work of turning out a couple of lights. He unlocked the front door and ushered us back into the brisk autumn night. My waist tingled where his fingertips brushed against me.

"Good night," Haylee said at the curb. "Don't do anything I wouldn't do." She winked and got inside her car.

We settled into Graeme's Audi, and I automatically pulled the seatbelt across my chest. He turned the key and the motor purred to life. I leaned back against the headrest, taking a deep breath against a sudden surge of expectation.

No business meetings. No cell phones. No strange, last minute interruptions.

Even with my eyes closed, I could hear the grin in Graeme's voice. "And what do you think she meant by that?"

"I have no idea," I said, managing a tone of perfect innocence.

His laugh was a throaty growl. I leaned forward, then, eager to be home. Eager to park in front of the Peabridge. To walk down the garden path. To fumble for my house keys.

And then we were there.

I reached for the light switch. "We don't need the light," Graeme whispered, centered in a pool of moonlight in my living room. His lips were already hot against my throat.

And he was right. We didn't.

21

W hen I woke, I lay in bed with my eyes closed, thinking I was suspended in a magical sort of movie reality. Early morning sunshine crept into my bedroom window, turning my eyelids crimson and warming my face like a honey bath. I was aware of my cotton sheets with every inch of my skin; every pore seemed awakened and energized, freed from the tangle of my usual pajamas.

I remembered to listen for Graeme breathing beside me, but I couldn't hear him. Fighting a sickening swoop in my belly, I contrived to roll over, careful to wrap myself in the top sheet. I took a deep breath to steady myself, and then I popped open my eyes.

Gone.

One quick glance confirmed that my clothes were strewn—strewn!—about the bedroom. So, I hadn't imagined that part of the previous evening's entertainment. But my dream date, my seductive Brit (who had kept up a steady purr of accented endearments through a level of activity that rapidly made me forget the entire English language) had disappeared.

I swore and kicked off the sheet.

I slashed my arms into the sleeves of my robe, cursing as the belt tangled around my waist. I was an idiot. A stupid, gullible idiot. Why had I let Graeme into the house? Why had I believed him when he whispered sweet nothings in my ear? Er, against the hollow of my throat? Okay, against every erogenous zone ever identified in any sex manual anywhere?

I couldn't even blame alcohol. My one glass of pinot noir had worn off well before Graeme's clock struck midnight.

No. I had deluded myself. Once again. I had let myself believe that Graeme was the one, that he was the solution, the salve. I was such an idiot. Swearing at myself, I yanked open my bedroom door.

And my heart nearly stopped beating.

The door to the basement was open.

Surely I would have heard Neko come home, drunk as he must have been on Mexican (or Colombian, or Argentinian) beer? He wouldn't have changed his plans to stay over at Jacques's place, anyway—not unless something had gone seriously wrong with the Frenchman.

"Neko?" I called downstairs, hating the tremulous note in my voice.

"Good morning."

Graeme. Answering immediately. Cheerfully.

Relief slammed into me so hard I needed to grip the door-frame to keep from falling. "Good morning!" I cried, and then I hurtled down the steps.

He had pulled on the khakis he'd worn the night before, and his white cotton shirt was wrinkled. He looked adorably sloppy with the tails untucked, like an incorrigible little boy who'd had enough of fancy family affairs. His hair was rumpled as well, and—truth be told—I could make out a few lines of fatigue around his eyes.

Well, I wasn't at my freshest either. It wasn't like either one of us had slept a great deal the night before. It took time to get used to another body in bed, to grow accustomed to sighs and snores and shiftings on a mattress. Not that I ever snored. Not me.

Graeme grinned. "I couldn't sleep any longer—jet lag—so I came down here."

"There isn't much to see," I said. "That is, if you aren't a witch."

"Oh, I don't know." He reached around me to pick up the book he'd been reading. I could just make out the flowery script stamped in gold on the worn leather cover. *Love Spells That Work.* What had Neko and Jacques been thinking leaving *that* around? Graeme touched the tip of my nose with the book's spine. "You've certainly cast a spell on me, Jane Madison."

I let him fold me into his arms. Into his arms, and then onto the couch. He circled his fingers around my wrists, keeping me from undoing the buttons that marched down the long front of his shirt. His warm lips distracted me with memories from the night before. I twisted on the couch to keep from slipping onto the floor, and that's when I saw it.

On the bookstand. In the center of the room.

A jasper necklace, entwined with sprigs of greenery.

"Stop!" I pushed Graeme off me with a vehemence that must have stunned him. He staggered to his feet, but I was already crossing the room, scarcely remembering to tug my robe back into place. My voice shook as I asked, "Did you put this here?"

Eyes widening, he glanced from the stone beads to my face. "What?"

"The necklace! The jasper! Did you put it there?"

"Why would I—? Jane, what's wrong?"

But it wasn't just the jasper. It wasn't just the threat of an anti-witchcraft necklace, or the herbs, which I could now identify as thyme and oregano, twining around the stone beads.

It was the book.

Or, more precisely, the *missing* book. My handbook on crystals was gone.

I wasted a moment looking for it, even though I was certain it had been on the stand the night before. I'd seen it beside Neko's mint concoction; I had specifically noted its parchment pages were safe from the cosmetic compound the guys had made.

"Did you move a book from here?"

Graeme was staring at me as if I had gone mad. "A book?"

"A leather-bound book. It was right here. On the stand. Where the necklace is now."

"The only book I touched was the love spell one. It was on the couch, draped over the arm. I was just going to close it, to protect the spine, and I started reading a few pages. But I didn't touch anything else. I *wouldn't* touch anything else." He closed his hands around my upper arms, lending me strength as I started to tremble. "What, Jane? What is it?"

I barely whispered. "Someone broke in here. It must have been last night. After Haylee and I left to visit you. Someone stole a book on crystals and left...that." I pointed toward the necklace.

He followed my trembling finger and then turned me around, so I couldn't stare at the mottled blood-red stones. "What is it?" he asked urgently. "What does it mean?"

It meant I was no longer safe in my own home. It meant David had been right, that the risk was increasing as we got closer to Samhain. It meant someone was working harder than ever to keep me from succeeding at setting the coven's centerstone.

"It means I have to call my warder."

"Your warder?" He sounded so completely confused that I was catapulted back to mundane reality. I must sound like a madwoman. Who worried about finding an unexpected necklace, or losing one little book? Who jumped to life-and-death conclusions on a morning when she should be stretching sex-sore muscles and contemplating breakfast in bed?

"I'm sorry, Graeme. This has to do with the coven. With the

witches I've told you about. That thing is a threat." I gestured to the necklace. "A sign to witches that they aren't welcome. That they might come to harm."

"Do you…" He swallowed hard, then looked at me without flinching, "Do you want me to do something with it? Throw it away? Take it to the police?"

I shook my head. "The police would laugh you out of the station."

"Jane," Graeme said, and I felt the tiny hairs on his knuckles as he brushed the back of his hand against my cheek.

"It's all right," I said, but I was pretty sure I was trying to convince myself. Not Graeme. "Or, it will be. But I need to get my warder here now." I caught Graeme's hand in mine. "And I don't want him to see you."

Graeme shook his head. "I want to help you."

"The biggest help is leaving. Don't make me explain why you're here."

His eyes widened. "If you think he'll be angry… If you're afraid he'll hurt you—"

I shook my head—a terse motion. An angry one. But I didn't even know who I was angry with. "No. It's not like that. But David thinks I've made…poor choices before. I don't want to waste time explaining us, when I should focus on finding my book."

Graeme still looked uncertain, but he nodded, reaching out to pull me close to his chest. His arms felt like a solid wall around me. I longed to lean against him—to collapse against him—for a long, long time. His fingers strayed to the sash at my waist, and I finally had to close my hands over his. "Graeme…"

He pulled back, his rakish grin nearly stopping my heart. "Call me. Let me know what happens."

"You know I will."

And he was gone. Up the stairs. Out the door. Gone.

I knew what I had to do. I'd done it once before, in a panic. Now, I measured out my power, poured it into a single steady stream of magic. "Neko," I thought, broadcasting my power like a radio beacon. "Neko. I need you. Home. Now." And for good measure, I included David in my transmission. After all, he'd sense the power I was spending. Better to invite him, than have him show up unannounced.

Not that I'd done anything wrong. This time.

I closed my eyes, the better to concentrate. "Neko!"

"No need to shout." He stood in front of me, surveying the basement with the wariness of a hunter. Without his silly Mexican accessories, his leather pants and silk shirt seemed sleek, dangerous. His eyes darted into the corners of the room, and his nose twitched warily. I couldn't help but glance down at my robe, wondering just how much Neko could sense about my escapades the night before.

I shivered and jerked my sash tighter. Neko was my familiar, not my jailer.

He found the necklace immediately. Stalking around the bookstand, he eyed the jewelry from every angle, his nostrils twitching as he recognized the thyme and oregano. He reached out one hand, a frown marring his smooth features, and he started to breathe through his mouth—as if he could sense more that way. As if the very air in the room could tell him what had happened. Who had been here, invading our privacy. Our safety. Our home.

"What do you sense?" David's voice was quiet, but I could hear the urgency behind his question. I wasted a moment, wondering when I'd become so accustomed to his presence that I didn't flinch at his silent arrival.

Neko cast his head to one side. "Nothing particular."

"What does that mean?" prodded my warder.

"I can feel *you*," Neko said, shoulders twitching in annoyance. "And Jane of course. And Jacques and me."

Jacques! Could he be the source of the eerie jasper warnings? That was absurd, though. He'd never shown the slightest interest in anything magical. He was interested in Neko's body and—just possibly—my familiar's mind. But Jacques had nothing to do with the threat in my basement.

"And?" David prompted.

"And...the coven."

I waited for him to elaborate, but I ultimately needed to prod: "The coven?"

"I can sense them here." He moved his hand in the air above the necklace.

"All of them? Like they held a meeting here?" I couldn't picture all those aristocratic women crowded into my basement. Their warders would have needed to wait upstairs, maybe in my bedroom. Their familiars would have been painfully obvious, lurking in the shadows of my too-small basement room. Everyone would have been disappointed in the caliber of my refreshments, unless a pitcher of watered down rum and a few dried-out vegetables on a platter were their idea of slumming fun.

"Of course not," Neko snorted, and my fantasy image disappeared. "But there's a...dusting. Like talcum powder, settled from the air."

"How many were here?" David asked, his eyes darting around the room, as if he expected to find malefactors still lurking in the corners.

"One?" Neko said, but he made his statement a question.

"When?" David said.

"I can't tell." Neko twitched and shook his head in exasperation. "My mind knows the jasper wasn't here when I left last night. But I can't sense how it got here. Something is blocking me."

I asked, "Could someone have made it materialize here? Without actually coming into the basement?"

David's eyes narrowed. "It's possible, but that would take a tremendous energy drain. Most witches don't have anywhere near that level of skill. Especially not working with something as antithetical to magic as jasper."

"But Teresa Alison Sidney——" I started to argue.

"Oh, Teresa Alison Sidney could do it." David nodded slowly. "She might be the only witch in the Eastern Empire who could. Aside from you."

I rubbed my arms with cold hands. My belly turned queasily at the notion that the Coven Mother herself might stalk me. "But why would she do that?" I asked, not caring that my voice was tiny. "Why would she try to frighten me like this?"

David glanced at me and seemed to awaken from his own spell. Squaring his shoulders, he crossed the room and settled a handkerchief over the necklace and herbs. The oily discomfort in my gut eased as soon as they were out of sight. "I don't think she is," David said. "There's no reason for her to intimidate you."

"But who…" I trailed off, realizing that if Teresa Alison Sidney hadn't made the jasper materialize, then someone actually *had* broken into my cottage.

"Were you home all night?" David asked.

I braced myself for his disapproval. "No."

Threading an even note of steel through his words, David asked, "Where did you go?"

"Virginia," I hedged.

"To the coven?" David's tone was disbelieving. "By yourself?"

"There are lots of other places in Virginia," I said. "Who says we went to the coven?"

"Who's 'we?'"

My lips clamped shut. I felt like a teenager, caught sneaking out after curfew. Neko glanced between us before he said, "Haylee." He flashed me an apologetic smile, shrugging as if to say his reply was for the best.

"Haylee James!" David's surprise was explosive. And a tiny part of my brain was relieved that he was so upset about Haylee. I just might get away without needing to admit I'd brought a man home after my excursion to the wilds of

Virginia. After all, David was my warder, not my father. He had no reason to police my romantic liaisons.

"She's my friend," I answered hotly.

"No she's not," David said.

"She's the only person in the coven who has actually reached out to me! She's the only one who acts like I might possibly be treated as an equal after Samhain!"

David's jaw tightened, and I knew from experience that he was barely restraining himself from making some unpleasant observation. He started three different sentences before he settled on, "Did Haylee come down here last night? Did she have any time alone with the collection?"

"Of course not! Neko and Jacques were here, getting ready for their party. Haylee and I left shortly after they did." I rolled my eyes. "David, Haylee wasn't alone in the cottage the entire time she was here." I flattened my voice, making it absolutely clear I would not tolerate more discussion about my only witchy friend. "It wasn't Haylee."

David sighed and ran a hand through his hair. That motion chilled me even more than the jasper necklace had. David only ran a hand through his hair when he was truly worried. When he actually believed I was in danger, that something might go terribly wrong.

"I don't want you staying here." His tone was flat. Absolute. "Call Melissa. See if you can sleep at her place for a while. Just until after Samhain."

I shook my head, even before he was through issuing his command. "No."

"She's your best friend. She'll understand."

Right. We weren't even speaking to each other. She'd be just thrilled to have me sleeping on her couch, to have my colonial dresses filling her closet. And I'd have a grand time, shlepping up here to the Peabridge every morning, walking the streets like some Revolutionary War re-enactor. "She won't," I said. "You can't make me stay with Melissa."

David must have heard the adamance in my tone. "Then go to your grandmother."

I pictured my pink bedroom, complete with little corners of tape that had once held up posters of dreamboat movie stars. "I can't do that. Besides, how would I explain it to her? She'd worry herself sick."

"Jane—"

"David," I countered. "I'm not giving in to them. Whoever they are. Let's just *say* Neko's right." My familiar yelped indignantly, but I rolled forward without stopping. "Let's say the warnings are from someone in the coven. Someone who broke in after Haylee and I left last night. That person wants to set me off balance. She wants to keep me from centering on my witchcraft, from being ready on Samhain." I firmed my resolve and raised my voice. "But I won't give in. I've got to stay here, to study. To center myself. To learn everything I can."

"Jane—"

"David, I've got less than three weeks." I did some quick math. "Nineteen days to prove myself. Don't disrupt that time. Don't make me turn everything *else* in my life upside down when I should be focusing on magic!"

I could see he was wavering. He looked at the hundreds of books, at my container of crystals. He actually looked at me— for long enough that I started to feel uncomfortable.

"If I let you stay here..." I nodded, encouraging him. He kept his eyes on me and reached into his pocket before he said, "You have to promise..."

He pulled out his keychain and cupped his Hecate's Torch in his palm. Both of us stared at the sleek silver lines, at the art deco design that seemed to glow with a light of its own. I realized once again how much I wanted to have my own Torch, how much I longed to be welcomed into the coven, to have this testing and judging and suspicion behind me.

David reached some sort of conclusion in his own mind. He

fumbled with the keychain, and then he passed the Torch to me, slipping his liberated keys back into his pocket.

"I can't take that!"

"Yes, you can."

"But it's yours!"

"It's mine, and part of my warder's powers are linked to it. Enhanced by it. I can keep better track of you if you're wearing it." He gestured with his ring, the smooth circlet hinting at the power that was his birthright. "Put it on a silver chain, and keep it close to your heart."

I felt a blush flood my cheeks, and I tried one last time. "I'm not allowed to have a Torch until the coven gives me my own."

"If you don't take this one now," David said evenly, "you might not last long enough for the coven to give you your own."

I swallowed hard, unable to keep from looking at the now-hidden jasper necklace. Whatever bravado I had mustered to argue against moving in with Melissa or camping out at Gran's, I really *was* disturbed that someone had broken in the night before.

I closed my fingers over the Torch. I could sense David's presence in the metal amulet; I could feel his quiet, calm presence emanating from the silver. I remembered when Gran had offered me her Torch, weeks before, on the bench near the Howard. I had told Gran I couldn't take her brooch; I had known its magic would clash with my own.

I didn't feel that danger from my own warder's charm. It wasn't opposed to me. In fact, it felt as if it had already melded with my own magical abilities. "All right," I said.

David didn't look happy over his victory, but he managed a nod. "Silver," he said. "Chain. Now."

I tried not to watch as he swept up the jasper necklace and the herbs, all the while using his handkerchief as a buffer. I didn'tt breathe easily until I had his Torch around my neck, warming a spot above my fast-beating heart.

22

D avid sat back on my couch, the hunter green fabric enveloping him like a cloak. He sighed like a man who had just finished consuming a porterhouse steak. With a loaded baked potato. Along with a bottle of aged cabernet. "Perfect," he said, favoring me with one of his rare grins. "I don't think we have anything left to review."

The past two and a half weeks had flown by—the fastest eighteen days of my life. Things had gone smoothly—surprisingly smoothly.

I hadn't found a single jasper ornament anywhere in or around the house. While I *did* continue to receive emails from my anti-witch stalker, I'd set up a filter to block them from my computer screen. (After all, there weren't any work-related reasons for anyone to send me messages with the words "coven," "safehold," or "centerstone.")

I knew David remained wary, but he hadn't policed me unfairly. I suspect he'd been reassured when I'd committed to working with him on a daily basis. Tonight, though, was the first time I'd heard him express actual contentment with the progress we'd made. I felt a bit like a lost little girl, uncertain about the kindly rescuer who was offering me a free ride home.

Even as Neko executed an elaborate, spine-twisting stretch, I asked, "Are you sure? I've still got fifteen minutes before I have to get back to the library."

While David glanced out the window toward the back of the Peabridge, Neko hissed his disapproval. My familiar was less than pleased with the amount of time we'd spent working, even if he understood exactly how much rode on my Samhain magic. "Why don't you astonish Evelyn?" David suggested. "Get back from your lunch hour on time for once."

I spluttered, but I could hardly come up with a snappy reply. In the past few weeks, I'd become an absolute star at stretching out my mid-day break. Anyone could tack on five or ten extra minutes by claiming to lose track of time, or blaming traffic, or complaining about slow service at a restaurant. But with the final phases of preparing for the centerstone working, I had routinely dragged lunch out to two hours.

By good fortune, Evelyn had let slip a few weeks ago that she loved a shot of cinnamon syrup in her morning coffee. Like the wicked witch I was, I'd used that knowledge to the utmost of my ability. Five minutes early, cinnamon syrup, and a dollop of whipped cream served with a wink and a smile—so far, I'd had no problem finagling the extra time to study setting the centerstone.

But now David said we were through. I couldn't believe him. "Shouldn't we go over the spells one more time?"

"You know them all by heart."

"How about reviewing the ingredients for the herbal wash?"

"You memorized them weeks ago."

"Practice casting a circle for protection?"

"You can do that in your sleep. Have done, since the jasper necklace. Right?"

I nodded, crossing my fingers to exclude the evenings I'd spent with Graeme. I wasn't going to cast any circle that would keep *him* away from me.

David went on, obviously unaware of that little duplicity.

"Besides, I'll be there. Me, and all the other warders. You don't need to worry about protection."

I was ready. Me. To face the coven and join with my sisters once and for all.

When I was in elementary school, I had dreamed of this moment. Not of joining a group of witches—I hadn't even known real witches existed. But of joining the in-group. The popular girls. The ones who were chosen first for the softball team, for homecoming court, for the dance team and all the other measures of popularity that we ate, drank, and breathed every day of our fraught existence.

I had never been one of the popular girls. Sure, I had friends. I'd spent enough hours texting to drive Gran to distraction. I'd gone to my share of slumber parties, and I could always find someone to hang out with at the mall.

But I'd never been part of the inner circle. The special core. The girls who set the trends and led the way and made all the rest of us jealous, no matter how much we'd protested to the contrary.

Now I was a little more than twenty-four hours away from my first real chance to join that clique. Tomorrow night, I would set the centerstone. Tomorrow night, I would join the coven that would support me and comfort me for all the rest of my witchy life. If I succeeded, of course.

Without conscious thought, my fingers fiddled with David's Hecate's Torch, which was hanging freely outside my colonial shift. I'd grown accustomed to the soothing feel of its sleek lines, its simple, swooping design. Soon, I'd have my own.

When I did, I could use it to nudge the coven in directions I thought worthwhile. After I'd settled in, I could question Gran's status, and Clara's. I could explore giving them back their own Torches, working with them to build their skills. It only seemed fair they should have *some* place in the coven, even if it was around the edges. Not everyone could be in the absolute center of the Popular Snobs.

I rubbed the Torch again and realized I was putting the magical cart before the enchanted horse.

I needed to set the centerstone before I started changing the slightest direction of Teresa Alison Sidney's coven. David's eyes tracked my hand, and then he shook his head. "I have to admit it," he said. "I didn't think you could make these lunchtime meetings work. But you were right."

"And?" I prompted, matching his slow smile with one of my own.

"And?" he asked, seeming confused.

"I was right, and? You?"

He actually laughed. Out loud. Like an ordinary man, instead of a grouchy, hyper-sensitive warder. He truly *must* be pleased with my accomplishments. "I was wrong. You've been better prepared for our sessions than I could have dreamed. I can only imagine how hard you've been studying each night."

Before I could lie, Neko his eyebrows arching as he studied his fingernails with nonchalance. "*I* can't believe you didn't need to spend every evening here. Studying the books in the basement."

I refused to glare at him—showing my anger would only tip my hand. Instead, I flashed a smile that was a single shade too tight to be sweet. "I'm a librarian. I study best in a library. It's habit, I guess. It's much quieter, and there are *far* fewer distractions."

I gave a pointed glance to Neko's throat, and the gold links of the necklace Jacques had given him only the night before. My familiar had the good grace to shrug and look away.

Distractions. If they only knew.

I shivered as I thought about how I'd seen Graeme every evening since he'd returned from London. Some nights, he arrived at my doorstep holding a paper sack from Dean and Deluca. Others, we met at one of my favorite Georgetown hot spots. On three different nights, he'd whisked me off to his place in Virginia, where he'd wined me and dined me and had his wicked way with me.

Or I, with him.

Whatever.

I was still perpetuating the Nate Poindexter charade. Pure luck had intervened to keep Neko from meeting Graeme so far. Luck, and Jacques, who knew about more parties in the Washington, DC metro area than any other ten people I could name.

Not that I was ashamed of Graeme, of course.

It's just that I still felt obligated to Melissa, bound by her stupid friendship test. Old loyalties died hard. I'd kept my promise despite the fact that I hadn't spoken to her in over three weeks—the longest time we'd gone without communicating in all the years we'd known each other.

I'd started to pick up the phone dozens of times, just to call her and make everything right. But every time I started to dial I remembered the way she'd dismissed my concerns. I thought about how she'd paid attention to everyone in her bakery, reaching out to them, helping them, before she even considered reaching out to me.

I thought about her having a phone, too. She could have called *me* any time in the past almost-a-month. Told me about more of her disastrous dates. Asked for commiseration, for an alliance against the men who broke her heart.

Demanded it, even, with a friendship test.

(Okay. When I was honest with myself, I silently thanked her for helping me keep my love life secret. I could only imagine what my overprotective familiar and warder would say when they learned about the new man in my life. There'd be time enough to deal with *that* disaster after Samhain.)

Before I could dwell more on my distractions, the phone rang. Neko perked up and said, "Jane Madison's grandmother."

I gave him a dirty look. Yes, Gran had been calling a lot, and she always left the same message. I just hadn't had time in the past three weeks to listen to more demands, to make more promises.

As the phone made another insistent ring, David waved me toward the handset. I guess we really *were* through with my training. The notion still set oddly in my mind, as I answered a cautious, "Hello?"

"Jane!"

"Oh. Hello, Gran." I looked at Neko, wondering if he truly *had* known she was on the other end of the line. I didn't think familiars could do that, but who could really say? He smiled innocently and resettled on the couch, tucking his legs beneath him. He and David started talking in quiet tones, and I took advantage of their conversation to concentrate on my grandmother.

"Jane, I am so glad I caught you! It's been *ages* since we've talked. Didn't you get my messages?"

"Yes, Gran." I sighed. "I've been busy."

"Too busy to return a phone call?" she asked tartly.

I made a face, feeling like I was about five years old. "David and I have been working together. A lot."

Gran liked David. Invoking his name was usually enough to make her forget extracting another dozen promises from me. True to form, her voice softened, and she said, "Well, dear, I was only calling because I found a great recipe for you."

"Recipe?"

"Weren't you going to start baking for the library?" Hurt feelings rushed back into her voice. So much for the magic elixir of David Montrose. "I could have sworn you said you would start serving baked goods on the first of November. I wrote it down on my calendar, in peacock blue."

Peacock blue. Gran always marked special events in the bright shade—my birthday, hers, the opening night of the school play. How could a shade of ink make me feel like a kid caught writing on the walls? With crayon. After several warnings.

"Yes, Gran, you're right," I hastened to respond, even though I'd completely forgotten about the bottomless pit that threatened to become the Peabridge Restaurant, with a mere side room of dingy books for the occasional lazy researcher.

"Then don't you think you should practice? Bake one or two things now, so you know what will work best in November?"

Damn. I *was* running out of time to launch my Freedom-From-Cappuccino campaign on the first. Well, I'd just have to get some baking done tonight. It would be soothing. Keep me from worrying about the coven too much. What could be easier than whipping up a batch or two of brownies?

I took a deep breath. "So, Gran, what's the recipe that you have for me?"

"It's called Homemade Turkish Baklava with Rose Water and Pistachio Cream."

I felt ill just hearing the name. "Baklava?"

"Homemade!" Gran enthused. "It takes forty sheets of filo dough, can you believe that? And a cup of butter. And a cup and a half of walnuts. Lucky for you, there are plenty of nuts in the store now that it's autumn. It shouldn't take too long to shell them. You'll be able to save money that way. Help out the Peabridge's bottom line."

Yeah, there were plenty of nuts in the store, and another one on the other end of the phone. Did Gran really think I was going to turn my kitchen into a baklava factory? She'd *raised* me —didn't she realize the disaster she was proposing? "Um, Gran," I said, trying to break the news to her gently. "I was thinking of starting off with something easy. Like brownies, the way we talked about at brunch."

"But Clara was over here when I found the recipe! She agreed that it sounded wonderful. She even cast her runes when she got home, and they came up Jera, Perthro, and Sowilo. It's destiny!"

I cast an exasperated look over at David and Neko, but they were carrying on a perfectly friendly conversation without me.

There'd be no escape from that quarter. I scowled and said, "I'm afraid I'm not quite up on my rune interpretations just now, Gran."

She clicked her tongue at my smart tone. "Jera is based on the harvest, Clara says. And Perthro is a sign of the feminine. Sowilo is the sun." She waited for me to say something, then continued with a touch of exasperation: "You should use harvested grains to pursue the feminine tradition of baking. In a hot oven." When I remained silent, Gran said, "Sowilo?"

"Sun. Oven. I get it," I said. "Look, Gran. Pastry chefs spend years learning how to make things like baklava. I don't think *Melissa* has even tried it."

Stupid. Stupid, stupid, stupid.

Sure enough, Gran swooped in for the kill. "Speaking of Melissa, have you phoned her yet?"

"I've been busy," I said through set teeth, and then I regrouped. "Gran, if I've been too busy to return your calls, then you know I've been too busy to talk to Melissa."

"It's just that you promised, Jane." She sounded utterly disappointed.

"Have I ever broken one of my promises?"

I could almost see her shaking her head. "No, dear."

"And I'm starting now." I glanced at my watch. Two o'clock. I was due back at the library half an hour ago. "I've got to run, Gran."

"Shall I send you my baklava recipe by email?"

Cruelly, I pictured her typing in the entire thing, hunting and pecking for each honey-soaked letter. "Why don't I stop by and pick it up? Some time in the next few days?"

"But what will you do for November first?"

"Brownies, Gran. I'm going to bake brownies. According to all the etiquette books, baklava is the traditional pastry for the *second* week of a bakery's existence."

She actually laughed and hung up, without wringing out any

more precious drops of guilt. When I turned around, Neko was staring at me with horror. "You're going to make baklava?"

My smile was sweeter than the most honey-drenched Turkish confection. With rose water. And pistachio cream. "Only if you and David are standing by to put out the fire and stop the floods and settle the earthquakes and handle every other natural disaster from the end of the world as we know it."

I left the men to their own devices and headed back to the library. Evelyn was standing by my desk, tapping her shoe and staring at the clock on my computer. I followed her gaze and winced involuntarily. 2:15. Whoops.

"Jane, could you come into my office?"

Good things never happened inside Evelyn's office. Well, except for when she offered me the cottage as a place to live. But I hadn't realized that was a good thing at the time. "Could I make you a latte first? We have a fresh bottle of cinnamon syrup."

"No."

One-word answer. That wasn't good. Not good at all.

She barely waited for me to sit down in the chair opposite her cluttered desk. "Jane, I can't help but notice you've been taking very long lunch breaks."

"I can explain—"

"The Peabridge is an excellent institution of higher learning. Our patrons depend on us to be here when they have questions."

When they want coffee. But I knew better than to say that out loud. I took a deep breath. "Evelyn, I've been working on our new patron program."

"Patron program?" The fact that I had an explanation—any explanation—stopped her cold in her tracks. "What patron program?"

"The new baked goods. Remember? We're going to start serving them on November 1?"

"Well, I knew we were going to launch something, but I wasn't certain we'd settled on the date."

"We have. Just today, I was speaking with a consultant about baklava. Homemade Turkish baklava with rose water and pistachio cream." I actually floated my hand in the air, adding a fillip to the pastry's name, elegant and yet familiar, as if I made it every day.

"Homemade—" Evelyn shook her head, like a terrier trying to knock dirt out of its ears. "But wouldn't that be terribly sticky? We don't want to do anything that might endanger our collection."

What? Protect the books in our *library*? What a fantastic idea! I resisted the urge to look at the paper coffee cup in Evelyn's trashcan, at the film of foamed milk that could just as easily have spilled over our holdings. "Well, if you think baklava might be too much…"

"I'm sorry, Jane. I realize you're putting a lot of hard work into this project. But I think we'd better to stick with something simpler. Maybe brownies."

Ha! I shook my head mournfully. "I suppose I *can* find another use for all those pistachios."

"There!" she beamed. "You'll see. We both want what's best for the Peabridge."

And the funny thing was, she was right.

I tried not to let her see my relief as I walked back to my desk. Truth be told, I'd been afraid she'd put me on probation—or worse. Now, all I had to do was make the revamped coffee bar a success.

No problem.

No problem at all, for a witch like me.

~

Twenty-four hours till Samhain, and I was pacing my kitchen like a madwoman.

I had pulled a dozen recipes for brownies off the Internet, and they all called for the same basic ingredients—butter, flour, eggs, sugar, chocolate.

I scorched the butter for the first batch, melting it before I added anything else.

I carefully measured the flour for the second batch, but neglected to remember I was doubling the recipe until after the glop was baking in the oven.

I broke egg shells into the third batch.

I spilled way too much sugar into the fourth batch, foolishly believing I could target a measuring cup held over a boiling saucepan of almost-batter.

I turned the melted chocolate of the fifth batch into an acrid pool of charcoal-tinged glue.

And I burned the sixth batch, leaving the perfect batter in my oven too long, forgetting the damned thing always ran hot. Very hot. Inferno hot.

As the clock chimed midnight, I sent Neko and Jacques to the all-night grocery store for more ingredients, and I collapsed at the kitchen table to drown my sorrows in the last remnant of a bar of Ghirardelli. Who knew how long it would take for the guys to get back? And who knew how many more ways I could ruin a simple batch of brownies?

I wanted to call Graeme. But I was the one who had told *him* I needed the evening off. He'd wheedled in that unbeliev-ably seductive way of his, but I held fast. I didn't want to chance staying up too late. Being too exhausted tomorrow. It really was for the best, I reminded myself for the thousandth time.

The knock, when it came, seemed to make the entire cottage shudder. After my heart slithered out of my throat, I darted to the front door, taking care to stay away from the windows.

Was this my jasper stalker? Had she realized I was alone and vulnerable, my trusty familiar scouting out grocery store aisles, with a robust, full-bodied distraction keeping him from hearing any frantic summons?

I closed my hand over David's Torch and looked out the peephole.

"Haylee!" I exclaimed, tugging open the door. "You scared me half to death!"

Her spiky hair was perfect—as ever—as she waltzed into my living room. She had draped a large cashmere scarf around her neck, flinging it over one shoulder with a perfect casual air. She sniffed as the door closed behind her, peering curiously at the disaster area in the kitchen.

I took advantage of her distraction to tuck David's Torch inside my blouse. No need for her to see his gift. No need for the coven to question my right to wear the symbol.

"So you sacked the kitchen in the midst of your terror?"

"Oh," I said, smiling weakly. "I'm trying out some new recipes. For work."

"I knocked loudly because I thought you'd be downstairs. Studying."

I shrugged. "I don't think there's much more I can cram in, in one night. I can either do the working, or I can't."

She laughed. "You know, I said almost exactly the same thing, the night before I was tested."

"What did they have you do?"

"I can't tell you. You aren't a member of the coven yet. Teri would kill me if I shared our secrets with a stranger." She smiled, but the words embarrassed me. I'd been presumptuous in asking. I hated the reminder that I was *different. Other.* Not one of the cool kids.

Yet.

Haylee reached inside the pocket of her impossibly slender slacks. "I wanted to give you something."

"What?"

"It's passed through generations of women in my family. My mother gave it to me the night before I was tested." My heart clenched at her words. Haylee was reaching out to me like a... sister. A true friend. "I know your mother and grandmother won't be there tomorrow. That must be hard for you—most witches can look around the coven and find at least one friendly face when they complete their testing. I wanted you to be able to look at this tomorrow, and to know I was thinking of you. That I've been thinking of you, ever since you first came to the coven."

She took her hand out of her pocket. I extended mine without thinking, palm open. I met her eyes and matched my lips to her smile. She opened her fingers to display a silver ring.

A plain silver ring. No engraving, no stone, and not a hint of tarnish. Absolutely no indication of its history or its meaning.

I shuddered as I slipped it onto my finger. The cool metal made my hand tingle, vibrate as if my flesh were awakening for the very first time. It fit snugly, occupying the place of an engagement ring on my right hand. "Haylee," I said, imagining the strength of the witches who had worn it before me.

"Good luck tomorrow," she said.

"I can't—" I started to protest.

"You can. And you will. Just look at it tomorrow night, and remember." Before I could say anything else, she gave me a quick, bony hug.

I asked, "Would you like to stay? Could I get you a drink? A brownie? Um, after Neko gets back?"

"No thanks," she said, and I think I detected a tremor that had nothing to do with witchcraft or covens or magical family-history rings. She looked into the chaos of my kitchen, and once again fought valiantly to hide her dismay. "I really have to be going. And you should get some sleep."

"I will." Before she left, I held out my hand, fingers extended to best show off the ring. "Thanks, Haylee."

After I closed the door, I sank against it, letting my knees buckle and my back slide toward the floor. It was happening. It was really happening. By this time tomorrow, I was going to be in the coven. Or out of it forever.

23

"Good riddance!" Neko said, slamming my front door. "They're all thieves! Vicious little thieves!"

"They're children," I said, stepping out of the bathroom. I had just fought, and lost, the fourth battle of the night against my hair. "They've been looking forward to Halloween for weeks. And they've probably been eating candy since they got home from school this afternoon. Cut them some slack."

"I'd cut them all sorts of slack, if they'd left a single Three Musketeers bar." Neko stared dolefully at the bowl of candy in his hands.

"You don't even like Three Musketeers," I reminded him.

"But Jacques does. I promised I'd save one for him."

"You should have taken it out before answering the door the first time." I returned to the mirror, tugging my hair out of its collapsing chignon and brushing furiously before starting again.

Secretly, I was pleased we had paid off a handful of trick-or-treaters. The year before, no one had dared walk through the library gardens to get to my cottage. I mused, "Of course, you can always try mugging some kids on the street. They're sure to have a few candy bars you can give your beau."

"I should just get him some of that nasty peanut butter taffy, the stuff wrapped up in orange and black wax paper. Serve him right, for abandoning me to door duty tonight."

I shook my head. I had long since stopped marveling at Neko's awareness of mundane details in our modern world, things like rock-hard peanut butter Halloween taffy that he couldn't have known all those years he'd been frozen as a cat statue in my basement. Nevertheless, I had to agree with his assessment of the revolting sweet. I'd always pawned mine off on Gran. She, showing perfect unconditional love, had accepted it with a smile and a hug. Years later, I'd discovered she actually buried it deep in the trashcan, so I'd never know she hated it as much as I did.

I eased a decorative chopstick into my thoroughly pinned chignon and reminded Neko, "Jacques wasn't the one who abandoned you tonight. You abandoned him. Remember?"

I could barely make out the words Neko muttered under his breath—more common knowledge he couldn't have absorbed when he was suspended in his statue form. And he hadn't learned it from me—I tried my best to avoid that type of language. Didn't always succeed, but I tried.

This time, I could empathize with Neko. Graeme had called me three times during the day, trying to convince me to change my mind and attend a Halloween party hosted by friends. Friends from work, he'd said, dangling a bait I would have snatched up any other night of the year. Finally—the chance to meet his colleagues, to find out more about his "acquisitions", to learn juicy office tidbits about my amazing mystery boyfriend.

A fancy-dress party, he'd called it in his droll British way. Costumes, he'd meant. I'd begged him to tell me what he was going as, but he'd refused, teasing that I'd never know if I couldn't be bothered to join him.

My frustration had only mounted because I couldn't tell him what I was really doing. I couldn't endanger the coven by advertising our working, by announcing to anyone—even to Graeme —that I was going to set the centerstone at midnight.

There'd be other parties, I tried to comfort myself. Maybe even more fancy dress. We could come up with costumes together—literary husbands and wives, musical lovers. Once I was officially in the coven, everything in my life would fall into its proper place.

I slid the second chopstick home and tried a tentative shake of my head. Everything stayed where it was supposed to, and I sighed in relief.

"So," I said, stepping back into the living room. "How do I look?"

I'd gone with black, of course. The heart and soul of my wardrobe, especially when I wasn't with Graeme. My slacks were lightweight wool. They should provide protection against the cool night-time breeze. I'd selected a silk blouse, one of the most demure garments I owned, with a placket that buttoned up to the neck. Fearing the midnight weather, and knowing I didn't want to be hampered by a coat, I'd added a wool sweater and taken care to smooth it evenly over my blouse.

My only concession to color was the deep blue of my sodalite earrings and necklace. I had chosen them specially, valuing their ability to provide clear sight and confidence. I worried I might need both before the night was done.

"Okay?" I asked.

"Perfect." I knew I should be pleased by Neko's approval, but his single word only made me more nervous. He never thought I was perfect. Anything but. He was obviously trying to calm me. To steady me. To help me through my testing with the coven so his own fate was secured.

Before I could demand an honest appraisal, there was another knock at the door. "I know, I know," Neko said, throwing open the door. "Trick or treat."

"Treat, thank you." David perused the bowl of candy, digging deep to see what we had available. "No Three Musketeers?" he asked, stepping into the living room and closing the door behind him.

"Not any more," Neko said, and he sounded so doleful I actually laughed.

"I'll buy you a Three Musketeers tomorrow," I promised. "A king-size bar, if you're good tonight."

"Oh, I'm good," he said, nodding vigorously. "I'm good *every* night."

"That's not what I meant!"

He winked at me slyly. Okay. So he was only trying to cheer me up. To distract me. But I laughed all the same.

"Are you ready?" David asked.

"Ready as I'll ever be." I looked around the room. "What am I forgetting?"

"I've already got the herbs in the car. And the silver flask of rainwater," David said. "You don't need anything else."

I'd given David a shopping list earlier in the day. Neko's feelings had been hurt until I'd tasked him with picking out the trick or treat candy.

"What should I do with this?" Neko asked, raising the almost-full bowl of candy.

"Just leave it on the doorstep. It's late for trick-or-treaters. If anyone comes after we're gone, they're welcome to whatever they want."

That was the smartest move. Otherwise, I'd be eating left-over candy for weeks.

Who was I fooling? I'd eat it all in three days and then swear off sugar for the rest of the year. Or at least until the stores started stocking miniature candy bars wrapped in Christmas red and green.

David quickly settled the three of us in his car. I tried to relax against the rich leather seats, forcing myself to take deep, calming breaths. David had a CD playing—piano music that was perfectly soothing and utterly boring. Chopin, maybe? Gran would know.

I leaned back and watched the roadside lights glint off the car's walnut trim. The Lexus seemed to pull us forward with a powerful magic of its own. David's keys jangled softly as he changed lanes. Involuntarily, I settled my hand over my heart, pressing against his Torch that I still wore. I closed my eyes and took another calming breath, and then I dared to ask, "Do you need it back?"

He glanced at me quickly before returning his attention to the road. "Only if you want me to take it. I don't want it to distract you during the working."

"I'm used to it now," I said.

"Then you can return it after you receive your own."

I smiled weakly. "You seem so confident."

"I've seen you work. I know how much time you've spent preparing for this. Our lunch meetings every day, your studying every night. You're ready."

Yeah, I wanted to say. Except I hadn't studied witchcraft at night. I shivered as I thought about Graeme, wondered again what costume he'd chosen for his party.

Oh well. No reason to confess to David now. No reason to let him know I was winging it more than he knew. Neko shifted in the back seat, but he kept silent. I whispered a quick prayer to Hecate, expressing gratitude for small mercies.

Before I was ready, we reached the long road that snaked up to Teresa Alison Sidney's house. We had plenty of time, and David pulled off to the side, extinguishing his headlights and turning off the ignition key. His face was lit only by the moonlight that streamed through the oak trees.

"You remember the layout, don't you?"

I nodded. He'd described it a dozen times. I said, "They've leveled the land near the creek-bed. It's out the back door of the house, down a flagstone path. We won't be able to see the house once we get there."

"The circle was set two weeks ago."

I looked at him curiously. "Have you seen it, then?"

"Of course." He shrugged. "We warders needed to make

sure there wasn't anything…unexpected when the boundary was placed."

Of course, I nodded to myself. How else would a coven prepare its new safehold?

"It's ready for the centerstone," he said confidently. "Ready for you."

The engine ticked in the night-time, cooling off as we waited. I took another deep breath, and this time I could smell the herbs in the cotton sack at my feet. Paper or plastic? I was certain the woman had asked David at the organic market. But the greenery was in natural cloth now, ready to play its part in the evening's magic.

"David?" I said, staring out the windshield at the trees arching above us.

He grunted a wordless reply.

"Thank you."

"For what?"

"For helping me. For having faith in me. For bringing me out here to the coven in the first place."

"They didn't give me a lot of choice, did they?" He smiled wryly. "Don't worry. You'll do fine."

I thought back to the first night I'd met my warder. He had thoroughly intimidated me, swooping in like a madman, demanding to know what I was doing with my powers. Since then, our relationship had mellowed. Sure, he pushed me. Pulled me sometimes too. Twisted me, even, into his version of what a witch should be, could be.

But underneath it all, I had come to believe—come to *know* —he was there for me. Would always be there for me. He wouldn't let me go forward with this working if he thought there was a true risk of failure. A real possibility of losing Hannah Osgood's collection. Of forfeiting Neko.

I tried to bleed off some of my nervousness by drumming my fingers against the dashboard. The moonlight glinted off the silver ring Haylee had given me the night before.

"What is that?" David had stiffened beside me.

"What?" His alarm startled me. "This? A ring."

"I can see that." His words were suddenly terse, tense.

"It's okay," I said, realizing he must suspect my jasper-stalker. "Haylee gave it to me last night."

"Take it off." He was angry with me. Furious.

"No! What is it with you and Haylee? Why do you hate her so much?"

His lips compressed into a narrow line. I read the stubbornness in his jaw, his refusal to tell me anything.

I'd never thought of myself as a rip-off-the-Band-Aid girl. I'd always been the sort to take a long, luxurious bath, to soak off a bandage with the perfect combination of bubble bath and aromatherapy oil. But now, with both the Lexus engine and the clock ticking, approaching midnight on Samhain, it was time to rip away. Time to get to the heart of David's antipathy toward Haylee. Especially if it had any potential to spoil the looming magical working.

I twisted my wrist, purposely moving my fingers to catch moonlight on the ring.

And something about that baleful light made David decide to yield. He took a deep breath and exhaled slowly, rubbing a hand from his forehead to his chin. He clenched both hands on the steering wheel, and then he collapsed back against his leather seat. Finally, he spoke.

"Haylee was my witch."

"What?" I couldn't believe I'd heard him right.

"Haylee was the witch who terminated me four years ago. The one who sent me back to Hecate's Court." The one who had condemned him to a life as an administrative clerk. Who had stripped him of his title and his pride. Who had made him question who he was and who he could ever be. Until I'd found Neko and opened up the Pandora's box of Hannah Osgood's collection.

"Why didn't you *say* something?"

"What was I going to say, Jane? Don't be friends with the witch who hurt my feelings? Don't hang out with the mean girls?"

"Yes! If that's the way you felt, you should have told me. I'd still make my own decision—"

"Why am I not surprised by that?" he interrupted.

"I'd *still* make my own decision," I reiterated, "but at least I'd have all the facts in front of me."

"Well, now you do." He sounded like a stubborn little princeling.

"And thanks for giving me plenty of time to think about them." I whined like a birthday girl, piqued that I hadn't received a rose on my slice of cake. I could match him in stubbornness, any day of the week.

"Children, children," Neko chided helpfully from the back seat. "It's time to move along. The clock just rang half past eleven."

What clock? I wanted to snap, as annoyed by my familiar's interruption as by his usage of the British phrase "half past." Graeme would have said half past. If he'd been with us.

But David didn't question Neko. He reached down and turned the ignition key, shoving the Lexus into gear.

I stared at the silver ring reflecting balefully on my finger. "I have to wear it now," I said, almost apologetically. "If you'd told me before… If I could have explained to Haylee… But if I show up without it now, it'll be like a slap in her face."

David didn't say anything. He just maneuvered the car down the rest of the long drive. I stared out my window.

Haylee and David. Well, that explained why he'd been so set against our friendship from the get-go.

But it didn't explain Haylee staying silent on the topic. It didn't explain her never mentioning that she knew David, much less that they'd worked together, in the intense intimacy of warder and witch. She should have said something to me. Should have filled me in a long time ago. Anger jangled my nerves, making my fingers feel as if I'd brushed them across a bed of nails.

My belly executed a sick little flop as David braked to a halt.

"David?" I asked, before he had a chance to unbuckle his seat belt. "What happens if I fail?"

He shook his head, staring out the windshield. Stress torqued his voice into an exasperated sigh. "You know all this. The coven will take possession of Hannah Osgood's books. The books and the crystals and all the other paraphernalia. Neko."

I shook my head impatiently. "No, I mean, when? Will I just blink, and they'll be gone?" I couldn't look in the back seat, couldn't force myself to catch my familiar's eyes in the midnight gloom. "Will Neko turn back to a statue instantly?"

Predictably, Neko growled, but his aggression tapered off to a high-pitched whine.

"Don't think about that," David said. "You won't fail. You'll be fine."

I might have believed him, if his face hadn't been carved into stoic wooden planes. My fingers mechanically followed his as he undid his seat belt, as he pushed open his door.

It seemed to take a century for us to walk to the site. Neko carried the cotton bag of herbs and the silver flask of rainwater, holding both close to his chest. A breeze had picked up, sending ripples down my spine to match the flossy clouds that scudded across the face of the moon. I was glad I'd put on a sweater.

David took the lead, glancing warily to the left and right. Neko stuck close by my side. I wasn't sure if he was seeking comfort from me, or offering reassurance of his own. It didn't really matter.

We crested a slight hill, and then we could see a circle spread below us. It was defined by stones that looked white in the moonlight, bleached, like driftwood abandoned on sand. Or bone.

I forced my mind away from that thought.

When I took a deep breath, I could still smell a faint tang of charcoal, aftermath of the warders preparing the site. My witchy senses tingled with the magic potential below me.

The magic potential, and the magic actual.

As we approached, two dozen shadows loomed out of the darkness. I started to clutch at David's arm, to call out a warning, but then I realized each black shape represented a witch, a woman clad in a hooded cloak that covered her from head to toe. As if responding to a silent command, they ranged themselves around the ring, close but not touching the soon-to-be sacred space.

Other shapes moved behind them—larger shadows, bulkier ones. Of course, each witch was protected by her warder. Each woman's personal guardian stood behind her, prepared to use whatever means were necessary to protect the magic working—the magic workers—on this eerie night of change and shifting potential.

David stopped when we were still several paces from the circle. I started to direct a questioning look at him—I feared my voice would be too loud if I actually spoke—but then I saw the shimmer of silver light before us.

Silver light, spread out in a second circle, in a shimmering dome that covered the inner ring marked off by stone. This was a protective band, a cordon guarding witches inside their sacred space. I looked for a warder knight, for a liquid sword of symbolic and actual warding. I found more than I'd bargained for.

Three steps to my right, suddenly visible against the inky darkness in a way that made me certain magic was afoot, was the tallest woman I had ever seen. She was clad in a silver robe held closed at her neck by a shimmering Hecate's Torch. Her hands were rigid in front of her, clutching the grip of a broadsword. She stared over my head, past me, *through* me, gazing into the endless night-time darkness. Without David saying a word, I knew I was looking at a member of Hecate's Court, at one of the elite arbiters of witchy justice.

David bowed low before her, with Neko and I following a heartbeat behind. "Lady of the East!" he proclaimed, as if he were the chamberlain at Cinderella's ball. "Lady of Air! We welcome your protection on this Samhain night. We ask that you watch all that transpires here and find Jane Madison worthy of inclusion in the Washington Coven. We ask that you protect our workings and bless them in the name of our mother Hecate. Guide us and keep us, illuminating the night before us with the power of your Torch."

The woman took her time inclining her head, looking for all the world as if she had come to life from some magical silver coin. "Welcome Warder Montrose. I hear your entreaty and agree to guard the workings of this night, as watcher of Air in Hecate's Court. May the Guardians of Air look kindly on your labor."

We bowed again, almost perfectly synchronized, and then Neko and I followed David one quarter of the way around the circle, crossing to the southern-most point of the circle. A man stood there—clearly the equal to the Amazon warrior we had just left. He was a full head taller than I, and his arms looked as big around as my thighs. He wore a cloak, too, and his brooch glinted balefully under the moonlight.

David repeated his salute, directing his address to the Lord of Fire. The official accepted our bows, agreed to protect us, agreed to watch over the magic we were about to undertake, agreed as watcher of Fire in Hecate's Court. He summoned the Guardians of Fire to look kindly upon our efforts.

The western edge had another woman, Lady of Water, and the northern edge was guarded by the Lord of Earth. He actually stepped back after agreeing to watch, and he swept his sword in a perfect arc, slicing open a doorway in the glowing silver ring. The hairs on my arms tingled as I stepped through, and I caught Neko swiping at his face, as if he were batting away the finest filaments of a spider's web.

David stepped up to the ritual circle, keeping his back as

rigid as a soldier's when he turned to offer me a hand. Neko scrambled forward under his own power, darting his eyes around the collection of witches, warders, and watchers as we glided to the precise center of the ring.

I swallowed nervously. This was it. Now or never. A dozen other clichés clattered inside my skull, like the slogans on over-wrought inspirational posters. *When you get to the end of your rope, tie a knot and hang on.*

There was a ripple across from me, and one of the witches stepped up to the circle's edge. She raised two hands to her cowl, pausing for a long dramatic moment before she cast back her hood.

Teresa Alison Sidney. Coven Mother. The woman I most needed to please before the night was done.

"Greetings, Jane Madison." Her voice was low and resonant, saturated with absolute confidence. She was a witch who would never need sodalite to bolster her certainty. "The coven welcomes you this Samhain night."

I bowed my head, trying to remember everything I'd read about ritual, about Samhain. All the appropriate witchy words had flown out of my head, though, and I had to settle for mundane ones. "Thank you." I cleared my throat, and repeated, "Thank you, Coven Mother."

"You see before you the centerstone of our safehold. You hold the power to set that stone. Do your working, Jane Madison, that all of us might see your worthiness to join our ranks, to be our sister, to enter into the heart of the Washington Coven."

Taking one step back, she returned to the circle she shared with the other witches. She raised her right hand, as if she were going to bless me, and all of a sudden, I heard a clock chiming the change of hours.

It was the clock in the Coven Mother's living room, the clock that had initiated the other meetings I'd attended. I did not know what magic Teresa Alison Sidney harnessed to bring the sound to us in our moonlit field; I was not certain how my ears made out the complicated notes across the distance. But I heard the tolling of the hours as I had on that first night, the deep insistent bass of the chimes filling my bones, resonating with every magical fiber in my body.

The witches around me felt it too. They stood straighter. They raised their hands to their own cowls. They lifted their faces to the moon.

And as the twelfth note echoed across the field, as Samhain dawned in the darkness, each woman in the circle cast back her hood.

Despite myself, I looked for Haylee. I was still unsettled by David's admission, newly uncertain about the woman's intentions. But she was the closest thing to a friend I had in the entire magical circle. Without conscious thought on my part, I rubbed the fingers of my left hand over her ring, tracing the unblemished silver as if it held all the answers, as if it could make everything right.

Maybe it was the ring that distracted me. Maybe it was a sudden gust of chilly October wind. Maybe it was the sound of the cotton bag of herbs, settling gently on the ground at Neko's feet, or the dull clank of the silver flask of rainwater.

But it took me a moment to realize that not only had the witches bared their faces, but their warders had revealed themselves as well. In my peripheral vision, each man stepped closer to his witch, each protector, stalwart and solid. There were two dozen witches. Two dozen warders.

But only one face penetrated the sudden fog before my eyes: Haylee's warder. Standing tall, directly behind her, left hand firm on the hilt of his magical sword.

Graeme Henderson.

24

I took three steps toward him before I realized I was moving. My face betrayed me, breaking into a smile by force of habit before my brain could freeze it, shut it down, force it into stony disbelief.

Absurdly, the first thing I could say was, "Fancy dress party."

Graeme inclined his head, the moonlight turning his blond hair to silver. He grinned bashfully, like a child caught lying about playing in a backyard pond. "As fancy as they come."

There was a rustle among the witches, a shift as every woman looked from me to Graeme to Haylee. And back to me. I felt the weight of all their eyes, the force of recognition as they realized some unscripted drama was unfolding, some unexpected spice for the trickster night of Samhain.

I clutched at David's Torch through my sweater, willing myself to breathe. Breathe. Breathe. Think of something to say. Anything at all.

I could not look at Graeme. Could not face his perfect smile, could not listen to the purr of his seductive accent. How many Fridays had he lurked outside of Cake Walk before he'd approached me? How long had he waited to acquire a gullible witch, along with a few squares of Almond Lust? How many times had he teased me, trying to schedule dates that he *knew* conflicted with my coven activities? Had he ever read a single one of Shakespeare's plays? Or had he merely used some warder's power to memorize the texts, to somehow protect his witch, to advance her interests by applying clever quotations?

My belly twisted, and my palms grew slick with sweat.

Avoiding his pale, pale eyes, I wasted a dozen heartbeats staring at the silver ring on my hand. What had Haylee said the night before? "I've been thinking of you, ever since you first came to the coven."

She'd been thinking of me. Manipulating me. Hating me— from the first moment we'd met. And she'd wanted me to know that tonight. Had given me the ring specifically to unravel me now, to destroy me and ruin everything I'd worked for. She wanted me to look on her gift and know I'd been betrayed, that I would never fit into her coven, never belong. She wanted me to fail.

I tugged at the silver band, ignoring the pain as it caught against my knuckle. I ripped it off and tossed it toward her feet. It landed in the grass, and I hoped she would never find it, not even by the light of day. "You knew!" I said. "You've known all along!"

"What? That you've been sleeping with my warder?" The anger in her voice sparked across the void between us.

Neko squeaked behind me. "Nate Poindexter is a warder?"

David glared him to silence before he said, "Haylee."

I had thought David was commanding in the past. He'd frightened me when he appeared on my doorstep on the proverbial dark and stormy night. He'd intimidated me when I reported to study sessions too hungover or too tired to work effectively. But if he had ever directed that precise and deadly tone against me, I would have fallen to my knees in terror.

Haylee blanched.

Haylee blanched, and Graeme swooped to her side, making a show of settling his left hand on the grip of his sword. How had I never realized he was left-handed? How many other details had I missed in the weeks I'd spent with him?

David did not spare the other warder a glance. "Your fight is with me, Haylee. You had no reason to bring Jane into this."

"I had every reason," she countered, and the tremolo in her voice might have been caused by the icy wind. "She doesn't belong here. She's an upstart and a rebel and she has no business joining the coven."

At last, Teresa Alison Sidney broke out of her immobility. "Haylee, what have you done?"

My so-called friend dared to look away from David. "Teri! You know it isn't right! I was supposed to set the centerstone!"

"The strongest witch among us sets the centerstone," Teresa Alison Sidney said. "That has been the way of all witches, since the first safehold was built."

"You promised!" Haylee's wail was like a knife scraping sideways on a pottery plate.

"The *coven* chose," Teresa Alison Sidney insisted. "You agreed, as one of the sisters. All of you chose to test Jane first. When—*if*—she fails, you'll be allowed to try. You, and anyone else who thinks she has the strength."

Haylee spluttered, and I realized I should be angry as well, furious that the Coven Mother considered my efforts likely to fail. But I wasn't angry. I didn't feel much of anything. I was still reeling at the extent of Haylee's betrayal.

I suddenly understood that she was the one who had arranged Graeme's limousine for our tour of the Washington monuments. She had phoned him that night at the Kennedy Center, after I'd worked my weather spell—after he had spied on my spell-casting technique. What had she gleaned from his report on my ability to manipulate the Potomac?

She had ordered him away from me that night, kept us apart. Because she could. Because she was a witch, and she could command her warder. Command him far more completely than she had ever succeeded in commanding David.

Had she sent him to London, then, to keep him even farther away? Had Graeme even *traveled* to London? I'd only contacted him on his cell phone. Perhaps he'd been sitting in his Arlington living room the entire time, just pretending to be overseas.

And about that Arlington living room, about the night Haylee had driven me to Virginia?

I closed my eyes, and I could see the look of surprise on Graeme's face when he'd opened his front door. I had thought his shock was from seeing *me* on his doorstep, but I'd been mistaken. He had not expected Haylee to lead me to his lair.

And yet, he'd adapted almost immediately. They had played out their scene like flawless actors. They had even chatted about his decor—interior design that Haylee must have done. He was keeping that stained glass lamp for a friend. I had no doubt the lamp belonged to Haylee.

And I had fallen for it. Fallen for him. I had let them fool me completely, let Graeme drive me home, take me to bed. And *Haylee* had let Graeme take me to bed then, too, because she had a larger plan.

The jasper necklace.

Graeme must have planted the jasper necklace—and stolen my book on crystals as well. While I slept the dissipated sleep of the sexually exhausted, he had wrapped the beads with thyme and oregano, harnessed the ancient protections against witches. Haylee would know them, of course. She would have mastered herbal knowledge as she chaired the coven's Gardening Committee.

Graeme had pretended concern, but he'd left before David and Neko arrived—left at my own benighted urging, before they could recognize him. Graeme was the reason Neko had sensed the coven around my bookstand. Who knew what other arcane knowledge Graeme had uncovered in my basement? What other magical information he had taken from me, passed on to the true woman in his life?

To his witch. The witch that wanted to best me now, wanted

me to fail at setting the centerstone so she could show her own strength.

I clutched the sodalite around my neck, using its energy to focus the vision unfolding inside my mind. I stared into Graeme's pale, pale eyes, and I felt a now-familiar shiver up and down my spine. A shiver I had first felt in Cake Walk, when Graeme recited his "nursery rhyme." *Keep our secret, silent be. Speak to no man, not of me.*

His warder's spell. His harnessed magic that had prompted me to live by Melissa's mundane Friendship Test. His power had asserted itself with shivering force every time I considered revealing my acquaintance with Graeme to any man. To David. To Neko.

Protected by my bespelled silence, Graeme must have left the jasper egg on my doorstep as well. He had sent the threatening e-mails, taking all the time he needed to compose Still Lifes with Jasper and Herbs, to photograph them and insert them into his anonymous electronic threats.

All so I'd be frightened. Intimidated. So I'd back down and leave the centerstone to Haylee. Or, at the very least, bungle the job so badly that she could step in and save the day—using my own knowledge against me.

I wanted to blame them. I wanted to appeal to the coven, to have my so-called sisters rise up in my defense. I wanted my warder and my familiar to stand beside me, before the other witches, the other warders, the watchers of Hecate's Court, so everyone would know that I had been wronged.

And yet uncertainty gnawed at the back of my brain. I had made this bed. I had accepted Melissa's juvenile Friendship Test. I had kept my relationship with Graeme secret, held it too close, treasured it too highly. I had let Graeme steal me away, package me up for Haylee to destroy. I'd been suckered by a smooth accent and a brilliant line, never even dreaming of harnessing my magical abilities to protect myself.

Grasping my sodalite, I could picture Graeme extracting his

business card from his money clip. The silver clip. The clip formed in the shape of Hecate's Torch. He had dared to reveal his alliance with the coven on the first day we'd met, but I had been too ignorant to recognize the message.

I took a deep breath and forced myself to meet his eyes. "Acquisitions, Graeme?"

He shrugged. "It seemed appropriate at the time."

A flood of shame and rage and embarrassment turned my mouth to copper. I finally dared to glance around the circle, to see how the coven was reacting. Some of the women were shocked to silence—they darted furtive glances between Haylee and me, between Graeme and David. Some of the women actually smiled, as if they had purchased tickets for a show and were enjoying the main event. And a few had moved to Haylee's side, surrounding her with a coterie of female support.

The Popular Snobs banded together, as always. They supported one another against any threat to their social status, any possible upset of their social prestige.

The warders took their cue from their witches. Most managed a neutral watchful gaze without betraying actual emotion. But a few cast admiring glances toward Graeme. I could imagine their locker room chatter. "Way to go, man!" "You totally had her fooled!" "Score!"

I'd lived this story before.

I was thirteen years old, attending my first boy-girl dance, celebrating some bar mitzvah at a downtown hotel. Brett Lindquist had asked me to dance. Brett Lindquist—the coolest boy in the entire school. I said yes before I could chicken out. Brett led me out on the dance floor and lurched from side to side, showing off the seventh grade equivalent of killer moves.

And then I saw the other boys. One called out, "Way to go, Brett!" and another whistled. A third boy sauntered across the dance floor, not even pretending to boogie. He sidled up to Brett and said, "Okay, man. You win. We never thought you'd actually ask *that* one!" A flash of money changed hands, the boy made an oinking sound in my general direction, and Brett strutted off mid-lurch.

I'd run out of the ballroom and up the stairs, into a bathroom where I locked a stall door and called home. By the time Gran pulled into the circular driveway in front of the hotel, I was crying too hard to explain what had happened. I was only able to tell her about my humiliation after a restorative bowl of chocolate mint ice cream, complete with Hershey's syrup, canned whipped cream, and—the grandmotherly coup de grace—a maraschino cherry.

Gran had marched over to her calendar and torn off the page for the entire month of September. She'd crumpled her careful handwriting, the immaculate peacock blue script: Jane's First Dance Party. She'd tossed it in the garbage, and we'd never spoken about Brett Lindquist again.

Peacock blue.

Like the peacock in the painting at the National Gallery of Art—the painting Haylee had shown me, had explained to me. I'd thought that we were sharing something special there, building a bond but all the time, she'd been exploiting me, searching for signs of weakness, for ways to keep me from succeeding at my magical task. For ways of cementing her best-friend bonds to the Coven Mother.

As if I'd been struck by another wave, I realized Haylee had charmed me as well. The tingle I had mistaken for excitement when she spoke to me at coven meetings, the jangle in my fingers, my entire arm, when Haylee brushed against me as she worked her magic. Her Dark Magic. Her unsanctioned magic. Haylee had made me compliant. She had made me accept what she did. She had made me stupid, even as I'd believed she was acting out of friendship, out of a desire to school a fellow witch.

But Haylee hadn't known everything. Clara had taught me more. Clara had told me about peacocks in *Eastern* art. She'd said peacocks could counteract venom. They could face down snakes. Traitors.

I closed my eyes and took a centering breath, clutching at my deep blue sodalite beads for confidence. I focused on the image of Gran and Clara sitting across the brunch table from me. Sharing dessert with me. Sharing stories of their lives, their love, their hopes for me. Even when the coven had slighted them.

I owed it to my mother and grandmother to finish this matter with the Washington Coven. I needed to set the centerstone. Set the centerstone, and complete my working, and not let Haylee or Graeme defeat me. I exhaled slowly, and when I opened my eyes, I was surprised to see my breath fog on the air.

The centerstone rested near the center of the circle. It was perfectly round, about two feet across, made of solid marble. Tiny crystals sparkled in the flawless white. Despite everything —my anger, my embarrassment, my growing physical exhaustion—the centerstone was beautiful. "By yon marble heaven," I whispered, quoting from *Othello*, "In the due reverence of a sacred vow, I here engage my words."

David caught my meaning and nodded slightly. It was time. Time to pass my test, or leave the coven forever.

I closed my eyes and took three deep breaths. I touched my forehead, my throat, my heart. When I reached out for the Samhain ritual words, they were easy to find, planted so firmly in my memory that I did not need to think, I did not need to worry. I knew them, and none of Haylee's calculations, none of Graeme's deceptions, could make me forget.

> "Witches gather, warders too,
> Ringing in a season new.
> Join together for this working
> Stand against the darkness, lurking.
> Pure of faith and strong of heart,
> Well-met sisters at the start
> Know Samhain power's, Samhain's lore,
> Driving through this coven's core."

With the first words of my incantation, Teresa Alison Sidney swept up her arms, figuratively embracing all who stood around the stone-marked ring. She clearly gained power from my words, weaving a bond between all of the assembled witches. Despite everything, my spell was working.

Neko stepped closer, bowing his head and huddling by my side. Heat radiated off his body, warming me back to life in the desert of the midnight chill. I rested my fingers on his shoulder, taking a moment to anchor myself against his sturdy strength.

And then I spoke to the centerstone.

"Heart of Stone!" I called to it, brushing my fingers over the flawless marble, relishing its solidity, its safety, its central core of Earth. It responded to its name, vibrating with a power that hummed through my sodalite necklace, whispering through the crystal wands of my earrings.

I raised my silver flask of rainwater high above my head, priming it with moonlight before sprinkling its Water across the perfect Earth circle. The Water added its own note to the stone's, a higher pitch, a perfect harmony that echoed in my mind. I helped the elements to meld, spreading my fingers wide, coaxing the Water to find the tiniest striations, the invisible gaps.

Only when the water shimmered like an unbroken pool of molten glass, only when Earth and Water were perfectly merged, was I satisfied. As if Neko could read my mind, he handed me the cotton bag of herbs.

I shook out the traditional vervain and rosemary, the radish that David had taught me about weeks before. I set them on the Water-melded Earth, arraying them across the marble in the complicated pattern of the rune othala, a diamond with two trailing legs. The symbol meant home and safety, security and abundance. The herbs added their own music to the working, a clamor of treble notes sparking off the harmony of Earth and Water.

Closing my eyes, I lifted my hands high above my head. I knew the motion would make David's Torch stand out against

my sweater, would let every witch and warder and watcher know
I wore a talisman not rightly my own. I did not care, though, as
I invoked the power of Fire, the cleansing element, the element
that sealed strength into the heart of the centerstone.

For just an instant, I contemplated letting my flame burn
brighter. I could make it flare toward the watching coven. I
could force Graeme to push Haylee behind him; I could manipulate him into doing something *I* wanted, something I desired.

Neko shifted beside me, though. As I harvested my strength
from his mirrored facets, I knew I'd be wrong to abuse my
witchcraft for the petty purpose of revenge. Instead, I bent my
wrists and directed a burst of purifying flame at the centerstone.

The herbs shriveled to dust. The rainwater sizzled into nothingness. The marble glowed gold, revealing its stony core for a
dozen heartbeats. Music surged in my mind, in my body, in my
soul, a sparkling crescendo that built to a single sustained note, a
perfect vibration.

From the heart of that clarion call, I summoned Air to blow
away the residue. Ash whipped into the night, leaving behind
only the acrid memory of burnt offerings. My summoned wind
flowed hot over the coven, giving them a moment's release from
the chill Samhain night. I released the last of the elements, let
Air slip away.

The centerstone was ready. It was primed, active, ready to
serve as the coven's protective base for years to come.

"Now!" I cried, and my voice was as wild as a crow's.

David stepped forward. He had promised me, weeks ago,
that I would not need to lift the centerstone, and he had not
lied. Half a dozen warders jumped to his side, ranging about the
marble with the precision of a military band. Graeme was no
fool; he kept his distance. He stayed by Haylee's side.

David issued some silent command, and the warders moved
as one, shifting the marble circle, easing it into the precise center
of the circle. I nodded when the placement was perfect, and the
men stepped back.

It was simple enough to raise my hands one last time. Simple enough to measure the crystal power of the marble. Simple enough to meld that power to the complex mixture of the earth beneath, to dirt and grass and underlying stone.

I closed my eyes to make the joining perfect, to feel the precise *ping* as the centerstone found its home. I breathed to steady myself. Once. Twice. Three times. Four. When I opened my eyes, every witch stared at me in awe. I wondered what they'd expected, if they'd thought I would succeed. If they'd hoped I would fail.

I spread my hands over the charged marble. "The centerstone is set," I intoned.

"So mote it be." The witches answered as if we'd rehearsed a script for months.

"Let all who would stand against the coven be turned away at the door."

"So mote it be." The warders joined in heartily.

"May Hecate be pleased by our working and look upon her daughters with joy."

"So mote it be." The watchers added their voices to the chorus, rocking the circle with the power of their affirmation.

The air was filled with the tinkling sound of breaking glass, and a million silver shards rained down upon us. Witches exclaimed and warders swore, and the watchers stood like statues. I blinked, more to clear my mind than my eyes, and I realized the Court's protective silver ring had been broken.

I reached out to capture a last glint of the spectral light. The motion set me off balance, though, and I would have fallen if David had not spun to my side, catching my arm with a confident iron hand. "Easy," he whispered. "Give yourself a moment to recover."

But I didn't have a moment.

Teresa stood before me. For the first time, I saw her as nothing more than an ordinary witch. A sister. An equal. "Jane

Madison," she proclaimed, evoking immediate silence from the babbling group around us.

"Coven Mother."

"We welcome you into the Washington Coven. We are honored to call you sister, and to have you stand inside our circle."

I forced my spine straight, taking my arm from my warder's grasp. "It's over then?"

"It is done."

"And the coven waives its claim to the property of Hannah Osgood? You recognize that I am the rightful owner of all the books and crystals and magical wares located in my home?"

Teresa smiled calmly. "The coven recognizes your right."

I pointed toward Neko. "And my familiar is bound to me alone? The coven stakes no claim?"

"The coven has no right to your familiar."

Teresa paused, apparently waiting for her words to register among all her witches. Then she gestured up the hill, toward her unseen home. She dispensed with formality and said, "Come on, Jane. Let's go back to the house. There's plenty to eat and drink there, and we can get to know each other better."

I ran a quick mental tally. Books, crystals, familiar.

That left my warder. I took a step back, so I could read David's face, stripped clean in the moonlight. We couldn't speak mind to mind. My powers did not stretch that far. But we knew each other. We had trained together. He had guided me, supported me, leaped to defend me when I'd been worst betrayed. I cocked my head at the slightest angle, asking a silent question.

Without hesitation, he nodded. Once. Firmly. Calmly.

I turned back to Teresa. "No."

"No?" She sounded as if she'd never heard the word before.

"I won't be joining you tonight. Tonight, or any other time."

She laughed. "But you're one of us now. You set the center-stone. Surely you know what that means."

"That you've used me to complete your work? To secure your safety?"

Teresa's perfect lips curved into a tiny smile, and I knew I was supposed to feel privileged. Honored. Special. "You're the strongest sister in the coven, Jane. The strongest witch in Washington, except for me. Think of what we can do together. You and me, Jane, sharing our powers."

I looked from Teresa to Haylee to Graeme, and then to all the other magical folk. "Teri," I said, relishing my unauthorized use of her nickname, "There is no way in hell I'll share any magical powers with you. I'm not joining the coven."

Now Teresa looked alarmed. "If this is about Haylee, you can be certain we'll address what she did. She had no right to try to sabotage your initiation."

"Teri!" Haylee exclaimed. She might have said more, but Graeme clamped his fingers tight around her arm.

Teresa gave her supposed best friend a dirty look, but then she addressed me with an honesty that would have seduced me a day before, weeks before, months before. "Jane, I'll admit I asked Haylee to find out about your powers. The coven needed to know your capabilities, your interests—what you could share with us, once we welcomed you in." Teresa's eyes narrowed. "But I *never* told her to use her warder. I never authorized that sort of gamesmanship."

Haylee spluttered for words, jerking her arm out of Graeme's grasp.

I dragged my disgusted glance from the pair of them. "It's not about Haylee," I said. "Not even about Graeme. It's about the coven, Teri. It's about witches setting up cliques for themselves. Counting people out, instead of bringing them in. Cutting women off from power—any amount of power—instead of helping them to increase whatever they've got."

Teresa swallowed hard, but she managed a shaky smile. "Jane, if you're talking about your mother and grandmother, I'm sure we can work something out. Now that you're in the coven, you and I can discuss their membership, just the two of us. I'm certain we can find a way to make everyone happy."

"That's just it," I said. "I'm already happy. And I have been all along, even without the coven. I guess, *especially* without the coven. Goodbye, Teri."

David and Neko caught their cues flawlessly. The three of us turned as one. We flowed up the hillside, past the gorgeous house, around to the waiting Lexus.

David opened the back door for me, and I remembered how I had collapsed after my first visit to the coven. I recalled dozing on my way home, utterly drained, unable to sit up, to speak, to control myself in any way.

This time, though, I was energized. I had stood up to Teresa and *gained* strength. "No," I said. "I'll sit up front."

I had walked away from the Popular Snobs. They had issued me an engraved invitation, and I had thrown it back in their faces. Me, the girl who always got the third out in gym class softball games. The girl who Brett Lindquist asked to dance on a cruel-joke dare. The girl who had never been quite cute enough, rich enough, popular enough to belong.

I didn't need them. I had set their centerstone, but I had no interest in their petty games. I had won.

Neko waited until David started the car before he pouted. "Couldn't we have gone inside for just a moment? Just long enough to grab a tray of salmon canapés?"

25

"Walk on in" said the sign on the door.

But sometimes it wasn't that easy. I dragged my toes along the sidewalk, feeling as shy as a preschooler at her first play date.

I'd awakened at 5:00 that morning, stunningly refreshed for having had a total of three hours of sleep. My first thought, upon consciousness, wasn't about the Samhain working. It wasn't about the coven, or about how I might live beside them as a lone witch. It wasn't about Haylee or Graeme or the cruel deception they'd played.

It was about brownies.

About six batches of burned and hopeless brownies—and the realization that I needed to have *something* for Peabridge patrons to eat when the library doors opened at 9:00. Either that, or I had to admit failure to Evelyn.

The night before, I'd set the coven's centerstone. I'd confronted the strongest witch in the Eastern Empire and told her I didn't want to play in her sandbox. I'd decided to stake a claim to an unknown, unknowable magical future. But there was no way in hell I could face the ripped and filthy brownie recipe that was glued to my kitchen counter with egg white and melted chocolate goo.

It was long past time I came to Cake Walk to make my amends. I shifted a bouquet from one hand to the other. I'd harvested the flowers from the Peabridge gardens—they'd be succumbing to a freeze in the next few weeks anyway. The bright crimson and yellow and orange seemed to glow from within.

Through the years, Melissa and I had joked that we should bring each other flowers on a very regular basis, because no man was likely to do so. I thought ruefully about the floral tribute Graeme had sent me after our first "date." I had been so pleased. So totally and completely sucked in.

I'd been such an idiot.

Would Melissa laugh at me now? Would she throw the bouquet at my feet, tell me to take my crappy offering and go away? Would she say she didn't want to be friends any more, that she was tired of investing more in our friendship than I did? Tired of someone who had thrown her over for a *guy*—and a lousy, lying scoundrel of a guy at that.

My stomach executed a queasy back-flip, and I thought about just taking the flowers home. I could always call Melissa later. We could limp through a conversation on the phone, grimacing separately at the awkward silences. In fact, I could send her email and avoid talking to her altogether. That way, I wouldn't interrupt her. I would be showing more respect for her. What did I think I was doing, anyway, showing up at the bakery first thing in the morning? That was her busiest time of day. If I took the flowers home, I would be considerate. Very, very considerate.

I turned away and took half a dozen steps before I realized I was being absurd. Melissa was my best friend—current spat be damned. Besides, she was my only hope, where emergency baked goods and the Peabridge were concerned.

Before I could lose my nerve again, I marched into Cake

Walk, tromped up to the counter and held out the flowers, as if they were the scepter to the throne of all England. "The quality of mercy is not strain'd," I quoted, hoping to prompt her into generous forgiveness.

"It droppeth as the gentle rain from heaven," Melissa replied, as if we'd been conversing all morning. She didn't even bother to cite *Merchant of Venice* as the source of my brilliant conversational gambit. It felt great to be back in the comfortable territory of Shakespeare. Stable. Familiar. Completely, utterly geeky, the way best friends can be without explanation. Without shame.

She accepted the flowers and smiled appreciatively. It took one twist of her wrist for her to locate the best view of the bouquet, the perfect angle to display the riot of color. "Thanks," she said.

I took a deep breath. "I'm sorry I stomped out of here that day."

"It was more than a bit crazy. Good for business, but bad for carrying on any sort of conversation."

"I should have called."

"So should I."

"I've been thinking about you a lot."

She smiled. "Yeah. I've been thinking about you too." She lifted a heavy glass dome and placed a trio of Bunny Bites on a pottery plate. "Want to try my new tea? Apricot Darjeeling."

"Do you mind? I mean, do you have time?"

"Oh, we'll probably get interrupted."

"Well, if it's good for business," I said, and she laughed.

So, that was easier than I'd thought it would be. But that's what best friends were really all about, right? We could reveal our inner selves. Admit our shortcomings. Show up at the start of a workday with a handful of flowers and a few stalks of autumn berries, and all would be forgiven.

It took Melissa seconds to fill a pot of water and add a handful of tea leaves. She took down a small tray and added my favorite pottery mug and a stainless steel tea strainer. I smiled as I took the tray from her, but I needed to catch a yawn against the back of my teeth.

"Tired?"

"I had a late night," I said. My understatement almost cracked me up. Maybe I was punchier than I thought.

"You'd feel better if you started the day with a few sun salutations."

"My back would never forgive me if I started the day with sun salutations."

She shook her head. "Yoga is good for you. You'll get better if you stick with it." I made a face, but she persisted. "They're having a special class at the studio this weekend. Hot yoga. They raise the temperature by ten degrees; it really increases the benefit of the workout. Come on…" she wheedled. "You know you want to go."

"I know I want nothing of the sort."

"Rock, scissors, paper."

"Melissa!"

But she had already folded her own fingers into a loose fist. Why did I let myself get roped into this sort of thing? I matched her hands with my own and counted to three before casting paper. She threw rock. "Paper covers rock!" I shouted. No sweaty yoga for me. Not this weekend.

Before Melissa could demand a new contest, or best three out of five, or five out of seven, or whatever it would take for her to be declared torture mistress of my weak and out of shape body, I pushed ahead with the secondary reason for my visit. "Hey," I said, reaching casually for a Bunny Bite. "Gran and Clara had an idea."

Melissa leaned back against the sink, gracious in her momentary defeat. "Let me guess. They have more secret relatives stashed in a closet somewhere. They can't wait to introduce you to Great-Aunt Edna and her triplet of witchy daughters, and they think Cake Walk would be the perfect meeting place?"

"Ha, ha. No. This one concerns you a little more directly."

"I don't like the sound of that."

"No, it's not bad. Really." Enough. Time to forge ahead. What was the worst that would happen? Melissa would say no, and I'd be stuck taking a trip to the grocery store for gummy lumps of partially-hydrogenated lard? I steeled myself and plunged into the entrepreneurial waters. "You know how things are crazy at the coffee counter at work? Well Gran and Clara thought you could help out there. We could cut back to serving just plain coffee, but we could sell Cake Walk pastries instead, to make up the difference. You know, lure patrons in with quality, rather than quantity of caffeine offerings. More profit for you. Less fuss for us."

"And we could all bask in the smiles of happy Georgetown matrons, strolling the streets and eating baked goods from the Peabridge to the canal." She completed my vision glibly, but I could see the idea appealed to her.

I put on my best wheedling voice. "We could print up a sign tolet people know the pastries come from Cake Walk. We could even keep your business cards on the counter, so people can contact you if they want to cater a party. It would be expanding your business, without expanding your business, if you know what I mean."

"It would be a lot of extra work," Melissa said, but her protest was half-hearted.

"Not for you! You would just make another tray or two of treats—send us a couple of samples from everything you've already made for the main shop." I shrugged, to convey just how easy it would be. "I bet it wouldn't add half an hour to your day. If that."

"Thou art a mocker of my labour."

I laughed, thinking back to brunch at Luna Grill, when I had thought the same quotation in response to Gran's suggestion. "Orlando," I said, rising to the Shakespearean challenge.

"*As You Like It.*" I bounced a little on the balls of my feet. "Come on. I'm serious. Let's try this."

Finally, Melissa nodded. "Okay. But let's call it a three-month trial. If the sales aren't worth it, or if it takes too much time…"

"Three months!" I toasted her with my tea mug, barely keeping milk-infused apricot Darjeeling from sloshing onto my fingers.

"When were you thinking of starting?" she asked.

Oh. There was that little detail. I glanced at the cake plates filled with treats, the refrigerated glass cabinet already arrayed to seduce early-morning snackers. "Today?" I offered her my most winning smile.

"Jane!"

"I tried to do this on my own! Really! I was going to bake brownies, but they didn't… Well, they didn't quite turn out…"

She was laughing. My best friend was laughing at me. My best friend was leaning against the sink in her bakery, folding her arms across her chest, shaking her head, and laughing at me. "Let me guess," she said when she could catch her breath. "You ruined three batches."

"Six," I said. "It might have been more, but I ran out of ingredients."

Before she could gloat, the door opened. Gran and Clara walked in.

"Oh!" Clara said, when I turned around to face them.

"Good morning, dear," Gran said, as if we met for Cake Walk tea and crumpets every morning.

"What are you guys doing here?" I asked.

Clara shuffled from one foot to the other, glancing from Melissa to me, not quite ready to answer. I took advantage of her silence to say, "See, Gran? I kept my promise."

"Of course you did, dear. It never crossed my mind that you would go back on your word." I rolled my eyes.

Clara stepped forward and said, "Jane, your grandmother

phoned this morning. She was eating her cornflakes when she looked at her calendar and realized last night was Samhain."

"Your calendar had an entry for Samhain?" I asked in disbelief. I'd never seen one that went beyond the Federal holidays.

"Of course not, dear," Gran said, shaking her head. "I *wrote* it there. Peacock blue ink, you know. Because it was a special day for you. Er, night, I suppose."

My eyes welled up. "Gran—"

Melissa looked at me, obviously lost. "Samhain? Wasn't last night Halloween?"

"That too," I said. "It was a Witches' Sabbath. The night I was supposed to be inducted into the Washington Coven."

"Oh!" Melissa said. "And from the way you just phrased that…"

"Let's just say, I won't be attending any coven meetings anytime soon."

"Oh, dear," Gran said, raising her hand to my cheek. "I'm so sorry. I think they were just being hard on you because they didn't like your mother and me. They had no right to make things so difficult for you."

She didn't know the half of it. And I didn't think I'd be telling her about Graeme and Haylee. At least not the whole story. "No, it's okay," I said. "Really. And it wasn't about you. Not exactly." I smiled at all of them. "I did set the centerstone. But then I realized I didn't want anything to do with the coven. Not ever again. I was the one who chose to walk away."

Melissa nodded, accepting my words at face value. I suspected it would take Gran and Clara a little longer to come around, because they knew how important Teresa had seemed to me. How important I'd thought she was to my happiness. To my life.

Pouring a mug of hot water for Clara's tea and a cup of coffee for Gran, Melissa said, "I'm sure there's a connection here somehow, but I have to admit I'm missing it. Gran realized last night was Samhain, and so both of you came down to Cake Walk this morning…"

"Well," Clara said, selecting a teabag from the astonishing array in Melissa's teak box. "We realized Jane wouldn't have time to do any baking last night. We knew she wouldn't be able to launch her new project at the Peabridge."

Gran straightened proudly. "So, we thought we'd come to Cake Walk to buy enough pastries to get the new program off on the right foot. I hope you don't mind, Jane. We only thought to tide you over until you have time to make the baklava."

"Baklava?" Melissa asked incredulously.

"Don't ask," I said. Before I could break the bad baklava news to Gran, the bakery door opened again.

"David!" Melissa exclaimed before I could turn around.

There he was. My warder. Looking none the worse for his long night's service and short night's sleep. "Good morning," he said, making one general nod, as if he'd fully expected to find all of us gathered in the shop.

"Let me guess," Melissa said.

David said, "I knew Jane needed something for the library, and I was certain she wouldn't have anything ready this morning."

"Wait a minute!" I said. "Doesn't *anyone* think I can bake a tray of brownies?"

"No!" They all said, in perfect unison.

As if on cue, Neko walked through the door.

"Oh," he said.

"Et tu, Brute?" I said, making Melissa smirk.

Neko looked over his shoulder, as if he expected someone else to be there, ready to receive my Shakespearean accusation of betrayal. Following his gaze to its logical extreme out the front window of the shop, I saw Jacques, huddling unhappily beneath an elm tree.

Melissa must have made the same extrapolation. Her jaw

tightened for a moment, and then she forced a smile. "Go ahead, Neko. Tell Jacques he can come inside."

I held up my hand. "You don't have to do that."

"Yeah," she said. "I know." And then she busied herself pouring coffee for David and milk for Neko, and a steaming hot chocolate for the Frenchman who would never be her boyfriend. When all of us had our beverages firmly in hand, she began to fill two pasteboard boxes, selecting pastries that would keep well at the library, even if they sat on the counter for the better part of the day. Which they wouldn't. I was certain.

I took advantage of the hubbub to pull David over to the corner. "Thanks," I said, setting my tea mug on a table.

"All in a warder's job description."

"No," I said. "It isn't." I reached inside my sweater and pulled out the silver chain that still bore his Hecate's Torch. "I guess you'll be wanting this back."

"No," he said. "Not really." I looked at him quizzically, and he shrugged. "It's a symbol of the coven. It was given to me when I was selected to serve my first witch. Haylee."

I wove the silver chain between my fingers. "You could have told me about her. About being her warder."

"No, I couldn't. Or at least there was no point in doing so." He shook his head. "Within the rules of the coven, Haylee had the right to cashier me. I disapproved of how she used her powers. I thought she was irresponsible, that she overstepped her bounds. But she was my *witch*. I was sworn to her. I didn't have the right to question her. There's no halfway point between a warder and a witch."

"That's an idiotic rule."

"That's the coven."

I longed to ask another question, but I wasn't sure how he would take it. Oh, hell. He'd stood by me through everything else. "And Graeme? Did he have a choice?"

David met my eyes calmly. Dispassionately. "The same one I did. He had a choice, and he made it."

Absurdly, tears started to clog my throat. "I'm sorry," I said, looking down at my twisting fingers. "It's just that I thought... When I was with Graeme, I let myself believe... I didn't realize..."

"They were cruel," David said. "Haylee felt threatened by you, so they were very, very cruel."

"Why was she *threatened*?"

He smiled as he shook his head. "You really don't get it, do you?"

"Get what?"

"Your powers. The breadth of them. The depth. Most witches are attuned to a single type of magic." He nodded toward Gran. "Crystals." And toward Clara. "Or runes. But you? You combine it all. You weave together crystals and runes and you bind them with spells. You toss in herblore like it's nothing. You call upon elemental magic as easily as you recite lines from Shakespeare. Jane, you heard Teresa Alison Sidney last night. The strongest witch beneath the Coven Mother sets the centerstone. And you're the strongest witch. By far."

"But why didn't you tell me that before?"

"And let you get lazy?"

I made a face. "Come on. I mean it. You should have let me know."

"My job is to protect you. But I also want you to be the best witch you can be. The strongest. The work you put in these past couple of months honed your powers. It let you see magical connections, links that you never imagined existed."

He was right, of course. Two months ago, I'd known almost nothing about herblore, about protective spells, about the ritual of setting a cornerstone. Now, I'd never forget any of that. David's plan had worked.

Still... "If I'm so strong, how did Graeme and Haylee work spells on me?"

"You had no idea they were allied against you. You never suspected they'd try to snare you in magic. With your defenses down—absent—you didn't stand a chance. Any witch can be caught by surprise."

"Even Teresa?"

"Yes. Even Teresa." He started to say the rest of her name, but he caught himself. Old habits were hard to break.

"Am I stronger than she is?" I asked.

He made me meet his eyes after I asked the question. Made me admit, even silently, that I was comparing myself to the Coven Mother, measuring myself against her. I saw him consider lying, consider telling me something good, then something bad. In the end, though, he shrugged. "I don't know."

It was hard to admit ignorance. I had certainly learned *that* lesson in the past two months. I could only begin to tally how much my ignorance had cost. If I had known my own strength, I would have had more confidence. I wouldn't have been so desperate for Teresa's approval. For Haylee's friendship. For Graeme's…for whatever I'd wanted from Graeme. (Sex? No, it had been more than that. Acceptance. Approval. Love.)

I shrugged. "You know I didn't mean to start all this."

"I know."

"I didn't mean to come between Teresa and Haylee."

"Things might have been different if Teresa ran a different sort of coven. If you'd had a different warder." He stared at the silver chain that was twined between my fingers, at the Torch resting against my knuckles. "When Haylee dismissed me, I was persona non grata in the coven. It's a hard life, Jane. It made me a hard person. It's not easy being out there on your own."

"But it's not impossible," I prompted.

"No. It's not impossible."

I squared my shoulders. "And this time, we'll be out there together."

"Together," he agreed.

I settled the silver chain around my neck, tucked the Torch inside my sweater. I might have walked away from the coven, but I wasn't ready to give up the symbol. Yet.

"Jane!" Melissa called, and I turned to face the chattering group at the counter. "Everything's ready to go!"

I scrambled for my purse, fishing out my wallet. "How much?"

Melissa waved me off. "We might as well start an account, don't you think?"

"That would be perfect," I said. "Absolutely perfect."

I made my farewells quickly. I didn't want to ruin my new Peabridge initiative by arriving late, and I still needed to change into my colonial costume. As the bakery door closed behind me, Melissa was freshening cups all around. Neko was begging for the filling from a cream puff or two. Jacques was proclaiming the perfection of the hot chocolate, with unbridled Gallic enthusiasm. Gran was telling Melissa about the recipe for Homemade Turkish Baklava with Rose Water and Pistachio Cream, and Clara was reminding everyone that some of the world's greatest mystics came from Turkey.

But David walked beside me, carrying my pasteboard boxes in easy, companionable silence.

AUTHOR'S NOTE

E lementary and middle school were rough for me.
    I was fortunate to attend an elite private school. We
regularly took standardized tests. We negotiated educational
contracts with our teachers. We wrote haiku and five-paragraph
essays in second grade. We learned French, and we staged plays,
and we conducted science experiments that I later repeated (in a
different city, in a different school) in high school.

I excelled at all those things.

But I was unhappy enough that I worked myself into daily
stomachaches, illness that was severe enough for my pediatrician
to prescribe medication. I only learned many years after the fact
that those little multi-color pills were placebos.

My distress had many sources but bottom line: I was
constantly mocked by classmates.

As a child, I was overweight. My mother took me to Weight
Watchers when I was ten, back when they required a meal of
liver once a week... (Oh, to be as "overweight" now as I thought
I was then...)

From puberty on, I was buxom, too. I couldn't get away with
wearing tube tops the way the popular girls did. And those cute
strapless sundresses with all the ruched fabric across the top?

Total non-starters for me. (My mom had a fix for that too—she sewed me a sky-blue sundress, adding pretty white-lace straps that were wide enough to cover my mandatory bra straps.)

Most importantly, though, I was terrible at sports. I couldn't run. I couldn't throw a ball. The two weeks every year when we competed for the President's Physical Fitness Award were the greatest recurring nightmare of my life. I could no more complete ten pull-ups than I could fling myself to the moon. And that massive rope that hung from the ceiling of the gym, with a skull-sized knot at the bottom... Let's just say I would be eaten by snapping alligators before I could begin to pull myself out of a dangerous jungle pit.

The only physical-education success I experienced at that school was when I was removed from gym class for three months to participate in a study conducted by a pediatric cardiologist. He wanted to prove that regular exercise could increase children's heart fitness. Rather than compete on the killing grounds of the gym floor, I rode an exercise bike in the weight room, exploring the wonders of *The Lord of the Rings* as I pushed my fitness limits on a daily basis. I mourned the end of that study and my return to regular class.

(As an adult, I discovered that my gym teachers could have done a lot more to support me and my fellow unathletic outcasts. They could have taught me how to run more efficiently and to throw more accurately. They could have helped me build core strength and arm strength, and they could have demonstrated techniques to achieve the feats they tested me on. I wonder how different my life would have been with a series of more engaged gym teachers. As it was, I just thought I was irrevocably broken.)

Where there are weaklings—as I was, literally and figuratively—there are people who thrive on power and strength. We call them Mean Girls now, but that phrase wasn't popular at the time.

I'm talking about the girls who orchestrated all of that gym-class aggression. The ones who stripped one of my friends naked in the locker room and threw her into the gym, jamming the door behind her so she couldn't return to safety. The ones who were appointed team captains in all our sports because they were so competent they'd overwhelm any single team if they were allowed to play together. The ones who glared and sighed and sneered when they had to choose me, last of everyone, for their teams.

(Lest you think girls have a corner on sadistic treatment of their peers, there were problematic boys too. One boy tied a girl to a flagpole using a jump-rope and left her there until a maintenance person found her and set her free. Another took to whispering things to me whenever he walked by: "Brown Nose" and "Butt Lick"—two phrases I had to ask my parents to explain.)

I was convinced I was a freak. No one else had ever felt the way I did; no one had ever suffered the way I had. Many days, I came home from school in tears.

My mother (gee, this is turning into an essay about Mom. I hadn't intended that when I started...) told me that *everyone* experienced the same feelings of rejection. Even Peggy Silven—the girl in our class who was friends with everyone, who got great grades, who pitched in softball games, and who taught me how to fold an origami "fortune teller"—even *Peggy Silven* came home crying to her mother.

(A few years later, Peggy left that school. I don't know if she chose to walk away from the Mean Girls, or if her parents made the decision for her, but I've often admired that choice and wondered what Peggy remembers of her years when we were classmates together.)

I later learned that my teachers were flummoxed by my classmates' cruelty. Teachers were aware of the problems, but they couldn't devise permanent solutions. Temporary gains—breaking out classes differently and changing some activities—were just that. Temporary. Many teachers and administrators just threw up their hands and said, "They'll grow out of it. Next year's class doesn't have anywhere near the problem kids this one does."

Even then, the situation wasn't completely bleak.

I had allies. Friends. A group of ten or so kids who thought like I did. Who read like I did.

At recess in elementary school, we had a game we called Horses. Each of us chose a different horse from an illustrated book—a palomino, an Arabian, a Morgan horse—and we enacted complicated adventures. We ran like horses (a combination skipping and running gait) and we protected our fort (a corner of the play area), and we nurtured invisible foals.

We wrote stories, too, sharing them with each other in nascent little writing groups. Those tales were written longhand, often in peacock-blue ink (everyone's favorite shade of Flair pen.) I bound mine, chapter by chapter, in color-coordinated Duo-Tang folders.

We had lots of sleep-overs. My best friend lived in an old house without air-conditioning, a novelty among my Texas peers. We spent our summer days roaming her neighborhood, taking refuge in a comic book store or at a drugstore lunch counter. We spent our nights staying up until the quiet post-midnight hours, telling each other stories as sheer curtains billowed above us, sucked toward the center of the house by a powerful attic fan.

Back at school, we inhaled the books in the library, reading and re-reading and re-re-reading some volumes until they fell apart. The "little kid" books were all kept in a glassed-in room, on waist-high shelves. That's where we discovered *Mrs. Piggle-Wiggle*, and *Charlie and the Chocolate Factory*, and *Twenty-One Balloons*. Maybe more importantly, that's where we found *The Black Cauldron*, the first fantasy series I loved.

We graduated to the middle-school books. Fiction was on shelves around the edges of the main reading room. We found Susan Cooper's *The Dark is Rising* and Ruth M. Arthur's gothics, and a tear-jerk version of an ancient Irish legend, *Deirdre*, by

Madeline A. Polland. We discovered Zilpha Keatley Snyder and EL Konigsburg. We read *The Hobbit*.

But we didn't just read fiction. We inhaled non-fiction, too. Dewey Decimal 920: Biography. 292: Greek and Roman Myth. 133.4: Witchcraft.

We fell in love with witchcraft.

There were the dry adult books that we could barely understand. But there were more immediate stories: *I, Tituba. Tituba of Salem Village.*

We were fascinated by the Salem witchcraft trials. By the power that one group of girls could hold over their entire community. By the grisly results as woman after woman was denounced.

The librarians never questioned our obsession with that pocket of history. They let us check out the same books over and over, only limiting our re-reads if someone had put a particular volume on hold.

I became so fascinated with the library, with the magical workings of the Dewey Decimal system, that I asked to skip my study hall so I could work in the library. I voluntarily carried home problem sets and other homework so I could spend more time with library books.

My responsibilities as a junior assistant deputy intern librarian-in-training started out very basic. I shelved books that other students had perused, returning them from a wooden cart to their proper places on the shelves. I checked out books to other students, stamping due dates on the pasted-in slips of paper at the back of each volume. I collected overdue fines and removed offenders' names from the log, sliding out thin strips of balsa wood typed with a student's name, a book title, and a due date. (Those strips gave a satisfying *snap* when they were broken in two, after proper payment was received.)

Over time, I was given more complicated tasks. I processed new books, folding clear, protective Mylar around dust jackets. I repaired damaged bindings. I added cards to the catalog, slotting in new fonts of information (and often getting lost in rabbit holes of research, following one subject matter to a previously unknown author, one author name to a book title, one title to an entire hoard of related subjects.)

When I received *The Silmarillion* for my birthday in seventh grade, the librarians let me wrap the dust jacket in Mylar, securing it with book tape to keep it pristine forever.

There was magic in the library. Magic in the books. Magic in my friendships, as we nurtured our stories and revised them and told them over and over again.

Along the way, we built a defense against the girls who tormented us in so many ways. Over time, our friendships protected us against the worst of the ignominy of gym class.

As we ran laps around the gym, we could tell ourselves we were hobbits, preparing for our journey to Mordor. We could pretend we were witches, working out spells to defeat our oppressors.

Along the way, we named our enemy. We called our tormentors the Popular Snobs.

I'm not sure how the name came about. Sure, the girls who ruled over us were popular. They controlled our social circles.

But they weren't really *snobs*. They didn't look down on us because they had more money or more fashionable clothes or nicer homes (although, in general, they did have all of those things.) They weren't haughty, in the way one thinks of a New York matron, sniffing down her nose at the hoi polloi.

Whatever the reason, the name stuck. Our enemies were the Popular Snobs.

Looking back now, it all seems ridiculous. Who cares how many sit-ups a person can do? Who cares if a run scores because a ball isn't caught? Who cares which child is left standing at the end of a game of dodgeball and which is nursing angry red burns from a deftly thrown utility ball?

The library I loved burned to the ground a few years after I left that school. It was rebuilt, in the same spot. I've seen pictures of the outside, but I've never ventured into the new building. I don't need to. I still remember exactly where the books I shelved were located.

I don't keep in touch with many of my friends from those days. I see a few of them on Facebook. I marvel at the pictures they post of their families, especially their daughters, who seem so much braver and stronger than we were.

Sometimes, I wonder how the Popular Snobs view those years. Do they regret choices they made? Do they defend their actions with off-hand dismissals—girls will be girls? Do they remember the stories differently, remember the stress fractures in their own families, within their own clique?

When I started writing *Sorcery and the Single Girl*, I knew Jane wasn't going to remain a solo witch. She had too much ability to be ignored by the women in power. She had to negotiate a balance with the Washington Coven.

I enjoyed creating Haylee James. Her casual cruelty felt familiar to me. Her dismissal of Jane's feelings was well-known. I *knew* the off-hand way she struck, the casual malice she deployed, solely because she could.

Haylee was a Popular Snob.

As the story grew, Jane protected herself the way I did. She surrounded herself with allies, with friends. She immersed herself in learning, in gaining knowledge so she'd never be trapped again. She emerged stronger and more free than any woman bound by the strictures of the Coven.

Because that's the lesson my friends and I really learned in that school library. We could write our own stories. We could build our own endings. And if we wanted them to be happy, we had the power to make them so, each and every time.

We still do.

Mindy Klasky
Arlington, Virginia
March 2020

MORE MAGICAL WASHINGTON

Jane and David have negotiated the Washington Coven for now, but there are more magical adventures afoot in Washington DC. Check out these other books in the Magical Washington universe!

∾

Magic and the Modern Girl

Jane learns a magical lesson the hard way: use it or lose it! Her neglected powers are disappearing, her handsome warder David Montrose is ignoring her, and her cat-like familiar has moved out of her home. Even her family life is in chaos. (Really, what octogenarian grandmother gets married—with orange-and-silver bridesmaid dresses?) Will Jane's last-ditch spell restore order to her world?

The Library, the Witch, and the Warder

David Montrose has a problem. Or two. Or three. Fired from protecting Washington's witches, he's stuck in a dead-end clerical job. His father says he's disgraced the family name. And instead of sympathizing, his best friend is dragging him into an all-out supernatural war. When David is summoned back to warder status, he must figure out how to juggle work, warfare, and warding—or all of magical Washington will pay the price!

Fright Court

Sarah Anderson found her dream job: Clerk of Court for the District of Columbia Night Court. But after she's attacked by a supernatural defendant, she's forced to take self-defense lessons from her boss, the enigmatic vampire James Morton. When a deceptively easy-going reporter starts to ask questions, Sarah wonders just what answers she's supposed to give. Will Sarah be able to create order in the court?

The Witch Doctor Is In

Dr. Ashley McDonnell, a witch, has lost her magical powers, just as the supernatural hospital she manages is threatened with being shut down. Life becomes even more complicated when Secret Service agent and newly turned vampire Nick Raines appears in the ER. Can Ash regain her magic when the vampire making her hormones hum may be the man sabotaging her career?

ABOUT THE AUTHOR

Mindy Klasky learned to read when her parents shoved a book in her hands and told her she could travel anywhere in the world through stories. She never forgot that advice.

Mindy's travels took her through multiple careers—from litigator to librarian to full-time writer. Mindy's travels have also taken her through various literary genres, including cozy paranormal, hot contemporary romance, and traditional fantasy. She is a *USA Today* bestselling author, and she has received the Career Achievement Award from the Washington Romance Writers.

In her spare time, Mindy knits, quilts, and tries to tame her endless to-be-read shelf. Her husband and cats do their best to fill the left-over minutes.

CPSIA information can be obtained
at www.ICGtesting.com
Printed in the USA
BVHW071331010520
579051BV00001B/35

9 781950 184149